Thirty-Three Days

by

Stephen B King

This is a work of fiction. Names, characters, places, and incidents are either the product of the author's imagination or are used fictitiously, and any resemblance to actual persons living or dead, business establishments, events, or locales, is entirely coincidental.

Thirty-Three Days

COPYRIGHT © 2018 by Stephen B King

Cover Art by *Kim Mendoza*

The Wild Rose Press, Inc.
PO Box 708
Adams Basin, NY 14410-0708
Visit us at www.thewildrosepress.com

Publishing History
First Fantasy Rose Edition, 2018
Print ISBN 978-1-5092-2110-3
Digital ISBN 978-1-5092-2111-0

Published in the United States of America

Acknowledgments

This book would not have been possible if not for the endless love and support from my wife Jacqui, and the tireless encouragement from my children. In particular Tania, who puts up with non-stop emails from me, always reads everything I throw at her, and responds enthusiastically.

Mica S. Cole gave some invaluable advice that dramatically altered Jenny's tale for the better, and I can't thank her enough.

Lastly, special thanks to Melanie Billings at Wild Rose, who saw the potential and offered guidance. She emailed me repeatedly, kept me informed at every step, and made the journey all the more enjoyable.

Thank you all,

~*Steve*

After three weeks of research,
Jenny O'Brien thought she was ready. The feeling of nervous expectation had followed her acceptance of what had started out being fanciful, then traversed through unbelievable, right on up to the doorstep of: You must be mad!

Well, I am as ready as I will ever be for my journey, I suppose.

But her fears and insecurities nibbled at her like a pack of baying dogs chasing a rabbit through the scrub. She was going to take the drug soon, and go to sleep; the injector lay on her bedside cabinet. Then she would wake up back in time thirty-three years, in her younger body.

Yes, folks, it's mad, isn't it?

The sound of her nervous giggle echoed around the barren walls of her lonely apartment and returned to haunt her. She still had trouble believing she had been chosen by a "Committee" some two hundred and thirty years in the future.

Oh, my God, why did I agree to this insanity?

She had initially refused point blank to help, vigorously shaking her head. "I can't, Simon, I just can't. I'm not the person you think I am. You want someone strong and courageous. Someone who isn't afraid to fail. I am the complete antithesis of that."

He smiled in the crooked way he had, which she quite liked, if she was honest. He then spent the next four days convincing her she was all those things and more.

Praise for Stephen B King

"THIRTY THREE DAYS by Stephen B King is a compelling, well-crafted story that blends a dystopian tale with time travel and adventure. A story of a future past with a powerful setting.

Readers will love Jenny and the fact that she is on a mission with deadly time constraints, and that the future of her future depends on her success. The story is well plotted and readers will enjoy the unexpected twists and the red herrings, the excellent pacing and character development. Stephen B King writes beautifully, combining vivid descriptions with great dialogues to create a realism that is felt through the setting, and characters that are infused with humanity. *THIRTY THREE DAYS* is a fun read."

~*Romuald Dzemo for Readers' Favorite*

Chapter 1
Time before Time

Simon Muransk's memory, for his thirty-three-day trip back into his past, never returned. Except for one moment as he neared death. Then, he almost remembered everything.

It was like looking through thick opaque curtains as he lay shivering and sweating in his bed on the farm, his fever ferociously high. He saw the outline of his memory for the missing time, as if it were a shadow through the drapes. If he could just stretch out a shaking, clammy hand, and pull them aside, he would remember it all. The sweat dripped from his brow as he trembled uncontrollably; he was close to a welcome death.

He'd caught a bad dose of Peruvian Flu two weeks before. At eighty-six years of age, it rapidly turned to pneumonia and he knew he was ill, very ill indeed. But since Cheryl passed away only the year before, he'd lost all will to survive. Simon had not called the doctor, or notified his children. He was content to let nature take its course, and for him be reunited with his wife.

The time had come when he remembered what occurred before he took the drug Bill convinced him to take, which sent him back in time thirty-three years. But he knew that to talk to people about time travel, and that he had taken an incredible journey on a very

1

important mission, would be enough for others to think him mad. There was no way he could have told his wife about it on his return, once his memory solidified. She'd never understand let alone believe him. And, because he was not able to remember what he did while in the past, it would have made his task impossible. She would have thought he'd gone insane. No, he decided it would be best to fake a total memory loss, rather than a partial one.

He remembered the task which had been given to him by a very persuasive Bill, but not whether he had achieved it. He had gone to convince Jenny O'Brien to take a leap of faith, as he had done. Only she could stop the oncoming Tsunami wave of disaster.

With the appearance of the spots on his wheat, which Bill told him was the initial stage, the solution to the impending doom of the future of every single plant on earth, was firmly in Jenny's hands. Had he been successful in convincing her to "Leap?" He had no idea due to the memory loss.

In his darker moments, he wondered if, with the appearance of the tiny yellow spots on his crop, it would suggest she had failed. Surely, if she had succeeded, would he have even planted the Destaine wheat in the new reality she would have been responsible for? But, the endless permutations of cause and effect of traveling in time baffled his aging mind, and he had long since given up trying to figure it out.

It was almost as if a breeze gently blew the curtains across his memory, just for a moment, and he caught a glimpse through to the past. He remembered Jenny's face, and her incredulous look, as he explained what her role had to be. The world's population was going to starve, if she didn't help.

He hoped, right before he slipped into oblivion, that because of his actions, Jenny would succeed, and save the lives of everyone living in the future.

****

August 2nd 2049, Perth, Western Australia

After three weeks of research, Jenny O'Brien thought she was ready. The feeling of nervous expectation had followed her acceptance of what had started out being fanciful, then traversed through unbelievable, right on up to the doorstep of: You must be mad!

Well, I am as ready as I will ever be for my journey, I suppose.

But her fears and insecurities nibbled at her like a pack of baying dogs chasing a rabbit through the scrub. She was going to take the drug soon and go to sleep; the injector lay on her bedside cabinet. Then she would wake up back in time thirty-three years, in her younger body.

Yes, folks, it's mad, isn't it?

The sound of her nervous giggle echoed around the barren walls of her lonely apartment and returned to haunt her. She still had trouble believing she had been chosen by a "Committee" some two hundred and thirty years in the future.

Oh, my God, why did I agree to this insanity?

She had initially refused point blank to help, vigorously shaking her head. "I can't, Simon, I just can't. I'm not the person you think I am. You want someone strong and courageous. Someone who isn't afraid to fail. I am the complete antithesis of that."

He smiled in the crooked way he had, which she

3

quite liked, if she was honest. He then spent the next four days convincing her she was all those things and more.

Once he had gone, returned to his farm in the future, she spent long hours, working at her desk in her one-bedroom apartment on the eighty-third floor of the glass and chromium steel building, The Monument Towers. She studied all the available history for the period she would be re-visiting and committed to memory all the necessary facts she believed she would need. Fortunately, a lifetime of study and lecturing students had given her near perfect recall.

The knowledge she was taking back in time was history but would be seen as fortune telling to others. Being able to recite events to come was a must if she was to have any success of convincing Iain, and more importantly, his son, Bradley, that she wasn't a complete lunatic.

Her trip was to be the last link in the chain, the final "leap of faith" Simon called it, and hence they called themselves "Leapers." Simon was the sixth, she was to be the seventh, and to her it seemed appropriate. Seven was her lucky number; she chose it for everything she could.

With a snap and twist of the alloy top, she opened a bottle of Margaret River wine, and poured a large measure into her crystal glass. She intended to finish the bottle before taking her ASX101 and going to bed, to wake up…in her own past. She still struggled to get her mind around the concept. At times, she wondered if it was not all part of some elaborate hoax.

She sipped her wine lovingly, rolled it around her mouth like a delicate truffle, then licked her lips once and swallowed. For a moment, her mind wandered into a daydream. She imagined fields with withered and dying plants as far as the eye could see. She sat up abruptly: Everyone could die. She shuddered at the terrifying image, and took another deep sip of wine, enjoying the crisp freshness.

Dry white wine was one of the two vices she allowed herself. Her cat Boof, short for Boof-Head, was the other. He was aptly named because that's what he was to her. He was currently asleep on her bed, but every two hours or so he would race around the apartment at breakneck speed as if his tail was on fire, sometimes jumping in the air and landing awkwardly, even rolling, as if he were a demented commando on steroids.

She enjoyed her wine. She found it somewhat ironic, her favored drink de jour was itself of the same ilk of what, in the future, would be called biological genocide, thanks to genetic modification. She sipped again, feeling incredibly naughty because this winery had embraced the technology of making plants grow faster, and stronger, in any weather or conditions.

Simon said there had been discussions within "The Committee" she should kill Bradley Reginald Destaine, if she could not convince him of the dangers to the world, if he continued with his research.

Shocked, she'd stood up, angrily. "No way, no-bloody-way, Simon," she proclaimed. "I teach kids, not kill them!" That sparked another long discussion into the night.

She wondered, not for the first time, if she could, if required, commit cold-blooded murder, no matter what the justification was, and she didn't believe she could.

She hoped upon hope she wouldn't have to find out. Jenny was not a killer, and didn't think she ever could be.

If she could somehow capture Iain's interest, a widower for over three years, she thought it might be so much easier to convince him to help her talk his son into not releasing his radically altered strain of wheat.

That was her plan, such as it was. Of course, at some point she would have to convince him and then his son of her sincerity—that she had traveled in time to warn them. She dreaded that with a fear bordering on hysteria.

While discussing at great length the mind-bending possibilities of time travel and the consequences of altering the past, she asked Simon the most obvious question: "Simon, when they were planning these "Leaps", why didn't they just organize one into a young version of Iain or Brad himself? Wouldn't that have been so much easier than an outsider trying to convince him to not make the discovery?"

He shook his head in a fatherly gesture, which seemed odd coming from such a young man. "Jen, that's a great question, and one I asked Bill, my tutor."

He dug into his rear pocket and took out his crumpled gray leather wallet. From inside he took out a carefully folded piece of paper and passed it to her. "I wrote this out having memorized it from the library obituary files from July 2020."

Nervously she opened it and read a hand-written excerpt from the Death Notices. Iain and son Bradley Destaine had been killed in a car accident after leaving a soccer game, when their car had been crushed by a heavily laden truck. The team had featured Bradley as

6

the star center forward, and father Iain as the coach. She read he had coached his son since he had taken up the game as a six-year-old. Family and friends hoped they would both now be at peace with mother, and wife, Simone, who had been taken tragically from them; a victim of breast cancer some years prior.

Destaine, Iain and Bradley
R.I.P.

Loving father, Iain and son, Bradley, tragically lost their lives in a vehicle accident following a soccer game last Saturday. Iain was Senior Coach at Queens Park Soccer Club, which featured Bradley as star Centre Forward, for many years. Both will be sorely missed.

Finally reunited with wife and mother Simone, who passed away after a long battle with Cancer.

All past members and players are invited to a memorial service at the club rooms before the home game 12.00 noon, 26th July 2020

Jenny looked at Simon's kindly but sun-weathered face. "That's so sad, they are going to die? Brad is going to make a discovery of such epic proportions and then die in a vehicle accident? Can't I stop it when I go back, warn them somehow?"

"Jenny, any change we make in the past will affect what has already happened in the future, because, as we now know, time is a continuum. If you save someone's life who otherwise would have died, who can say what will occur. One alteration now could cause fifty others down the line and have some sort of huge domino effect. Maybe they will be good changes, maybe they won't. The whole reason for ASX, and us taking it, is to save humankind from the Yellow Spot Blight. Anything else? Well that's up to you and your conscience in your allotted thirty-three days."

"So, are you saying I shouldn't save their lives?"

"I'm saying it will be your call when you are there. People will not, and cannot, judge you because whatever changes you make will become their new reality. No one would know any differently. Just remember this though, Jenny." He paused to gather his thoughts. "When your thirty-three days are up, the young you won't remember what the older you did. It will be as if you've been asleep, and, as you know, your dreams disappear sometimes after waking. Similarly, when you wake up, back in your future, within hours you won't remember what happened in the past. If you are successful, you alone will have saved the future of every person, animal, and plant on earth, but you won't know it. So, you do whatever feels right to you in the past, and damn the consequences."

Chapter 2
The Sands of Time

Day Five, August 6th 2016

Saturday afternoon, the weather was cold, wet, and unbelievably dreary, as Jenny stood on the concrete outside the clubrooms. She stood, shifting her weight from foot to foot, under the leaky iron roof of the veranda, at the Queens Park Soccer Club, watching the game. Her hands were stuffed deep in her red parker jacket pockets to try to stop frostbite, or at least chilblains, setting in. Her fluffy lined hood was pulled up over her long blonde hair, in a forlorn effort to keep out the wind. She wore jeans, and runners, and wished they were twice the thickness.

Boy, am I feeling the cold? Nope, I'm way beyond that. I'm freezing.

Adding to her lack of enjoyment was the fact that she didn't know too much about the sport, though she had been reading up on it and watching games on TV over the preceding days while she had been adjusting to her new time stream.

She didn't understand why the referee had just blown his whistle. To add to the confusion, a man alongside her screamed out at the top of his lungs: "That was never offside, ref! You need fucking glasses!"

This sentiment was echoed by other, clearly partisan supporters making up the hundred or so spectators sitting on plastic chairs or standing rubbing their hands together under umbrellas, trying to keep warm. She grinned as more and more insulting, crude, but none the less humorous insults where shouted out at the poor hapless referee. Jenny had no doubt he would be wondering why he did the job in the freezing cold rain, only to be jeered at by the onlookers.

Some of the predominantly male crowd around her were quite funny, and the comments they shouted out frequently, were very, very colorful. There had been such verbal abuse as: "Fuck off, ref, that was no foul." Another: "He's been doing that all fucking game, ref." But her favorite had been: "Are we watching the same fucking game, ref?" The word fucking was used in every single insult.

When the last one had been screamed out by a short elderly man on the veranda, she was hard pressed not to break out in a fit of the giggles. In doing so, she would have needed to go and pee, and she didn't fancy doing it here. God alone knew what state the women's toilet would be like, and she had no desire to find out, thank you very much. So, she bit her lip, held her laughter in, and kept her focus on the back of the man she had come to see, Coach Iain Destaine, when she wasn't trying to keep up with the game.

Since waking up in 2016 she felt somehow lost for a while, everything was so different to the world she left behind. She retained her younger memories, though her future consciousness was far more dominant. So much technology had raced on in the future, she needed time to settle in and adjust to the older ways of doing things. She had gone to work, though people there barely noticed her, as per usual. She performed her tasks as usual, with most of the other lecturers barely acknowledging her presence. She tutored her students and slowly gained in confidence to think she could carry out her day job, while after hours would be the mission she had traveled thirty-three years to carry out.

In some strange way, she was...very different. Though essentially the same person, she now possessed a wiser head on a much younger set of shoulders. She had knowledge of future events and where her life was heading—sadly, pretty much nowhere on an emotional level. There were things she hadn't known at thirty-five, but now she did.

She had to watch herself constantly in conversation, but after five days of living in the past, she believed she was ready to meet the man she had come to see. The thought of doing so still terrified her.

She was not, and never had been, comfortable with men in any sort of...close way. The upcoming meeting would be the most difficult thing she had ever attempted, and way beyond her comfort zone.

Iain pranced up and down the touchline, in the pouring rain, barking out orders to his players, who clearly respected their coach and did what he extolled them to do. Currently the score line showed the home team was losing to the much more fancied Bayswater United, one goal to two. Jenny studied the club's history before she took her "Leap", and Queens Park men's team would go on to win this game four to two. Hoping Iain would be in a good mood because of the coming victory, Jenny believed today would be the best time and place to meet him.

Jenny wished it hadn't been so cold, so she could have dressed just a little more nicely, to be able to more easily attract his eye. She wanted to give him just a hint of cleavage, not that she intended to be in any way slutty; that was beneath her. But if she had worn her first choice in clothes, quite simply by the end of the game, she would have resembled a very large, blonde icicle, and she was quite sure he wouldn't be attracted to that shade of blue.

Her thoughts were interrupted by a man who nudged her arm before speaking in some sort of English accent. "Hey, Darlin, you look freezing, let me get you a drink from the bar. We've got Vodka Black, one of those should warm you up."

She turned to look at the short man wearing an old-style cap which she thought was called a 'duster'. He was unshaven, looked to be in his fifties, and wore a thick ex-army trench type coat to keep out the winter chills. He held a can of what looked like Foster's Beer wrapped up in a cocoon of neoprene, a stubby holder. It was designed as much to keep the holder's hand warm, as to keep the can cold. He was much older than she was, and she could tell this was an offer of genuine friendship and welcome for a fellow supporter, rather than some obscure method of chatting her up. She thought he'd realize he hadn't a hope in hell of scoring that goal. She nearly giggled again at the pun she just thought of, and before she could stop, found herself saying: "Thank you, so long as it's in one of those holders, a Smirnoff Black would be great thanks."

"You guard my spot next to you, Missy, and I will be right back with one for you. My name's Geordie by the way, I'm the volunteer bar manager here." No

12

sooner had he said the words, she recognized the folly of her acceptance of his offer. She was already close to needing the lavatory, and a cold drink would, no doubt, tip her over the edge.

"Thanks, Geordie, that's very kind. I'm Jenny."

In a matter of minutes, he was back and thrust in her hand a similarly clad bottle of pre-mixed Smirnoff, which she gratefully accepted. She offered money but he shook his head, "Nay Missy, your first one is on the house."

Now if I could just get a hot bacon and egg sandwich to warm me up I'd feel almost human again.

"Which one's your feller, Missy? My lad's the number four, Mickey, my only boy. He's not having the best game of his life so far. He was the clod who gave away the penalty, fucking idiot he is." He smiled as he said it, before adding: "Scuse my French, Missy."

"Geordie, I thought the ref was looking the other way when he blew his whistle for that. Oh, and it's okay, I've heard the word before." She chinked the side of her bottle of vodka with his beer can and took a drink.

He laughed outrageously. "Oh Missy, you're a woman after my own heart, if I were single and twenty years younger, you'd be in trouble, make no mistake."

She laughed back as the ref blew his whistle to signify the end of the first half, which meant they could escape the cold by going inside the clubrooms to warm up, before the second half started. "Geordie, if I were twenty years older, even if I were married, you'd be the one in trouble." She winked and was rewarded with another healthy laugh.

"You stick with me, Missy, you don't know

anyone here, and I'll keep you company, and keep the riff-raff away. You're a bonnie lass and it will be like flies around a honey pot once the players finish the game and shower up. That is if you're staying till after the game?"

"I could be tempted, Geordie, but I'm freezing out here."

"Well my missus works the canteen, and the hamburgers are not bad, or she does a wicked chips 'n gravy, and home-made sausage rolls."

"Oh, you know what? I've not had chips 'n gravy since I was at school, and this is just the weather for something like that. You talked me into it, you smooth talking man." She chinked his can with her bottle again, and they both shuffled inside the clubrooms, out of the howling wind, and away from driving rain.

Two minutes later, she saw over Geordie's shoulder, Iain enter and walk up to the bar. She had a sudden inspiration. "Would you excuse me for a minute, Geordie, I'll be right back."

"Well your chips are on their way, so don't be long, there's nowt worse than cold chips 'n gravy," he answered at her departing back.

At the bar, Jenny took a deep breath to steady her nerves and thrust her hands in her pockets to hide her shakes. This was it, her first introduction to her target and she felt petrified.

Iain took a sip from a glass of what looked suspiciously like straight scotch, obviously, to help keep the cold out during the rest of the game. "You look worried, Coach, but you shouldn't be. A little birdy told me something very special is going to happen in the second half."

14

He turned, glass in hand, and looked pleasantly surprised. She had shrugged her hood off when she entered the bar area, and her long hair hung down around her shoulder, damp, but not wet. She usually wore it tied up in a bun, or a ponytail, but today some inner sixth sense told her to keep it down. She smiled her best possible smile as she tilted her head to the left.

"Well, what did your little birdy tell you?" he asked, and she was immediately taken with the warmth and timbre of his masculine voice.

"You really, really, want to know?"

"Yes, I really, really do. What's your name, I haven't seen you round here before?"

Here it is, now I've got to come up with the reason why I would suffer the freezing cold weather to watch a stupid game of soccer at a club where I don't know a soul. "My name is Jenny, and my younger brother is coming over from Melbourne soon. He is a state player over there, and he asked me to scout you, and this club out as a potential place for him to come and play next season. Apparently, his best mate used to play here, and he speaks very highly of you as a coach. So, I thought I'd come and check it out, on his behalf."

"Must be Billy Slyman, he's the only one I know of who moved to Melbourne that played for us."

"Yep, he did say his name was Billy." *That's a bit of luck.*

"Well, Jenny, please forgive me for running out on you, but I've got to get to the change rooms and try to fire up my boys. See if we can't turn this game around. If you are here after the game, I'd love to chat with you about your brother, we could do with an ex-state player."

15

"But, I didn't get to tell you what my little birdy said."

Iain smiled. "Well, you better make it quick. I only wanted a drink to warm up."

"Okay, here goes. It's going to be tight, but about half way in they are going to have a player sent off for a pretty awful foul, but don't worry, your man won't be injured. The good news is it's going to give your boys the lift they need, and your son is going to be a hero. He scores twice and a guy named Simmo scores another, and you win four goals to two."

He stared, open-mouthed, then laughed. "Wow. Now that is some little birdy. That's the best story I've heard in a long time, Jenny. Forgive me, please, I've got to go, but I hope you're still here after the game." He downed the last of his scotch, turned on his heel still smiling and shaking his head, walked back through the milling crowd.

When Jerome Selcock was fouled at the seventieth minute mark, causing the referee to yank the red card from his top pocket to send off the Bayswater offender, Iain turned and hunted for her face in the crowd. Their gazes locked onto each other. She shrugged exaggeratingly, and held her arms open wide as if to say, "What?"

He shook his head and turned back to the game with a strange, bemused look.

By her side, Geordie, now on his fourth beer while Jenny nursed her second vodka, was almost beside himself screaming out obscene insults at the offending player. For the first time in the game, the home team supporters were as one in congratulating the referee for getting a decision right.

The noise quietened down as Bradley Destaine stepped up to take the free kick from just outside the box, as five men built an impenetrable human wall ten yards in front of him.

Even though, thirty-three years into the future Jenny had found the match report and read it, she too felt a thrill of excitement course through her as Brad stepped back away from the ball, a look of deep concentration on his face. He was a good-looking and very fit young man with short, curly dark brown, unkempt hair. Having conducted so much study on the family, she felt as if she already knew him.

His foot made perfect contact with the ball, with the right amount of power and curve to take the ball up and over the wall. It dropped just in time to go under the crossbar and away from the diving goalkeeper, into the back of the net just inside the top left hand corner of the goal. This time when Iain looked for her, she held up two thumbs and smiled. He smiled back, still with a strange look on his face, as the rain took that moment to come down even harder than it had before.

As she predicted, Brad scored the next goal after weaving past two defenders and taking a shot from a forty-five-degree angle to the near side post, while the goalie anticipated he would go to the far side. Even Jenny jumped up and down with glee and clapped her hands when he scored, and suddenly, she understood what soccer was all about. One single goal was so intrinsically important; it could mean the difference between winning and losing, or to the true devotees, almost life and death.

Iain was so overjoyed with his son's performance he ran up and down the touchline whooping and hollering like a schoolboy, and Jenny's world of perception, just for a moment froze. In some way, she could not comprehend she experienced an out-of-body experience unlike anything she had ever known before. Perhaps it was a side effect of the ASX101, but everyone watching and playing the game was suddenly halted, and she could experience everything. She sensed the joy of the spectators, but more importantly, she could feel the pride and love of a father for his son, and she was humbled by it. She had traveled thirty-three years to meet them, but nothing had prepared her for that one moment when she felt somehow part of their family.

Bayswater's spirit had been broken, and they were incapable of scoring the goal which would give them a draw. When a corner was taken by Brad, a short stocky player rose high above the pack to head home the fourth goal.

That must be Simmo.

She screamed her delight at the goal, along with the crowd.

The spectators under the veranda were overjoyed and delirious with happiness, cheering and screaming their glee. But, there was one person who did not celebrate the goal: Iain. For what felt like minutes, he stared at Jenny, and she worried for an initial contact, maybe she had gone too far. She stared back, his gaze questioning, while hers was non-committal.

She made up her mind what to do, mostly through fear, but partly as a strategy, and the moment he turned back to the game, she spoke to Geordie and said her goodbye. "I have to go, Geordie; is next week a home or away game?"

"Tough game next week, Missy, we play Floreat Athena, at Floreat. We generally lose to them."

"Well. Something tells me this is our season and this time we will win. I will see you there. Thanks for keeping me company, and for the vodkas; it's time I left. Would you do me one last favor, please?"

"Aye, Missy, I reckon I would do you a favor, so long as it doesn't get me in trouble with the law, or the missus." He winked as if he had been in trouble numerous times with both.

She took a page from a small notebook in her handbag and wrote her name and mobile phone number on it. "Would you please give that to coach Iain after the game please? I spoke to him at half time and he showed interest in picking my brother as a player for next season. Please tell him I'm sorry I had to go."

****

The sound of her phone ringing startled her and the cat on her lap, as she watched a movie on TV. Jenny was unused to nighttime calls. She answered nervously: "Hello?"

"Why did you run away before the end of the game?" Iain asked in his masculine, craggy voice.

She breathed a long sigh of relief and tried to calm her nerves. "I didn't so much run away, well okay, I suppose you could call it that, but when my prediction turned out to be so true, I guess I thought you would think I was loopy."

"Well, I admit, it was spooky. Weirdest damn thing that's happened to me in a while, for sure. Do you often do things like that, predict the future, I mean?"

"As a matter of fact, Iain, yes I do."

"Well, if you ever get an idea what the Saturday

lottery numbers will be, you let me know, okay?"

"Hmm, well I have your phone number now; it showed up on my display. So yes, I could send them through to you, easy. Of course, we'd have to split fifty-fifty."

He laughed, but she didn't. Jenny had memorized the next few weeks' numbers and could easily give them to him. When he paused, she felt the need to fill the void. She had to be careful not to scare him away at the first hurdle. She was beside herself with delight he had called.

Slowly, gently. "So, I think the real reason you rang was to ask about my brother?"

"Umm, yes, I did, of course yes. Umm, what position does he play?"

At age thirty-five, having studied hard through the years when most people were at the height of their sexual activity, Jenny: version one, did not have too much experience in meeting men, let alone being bold enough to try to date one. There had been the odd occasion when men hadn't been put off by her frosty, intelligent demeanor at university, but for whatever reason, she hadn't felt the need, or want, to go any further. There were always more important things to do.

In Jenny: version two, she knew what went where, and why, very well. She also possessed a mature mind but inhabited a much younger body, and amazingly she had an inkling Iain was interested in her, which was a revelation hard to comprehend. It was exactly what she had hoped for, but that didn't make it any easier, she still felt nervous. He sounded just a bit flustered, in a very nice way, just like a kid caught with his hand in the cookie jar. She decided to tease him a little.

"Aww, and here I was, hoping you called to ask me out to dinner." She giggled, just enough to hopefully let him know she was kidding, but also, if he asked, she would probably say yes. "River, that's his name would you believe? Don't ask me how mum and dad dreamt up that. He's a goalkeeper, and from what I remember when I watched him play, a pretty good one.

"A goalkeeper? We can always use a good goalie. I'd be very keen to have him with us. And you Jenny, do you play? We have an excellent women's team here."

That's a curve ball. "No, Iain, it's not for me anymore, I did my knee in my twenties, and I figured once was enough. These days I just enjoy watching. Mind you, I wouldn't mind being a coach's assistant, not that you probably need one."

"I think you're teasing me. No one these days wants to be an assistant. It's hard enough to get volunteer linesmen, let alone a helper."

"I'm not teasing. I'd like to do it. Maybe we could discuss my wages."

He laughed long and hard. "Wages? I do it for love, Jenny. Sometimes the club buys me a scotch on a cold day; otherwise it's just for the love of the game. The main bonus for me is it keeps me close to my son. Since his mum died, well, we kind of lean on each other. He finishes University soon; he wants to feed the world and save starving nations. He's been offered a position with the CSIRO, that's the Commonwealth Science and Industrial Research Organization, as a microbiologist. I'm very proud of him."

"Wow, not only a great soccer player, but he has brains too. He must take after his dad. I'm so sorry to

21

hear about your wife, I had no idea." She bit her lip, hating her lies and deception, but knowing it was important.

"Not too many brains here, Jenny. I'm just a humble sub-contract truck driver. No, I reckon he took after his mother. She was the smart one. No need to be sorry, you weren't to know. She died, aged forty, from breast cancer, over three years ago. It was a pretty tough time for Brad; he was very close to his mum."

"It must have been awful for you both. I can see why you are so proud of him."

"I'm sorry, I must be boring the pants off you, talking about Brad and me like this. It's a pretty good way to scare my new helper."

"Well, Iain, I do still want to be your helper, I think I'd really enjoy it. Secondly, you're not boring me one tiny bit. I think it's nice the way you talk about your son, and your late wife." Her face turned red as she could barely believe what she'd said. She had never been so forward in a conversation with a man. Somehow, in a way she could not understand, it also felt right.

He laughed, she joined in, and they spoke on the phone for another hour. Jenny felt herself becoming more and more attracted to him, and suspected, though her logical brain refused to accept it, those feelings were reciprocated. She was shocked, and happily surprised when out of the blue Iain cleared his throat.

"Jenny, umm I'm not used to this, but, would you like to come out to dinner with me tomorrow night?"

"Oh yes please, I would."

It was only later she worried she had sounded too eager. But, Iain had invited her to dinner, and she believed in her heart they both felt the connection of mutual attraction. She had taken her first step, and was very, very proud of herself.

Chapter 3
Time and Place

Day Six, August 7th 2016

In some ways, coming back thirty-three years was difficult for Jenny, yet in others it wasn't. She was a sixty-eight-year-old woman in a thirty-five-year-old body. On the plus side, she had wisdom of years, maturity, dignity, and the ability to think less emotionally. But uppermost in her mind was one fear: She had to be careful she didn't come across as an old woman to the forty-three-year-old Iain, or worse, say something which gave away her mental age.

Her mind raced as she stood in only her underwear, before her wardrobe, deciding what she should wear for her dinner date. Part of her wanted to be conservative, as she always was every single day of her life. Another part of her felt that under the circumstances she should be more adventurous. She wanted to be more provocative, if such a thing was possible. She had to keep reminding herself she only had twenty-six days remaining in which to somehow convince a father, who clearly adored his son, to help her tell him if he kept going on his career path he would kill every living thing in the world.

Suddenly, the enormity of her task made her tremble with fear. *What if I blow it?*

Simon had told her there would only be this one chance, and if she failed to convince Iain and Brad, how could a second attempt succeed? It had taken seven people to take an enormous leap of faith in the word of a total stranger and inject themselves with an unknown drug that had been cooked up in a kitchen. Simon told her if she was unsuccessful, and another attempt was launched, the next "Leaper" may have an entirely different method of stopping Bradley Destaine.

It took time to believe sufficiently in Simon, to make the commitment herself, and then only had a few short days with him before his time ran out. He had, like his predecessors, manufactured the ASX, for her to use, without any form of pharmaceutical training. Each "Leaper" had to memorize the formula, then when they awoke in the past, locate the ingredients and equipment, then synthesize the drug. At least she didn't have that task.

Here she was on day seven of her allotted thirty-three, worrying what to wear, not working in a drug lab. She suddenly giggled, and with the laughter came some relaxation.

She did have a fallback position, which she refused to consider each time it lurched to her mind unbidden; she could murder Brad. But she didn't believe it was an option. It sounded easy when you thought about it quickly, but could she do that?

It would mean spending most of the rest of her life in jail, and the chilling harsh reality of the thought of murdering such a gifted, and lovely young man, made her giggles stop dead in her suddenly dry throat.

It was too much, and in a fit of pique she threw the dress across the bedroom to flutter against the blinds across her window. *Why Me? Damn Simon, and every "Leaper" before him. How dare they lay this monumental task at my feet? Who gave them the right?*

She sat on the edge of her bed, put her head in her hands, and wept with frustration. At first they were tears of anger, and then fear she would fail. If she did, it would no longer be Bradley Destaine who was responsible for total world annihilation, but her, Jenny O'Brien.

How can that be fair?

She remembered back to the pivotal conversation she had with her tutor, the one which caused her to finally agree to take the challenge:

"Simon, I don't think I can do this. Please, just find someone else. I can't possibly murder a young man for what he might do."

"I know, Jenny, I don't think I could either. But, it's not what he might do, unchecked it's what he will do. In fact, for us he has already done it in the continuum we come from. I can't just find someone else, this path was plotted by people far into the future, and I have no time to find someone else and convince them."

"But surely anyone around my age would do? I can even help you, and if you run out of time, mix up another batch and come back, we can find someone suitable together, I will help."

He shook his head. "I'm sorry, but I can't do that. This is my last "Leap"; it's down to you, now."

"Don't lay this on me, It's not my fault, and I'm not a murderer. I teach kids; I don't kill them. You must find another candidate."

He stretched across the table and took her hand in

his, and gently squeezed. "I didn't say I wouldn't, I said I can't. In 2247, when ASX101 was being tested, they sent someone back twice. He died after a period of total insanity. For some reason, the human system can't handle leaping a second time. This is my one and only shot. If you choose not to take your "Leap", then you must find someone else who can. If you're completely sure you won't do it, then that's your call, I understand. But I've come a long way because I think you can. The fate of the future of mankind is in your hands. I am not expecting or asking you to kill anyone, just convince him not to modify the wheat."

She stood up before slowly walking over to the now crumpled up dress she had been intending to wear in a heap on the floor. She had twenty-six days to find an alternative to murder.

Damn it, I will, even if it kills me.
****

She opened the door to his knock three quarters of an hour later and was pleasantly surprised at what she saw. He was a handsome man, graying at the temples, tall, slim and fit looking. Jenny had to admit his choice of clothes was good too: pale blue shirt, red silk tie, hound's-tooth sports jacket, and blue jeans. "Hi, Iain, come in, do you fancy a glass of wine before we go?"

"That would be very nice, thank you. We're going Vietnamese. It's Brad and my favorite place. The décor leaves a bit to be desired, but it's fantastic food, cheap, and you can bring your own wine. So, what's not to love about it?"

She poured him a glass of white wine, while nodding, "Vietnamese sounds pretty good to me, Iain. To be honest I haven't had it for a long time. Not because I don't like it, just never had an opportunity to go really. If I'm honest, I have to admit no one has offered to take me out for dinner." She held up her glass, and he did the same, they both sipped, looking at the other from above the tilted Riddell's.

Her gray scruffy-looking cat walked between them, sat and looked up at Iain with disdain, before standing, turning away and showing him its rear end.

"That's Mister Sanchez checking you out. I think he approves." She grinned, biting her lower lip.

"Mr. Sanchez? Why do you call him that?"

"What? You don't think he looks Mexican?"

Iain had been taking a sip of wine and choked as he burst into laughter.

"Seriously, his whiskers droop," she added. "So, to me it looks like one of those Poncho Villa type moustaches. It was going to be Sanchez or Valdez, so I tossed a coin."

He had been recovering, but that set him off again, and he looked to be struggling not to spill his wine.

Jenny loved his laugh. It was one of those, I don't give a damn, and I'm going to laugh my head off types, unlike other men who almost felt guilty so they made their laughter quiet. She smiled broadly, and sensed they were going to have a good night.

****

"Goodness, Iain, when you take a lady out for dinner you really go all out, don't you?"

Jenny looked around the dimly lit interior of Hoy Anne's Vietnamese Restaurant. It was in a Leederville laneway off the main entertainment strip. The first thing she noticed was few of the plastic chairs matched the tables, let alone each other. They comprised different styles, some with high backs, and others low, though it was fair to say the majority at one point in their lives—were white. Now they appeared an ashen shade of gray. The next things that didn't match were the tablecloths which had been slung haphazardly over different shaped plastic outdoor, patio tables. Each had a small water-filled vase with some type of lily immersed, to brighten up the otherwise very drab interior.

"Don't pass judgement until you try the food," he said, sounding very nervous, as he squeezed her arm with his left hand, while his right held the two-bottle wine cooler bag.

Jenny hoped she hadn't insulted him, but she couldn't stop making sarcastic comments, her way of trying to be humorous. She was so shocked any man would bring a woman to a place like this on a first date.

"Okay, I'm trusting you, but the ambulance phone number is programmed into my phone if we both get salmonella." She grinned to let him know she was kidding.

She looked forward to eating, as she figured the only reason anyone would come to such a drab and dreary looking place was if the food was good. "Do you think they can fit us in without a booking?"

He grinned. Barely six of the twelve to fourteen tables were being used. Before he could answer a small elderly woman approached and bowed. "Welcome back Mister Iain, lovely to see you again. Just the two of you tonight, you no bring Mister Bradley?"

"No, just us, Tuyen. This is Jenny."

"Welcome Miss Jenny, please come, I will give you best table in the house. The one furthest away from kitchen, then you no hear my husband yelling at the help." She turned and led them to a small outdoor setting with a pink-and-yellow checked plastic cover. There was no cutlery, just chopsticks and a small side plate

Jenny instantly liked the woman, and her sense of humor. "Tuyen, that's such a pretty name, I've never heard it before. Does it have a meaning?" she asked as she sat on one of the formerly white chairs.

"In our culture, Miss Jenny, all female names have meaning. Tuyen means Angel. My husband think I got wrong one, should be she-devil." She laughed at her own joke and Jenny joined in. "Look like you need wine glasses, I get them for you."

"Oh my God, what a lovely woman, she is worth the price of admittance alone, I'm so glad you invited me here, Iain, even if I do end up on the toilet all night."

Iain took out both bottles of wine, one white, one red, from the cooler. He lowered his voice to just above a whisper. "Look around, Jen, what do you notice about the people?"

Trying to appear as nonchalant as possible she looked around the room, and suddenly understood. She lowered her voice as a co-conspirator, "You are not referring to their height, are you? It's because they're all Asian, is that what you mean?" She liked being huddled close together, whispering like kids, and she noticed the scent of his cologne, and liked it too.

"All the times Brad and I have been here, I've never seen another Aussie. But, when you look at the furniture, you get why they would rather go somewhere else. There is only one reason why mainly Vietnamese people come here: because the food is so good."

"Okay, well, I've got to admit, you've well and truly got my interest. I can't wait to see a menu, oh, and I hope they have pictures so I don't have to try to pronounce the words."

"Ah, yes, well, that's something else. They don't do menus here."

"Right, what is it then, electronic tablets?"

"No, not as such." Once again he laughed in his I-don't-give-a-damn way, which she found so endearing.

"Iain, you're killing me here, how do we order?"

Before he could answer, Tuyen returned with not two, but three wine glasses and an ice bucket, then placed them on the table. Iain poured her drink from the chilled bottle of white, and two from the red. He passed one to her, the second to Tuyen and picked up the last. He lifted his glass so Jenny did the same, noticing the other woman did too. Almost as one the two said, "*mot, hi, bah, yo*," before lifting the glass to their mouths and taking a drink.

Not to be outdone, Jenny drank too, feeling just a little left out, though she held a fascination for whatever it was that was going on in this dimly lit room, in the heart of bustling Leederville.

"Jenny would like to see a menu, Tuyen."

Jenny noticed Iain take another sip to hide his silly-looking grin.

Tuyen bent at the waist, careful not to spill her wine, as she burst into a loud cackling laughter. Despite her confusion, Jenny joined in. There was something odd going on, and while she had no idea what, she could see the funny side of the conspiracy between her date and restaurateur. Jenny thought of it as: let's play a joke on the western woman.

"She funny lady Mister Iain, you should marry her." She turned, shook her head, and walked away, taking her glass of wine with her.

Jenny turned to her date, who shrugged, spread his arms wide and said, "What?"

"If you don't tell me what's going on here, firstly I'm going to give you such a punch on your arm, and secondly I'm going to march into the kitchen and ask Tuyen."

"Okay you win. Well firstly the toast, *mot, hi, bah, yo* means one, two, three cheers. It's a tradition if you're drinking with Vietnamese people. You toast before each time, and, boy, do they love to drink. I warn you, try to avoid getting into a session with them, they're very good at it. The lack of a menu's is because when you come here, you don't choose what you will eat, the chef, Tuyen's husband, decides. I have never, not once, had a meal here that wasn't superb. By the way, I hope you like fresh chili."

"Wow, really? Oh, my God, I'm so looking forward to this, Iain. Thank you so much for bringing me. I love chili, bring it on. How on earth did you find this place?"

The change in Iain was instantaneous; his happy smiling face turned dark and sad looking as he stared down to his glass and twirled what wine was left in it. He snapped out of it, and shook his head. "Sorry, I thought this would be easier than it actually is."

Her heart melted as she could see the pain etched in his face. She could tell the place meant something to him and his late wife. "I'm so sorry, Iain, you don't have to talk about it. Let's just enjoy the meal, and the company."

"No, I'd like to explain, Jenny, bear with me, and so long as you don't get mad at me for coming here with you."

"Get mad at you? Heck Iain, in my sixty plus years this is the most interesting restaurant I've ever been in." No sooner were the words out of her mouth, Iain jerked his head up to stare. *Damn, damn, damn.*

"Sixty plus years? Just how old are you?

"Did I say sixty? I meant thirty, slip of the tongue, sorry. I'm thirty-five, Iain. Don't tell me you think I look in my sixties."

They both laughed at how ludicrous it would be if she was that old.

Dodged a bullet there. She breathed a deep silent sigh of relief.

He nodded then slowly topped up their glasses. Jenny wondered if it was to buy time as he gathered his thoughts. Before he could begin his tale, Tuyen arrived with a tray balanced on her arm.

"*Goi Cuon,*" she said, as if everyone but the dumbest people in the world knew what she meant.

A small plate appeared in front of Jenny with three quite large, but somehow delicate, soft spring rolls, so clear she could see the glistening prawns and various salad greens and herbs inside.

Alongside sat a small bowl with some form of dipping sauce, which by the slices of garlic, chili and fresh herbs floating could only be homemade and fresh. It all looked divine, and she watched as Iain was served with his. Tuyen bowed as Iain and Jenny both said thank you, then she left them alone again.

"Vietnamese Spring rolls, we would call them," Iain informed her. They both picked up their chopsticks

33

as one and snapped them apart. Jenny was not the most proficient with them but she managed to pick up one of the rolls and successfully dipped it in the sauce and took a bite. Her mouth was instantly ablaze with flavors, none of them overpowering the other. It was fantastic.

She put the uneaten spring roll half and chopsticks on her plate and closed her eyes to savor the merry-go-round of tastes going on in her mouth. When she opened her eyes, Iain was smiling broadly.

"Okay?" he asked.

"Okay? No, it is soooooooo much better than okay. It's like...bloody hell, like my mouth just found out it's alive. Now stop talking to me, you're distracting me from the best thing I've had in months." In another moment, the last half had been dipped and was being rolled over her tongue. She confirmed the first taste was no mistake; it was seriously good.

It would, have been sacrilegious to speak until the last morsel of spring roll had been dipped and eaten, and Jenny wondered what was best: the roll itself or the dipping sauce? To find out, she put the tip of her index finger in what little remained of the liquid and tasted it, but that was futile as she hadn't tasted the roll without dipping it. It didn't matter, she had never had anything quite like it before, and she couldn't wait for what arrived as the next course.

She put her chopsticks down, and cleared her throat. "There's a problem, Iain. The trouble with starting with something that good is, inevitably, it must now go downhill. I think we should leave, and not risk it happening."

He grinned with a smug, happy look on his face.

He picked up his glass, and she matched his movement as she remembered the toast. As one they softly said: "*mot, hi, bah, yo,*" and drank.

Behind them a family paid their bill at what passed for a counter, as Iain began his tale. "Brad was ten when Simone and I took our first holiday together. We married young and she fell pregnant quite early in the piece, so money was never plentiful enough for an overseas trip. As for why we chose Vietnam when we finally could afford one? Well, Simone's father was killed in the war there at the battle of Long Tan. He was based at Da Nang and it kind of seemed proper we visit by way of paying our respects."

It occurred to Jenny, in a flash, what an incredible man he was, and *chink*: a small piece of her heart was lost to him. She reached across the table with her right hand to touch his left. She closed it over his and felt the wedding ring he still wore; she squeezed gently.

"It's an amazing country, Jen, beautiful, and the people? They are just so genuinely warm and welcoming. We fell in love with the place, loved Da Nang, and we spent a lot of time in and around Hoi An, which is a very historical town about an hour away. We returned the next year, then every year after. Brad and I still go at the end of the soccer season; it's like a pilgrimage for us.

"So, anyway a while back, this place was mentioned to me by a Vietnamese man I deliver to, and because the name was so like the town's name Simone and I loved so much, Brad and I ventured here to try it. The rest is, well, history. We come here quite a bit. Tuyen treats Brad like he's her own son. It's quite remarkable to see her get all mother-hen over him." He raised his glass and once again, she matched him. "*Mot, hi, bah, yo.*"

At this rate, I'm going to be rolling drunk. But, I can't imagine a nicer way for it to happen, than right here with this man.

"That's a wonderful story Iain. I am so sorry about your wife. I've never been married myself, to be truthful, never even had a man who stuck around. I suppose I've always been tough to get along with. I not only teach during the day but devote some of my nights to tutoring gifted students and mentoring others. I guess you could say we have something in common, helping gifted kids I mean."

"Jen, if a man wouldn't stick around you, then I think that's well and truly his loss."

She was saved from responding to such a lovely complement when Tuyen arrived to take the plates. "You still want menu, Miss Jenny?" She asked, before cackling again in the funny way she did.

Jenny looked up, "Tuyen, if everything else to come is as good as those spring rolls you can serve me what you like and you won't hear a word of complaint. Please thank your husband for me. They were sensational."

"Okay, I tell him you no like the *Goi Cuon*. Make him try harder for next course." Then she left laughing again.

"You know, Iain, I feel sorry for all the people who will never know this place is here. Especially the ones who look in the window, as I would have done, and walked on."

"I don't. If word got out how good it is, we'd never get a table."

"Amen to that," and she held her glass up. There was just enough in it for one more toast. "*Mot, hi, bah, yo.*" Then her glass was empty, and Iain topped it up again, then his with red wine.

"So, I think I need to re-schedule some students around, what nights are training?"

"You mean you're still serious? You still want to be a helper? Wow. We train Tuesday and Thursday from six thirty to eight thirty. I saw you talking to Geordie. Well, Brenda, his wife, does some food for the boys for which the club charges ten dollars and we have a few drinks. Usually the night's over between nine and ten. You really were serious?"

"Oh yes, I'm serious, well for a month anyway, I may have to go away for a while after. But while I'm here, Iain, I can't think of anything I'd rather do in the world than be with you…and help your team."

His face dropped, and she could see the sadness in his eyes. "You have to go away? I thought it was too good to be true. Oh well, there are only four games left this season anyway."

"I said might; it's not set in concrete yet. And um, well you can have me for the next four weeks, if you want to. I just decided to stop all my tutoring for a while. If you like, if you umm, wanted to keep seeing me, you could.

There was a drawn-out silence. Iain sipped his wine again before he spoke: "I've never invited anyone else here, Jenny. Since Simone, I've not dated anyone, not even considered it. Then out of the blue, you rocket into my life. Yes. I think I'd like to see you again. You know it was Brad who helped convince me into this? He said three years is long enough to be a hermit. Kids,

37

huh? Sometimes they know more than their parents."

Chink. That's another piece of my heart gone.

"Tell me about Brad, Iain, he sounds like he's one amazing young man."

Tuyen appeared as if by magic carrying her tray again, with two steaming clay pots and a larger bowl of rice perched on it. As she placed the bowls on the table she said: *"Ca Kho To."*

Iain smiled; clearly he remembered this dish from a previous visit.

She looked questioningly, but he just smiled the same grin and stayed silent. Tuyen spooned rice into their individual bowls and took the lids off the clay pots. The odor which emanated from within was unlike anything she had experienced before, sweet yet sour with the hint of fish, chili and garlic. Once Tuyen left, Jenny copied Iain as he spooned the mixture of large lumps of caramelized fish and vegetables in a thick sticky, glutinous broth on top of rice.

The spring rolls were fantastic, but this dish is spectacular, oh my God.

The complex but subtle and distinct flavors rolled over her tongue, each one trying to outdo the other. The chili raised mist to her eyes, and the garlic took her breath away. The fish was soft and flaked in her mouth and tasted so sweet, yet sour. She sat back in her chair and looked up to see Iain was close to laughter. *My emotions must be written all over my face.*

"So, you're not enjoying it then?"

"Not enjoying it? Are you kidding me? This is the best meal I've ever had in my life. How does he cook this fish?"

"No idea, he doesn't speak a word of English, or so

Tuyen says. Even if he told you, unless you know the language you're never going to find out. I stopped wondering a long time ago. I think of it as a bit like watching a magician; if you ever found out how he did his tricks you'd feel disappointed. It's enough for me to just enjoy."

She nodded at his wisdom and picked up her chopsticks again. Every mouthful was a delight, and the rice absorbed the flavorful broth. There was more to come, a hot spicy noodle soup arrived the moment the fish dish was finished, and then Jenny's eyes did water from the chili. That didn't stop her though; she drained her bowl only stopping to make toasts with Ian and drink more wine.

"No more, I'm full," she told Iain after swallowing the last spoonful of soup. "Oh my God, what a meal. Can we come back again?"

He smiled a very lopsided smile; he didn't look happy. "I guess we could squeeze it into one of our nights left. So, where are you going then?"

She looked across the table; his face showed a tinge of sadness. How could she answer that, without lying? She could not afford to drop the future 'bomb' on him too soon. It was ironic that to gain trust she had to tell lies. She remembered a teaching exchange program which was announced every year that held no appeal before, but now was the time to use it. "It's a teacher exchange program, if I get offered it, and I accept, I'd be going to the States, and we get one of their lecturers to replace me here."

He nodded, "Yeah, I can see why you'd want to do that. Well, I better get the bill and get you home. We both have work tomorrow."

She grabbed his hand and held onto it, stopping him from rising. "Hey, Iain. Did I do something wrong? Seems like suddenly you want to get rid of me, what happened?"

His shoulders sagged, and he had that schoolboy hand caught in the cookie jar look again. "I'm sorry Jenny. I'm way out of practice with this sort of thing. I suppose I just hoped, well, you know, we maybe had a chance of something."

"Maybe we do."

"Not with you going to America, we won't."

She looked deeply into his eyes, "So, make me want to stay."

****

The ride in the taxi back to Jenny's small home was somber, despite her holding Iain's hand all the way. He seemed more than distracted, and when she made conversation he gave non-committal answers. The sparkle so evident in his voice, eyes, and manner earlier was gone, and Jenny cursed herself for telling him they only had days remaining. Her intention had been to build some urgency, so they could see each other every night, rather than every few days. Time was ticking away. She worried it may have backfired and he acted as if to avoid future hurt he chose to cut ties now.

If she couldn't snare his emotional interest in her, then all she had left was the truth, and that was scary. She worried deeply that his love for his son, and respect for his dream to feed the starving world, would outweigh any belief in her story of future devastation and time travel.

She stared out into the night, hoping for a change in him, but fearing there wouldn't be. She'd had a wonderful night with him, and despite everything else, that was the tragedy. She would have loved to have met him, as herself as she was in this time zone, without her "Leap". Maybe then, back in 2049 she wouldn't be so lonely, with only her students and cat for company.

She thought of all the things she had missed out on in a lifetime spent alone. Her studies, and following an intellectual, academic life had seemed more important at the time than a relationship with a man, but, if only she had met Iain. She'd been foolish, she suspected, with a heavy heart.

"Iain, please don't let this be the end, I've had an amazing night with you."

He turned, smiling faintly, "I had a good time too."

"Will you come in for a coffee?" She gave him her best smile, unused as she was to giving men a 'come hither' look, as her mother would call it. But he just stared back and shook his head."

"It's not you, it's me, Jenny. Simone died three years ago, and this is the first time I've gone out with someone else. I feel like I'm not being fair to her memory, or you, hoping you might give up your trip to the States. I'm just confused, and I think I just need a little time."

"Ah, yes, time. If only there was more time."

"I will see you Tuesday, at training, maybe we can talk afterward, if you still want to help, that is. Maybe everything will look clearer then, I hope so because I'm just so lost at this moment."

Chink. Another piece of my heart gone. Why does he have to be so wonderful?

"Okay, Iain, I understand, I'll see you Tuesday night."

Chapter 4
Timing is Everything

April 19th 2055, Zimbabwe, Africa.

How could something so promisingly good, turn out to be so bad? President Omba Mubanty, The President of Zimbabwe looked out over the dead and dying fields of wheat.

He was on his way to a meeting with the best agricultural brains his country had, to try find a way to halt the progress of whatever disease was killing the wheat crops in this area of the savannah. For twenty-six years, farms had planted the wonder grain provided as a gift from the Australian Government, and starvation and poverty were now things of the past.

Droughts and floods had not halted the growth of the crops, which after the first year's assessment, had been granted to more farms across the nation. The wheat had thrived no matter what disaster Africa's weather threw at it.

After generations of despots and warlords who had raped and pillaged his beloved country before him, he brought wealth, security, and safety to his people. Under his rule he welcomed the help from other more fortunate countries than his, and had not syphoned it off into his own bank accounts.

His father sent him to school, and then University

in Melbourne, and he studied hard and loved the Australian people, and their values.

When he returned home, it was to a bankrupt country which had been at civil war for decades, and he worked hard to gain the people's trust. He alone led them out of the darkness and into the light. He convinced the warlords and militia to put away their weapons and open farmland as the only way forward. It was a long, slow process, but he prevailed and gained the respect of everyone. When the next election was called, despite threats and wholesale killings of all who were called 'dissidents' by the government in power, he won a landslide vote.

Once in power he begged the Australian Government for help, and they gave him the 'Destaine' grain, rather than financial aid. The Foreign Affairs Minister of the day touted the adage: "Give a man a fish and he eats one meal, teach him how to catch fish and he eats for a lifetime."

That had been in line with Mubanty's own beliefs, and he welcomed the wheat with open arms. Within five years, more farms took on the wonder grain, and within ten, starvation was obliterated. They became an exporter of the grain to other African Countries, which had built wealth for all, and allowed for new hospitals and schools to be constructed. The country had changed for the better, Mubanty felt very proud of his achievements, and he was adored by the people.

But then, just when things appeared so perfect, the first cases of yellow spot had appeared and the yields had declined at harvest. They had stockpiled plenty of fresh grain so the farmers just shrugged and re-planted. But the next harvest was worse.

But then, a farm in the Eastern part of the country, reported an entire field of Destaine, comprising some six hectares, had turned brown and shriveled up. The other fields surrounding it were fine, but the yellow spot had increased its presence significantly. They harvested as normal, sprayed with pesticides, and ploughed into the soil the dead wheat, and planted again believing it was some random outside cause.

The field which had been ploughed over, stayed like a barren dessert, but no one placed significance in that until later.

The next harvest was better, as was the one after, but this year it was over twenty hectares which died, and everyone worried.

Mubanty had always been a benevolent man, but now he faced an uncertain future as the Blight spread to other farms. He could have reported it to Australia and ask for their help, but instead he chose to keep it secret to save face. Meanwhile he hired biologists and experts to form a committee with one objective: to find a solution.

"The Yellow Spot Blight" as it was to become known, took its foothold in Zimbabwe, destined to be the country blamed for many years as the originator of the plant disease, which, in time, would threaten to destroy the world.

****

November 14th 2112, Nebraska

Nebraska Farmer Carl Ontario held the corncob he had just plucked in his hand and studied it. *What the heck is that?*

He stood among row after row of corn stalks dancing as one in the morning breeze. Each day he walked into a different area of his crop and picked a cob to check for ripening. It was an old-fashioned way, but it was how his father and grandfather before him had done it. If it was good enough for them, it was good enough for him.

He saw some yellow spots on the corn ears inside their protective green sheaths, and he had never seen the like of it before. If he hadn't caught the tiny yellow spots glinting in the sunshine, he may have harvested next month and not been any the wiser. He tucked the corncob in his denim overalls pocket and walked three rows deeper and took another one from the stem. He ripped the husks away and there it was again. But five rows further in, the cob he picked didn't display the spots and he breathed a sigh of relief. The problem, if it was a problem, was in one area. Perhaps it was a bug, or weather related, some form of mildew?

The next thought was one of worry. If he reported it, as he should, to the Department of Agriculture, they might shut his farm down as a precautionary measure while they spent the next few weeks or months investigating further. They could burn his crops to stop whatever this was from spreading. He had seen it happen to other farmers who suffered outbreaks of disease. While the government always promised compensation, it was never enough, and never paid on time to avert financial catastrophe for the farmer. They always ended up bankrupt with the bastard banks foreclosing.

He decided to say nothing, but to watch and wait and see if it got any worse.

****

June 24th 2181, San Francisco. USA

45

Julian Michaels, aged sixty-nine, sat open mouthed while at a window table in the revolving restaurant called: The View.

It was aptly named as the building sat on the Northern bank of the San Francisco Bay and on days when the fog wasn't too bad, diners could watch Fisherman's Harbor, Alcatraz Island, The Golden Gate Bridge and the city itself go by at a steady two miles an hour. By anyone's definition it was spectacular, as was the five-star food served there.

A lunch booking for a table with a view would need to have been made at least a month before on any midweek day, and over three months' prior for a weekend. Dinner bookings were only slightly better on weekends, but during the week sometimes, a patron could get lucky and secure a cancelation, though they were very rare.

Good quality fresh vegetables were becoming more expensive to source because of The Blight which was affecting varied crops in odd areas. Everyone complained about it, and the government promised they were doing everything possible, but some things which had been cheap and common only a few years before, were now outrageously expensive or not available at all.

Julien Michaels was the guest of the much younger and extremely wealthy property tycoon and developer, Henry Van Anst III. Henry had a table permanently booked for lunch on the second Tuesday of every month, and would decide, often at the last minute, whom he would invite. Everyone in San Francisco knew Henry by reputation. In business, he was a shark, and never took prisoners. It was said he was great fun at parties, and he was renowned for his sense of humor and ability to play the most elaborate, and sometimes expensive, practical jokes on unsuspecting friends.

When Julien's secretary told him, he had an incoming call from Henry Van Anst, he worried. Julien did not move in the same circles; he was a very small time realtor who specialized in apartments for first time home buyers. With heart in mouth he took the call and was shocked to his very core when Henry didn't waste time on pleasantries.

"Julien? I know you don't know me, but I'm sure you're aware of me. I will come straight to the point, there's no sense mucking around is there?"

He didn't wait for a response, just carried on, treating his own question as rhetorical. "Tomorrow, one o'clock I want you to come to lunch as my guest at The View. I have an offer for you and, if you take it, I will pay you one million dollars for one day's work. What do you say, shall I pencil you in?"

"I, err, umm, well, yes, I err...*what*? One million dollars for one day's work?"

"Mention my name at the desk on the ground floor when you arrive, and they will escort you up. See you then Julien, I'm looking forward to meeting you." And, much to Julien's astonishment, the connection was broken.

He couldn't sleep that night, and kept his wife awake by asking her every hour or so what she thought Henry Van Anst could want with him. By three in the morning she lost her temper and told him: "Julian, if you ask me one more time you won't be going to see Henry Van-fucking-Anst, because I will have throttled you."

Charlene was not the kind of woman to make mad, or cause to lose sleep, and Julien knew well enough not to wake her again. Instead, he got up and sat on his balcony until the sun rose above the gray skyline, worrying what he had done to cause the interest, and invitation of one of the leading business lights in the bay area.

Julien thought lunch was the best meal he had ever experienced in his life. After the main course of perfectly prepared saffron lobster tail with truffle glazed asparagus tips and a salad of just wilted cilantro with Danish ham, cherry tomatoes, and crumbled Danish feta cheese, Henry placed on the table between them a vial of rose colored liquid which he took from his extremely fashionable Italian red leather bag.

"I have here a contract, already signed by me to pay you, in cash, one million dollars, for you to work for me at my home, for a twenty-four-hour period. That will follow a couple of days studying history with me. Not only will I gladly pay you this sum, but I can tell you if you accept, you could be instrumental in saving the entire future population of the planet. What do you say?"

Two hours later, Julien Michaels agreed to be a "Leaper."

Chapter 5
Time Out

June 15th 2018

Bradley Destaine walked out of the conference room, calmly shut the heavy oak door behind him, then fist pumped the air. He had the urge to scream at the top of his voice: "*Yes, who's your daddy?*" but they would hear him back inside if he did.

They had approved trials of his wheat in five different locations around the state. Sure, it was only at quarantined testing stations and there was a lot more work to do, hoops to jump through and red tape to cut. But he had won the right to a trial, and this was a big day. They had approved changing the designation of his grain from the computer-generated letters and numbers to the word: Destaine, which acknowledged him, as the person responsible for its discovery.

He considered phoning Lyndsay but thought better of it. With bitterness bordering on rage he shook his head. She made her choice and it excluded him from her life; though he still felt the pain and bitterness of separation. She should have accepted how vital his work was and stood by him because of it.

Typical, now I can slow down she's living with Eamon, or Aemon, or demon; however, he spells his fucking name.

It was too late for them to have a second chance; she'd burned her bridges and no matter how much Brad missed her, he could not forgive her treachery.

In his quieter, more reflective moments, he supposed he couldn't blame her for getting bored. He worked long hours because he had been close to a monumental discovery that could save millions of lives. There was no way he could slow down, let alone stop, when he alone held the key to feeding drought-stricken third world nations. They fought, many times about it, but he couldn't, wouldn't, cut his hours when he sensed he was so near to the pot of gold at the end of the rainbow.

His wheat was amazing. It repelled problems like mold and staining from heavy rains at the wrong times, or lack of fertilizer and drought. It withstood attacks from the most virulent insects and bacteria he could throw at it. He had engineered it well. During a period of lying dormant, it learned to adapt, then, when it did bounce back, it was immune.

It was remarkable, and today, finally he had shown his bosses it was time for clinical trials out in the open. They would see how fantastic his discovery would be in uncontrolled weather conditions, and he could get the recognition he deserved. He heard whispers there was considerable corporate interest, and financial reward on offer, and he would ultimately receive a percentage, which could set him up financially for life.

Brad whistled a tune as he walked with a spring in his step, back to his shared lab and office, throwing off his dark mood and angst of losing Lyndsay. He wanted to phone his father to tell him the news; he would be thrilled to hear of the success. But, his father wouldn't answer his phone while driving the truck. Bluetooth was a technology alien to his father, who stayed firmly stuck in the nineties. Better to wait for his lunchbreak and call then.

He sat at his desk and thought about his father and how much that relationship meant. For as far back as Brad could remember his dad had been there for him. Not only providing the money to go to university and study, but helping with assignments, urging when he needed to be forced, and praising when he had needed that, too.

When his mother died after the agonizingly slow march of breast cancer, Brad could have thrown everything away, and would have, if it hadn't been for his father. He offered simultaneously a shoulder to cry on, a sounding board for his grief, a mentor for his studies, and a loving friend to help support and propel him forward.

He was saddened that his father spent so much time making sure Brad was all right; he had shelved his own life. He never dated another woman, and yes there was a time when Brad wouldn't have been comfortable with something like that. But, eventually, he would have understood, if not welcomed it. But his father got out of the habit, or worse, accepted his lot in life to be single.

The times he talked to his father about it, he would say things like: "There will only ever be one woman for me, Brad." Or "I had my one true love, there won't be another." Brad loved and respected him, but he wished there could be someone else for him to grow old with.

While his father started to show gray at the temples, he wasn't overweight, and was still a good-looking man. Surely, he would be a great catch for a woman in his age bracket? But if he wasn't coaching at soccer training or on match days, he wouldn't leave the house for any reason other than work, which was sad.

Despite whatever success may come Brad's way, he wished his father could find some happiness, but he had to admit, he had his doubts.

****

Day Seven, August 8th 2016, 12:27am

Jenny lay awake in bed, on her back, with her hands behind her head, staring up at the dark ceiling, saddened by how the night had gone wrong after it had started so well. She liked Iain and was deeply disappointed that he'd refused to come inside after dinner. It had been many years since she had made love with anyone in her thirty-five-year-old world, longer than she cared to remember. And between her now age, and when she made her "Leap", it hadn't happened then either. She had never all but thrown herself at a man only to be refused, well, not since her student days. Even forgetting the plight of the future of mankind, she felt like she had lost something so very important.

Her thoughts raced around inside her head, trying to make sense of it all. She had feelings for Iain, who she could only have met because of time travel and she was very unused to such emotions. If she had not come back she would not be experiencing this sense of loss. She blamed herself completely for the breakdown and cursed her lack of good judgement in telling him they only had limited time together. With the benefit of hindsight, she should have said nothing.

Then there was the other problem. It seemed the only way to enlist him as an ally to talk his son out of the course of action he was destined to follow meant she had to be dishonest, and she hated that.

True, he assured her the problem of her going away didn't affect his desire to see her in the interim; he thought he was being unfaithful to the memory of his departed wife, Simone. It had been only three years since she died, and while Jenny had never loved anyone, she could well imagine if she had she would probably never get over his death.

How could I possibly have thought I could win Iain's heart, and then jointly stop Brad? The whole thing was madness and I should never have agreed to try.

She'd blown it. She sensed that in her heart, and she felt like she should cry. Her failure not only affected her life, now and into the future, but all of civilization two hundred years hence.

Should I care?

The end of the world didn't affect her; it was in the very distant future. She could just not worry about it. Why not live out the remaining days in her younger body, as if it were a holiday, and simply not care about the consequences. But, she did care, which was why she took the "Leap" in the first place.

No doubt that was why those desperate men, who so cold heartedly plotted her course two hundred years in the future, chose her. They knew she would want to be a part of saving the world. She was an easy mark for them, she supposed. She spent her whole life trying to teach students about the environment and trying to instill a sense of responsibility within them. The inhabitants of the planet had a duty to care for the damned place. She pounded her students non-stop to believe future generations relied on them to ensure they could live in the sun, and not the darkness.

She felt, with some amazement, a single tear trickle slowly down the side of her face. *Oh, my God, am I crying over him, or the future of the world?* Without any doubt in her mind, it was over Iain. *How can that be?*

At twelve thirty-six in the morning, the sound of the text message tone of her phone shrilled and made her jump. She had to stop herself, again, from thinking as her sixty-eight-year-old consciousness dictated, and realize she was a thirty-five-year-old woman. She scanned her memory with a growing excitement in the pit of her tummy. Jenny was not in the habit of late night text messages in either time stream. Ergo, there could be only one possible explanation: Iain.

She leapt out of bed and tripped over her long nightdress which had tangled around her feet with the sheets. Fortunately, she recovered before she fell sprawling across the floor. Once in the darkened living room she frantically looked around to see where she had left her phone. The text tone had stopped, so it couldn't direct her to it. The room was lit by faint moonlight filtering through the curtains and she couldn't see her handbag anywhere.

She raced to the light switch, then spent precious seconds blinking rapidly trying to let her eyes adjust to the sudden brightness. There was her handbag, on the recliner armchair. It looked sadly forlorn and abandoned, and she remembered she had tossed it there in a state of near depression when she had come home.

Within moments she held the phone in her hand, jabbed the home key and entered her code to turn it on: *Incorrect Code—Try Again.*

Fuck, fuck, fuck, fuck and fuck, she chanted in her head until she had cleared the screen and, more slowly this time, put in 7777. The screen lit up, and there was what she hoped to see:

—I know you are asleep but I just wanted you to know I'm laying here, in bed, not tired. I am kicking myself for being a dummy and I wish I was there with you. I'm so sorry my stupidity made our night end on a downer. I had the best time I've had in years with you, and I just wanted you to know. I hope I haven't blown it.—

Oh, my God. She felt tears trickle down both cheeks. She was elated, so much so she felt she could scream with joy. She sat back in the recliner, squashing her handbag, but didn't care. She thought how she should reply. The seconds dragged into minutes, her mind racing, thinking, tapping, then correcting until she had it how she believed it should be.

—I'm awake too, and I thought I was the dummy, not you. I'm so sorry for telling you about me maybe going away. I do understand how tough this is for you, after losing Simone. I had a wonderful night, and not just because the food was divine. I enjoyed your company. I want you to know I'm patient. I believe the best things in life are worth waiting for, and I will wait for you to feel ready to take the plunge again into the dating pool.—

Time dragged very slowly for Jenny while she stared at the phone, willing it to 'chirp' its message tone again. She saw, with horror, she was biting her thumbnail; she hadn't done that since school days when she was studying for exams. She took a slow, deep breath, and told herself to calm down. She was an adult, not a child with a crush. When her phone did sound and vibrated its announcement, Jenny was so taken by surprise she almost dropped it.

Wouldn't that be hilarious; smash the damned phone so I can't read his message?

—You're a funny lady. Take a plunge in the dating pool? LOL—

She laughed. A genuine, happy, ecstatic laugh. Once again, she had tears rolling down her cheeks. *Oh, my God, what is the matter with me?*

—Yes, come on in, the water's fine. I know CPR too if you get in trouble.—

—You know Brad was waiting up for me when I got home. He asked me how the date went and I told him I think I blew it with you. He called me a stupid dork. I think he's right.—

—He's not. You didn't blow it, and I don't think of you as a dork, though it is a cute nick-name.—

—So how about another date tonight?—

—I'm in, what did you have in mind?—

—Barbeque, my house. Brad wants to meet you.—

—I could rustle up a potato salad; I think I remember how to make one.—

—Really? Wow.—

—What, you think I can't make potato salad?—

—No, no, no, I was surprised you said yes so easy. I had all these things I was going to say to convince you when you said no.—

—You realize we are texting like teenagers, don't you?—

—Yeah, it's fun, isn't it?—

—Yes. You should see the massive smile on my face.—

—So, take a pic and send it to me.—

—You're kidding me; you want a selfie? In my nightie? I don't do selfies.—

—MMM is it see through?—

Her face reddened deeply. He wants to see my body! A part of her wanted to show him, and she was shocked at that. This was not who she was, or how she behaved. Then, in the next instant, she decided that in her sixty-eight years, maybe she should have behaved this way, at least once.

But her nightie was far from sexy, it resembled something her mother, or even her grandmother might have worn. Before she could change her mind and chicken out, she flipped both straps off her shoulders and let them slip down. She then thrust her arms against her sides to stop the halt. Sexy was one thing, topless something else entirely, she was not ready to take that leap.

—Are you still there? Did I go too far? I'm sorry I was only kidding.—

No, you weren't, buster. You were flirting, and hoping I would flirt back, and oh my God, I am going to.

With trembling hands, she switched her phone to the camera option, then turned it around, aimed and smiled her best smile, before thumbing the capture button. Jenny argued with herself whether to look at the photo first, but, if she did, she would then never find the nerve to send it to him. Within seconds it winged its way to Iain through the ether and only then did she look at what she had sent.

Oh my God! She stared at the picture. Her hair was all over the place, understandably so, as she had been in bed only minutes before. Her eyes were puffy, her cheeks red and her floral flannelette nightie, which resembled the curtains that used to adorn her late grandmother's home, only barely concealed her nipples. But, somehow, incredibly, she looked hot. Damned hot. A line she remembered from a movie, though which one escaped her memory. She bit her lip, her mind racing, what if he doesn't like what he sees?

—*You're beautiful.*—

—*Cut it out, I'm a mess, you're being way too kind.*—

—*You have stunning breasts, my God you are realy beautiful Jenny.*—

—*Seriously stop it now, I am blushing. I've never done anything like that before, just so you know.*—

—*I'm going to be staring at you when I go to sleep.*—

—*Well that's not fair then. I don't have a pic of you.*—

—*Okay, I can fix that, your wish is my command.*—

The next message had a picture attached. She opened it up and smiled, while biting her lip. *Oh my God, he is sooooooo handsome.* He was sitting up in bed, his bare chest was not too hairy, and he wasn't overweight, though his hair too was messy, but on him it looked good.

—*You know that's not going to help me sleep, you know that, right?*—

—*I have no idea what you mean* ☺—

—*Yes, you do. I want to run my nails over your chest.*—

—*You are one incredibly sexy, beautiful woman.*—

—*Aww shucks. Will you quit it with the*

58

compliments, I'm not used to getting them.—

—Well I can think of two things to say. One, I have no idea why men haven't said that and more to you, clearly all your academic male friends are blind. Secondly, you better get used to it, because I'm going to be saying it a lot.—

—Promise?—

—Promise.—

Jenny sat back in the chair and shook her head. Her older self, let alone her younger version, had never experienced anything quite like this. Her heart raced, she felt on the one hand so wonderfully excited, yet on the other she missed Iain, yearned for him, and longed to be with him. She wanted to feel his lips on hers, his hands on her body, and more. She shuddered deeply, even sadly as realization dawned on her. This would not, could not last. She would wake up from this dream and not even remember it had happened in only a few weeks.

—You know it's after one in the morning, and we both have work tomorrow, I mean today. I'm so glad you texted Iain, even though I'm not going to sleep well, I need to try.—

—Me too. I have to be up at five-thirty. Thank you for sending the picture, I will treasure it. So, can I pick you up and at six? Will you have the potato salad made by then?—

—Oh, I think I can manage that. Six o'clock will be fine. I'm nervous about this.—

—What, making salad?—

—No, dummy. Meeting Brad. I hope he likes me.—

—How could he not? Remember he told me I was a dork when I told him I blew it with you. He is going to

love you, don't worry.—

—I hope so. Night, Iain, see you at six.—

****

Jenny doubted she got more than two hours' sleep before the alarm clock/radio woke her with the cheery morning radio announcers laughing at their own humor, and playing songs she had listened to many times before.

Her first reaction was to shut off the radio, and then go back to sleep. When she woke again she could call the university and feign illness. The idea had merits, for sure. But then, inevitably her thoughts turned to Iain, and she smiled. Then she didn't feel so tired any longer.

He said he liked my breasts. Her skin glowed as she warmed from head to toe as she remembered how naughty she had been. Lying in bed, stretching, she looked down at herself. As if by magic, the neckline of her nightie had bloused out, and through the gap she could see her thirty-five-year-old left breast, and her nipple was stiff. If Iain liked them when they were partially hidden, what would he think when he uncovered them, and held them in his big strong hands. *Oh, my God, how would he be when he kissed them?* She closed her eyes and imagined that.

She imagined him suckling from her, holding them in his hands, softly caressing her, kissing first her lips, then her breasts and back again. Her lower tummy tingled and she squeezed her thighs together. She was turned on, incredibly so, and she couldn't, for the life of her, remember when she had last felt like this in either time stream. She wanted to lift her nightie and slip her hand inside her panties, which was another shock for her once near puritanical mind.

I must stop this, right now. I'm not some adolescent schoolgirl, I'm a sixty-eight, no...No I am not. I am a thirty-five-year-old woman. She gave into the feeling. Jenny sat up and wriggled the ugly nightdress off and threw it across the room toward the bathroom door where it fell unceremoniously to the floor. Laying back she lifted her bottom from the mattress and slipped her plain white cotton panties down to her knees then snaking her legs alternately until she got one leg free of them. With the other she flicked them away to join her nightie on the floor. She was naked and she felt so bad, yet good, as one hand closed over her left breast and her other touched her incredibly silky velvet wetness.

Oh, my God. I wish Iain could see me now. Maybe I will send him a picture. She couldn't possibly do that, but the thought of being so naughty, forced her excitement to build even higher.

****

Jenny was tired at work; she did not know how she was going to make it through the day. The morning dragged its heels all the way through. While she lectured, berated, laughed at, and cajoled her students, in the back of her mind was a dilemma. True in the grand scheme of things, like the end of civilization, it was a minor one. But, on a personal level, it was momentous. She did not possess any underwear she wanted Iain to see her in, let alone remove! The thought of him seeing her semi-naked filled her with dueling, competing wonders. It turned her on incredibly so, and it was a unique experience. To be so excited at the mere thought of Iain was wondrous. But, she didn't want him, at worst, laughing, and at best, pitying her because her underwear was far from elegant. Sensible, is how she would describe it, and that was being complimentary. But what to do about it in the time she had before six?

Once she finished work she would barely have enough time to stop at the market to buy the makings, so she could follow her mother's recipe for the potato salad she had promised. *Why did I even do that?* The bloody thing needed to be cooked, then cooled, before she could add the other ingredients. It would be such a rush. She felt better when she made the decision not to make the mayonnaise, but to buy a bottle. Her mother would be horrified, naturally, but time was too precious, and if she ever mentioned it, Jenny would lie.

The thought of her Mother caused her to stop short, and she shook her head at the confusion of time travel. Her Mother lived in Melbourne, and other than occasional phone calls, they rarely caught up. It wasn't that they didn't like each other; it was more their family was…stilted. Brains was their family's watchword, not emotion. So, it was hardly likely Jenny would be conversing with her mother in this incarnation and would forget everything when she left to go back to the future. Ergo, conversations about the lack of homemade mayonnaise being in or out of the damned salad was simply not going to happen. She shook her head at her own silliness.

After work she had to buy the ingredients and prepare the salad. Then, she had to find time to shower, do her hair, shave her legs, and, she blushed and grinned at she thought: trim her bikini line. That sensual mental image guided her back to what underwear she could possibly wear, because she hoped to let Iain see it as he uncovered her body.

Suddenly a plan occurred to her and she breathed a sigh of relief. The distance from the UWA campus, to The Claremont Shopping Quarter should be close enough to drive to it in her lunch break, so long as she could get a parking bay. She shook her head with wonder at her audacity. The Claremont Quarter was not somewhere she would normally buy clothes—let alone underwear; far too expensive for her tastes and budget.

But, this is an emergency, so damn the cost.

She remembered going there for a colleague's farewell lunch the year before. The rather lovely café they had eaten at was close to a chic looking intimate shop called Secret Desires and she remembered thinking that some of the things in the window did look very movie starlet like.

Jenny had always been a woman who believed clothes and underwear were a necessity, rather than something worn to attract and titillate the opposite sex. A bra was for comfort and to stop unnecessary jiggling in front of her students, not titillating a man. Now she was wondering if she had spent her sixty-eight, *there I did it again,* thirty-five years on the planet living in a fugue. What had she been missing out on? This feeling of barely suppressed excitement was worth more than all the tea in China, as her mother always used to say.

So, she would skip eating lunch, whizz to Claremont instead, throw herself on the mercy and experience of a staff member at the lingerie shop, then get back to Uni. Problem solved, and she faced her students in a happier frame of mind.

****

Oh, my good God.

Jenny stood inside Secret Desires, slightly out of

breath from rushing through the crowds after almost running from the car parking spot she had eventually secured. She stared at all the underwear sets on display, feeling lost and confused. They ranged from the demure to silky sexy to the satin harlot. There were even playful nurse and police outfits. She felt like a fish out of water. She would have run away and canceled her date with Iain were it not for a woman at that moment coming to her rescue.

"Hi, I'm Janet, forgive me for saying so, but you look a bit like a deer caught in the headlights. Don't worry, I'm here to help, what can I do for you?"

Jenny turned to see a tall beautiful woman with long full brunette hair, and big brown eyes, smiling at her. Janet looked to be in her early forties, and by her dress and manner she appeared so much worldlier wise than herself. Jenny experienced a shiver of terror and embarrassment at her predicament in front of such a sophisticated woman.

"Thanks, but umm, I'm just looking around."

"No, you're not. If you lose your courage and walk out the door you'll never come back, we both know that. Now I want you to put yourself in my hands and tell me what caused you to come here. Let me help you."

Jenny looked around nervously, thanking her lucky stars the shop was empty. "I umm, have a date tonight, and ummm I don't have anything, you know, underclothes wise, I want to wear, for umm, him to see."

Janet beamed the biggest seemingly understanding smile, which helped calm Jenny's frantically beating heart. "Oh, you lucky thing. Special man?"

Jenny nodded, not trusting her voice to not quiver if she spoke out loud.

"First time he gets to sample the woman you really are, and you are not used to that kind of attention?"

She nodded again, as her skin reddened with embarrassment; she wanted to run and hide.

Janet took both Jenny's hands in hers and squeezed them warmly. "You are so going to love it, and you've come to the right place. You and I are going to drive him wild and make him want to spend the rest of his life with you. Now tell me the first thing that comes into your head when I ask you this. Favorite color?"

"Yellow."

Where the hell did yellow come from? Jenny wasn't sure, but had to admit that she did like it, but in underwear? No way!

"Oh good choice, especially with you being blonde. I have just the set for you, come with me." She dropped one of Jenny's hands but kept hold of the other as if she feared Jenny might run away. She led her to the rear of the shop where the change rooms were. She opened the louvered door and firmly guided Jenny inside the cubicle which had the main wall mirrored. "Now, I'm going to guess two things, are you ready?"

"Yes, as ready as I'm ever going to be, I suppose."

"Good girl. Now, first guess you are a 34C?" Jenny nodded. "Good, second one, I'm thinking you are more of a bikini woman rather than a thong?" Again, Jenny nodded. "Sensational, okay, clothes off, I'm going to get something for you to try on. Trust me; he will be eating out of your hands, and everywhere else, when I'm done with you." She winked before turning on her heel, leaving Jenny to undress.

It was all a bit overwhelming, but, she had come this far as another of her mother's sayings entered her mind unbidden. In for a penny, in for a pound. She began to unbutton her shirt with trembling fingers.

"Good grief, where did you buy those awful things? Get them off, you are far too beautiful a woman to wear underwear like that." Janet re-entered the change room cubicle to see Jenny standing with nothing on but her white sensible bra and cotton panties. If she wasn't embarrassed before, those words smashed home to Jenny how she had been living her life, and her skin turned an even darker beet red, with shame.

"Now, now, don't feel like that. Looks like you found me at the right time. I want you to think of yourself like a caterpillar, but when I'm done with you, you will be more like a beautiful butterfly. Come on, get those things off, and try these."

From behind her back Janet held up a small plastic hanger with bra and panties of the finest, most beautiful lace, in the palest tint of yellow, and suddenly, Jenny wanted to see herself wearing them. She took her underwear off while Janet unclipped the items from the hanger, and there was another first. She'd not undressed in front of another woman since school PE lessons.

Janet held the bra out so Jenny could put her arms through, then twirled her fingers to tell Jenny to turn around so Janet could do up the clasp. *Oh, my God.* She stared at herself in the mirror wearing the new bra. Her gaze tracked from her breasts up to her face, and then to the smiling brunette standing behind her.

"See? I told you. Now, just let me just do this, hold still."

The woman's fingers pinched at the thick black

elastic ring which held her ponytail firmly in place. Then she slid it off, and her fingers rubbed and mussed up her long hair. "Don't wear your hair up tonight, brush it and leave it flowing free, you have beautiful hair. Now just slip the panties on, I'm sorry, but you have to put these disposable ones on first." She shrugged as if to say it's the law. "Now, let's see the full picture."

She stepped into them and slid them up, wishing she had trimmed earlier in the shower, but because she had lost time playing with herself she would have been late for work if she had. She turned slowly to face Janet biting her lip, almost to the point of bleeding.

"Ta dah! Oh, my dear, if I were a man I wouldn't be able to keep my hands off you."

Jenny turned back to the mirror and stared open mouthed at her reflection. It was true, she was transformed. "I'll take two hundred sets," she joked.

Whatever these skimpy items cost, it will be worth every cent.

She couldn't stop looking at her body. The silky lace was the perfect combination of see-through and tease. It showed enough, but no more. She could not have dressed like a harlot. She couldn't help it, she raised a hand to her breast, the same one she had squeezed as she orgasmed that morning and felt how soft the material was. "Oh, Janet. I'm so glad I met you. Why didn't I do this years ago?"

"Better late than never. Now I'm going to get you another set in white, and one more in black. But, I know they are pricey, so I'm going to give you three sets for the price of two in hopes it brings you back to me in future. Promise me, no more wearing those ugly things, unless it's that yucky time of the month."

"I promise." And she meant it. But a sudden flash of understanding swept across her mind, though fortunately, Janet had left the cubicle, so didn't see it. In twenty-six days' time, Jenny wouldn't remember where this shop was, so how could she go back? She would have to make a diary. So, when she woke up she could read all the wonderful things she had learned and experienced while she had been asleep. It would help her younger self through the transition. It was a shame, but there was nothing she could do about the memory loss for her older body.

She was late back for her next lecture, and she apologized profusely to the students. She had always been very hard on those who arrived late, so the irony was not lost on her. "You all have one I'm allowed to be ten minutes late to Ms. O'Brien's lecture card you can play in the future. But one only mind," she said sternly, and noted the smiling faces. She had no doubt it would be used against her at some point.

The remainder of the afternoon dragged even more slowly than the morning session had. She couldn't wait to get out of class, make the promised salad, shower and dress in her new underwear.

****

Jenny needn't have worried. She made it with ten minutes to spare. At precisely five-fifty she poured herself a much-needed glass of wine, took a long sip and breathed an enormous sigh of relief.

The salad, which comprised of potato, eggs, triple smoked diced ham, finely grated Swiss cheese and, unfortunately, shop bought mayonnaise, though she did add a touch of sour cream to it, sat in the fridge. It stood almost proudly, she thought, in her best glass bowl, covered in cling film. When she had treated herself to a taste test earlier she had nodded, not too shabby at all. It would be all the better for letting stand for a while too, so the Smokey flavored ham could infuse with the eggs and mayonnaise. She was happy with it and thought it would pass muster. *Why am I coming up with all my mum's old sayings?* Pass muster had been yet another one of her favorites.

It dawned on her, as she swallowed the spoonful of rather yummy salad, she had skipped lunch and breakfast and was hungry. Proud of herself, she resisted the urge to eat a full bowl.

For the umpteenth time, she walked over to the mirror to make sure she looked okay. Naturally, she had agonized over what to wear above the stunning underwear but believed she had found the right balance.

She wanted Iain to like her, and be attracted to her, but at the same time she would be meeting his son. She didn't want to come across as some sort of vamp who was trying to replace his departed mother with a new version. It was a tough mix, and one more thing which Jenny was unused to in the cloistered life she had led. Normally she dressed for two things only: her work or her cat, not men, and most definitely, not a man's son.

She looked at her reflection. She wore very pale beige corduroy jeans, nearly bone color, but not quite; and she wished they were white. Once she overhead three male students talking about a girl who had walked past them wearing white jeans. They had made it sound like it was the sexiest thing in the world, and Jenny, much to her ongoing surprise, wanted to be sexy for Iain. But alas, she didn't own any, so it had to be the bone ones. She did wear white colored sandals, with two-inch heels, because Iain was tall, and she didn't want to feel too short alongside him standing at his barbeque. On top, she wore a black snug fitting polo-necked jumper. There was no cleavage, which she thought appropriate for meeting Brad. There was no hint of the devastating underwear underneath, that was for Iain's eyes alone later. But, the long-sleeved top being snug fitting, and the bra being such delicate material, her breasts looked fantastic, she had to admit.

Jenny took Janet's advice and left her hair down. She blow-dried it after finding the hair drier at the back of the vanity cupboard, covered in dust from lack of use, and was quite pleased with the result.

Oh, my God, oh my God, oh my God. She panicked as her doorbell chimed its merry song. He had arrived to pick her up. She took three steps away from the mirror toward the door then dashed back for one last look. She took a deep, calming breath, and left the bedroom to let him in.

Iain did a double take when she opened the door. The hunger in his gaze was unmistakable, and for the second time that day, and probably in her life, Jenny felt undeniably sexy. His look of approval was so wonderful, she couldn't help herself, and she flung her arms around him and hugged him tightly.

Oh, my God, this feels so right. She reveled in his arms; he smelled so manly, and his body was so muscular. Instinctively, as if orchestrated, suddenly and wondrously he was kissing her. He stood several inches taller than her; his arms held her as she could only have dreamt of in the past. When his lips found hers, she was aware of so many things at once and stupidly it was like a list flitting through her academically trained mind. He had brushed his teeth, and tasted minty. He had not had a drink of alcohol, her breasts were nicely squashed against his chest, and his hands were located firmly on her back, one just above the swell of her bottom, the other across her bra strap. She was breathless and heady, and if he wanted to, he could strip her naked right there and then.

As if by some secret agreement, their lips parted, and his tongue entered her mouth. Jenny suddenly knew what heaven was like. His hands softly caressed, and explored her back, and she used both hers to squeeze back, communicating her acceptance. She kept hers still, one on his shoulder, the other on his hip, as his right hand caressed lower to fondle and hold her bottom.

Oh, my God; he is feeling my bum. His big strong hand was opening and closing over her left buttock, and she moaned into his open mouth. His left hand slid from the center of her back and now pressed firmly on her shoulder blade. This forced her right breast against his chest. Her nipple was harder than she had ever known it to be and suddenly she was aware of his hardness against her lower tummy.

Boy, he does really want me.

Their first kiss could have lasted hours. Time had stopped still for Jenny and she relished the wonderful tease of his lips, tongue, and hands on her body. When it did come to an end, she was out of breath, and, she noticed with utter joy, so was Iain.

"Now, that's what I call a welcome," he said, and Jenny was delighted by the croakiness in his voice.

I did that to him? One kiss and he lost his voice?

She had never felt so fantastic. If this was a drug she was now an addict. "I missed you," she whispered. "Would you like to come in?"

"No way, Jose. If I come inside, I couldn't stop myself, we would kiss again, and then again, and then I'd be taking your clothes off. Much safer if I stay here. Brad is waiting for us."

It was obvious he meant it, and, incredibly, unbelievably, she had mesmerized him. She agreed; if he did come inside, they would be in bed within minutes. Now, she firmly sat on cloud nine, and as much as she wanted him to make love to her, she wanted it to be mind-blowingly special when they did. It would be all the better, for waiting just a little longer for that to happen. Brad was waiting, and he was her reason for coming back in time.

She took two steps back away from Iain, back across the threshold, knowing she had to tease him more, wanting him to feel as she did. What they had was special. "So, if I lifted my top up, you wouldn't be able to resist me, Iain, is that what you mean?" She firmly grasped the hemline of her jumper and looked expectantly.

He nodded, dumbly, and stared as she slowly, inched up one side, and then the other, back and forth until he could see her tummy, though she stopped short of her bra-covered breasts. The look on his face was priceless. This power she held over him was totally alien to her, and she loved it.

"Well, we better not keep Brad waiting then, had we?" Her voice was husky, and still breathless. She lowered her top, just as slowly as she had raised it. "If you're interested though, you can take my top off later…if you're interested."

"If I'm interested, did you say? Did you ask me *if?* You're such a tease, Jenny. It's taking all my willpower not to chase you inside and close the door. I hope you realize that."

"Correct answer, sir. I will get the potato salad, and a jacket, and we better go. Apparently, Brad is waiting. I'm hungry, and not just for steak and salad." She winked before turning and dashing inside.

She had an inkling, as she walked away, he was checking out her bottom in her jeans. She looked over her shoulder and smiled at the look of knowing he had been caught sneaking a peek, which appeared on his face. She waggled a finger, smiling, so he would know she was kidding.

When she turned the corner into the kitchen out of sight from him, she fell back against the wall and put a hand across her open mouth. She wanted to scream loudly, incredibly loudly. What had happened? This was not the Jenny she had always been, this was not how she acted. This was a new version of her.

She was operating on her feminine instinct alone. She could not possibly have planned this. She had no knowledge of love and the nuances between men and women other than what she had seen in movies. Sure, she had been with a couple of guys when she had been a student, but it had been nothing like this. This was sooooo elating. *Is that even a word?* She didn't care. Elating described it and it was enough. Damn the future, and damn whatever happened at the end of her thirty-three days, this feeling she was experiencing was enough. *He wants me, and I want him.*

She lunged off the wall, calmed her beating heart,

and opened the fridge door and took out the salad. *Should I take a bottle of wine? What is protocol for this sort of thing, would he be offended if I did?* She stuck her head back around the corner. "Hey, Iain," she called out. "Shall I grab a bottle of wine for the three of us?"

"I've got plenty. Promise you won't laugh but I stopped in at the bottle shop after work and bought twelve bottles, six different varieties so I was sure to have one you liked."

Oh, my God, he did that, for me? Chink. It hit home to her, Iain was as unused to being with a woman as she was unsure of being with him. He worried about what wine to get?

It was an alien idea that a man so sexy and good looking as Iain would even be interested in boring, mousey her. Let alone he would agonize over what wine to have. Where she was on cloud nine earlier, she now amended it to cloud twelve. "I can't believe you went to so much trouble over me, Iain. That's about the nicest thing anyone has ever done for me."

"Seriously, Jenny, you really need to get out more. You're an amazing woman, and I have to keep pinching myself this isn't some kind of weird dream I will wake up from, and you will be gone."

That hurt her. Cut her to the bone, more deeply than she could have imagined possible. Soon, she would wake up, and would be gone from him. She blinked back tears, and not just for the loss she would experience, but for his. "Umm, I just need to pop to the loo before we go, won't be a sec."

In the bathroom, she stood in front of the mirror and gave herself a good talking to in her mind. *You are here for the future of the planet, now buck up girl. It's okay to enjoy your time here, it's okay to fall for him, and it's okay for him to fall for you, because if you succeed, you will save millions, upon millions of lives. Now get out there, enjoy this wonderful man and the experience, and focus on what you need to do.*

Did those strong words make her feel better? Not really. But it did put things back into perspective. She would not remember this thirty-three days, so she had to enjoy it while it lasted. She nodded at her reflection, and even gave herself a wink. Luckily, she didn't wear make-up otherwise she would need to re-apply her mascara.

Two minutes later she had a jacket over her arm and the bowl of potato salad in her hand. She met him again at the front door with a smile. "Let's go meet Brad, God I'm wetting myself with nerves over this, Iain."

"Jenny, Jenny, Jenny, what am I going to do with you? You really don't know how gorgeous you are, do you?"

She shook her head, and answered with total sincerity: "No idea whatsoever, could you keep telling me, just so I don't forget."

"You know when we get back to my place, Brad is going to love you, just like I do."

There, he said it again—the L word. *Does he love me, already? Nah, it's just a turn of phrase, I'm sure. A man like him doesn't fall for women like me, and even if somehow, someway he did, it wouldn't be so soon.*

"Well, if he doesn't, I'm going to hold you responsible then. Let's go, take me into the lion's den, I'm ready." She put her free arm through his and they walked to the driveway, where Iain's white Holden

Commodore sat patiently waiting for them.

"Did you clean your car especially for me, Iain, or do you always keep it so nice?"

He looked crestfallen, and she melted even further. *Chink, there goes another piece of my heart.* "Sprung. I took it through the car wash this afternoon on my way home after work."

She stopped in her tracks and turned then tilted her head to one side. "Seriously? I was just kidding. You washed the car just to pick me up in it? Oh, my God Iain. I'm so impressed already. Ask to marry me and I will say yes."

She giggled loudly, and he laughed too, but just for a split second she wondered if he would ask. Luckily he didn't, but he did open the passenger door, like a true gentleman, and she felt yet another chink as a further piece of her heart fell.

In the car, and underway, she noted he had not just washed the car but deodorized it too; there was a lovely smell of cleanliness, which put her own Hyundai to absolute shame. "So, tell me about Brad, what do I need to know?" she asked, as she placed a hand on his thigh and enjoyed the warmth through his denim jeans.

"I think one of the reasons we are so close is he takes after his mum so much." He glanced up at her quickly. No doubt to make sure he hadn't said something wrong by mentioning Simone in such a way. She squeezed his thigh, letting him know he was fine to talk about his wife with love.

"In some lights, with some of his expressions, he reminds me of her so much. He is smart, smart as anyone I know, and I don't mean just brainy. He is funny, sharp sense of humor, quick on the uptake. He has a girlfriend, Lyndsay; she adores him. She will be there tonight, and she sleeps over quite a lot. I didn't mention it, and I hope it's okay with you?"

"I'm going to be a guest in your and Brad's home. It's not my place not to be okay with whomever you invite. But, I can tell you I'm so happy I won't be the only woman there. You mentioned to me before he had a dream to feed the world?"

"Yeah, he's one hell of a kid. For years now he has had this idea he could change the way plants grow, improve them using genetics. Make them impervious to bad weather, grow faster, and give more of a harvest. Even be unsusceptible to pests and bugs. He wants countries like Africa, and the poorer Asian ones, not to have to worry about basic food supplies. It's his dream. He says man has been skirting around the edges for years now. What with cloning sheep, modifying Canola, things like that. He says we have the knowledge to make a difference. He has been working on something for a while now at university, and the CSIRO are very keen to hire him."

"Oh, I'm sure he will make a difference, Iain." *If only you knew how much he will make.* "So, what area do you live in, where are we heading? I can't wait to see your house."

"Canning Vale. We built there ten years ago. I never had the heart to sell and move on, and I thought it would be good for Brad to be in the same house after his mum passed away. You don't mind, do you?"

"No, Iain, I don't mind at all, it's your home, why would I mind going? Honestly I'm just so happy to be invited, I genuinely feel privileged."

He turned toward her, and she smiled back. "I've

never taken anyone else there, you know, a woman, I mean."

"Then it makes me feel doubly proud. You said Brad already has a job lined up with CSIRO, how did he manage that before he has even finished university?"

"He did the last three years there for work experience and university placement. They made the offer after he made a presentation to them on what he is working on in his own time. One of our spare bedrooms is his study, come lab, come workroom. Don't ask me any technical stuff; he doesn't talk about that side of things, and if he did, I wouldn't understand it anyway. His thesis is on genetically modified wheat, and when I attended the information night, one of the managers said they were incredibly impressed with him, and especially his thesis. They think he could be onto something quite extraordinary."

"Wow. So, they have set up funding for him already?"

"Yes, apparently so. Naturally he is chomping at the bit."

"It's not my place to say, but as you know I teach Environmental Studies. There is a lot of fear and worry about the potential long-term effects of genetically modifying basic food supplies. Historically, man does not have a good track record with interfering in the natural order of things."

"Oh, I'm so looking forward to long discussions between the two of you."

"Me too, but what do you think?" She wanted to know if he would be an ally in the discussions to come.

"Me? What do I know? I'm just a truck driver; he has the brains. I'm not even sure with what you mean by the track record we have."

"Well, a couple of things come to mind which have dramatically affected us here in Australia. Cane Toads for one thing."

"But they weren't genetically modified, surely?"

"No, but they were introduced into the sugar growing areas of Northern Queensland in 1935 in a hope to combat a beetle which was at the time devastating crops. The beetle eats the leaves of sugar cane, but the larvae which live deep in the ground, eat the roots, too deep for normal pesticides. So, just so people can have lots of sugar in their soft drinks, make cakes with, or sprinkle on their breakfast cereal, the cane toad was released to attack the beetle. About one hundred of them were set free, apparently under strict control, in and around Cairns and Innisfail. They originated from Hawaii, and they have since spread like wildfire, killing many native species because of the toxin on their skin. They look good to eat, and they are slow, therefore easy to catch by carnivores, and boy do they breed! You bet they do. But one bite on their toxic skin and the predator dies. They have marched north and westward, killing pretty much everything that tries to attack them.

"They have been described as 'the greatest risk ever to Australian biodiversity.' That was the Kakadu National Park's risk assessment, by the way, in the Northern Territory, which shows how far they have traveled. They now reside in the North of Western Australia, gaining something like thirty miles a day, and spreading south. They will be in Perth before you know it. Think about the geography, and the landscape, Iain, and you will realize they have traveled something like five thousand miles. The government of the day did not contemplate the future risk, only the short-term benefits."

"Hmm, I see. I hadn't thought of that before. But surely we have stricter controls these days, don't we?"

"Ah, but do we? I'm not so sure. When there is big money involved, the promise of massive profits tends to make people in authority turn a blind eye. There are lots of other examples."

"Such as?"

"Foxes, goats, camels, rabbits to name a few, all imported into our environment, for some short term gain or other, and all have devastated our ecology, and bred out of control. Australia has a unique eco-balance and when something is introduced which doesn't belong, the effects can be catastrophic, and far-reaching. Honey Bees, and European Wasps are so firmly entrenched they are now impossible to eradicate, and the list goes on and on. The Fire Ant is a particularly nasty threat but is so far contained in Northern Queensland, for how long no one can guess. They have a poisonous sting which can kill humans, and if, or should I say when, they break out, it could cause a massive problem for us. Living underground as they do, they can be very hard to stop, if not impossible."

"Jesus, I can see I might have to come between you and Brad at the dinner table."

"Oh, I think healthy debate is a good thing, don't you?" She squeezed his thigh again. She did not want to get too heavily involved in discussions of a nature which might affect their relationship. Not too early in the piece anyway. There would be time enough in the weeks to come.

"But Brad wants to be a savior to the world's food supply needs, not hurt it further."

"Very true, and it's to be commended, Iain. But, history is littered with good intentions having turned bad. There is the age-old debate about progress. 'Just because we can, doesn't mean we should.' "

"But, who has the right then to make those decisions on behalf of the rest of us?"

"And therein lies the problem, Iain. Who indeed should determine it? That's why some of the things are in the mess they are. As an environmentalist, I just want to make sure there is something left for our kids, and their kids. I'm not necessarily against progress, but some things are best left as they are. Nature is in balance, once it goes out of that state, who can say where it will end?

"Hydro-Fluorocarbons are another good example. In the sixties, they were the propellant used in spray cans; it was a cheap way to be able to spray deodorant. But they were destroying the ozone layer and who would have thought it? They were banned worldwide, thankfully. Today, the layer is slowly recovering, but if we didn't have the benefit of those studies and act on them back then, the incidence of some types of cancer, particularly skin cancer, would be vastly worse than they are today. Oh, I'm so sorry Iain, I didn't mean to mention cancer because of Simone, please forgive me."

"It's okay, it's no problem, I'm really enjoying this discussion, tell me more."

"All right, but be warned, once you get me started I find it hard to stop. Let me ask you a question, what do you think about antibiotics?"

He glanced at her with a strange look on his face. "They have saved numerous lives, what's wrong with them?"

"Well in some instances, undoubtedly they have saved lives. But, more realistically, in most cases all they've done is hasten a person's recovery. We get sick, the doctors prescribe them, and we get better. But we now have people who are developing allergies to them, and the incidence is growing exponentially. Worse, we have bugs which have now mutated so much they can defeat the drugs. So, the germs are now not only immune from antibiotics, but are far more virulent than they would be had they been left alone. If we had evolved a natural defense to some illnesses, they may well have disappeared by now.

"Polio is coming back, having almost been eradicated through a worldwide immunization program. Thanks mainly to Rotary International's work, and right there is a truly benevolent effort. It was commendable and is a prime example of good intentions. But, the strain of Polio we are now seeing has no cure, and you cannot immunize against it.

"You see Iain, things mutate, it's the natural order of things. When we look at bugs and parasites, it is the intention of the parasite to live off its host, not kill it. When the parasite kills, it effectively commits suicide itself and therefore does not fulfil its basic quest to live and survive. So, given time, humans can develop immunity, and the parasite gets to live within us, and everyone is happy. Naturally, some people will die along the way and of course that is tragic, but globally, or for the benefit of the population it could be argued antibiotics should be banned. The human gut has billions of bacteria which initially were dangerous, but now we have learned to live with, and some we need to survive now. Another problem with antibiotics is they can, in some cases, kill the good bacteria residing inside us. It's a complex issue, Iain, and there are no easy answers. One thing's for sure, the drug companies have made many, many millions of dollars along the way.

"So, bugs mutate usually, but most eventually adapt without killing the host. When man interferes with nature, and worse modifies it, he can take away that aspect."

"I don't know what to say, except I am loving listening to you, and we are nearly home. Can I kiss you before we go inside?"

"You must be a mind reader; I was going to ask you the same thing."

****

She felt more nervous than any time in her life, bordering on terror, holding her potato salad, as Iain unlocked the front door with his key. There was music coming from inside, though she was in such mental and emotional turmoil she couldn't tell who had sung it and what the song was, but it sounded like a ballad she should know. They lived in a nice-looking house, with a neat and tidy front garden made up predominantly of lawn and flowerbeds full of native shrubs.

"We're home," he yelled out as he opened the door. "Better get dressed if you're naked."

"Oh my God, Iain, how can you say such a thing?" she whispered.

"Because I once walked in and they were naked," he whispered back, and winked.

He held the door open for her to step through. *Here*

goes nothing. She walked into a warm, welcoming lounge, with comfortable furniture which looked just right for the room. She had no idea what she had expected, but this was so normal. Against the far wall was a gas space heater, with a mantel shelf over it. Above, was a very large framed picture of Iain and Simone on their wedding day. They were holding hands facing each other, leaning back at an angle away from each other, her in her wedding dress, and him in his tuxedo and bow tie. Their faces radiated happiness and the massive weeping willow tree which surrounded them gave the picture an ethereal, make-believe look.

"Oh my God, Iain, Simone was so beautiful." She stood and stared.

"So are you." He put his hands on her hips from behind.

She turned into his arms, tilted her head to one side, "So, Iain, when was the last time you had your eyes checked?"

"I'm still trying to figure out if you actually don't know how beautiful you are, or you're just so modest you have to make jokes about it."

"I'd go with the former, if I were you." She kissed him as a reward for saying something so blatantly untrue, just to make her feel better. Then immediately she felt guilty because she was doing it in front of a picture of his wife. It was somehow sacrilegious. She broke away, quickly. "Sorry."

"What are you sorry for?"

She raised her gaze and nodded her head backward to indicate the picture. Then she stepped away and placed a finger over her lips.

He burst into spontaneous laughter. "You are so

gorgeous." He tried to grab her, but it was still so wrong, she deftly stepped aside and shook her head.

"Should I turn the picture to the wall? Will that make you feel better?"

She gasped. "No, don't you dare."

"Okay, now listen to me. Seriously, just listen. Simone has been gone over three years now, and for the longest time I was dead inside. If it wasn't for Brad, I think I would have gone to join her, but I didn't. From time to time I still talk to her." He held up his hand to stop her, "Okay, so maybe she doesn't talk back literally; I know it's in my head, but I mean in my mind and my heart we do still talk, mostly about Brad. I've lived my life since just going through the motions, and then *whammo*, out of the blue, you walked into my life to ask me if your brother can play in my team. I'm not dumb, Jenny, and meeting you was like a bolt of lightning hitting me. My mind was like frazzled or something. But that night, after the game, I sat on the back patio, alone with a glass of red wine, and I talked to Simone about you, and you know what she said?"

She felt a dawning horror as to what he might say next, but she had to know. "Oh my God, Iain, no, what did she say?"

"Nothing, nada, not a word. Because I think she has moved on. She could see inside me, and could see I had feelings for you, and I think her not answering was her way of accepting it. It's okay to hug me in front of her picture, I think she would not only be happy for me, but she would approve of you. Hey, how could she not approve of you?"

She stayed silent for a while, not knowing how to answer such a statement, then she shrugged, "Do you know what I find hardest to believe?" She could tell she had his interest.

"No, what?"

"You actually said the word 'whammo'. You are my kind of nut case." She smiled her best smile, tilted her head back to the other side, and flicked her hair from her face.

She could see by Iain's look, he was smitten with her, but how or why was beyond her comprehension, so she made a conscious choice to enjoy it, and go with the flow. Yet another of her mother's sayings. "This potato salad is getting awfully heavy, and I could really do with a wine."

He took the bowl from her in one hand, and wrapped his other around hers, then led her from in front of the picture, out into the living area, where Brad and his girlfriend were sitting on the couch, playing a computer game on the big flat screen TV.

They both stood up, tossing the hand controllers to the side. "Brad, Lyndsay, this is Jenny."

Jenny froze, terrified, though why, she had no idea; unless it was that she was face to face with the man who was destined to destroy the world. She stood still, in the middle of the room, feeling stupid but incapable of doing or saying anything. She wanted to run away.

He is so goddamned ordinary; he isn't a monster mass murderer. He is just an idealistic, beautiful young man.

"I'm really glad to meet you, Jenny," he said, and he showed a huge grin. "You've got no idea what you've done to the old man. He can't shut up about you."

Lyndsay elbowed him in the ribs, making him

grimace, and suddenly everything was all right. Jenny let out her breath in a whoosh, they were a normal everyday family, and she was being welcomed.

Jenny found her voice, "Brad, you have no idea how glad I am to meet you, and you too, Lyndsay. And, as for him not being able to shut up about someone." She made the shape of a pistol with her fingers and pointed them at him. "You, buster, you have one proud father."

"Aw shucks, stop it. Now, what should we call you: Jenny, Aunt Jenny, mum to be or Ms. O'Brien?"

"Bradley Reginald! That is so rude." Lyndsay poked him in the ribs again. "He doesn't mean to be rude, Jenny, he truly hasn't shut up about you coming for dinner." She crossed to Jenny and gave her a hug. "We are glad to meet you," she whispered.

Brad smiled a disarming smile. "I'm just kidding. I guess we are a bit freaked out. Not used to dad having a girlfriend. We thought he would be a bachelor for the rest of his life."

"Well, thank you both so much for welcoming me, and Brad, I feel like I'm the lucky one, not him. Oh, and feel free to call me Jenny—that's my name."

"Right, well if you lot are going to talk about me, I'm going to get the drinks. White or red, Jen?" Iain put the potato salad on the kitchen bench and headed toward the oversized double door fridge.

"White please"—then remembering the multiple choices he had bought added—"a sav-blanc, or sem-sav blanc would be wonderful, thank you."

Brad took her arm, and led her to sit on one of the couches, "You know Dad said you were beautiful, and I wondered just how lovely a woman can he attract at his old age, but boy, he wasn't lying."

"Oh, now I see where he gets his bullshit from, it must be hereditary; he gets it from his son."

The ice was broken, the four of them laughed, and the tone was set for the night. She liked Brad, and his lovely girlfriend Lyndsay, who was clearly as much in love with him, as he was with her. It was all so surreally normal, it made her think she was inside a dream, rather than trying to stop the end of the world, and Jenny loved being there.

A half hour later, she stood next to Iain, while he cooked some steak and fried onions on the hot plate of his barbecue in the back garden. He wore an apron which every time she looked at him gave her the giggles, possibly exacerbated by the three glasses of wine she'd drunk on a very empty tummy.

The apron was black and in bright red letters was written a list of cities: *PARIS * LONDON * RIO DI JANERIO * NEW YORK* and then the killer: *CANNING VALE.* While it was, true Jenny didn't know too much about the suburb of Canning Vale, to compare it to the great cities of the world was just so damned funny.

"I love your son, Iain, and I can see why he is the apple of your eye. You're right; I can see some of his mother in him too."

"I was a bit worried he might have offended you when he started. I promise you it's just his way, he is always trying to be funny, but he has spent so much time studying sometimes his social skills are lacking. He's a good kid though."

"Oh, as someone who lost years studying for my three Master's Degrees, I get him, don't worry about that. I knew it was his way of being humorous. I still struggle with people and interacting with them. All the harder for me because I've never left the academic world. When I finished studying at UWA they offered me a lecturing position, and as it was what I'd always dreamt of doing I jumped at it. As you can imagine, all the people I know are either students or teachers. To be honest I find the students an awful lot more interesting than the lecturers. We are a boring lot, trust me."

"Jen, of all the words I could think of to describe you, boring is not one of them."

She stared back. *How come he always says the perfect thing?* He glanced up and caught her looking and smiled, then busied himself turning the onions so they didn't burn.

"Okay, go on, tell me five of them?" she said, then sipped from her wine glass to hide her grin

"Five what?

"Five words you would use to describe me."

"Easy, but only if you do the same. Here goes: Sexy, gorgeous, kind, loving, intelligent, beautiful, interesting, shall I keep going?"

"Oh my God, Iain, I am so not those things."

"You say 'Oh my God' a lot, don't you? You also spend so much of your time putting yourself down, you don't see the wood for the trees. And for a tree hugger, that's not a good thing."

She gasped, loudly, because for the first time in sixty-eight years, it dawned on her, she did say it a lot. She turned red, from head to toe. Iain dropped the tongs onto the barbeque and turned. He held her and she felt his strong arms envelope her body.

He whispered, earnestly, "Babe, I'm so sorry. I didn't mean to offend you. I love that you say it so much. I think it's cute, and it's so you. It's like everything I do and say amazes you. Please don't be upset. Honestly, don't change, don't feel conscious of it, and don't ever stop saying it to me."

Chink, there goes another little piece of my heart. I won't have any heart left at this rate.

She swallowed the lump which had come into her throat and blinked back tears. Could there ever be another man as perfect as this one?

She leaned her head back and stared into his ice blue eyes, she could see the honesty and sincerity there, and she kissed him. She put everything into it, to communicate how she felt about him, with her lips, tongue, hands, body, and mind. She knew right then she loved him.

Through the misty cloud of emotion, as they kissed breathlessly, Brad's voice filtered through: "Hey you two, cut it out. The steaks are burning and we're starving in here. Jenny, stop it, put him down right now; you don't know where he's been."

They broke the kiss, giggling like kids caught by their parents, yet it was the other way around. She punched his arm, lightly, "I am *not* a tree hugger."

He picked up the tongs and immediately dropped them as they had become hot while resting on the hot plate. "Fuck," he said, then followed it up with the obligatory, "Oops, sorry I didn't mean to swear."

She took another swig of her wine, which almost finished the glass, "Its fine, I've heard the word before, you know. I often use it myself, mostly in my own head though. Usually it precedes or follows that, 'oh my God' thing I do. But, Iain, there is one time when I want you to hear me say it, can you guess when?" She giggled in an evil way, so he would know she was talking about sex.

"Oh my God, Jenny! You don't mean what I think you mean, do you?" They both laughed as he mimicked her. "Okay, we're done here, let's go eat."

****

The meal was good, and everyone made a fuss of Jenny's potato salad, even Brad. "Jenny you need to give Dad this recipe, its brilliant."

She blushed, unused to such complements. "Really, it's nothing special, just my mum's way of doing it, but I'm really glad you like it."

"Can I have the recipe too, Jenny? I'm loving it too and seeing as he likes it so much it looks like it might be part of our staple diet once we get our own place." Lyndsay added.

"Of course, you can, I'd be delighted to hand over the baton. When are you both thinking of moving into your own nest?"

Jenny had discovered the couple were destined to break up, from her studies in the future of their Facebook posts. Jenny felt saddened, having met them, to realize because of the long hours Brad was going to be working, Lyndsay would get bored and fall for another man. He would throw himself into his work, spending up to eighty plus hours at the lab a week, which would be the catalyst for making his breakthrough.

"Well, I start work at the Commonwealth Scientific and Industrial Research Organization in three months' time, but Lyndsay has another year for her law degree. My starting pay is okay, but not brilliant, so we are thinking in about a year from now we will have saved up enough. Dad can't wait to get rid of me, especially now you're on the scene, hey Dad? He wants lots of play dates with you, Jenny."

Jenny smirked when Iain blushed at his son's forwardness, *oh the honesty in youth.*

"Well, son, I can promise you one thing, you won't be walking in and catching Jenny and I naked on the couch doing a horizontal folk dance."

Jenny had been taking a sip of her fourth glass of wine, when Iain's words made her laugh so hard it traveled up her nose and made her choke. This made everyone else laugh at her expense as she alternated between trying to catch her breath, cough, and stop giggling. Meanwhile it was Brad and Lyndsay's turn to blush.

Once the meal was finished Brad asked Jenny a question which took her by surprise and she struggled with a reply that would make sense, yet one she could point to later as early proof she was from the future.

"So, Jen, we all want to know, how the hell did you know what the outcome would be in the second half of the game, right down to who would score what goal?"

"Oh, your dad told you, did he?"

"How could I not, Jen? It was just about the freakiest thing that's ever happened to me," Iain replied, nodding as he raised his glass to his lips. The table was silent, waiting for her to explain.

"Look, umm, it's hard to explain, especially as I hardly know you all. I suppose the best way to answer is to say I get, um, like visions. I watched the first half, and just sensed, what was going to happen in the second. Your dad looked so down about it, and it was so cold and wet, I thought I would cheer him up. I can't explain it much better. I know quite a lot about the future, as it happens."

"Go on, then tell us something else, oh Prophet Jenny." Brad leaned forward with his elbows on the table edge. He was challenging her and she wondered now she had dug this hole, how she could get herself out of it. It was way too early to talk about the future. They would think her mad if she did.

Maybe, this is a good thing; it could lead into deeper discussions if I handle this right.

"I think you're teasing me. Brad, you think I'm making this up, don't you?"

"Well, Jen, I wouldn't go that far, but my life is all about science, not mumbo jumbo. I am interested in how you could predict a game of soccer results and name the scorers."

"You know a hundred years ago, radio would have been called mumbo jumbo, and mobile phones, space travel, and how about TV?"

"That's my point, all of that is science."

"Mine too. The point is things we don't understand today; science can explain tomorrow."

"Like seeing into the future? That's rubbish, Jen, no offence intended."

"None taken, I promise. Okay, if you are sure you want to do this, let me think for a minute." She took another drink of her wine. She was close to her limit, perhaps it blurred her judgment. "You met Lyndsay in the library, but not at Murdoch University, in the city. You had gone there with another girl...she has a strange name, foreign? Heidi?" She nodded. "Yes, Heidi. She was taller than you, which you didn't like, but she was pretty. But then, in the...ummm,

Philosophy section? You literally bumped into Lyndsay. In fact, you knocked the books out of her hand. Then when you both bent to pick them up you banged heads. That was when you first laughed with each other, and you've been laughing ever since. Lyndsay snuck you her phone number, while Heidi had her head buried in a book, and the rest…is history."

The three sat, open mouthed. Jenny took another sip, feeling quite smug. She had gleaned the information from their Facebook posts.

"No, fucking way." Brad choked.

"Bradley, there will be no swearing at the dinner table, thank you," Iain interjected.

"Yeah, but. No way could you know that stuff, no fucking way. Oops sorry, Dad, and Jenny, it just slipped out."

Lyndsay looked deeply troubled, and Jenny worried she had gone too far. She suddenly had an idea of a way to make it less personal. "Iain, quick give me a pen and paper please. I need to write something down.

He crossed to the kitchen drawer and took out a spiral notepad and pencil. Silently he put it in front of her, opened at a clean page. He too looked a little troubled. Jenny had to put on an act now, or she feared she might lose them. She put down her glass, picked up the pencil, leaned back in her chair, and closed her eyes. She didn't want to give them all six first division numbers for the following night's lottery and turn them into instant millionaires. But, she had memorized all the upcoming draws, for an occasion as this. With her eyes still closed she quickly wrote: 7-13-28-44 and after a pause number 3. She then put down the pencil and shook her head. "Sorry, I can't see any more."

"What are they, Jenny?" Brad asked.

She paused for effect and took another sip of her wine. "They are five of the seven numbers which will be drawn tomorrow night in the Tuesday Oz Lottery."

The three all spoke at once, and she had a hard time making out what each of them said. She held up a hand, she needed to lighten it up now. "Look guys, I don't have two heads. I'm not a witch, just sometimes I just see things. Maybe I'm wrong about this, maybe they won't come out. I can only tell you what I see. Now, I think I may have had just a little too much wine. Would it be okay if you took me home now, Iain, please?"

****

In the car, after the cool air hit her, she realized she was almost drunk. She prayed to all the gods she could think of to help her not be sick as her vision danced and spun. Once Iain got inside and clicked his seat belt on she snuggled into him across her seatand was asleep in minutes.

She awoke as the car turned into her driveway, her head fuzzy. Iain helped her from the car, "I loved tonight meeting Brad and Lyndsay, I'm sorry I came over so tired."

He leaned her against the wall beside the door and asked her kindly where her key was.

"Where's my bag? Keys in my bag, I'm sorry, Iain, I skipped lunch." She waggled her finger from side to side exaggeratedly, "I was out buying underwear, 'specially for you to see. Take me to bed, Iain, I want to be with you so badly."

He laughed softly, "Well let's get you inside. I've got your bag here, let me find the keys." Once he found them hidden in the clutter, he opened the door and with his arm around her, supporting her, he led her inside to the kitchen, and kicked the door shut with his heel. "Now I think you need some water, lots of water." He left her standing by the sink and opened cupboards until he found a glass, then filled it from the tap. "Come on, drink up."

"Only if you promise me I haven't stuffed things up with us by drinking too much. Take me to bed. I think I love you, Iain."

"I want to stay, and make sure you are all right. You haven't stuffed anything up. If you tell me you love me in the morning, then I will believe you. Now drink up, that's an order."

"Aye Aye, sir." She saluted, then finished the water and held out the empty glass. But instead of taking her to bed, he filled the glass again and held it out. "Really? Another one?"

"Trust me, you will thank me in the morning."

This time it took longer and when she stopped halfway through, Iain shook his head. Chastised, she finished the drink. He took the empty tumbler from her and turned to the sink, when he turned back she had stepped closer to be directly in front of him. She wrapped her arms around him and buried her head in his shoulder. Desperately she whispered, "I do love you." Then they were kissing, and she fumbled with his shirt buttons, desperate to touch his bare chest, the same chest she hadn't been able to get out of her mind since he sent her the picture.

An hour later, she slept in his arms, both naked. Her last thought before sleep overtook her was: *I must go and thank Janet; the underwear worked like a charm.*

Chapter 6
To the End of Time

Day Eight, August 9th 2016

Jenny was having a horrible dream. Images of sun ripened wheat fields were burning, and smoke billowed to the sky forming clouds and blackening the sun. From within the roaring flames came the agonizing sounds of screams. Adults and children alike, burning to death, while the fire spread uncontrolled.

Firebreaks were useless. The wind blew smoldering embers ahead of the flames, and together they raced eastward. Farmhouses ignited from gas bottles, with huge explosions, while the residents baked within them. Whole towns disappeared in the widely spreading holocaust. The air was rancid with the smell of burning bodies as fire leapt from house to house.

People attempted escape in cars, but the flames found them. Petrol tanks ruptured with the heat causing fireballs which traveled through the air like mortar shells. A vineyard received a direct hit, and the grapes exploded on the vines as the flames licked along the wire trellises, hopping from one row to the next.

Iain woke her gently shaking her shoulder. "Wake up love, you were having a nightmare. You kept yelling out about how the wheat fields are on fire and it will kill us all. It's okay; you're safe here with me."

"Oh my God, Iain, it was awful." She couldn't stop the tears. It had been so real; she could still hear the screams of the people burning to death, as they echoed through her mind.

He held her tightly, she on her back, he on his side, cuddling her. She was so glad he was there to comfort her in her hour of need. Slowly the horrific images faded as she came back to reality. Jenny's heartbeat slowed back to normal eventually, as she became aware it was the early hours of the morning, and Iain was with her. She remembered they had made love. *Oh, how we made love.*

She kissed his shoulder, where the skin was so tight across it, and she snuggled her body so she could touch more of him along his torso. "I'm okay now, it was just a dream."

He looked down with a smile that lit up his face. His hand appeared as if by magic to gently caress her cheek. With his index finger, he wiped away an errant tear. "You're so beautiful."

She blinked and whispered back, "I'm in love with you, I hope you don't mind."

"Mind? Do I mind one of the most stunning women in the world is in love with me? Oh, yeah, I hate that; you gorgeous dummy."

"I didn't get a chance to ask you before you took them off me, but did you like my underwear? I got them for you especially, so you could remove them. Crazy huh?"

"Yes, I did, I loved them. They made you seem even more wonderful. But, I must say, you could have been wearing chain as a suit of armor and I would have found you sexy. It's been a lot of years since I made love."

"Well, you haven't lost your touch, not that I've been active either, just saying. Maybe we both need lots more practice though, hint, hint."

"Oh right. I don't do it in four years or so, but you think I can manage it twice in two hours?"

She snaked her arm beneath the covers, touched his hardening penis resting on her hip, and she gripped and stroked him gently. "Well, I'm willing to give it a try if you are." They kissed; long and hard. While still holding him, she guided his body on top or her, her ankles griping his thighs, and she helped steer him back inside her warmth.

When she woke again with the alarm clock radio playing a Bon Jovi song, he was gone; she was alone. For someone who spent sixty-eight years single, she had no idea the depth of loneliness she could feel to wake alone after making love twice during the night.

The rising sun shone through the gap in her opaque curtains where she had neglected to close them properly the night before. *How could he leave without a note to say bye-bye? Maybe he left one in the kitchen.*

Nude, she dashed out of her bedroom, and there on the breakfast bar, resting against her handbag, was a single sheet of paper, torn from a pad he must have found in her desk drawer. Her heart gave a little flutter, and she smiled. Relief flooded through her; the note meant it had been more than just sex for him too.

She snatched it up, tilted it to the light, and read his very neat handwriting:

Dearest Jenny

You looked so angelic, asleep, especially after your nightmare, I didn't have the heart to wake you to say thank you for the best night I have had in more years than I care to remember. I must get home, get changed and get to work—my truck won't drive itself, though I'm not sure how I will get through the day with so many thoughts of you I know I will have.

When you told me you loved me, I wanted to scream back I loved you too, but for some reason, I couldn't. I know I feel it in my heart. Maybe it was images of Simone, maybe it was because you had so much to drink I was scared you were saying something that in the cold light of day you would regret. Whatever, Jenny I LOVE YOU.

Oh, my God (I love you say that so much) you are so too good for me. You asked me to come up with five words which describe you—I could come up with five hundred. You are so intelligent, and you care about so much in the world that up until now I've turned a blind eye to. I want you to teach me to care too.

If this has been all a dream, and I wake up from it, I would be so incredibly sad. I love you Jenny, and I don't want to think of a life without you in it. I hope you turn up to training tonight at the club. There is no one in the world I would rather have as a helper.

I love you

Iain

XXXXX

Oh, my God, Iain, you wonderful, fantastic, beautiful man. Boy when you leave a note, you really leave a note.

Suddenly, she cried, happy tears, there was yet another of her mother's world famous sayings.

She had to reply, just had to. She rummaged in her bag for her phone and this time got her code right first

101

time. She opened the text message application, and their last conversation and picture showed on the display. Without a second thought, her fingers flew over the keyboard.

—*I'm standing here in my kitchen, stark naked, because I had to find the note I knew you would leave when I woke up and you were gone. The words THANK YOU hardly seem enough, but they are all I have. Thank you for a beautiful night, thank you making sure I got home safe, thank you for making love to me TWICE (you Demon) but mostly, thank you for telling me you love me. I've never been in love before, isn't it wonderful???? I LOVE YOU.—*

—*See you tonight, your loving helper, Jenny.—*

She hit the send tab, then tossed her phone aside where it lay resting on top of her handbag. She glanced at the clock to check she wasn't running late, and realized she had a headache. *Wow, how come I didn't notice before?* But it was obvious why she hadn't: her emotions hadn't permitted it.

She crossed the kitchen to her pantry, and right at the back of the third shelf there was the bottle of pain killers. She dropped one horse-sized pill into a glass of water, and watched it fizz, then swallowed three headache tablets as she drank it down. As she put the glass down she realized she was still naked, and right there was a first. This was *not* the Jenny who walked around her apartment naked; this was the Jenny who walked around covered from head to foot like some Muslim woman in a hijab. But, she had to admit she felt somehow liberated. Is that love? She didn't give a flying fig; she was too involved with the ride to worry about the end of it.

She skipped. *Yes ladies and gentlemen, I'm skipping! Into the bathroom!* She turned on the taps and stepped into the hot shower to get ready for work, although she had no idea how she would get through the day.

She washed her hair and soaped her body. When her hand touched her intimate part—another of her mother's expressions—she suddenly froze. *Oh my God, oh my God, oh my God! He came inside of me—twice!*

Sex hadn't figured much in Jenny's life for so long she did not have use of the birth control pill. In fact, she had not made love in any form for many years. Yes, she had wanted to make love with Iain, but, if she been sober, she would have asked him to wear a condom. Somewhere in the back of her bedside drawer, possibly out of date from lack of use, was a packet of the bloody things.

She bought them, was it six years ago? Or seven? She couldn't remember, but she had been in the supermarket one day, shopping for something to cook for her dinner and she just happened to be in front of the myriad of different types of condoms. Who knew there were so many different types? Then she experienced a flash of memory from a phone call with her mother some time before.

Right in the middle of a conversation about, of all things, one of her more gifted Asian students, her mother blurted out: "I hope you have condoms in the bedside drawer, you know, just in case."

Jenny almost wet herself with laughter, just in case? Just in case of what?

Her love life, or lack thereof, was kind of like looking for water in the Nullarbor Plain, which was a desert. Jenny did not 'do' sex, she taught, she told herself. But, there she was, a few weeks later standing in front of the condom display looking at the colors, textures and sizes, in her local supermarket.

Who even knew they came in different sizes? That thought made her laugh at her own humor. Came in different-sized condoms, now that was funny.

She was suddenly aware of a man standing beside her and she grabbed a packet of twelve and lurched away, blushing, still trying to stifle her laughter at her sparkling wit.

Twelve? I'll be lucky to use one of them, but twelve?

When she got home, she knew she had just wasted fifteen dollars and ninety-five cents, but she shrugged and tucked them in the back of her bedside drawer, behind all the unsexy pairs of panties she owned, just in case. Then she proceeded to forget all about them.

She was not on any form of birth control, and Iain ejaculated several million little Iains inside her body. Was she fertile? When was her last period? That was a real problem for her sixty-eight-year-old consciousness; when had her thirty-five-year-old body last ovulated? For the life of her, she couldn't remember, and she started to panic.

Okay, she calmed herself after a long deep breath as the warm water cascaded down. There was such a thing as the morning after pill. All she needed to do was stop at a pharmacy on her way to work and buy one. There, problem solved.

Her hand was still stroking herself, and she contemplated not stopping for a while, but her phone chose that moment to chirp its announcement of a new text message. *That will be Iain.* She smiled and finished her shower almost frantically so she could go and see what he had replied.

—*You are such a tease. You had to tell me you were naked, didn't you? Now all I can think about is your body, thank you very much. Yes, it is wonderful being in love again, especially when I thought I never would be. Life is fantastic. You thanked me, well, thank you for coming into my world.*—

Isn't he beautiful? Isn't he just so god damned wonderful?

They swapped a few more texts, and would have carried on, but Jenny noticed the time. *Yikes! I'm gonna be late, again.* She sent a final message then flew into her bedroom and dressed for work.

She made it to UWA and her first lecture with bare seconds to spare and began her lesson about the ecological pitfalls and problems encountered by, and still facing Yosemite National Park. Despite attempts to leave it as an undisturbed natural wilderness, man had left his indelible stamp.

She hadn't stopped at the Pharmacy and didn't give the morning after pill another thought until later. By then, it was too late. Iain had either impregnated her or not, and that made her realize young Jenny wouldn't remember this when she woke. *If I'm pregnant, I won't even know until the morning sickness starts!*

She determined then she *must* write a diary, so she would know what she had gotten up to while asleep, it was all just so confusing.

****

If the previous day dragged, this one was dreadful. It was not helped by Jenny feeling so tired having enjoyed two very late nights on the trot, which she was unused to. Ten thirty was normally past her bed-time, and the minor hangover exacerbated her tiredness. She thanked Iain by text, for making her drink the water. There was no doubt it had helped with hydrating her. All in all, it could have been worse, and feeling under par was balanced by her fantastic emotional mood.

Football training was fun, more fun than she could ever have imagined possible, even though it was cold, and damp. It was obvious to her, if she wasn't so in love, and had a job to do, she would have thought it downright miserable, but for the men who treated her as if she was a long-lost friend.

She didn't have a clue about football. She learned quickly she couldn't call it soccer to the devotees—it was football. She fetched balls, accompanied guys for a jog, help set up training cones in rows and triangles and a heap of other things as per Iain's animated directions. She found it was wonderful for her own fitness too, as she joined in the warm up exercises and found it helped with her tiredness.

The guys were good fun. They were led by Brad calling her 'Mummy-Jen' and by the end of training session the whole team had joined in, which made her feel special. When the clouds opened ten minutes before finishing time, Iain, who Jenny thought must have been exhausted too, called an end to training. The players ran through the increasingly heavier raindrops—the men to the change rooms, carrying some equipment, while Jenny and Iain picked up the remaining balls and paraphernalia.

Later, they all tumbled through the double doors and swarmed to the bar, where Geordie stood waiting.

As one, the boys called out what they would like to drink, but Geordie just shook his head and said loudly: "Aye, well you can all bloody well wait your turn, you uncouth lot. We have a lass with us. She's come out to help you train in this crappy weather, and she gets first drink, right? Now Missy what will it be?"

The mere idea of an alcoholic drink made Jenny's stomach lurch, she was not going down that path three nights on the trot. "Thanks Geordie, can I just have an orange juice please?"

"Aye Missy, you can, but I'll tip a drop of vodka in it for yah; help keep the weather out." He winked while the players all turned and stared.

Out of the corner of her eye she could see Iain laughing and her resolve crumbled. "That would be lovely, Geordie, thank you, but just a small one."

Iain put his arm through hers and guided her to a big round table. "So, how's the willpower going?" he asked looking very innocent.

"I tried saying no, you heard me, but you are an evil lot in this club. Though, I love you all. I've had fun tonight, Iain, I'm so glad I volunteered."

"So am I. Unfortunately, it was one of the few things Simone didn't get into, so I'm really enjoying that you are." He smiled just as Brad arrived carrying her drink, and a glass with a large shot of scotch in it for his Father.

"It was great having you here tonight, Mummy-Jen, the rest of the boys hope the old man here doesn't upset you so you stick around."

"Hmm, well it all depends; if you keep calling me Mummy-Jen, I won't." But secretly, she loved the name.

She almost choked on the amount of Vodka hidden in the orange juice as she dared to have a sip.

No sooner had most the players sat down, then Brenda appeared from the rear carrying two large platters. One piled high with homemade sausage rolls and the other with thick cut potato wedges with bowls of sour cream and sweet chili sauce for dipping. Like a flock of seagulls feeding, hands appeared from everywhere to grab some the moment the trays hit the table.

Being such a dreary and cold night, the hot food was welcomed enthusiastically by the group, and the trays emptied quickly to be replaced with two massive saucepans with ladles sticking out of them. Jenny could tell one of them held a curry by the wonderful smell emanating from it, while the other overflowed with fluffy steamed rice. Geordie distributed bowls and spoons and the constant ribbing and humorous insults between the players stopped while everyone ate.

While Jenny savored her meal, she took a few moments to look around the team, and became aware of a feeling in the pit of her stomach. She struggled to identify what it was, and what it meant. It was a sense of belonging, almost like this was an adopted family. She looked from man to man while they ate and marveled that without question, they had accepted her into their throng. They all joked with her and had given her a nickname. Surely there could be no better sign of acceptance? Granting her a name within a team environment was like giving her the secret handshake, or key to a hidden society front door. This was something else she had not only never experienced before, but in her hermit like lifestyle, she could never have imagined. She was faced with the realization of a wasted life; it was a watershed moment.

"Penny for your thoughts," Iain said gently, which broke her reverie.

She shook her head to clear it. "I was thinking I've never felt this good in my life, Iain. Since I met you, you've quite literally turned my world upside down. Everything has changed for me. I will never be able to thank you enough."

"You realize, I hope, the feeling is mutual. You've come rocketing into my life like a freight train out of nowhere. I can't stop thinking about you when I'm not with you, and when I am with you I keep pinching myself to make sure I'm not dreaming."

She wanted to kiss him but the mood changed when Brad shouted out: "Fuck, lads. The next round is on me. I just won eighteen hundred dollars on the lotto." He looked straight at Jenny, his phone in his hand on which he must have used the internet and checked the results. He had a look of wonder on his face. "We need to get you drunk more often Mummy-Jen."

Jenny blushed, as among the cacophony of sudden noise everyone asked what Brad meant, and at the same time congratulate him on his win. She stared back at Brad and shook her head, willing him not to tell the crowd she had given him the numbers. He gave an imperceptible nod back.

"We were talking numbers last night after dinner and on a whim, I did a systems entry on some Mummy-Jen dreamt up. I got lucky and I got four and a supplementary, and because it was a systems game it payed several times. Geordie? Get everyone a drink on me, please."

Iain placed his hand on her thigh and squeezed, while the congratulations were called out around them. Jenny suddenly felt very sad: She would lose all of this, camaraderie, when she told them the real reason why she was there.

****

They hadn't discussed what they would do after training, and Jenny was torn between wanting to spend more time together and going home to her own bed to sleep. While they were sitting at the table there hadn't been an opportunity to speak privately. Some of the players wanted time with Iain to discuss football, both the previous game, and the next one on the coming weekend at Floreat. With little interest in the next game, and already knowing what the score would be, she felt herself becoming drowsy. The clubrooms were warm; they guys had formed their own little cliques and one or two girlfriends turned up to spend time with their men.

By ten o'clock it had wound down. Most had left when finally, Jenny and Iain found themselves alone siting at their table. He took the final sip from his glass of scotch and gazed into her eyes. "You look just about as tired as I feel."

"I am. Two late nights on the trot and I'm done in. God, I feel like I'm twice the age I am." That was funny and she almost laughed out loud, because she was twice as old.

I want to ask you back to my place, but, for a couple of reasons I just can't bring myself to yet. I think I need just a little longer before I take you into the bed I shared with Simone. I hope that doesn't upset you."

"I understand, Iain. No, I'm not upset in the slightest. One of the many things I love about you, are your emotions. When it feels right, it will be fantastic. There is no need to force it. Besides, there is Brad to think of too."

"True, and that is the other thing. I know he really likes you, the Mummy-Jen thing is really his way of admitting it, but I'm not sure how he would feel if you were there in the morning, too quickly as a real mother replacement."

"Well, there is always my place until it feels right for you."

There was a pause, and Jenny could see the internal war going on behind his eyes. "I want you, tonight. I want to be with you, and spend the night with you, holding you while you sleep. But I'm going to pass. I'm tired, I didn't put any of my work clothes in the car so I would have to leave your place at four to go home and change to get the truck out on time. How about an early night tonight and we get together tomorrow night, and I will have some things with me so I don't have to leave at the crack of dawn?"

"Well, I'd better check my calendar." She grinned. "I do have all of those other offers from suitors to consider." She made a pretense of looking at her phone. "Nope, it's all good, I can fit you in."

"You might joke, Jenny, but I'm still amazed you are available, and that you want to be with me."

"Hey, Bucko, stop putting yourself down. I'm the lucky one."

Iain, shook his head, then shrugged. "Whatever force it was that brought us together, I will be eternally grateful for."

Brad sauntered over from the bar with Geordie, being the last two men in the clubrooms and sat down with them. "What about one more for the road, Missy, before I shut up for the night, and while Brenda is cleaning up in the kitchen? Brad is still buying after his lotto luck."

"Thank you, Geordie and Brad, but I'm so tired I daren't have another drink, I still have to drive home," Jenny replied, while Iain too held up his hand to say no.

"How come you're so tired, Mummy-Jen?" Brad asked, a mock innocent look on his face.

"Oh, I don't know, may be something I drank which disagreed with me."

"I just noticed Dad looks really tired too. Must have affected both of you." He grinned at them and burst into laughter when they both blushed guiltily.

Geordie interjected: "I feel like I'm missing out on something here."

Brad was in fine form with his jocular, irreverent manner, and jumped in before Iain or Jenny could answer.

"Well, Geordie, it's the strangest thing. But Mummy-Jen here was over at our place for a barbeque last night, and maybe drank one too many glasses of wine."

Jenny couldn't help herself but interrupt to save face. "Geordie, I made the mistake of skipping breakfast and lunch yesterday, then by the time we ate I had way too much wine, but G.I. Junior here will probably never let me forget it."

"You bet I won't, Mummy-Jen, but only because I think of you as part of the family." He winked and smiled. "So Dad took her home, fortunately for me, not till after she gave me some numbers for tonight's lottery, and that's the real reason I'm trying to get her drunk again tonight. But Geordie, I didn't hear Dad get home until, oh, it must have been what, about five a.m., Dad? I just hope he didn't take advantage of my future mother because she was a little under the weather."

While Jenny felt horrified at his sense of humor, which was nothing more than sarcasm designed to embarrass, Iain rode to her rescue.

"Geordie, did I ever tell you about the time I knocked off work a bit early because I was coming down with the flu?"

Now it was Brad's turn to show embarrassment, and Jenny was pleased to see him squirm. It was obvious Geordie knew exactly what was coming; he feigned exaggerated innocence. "No, Iain, I don't think you ever did, what happened?"

"Well, I walked in to my own home, as you would too, Geordie, unsuspecting, and saw Brad and Lyndsay on the couch. You've met Lyndsay haven't you Geordie?" He nodded, while Brad wriggled on his chair and Jenny smiled at his discomfort. Turnabout is fair play.

"Well, I'm not exactly sure what they were doing, but it looked like some sort of naked yoga exercises. Good-looking girl Lyndsay, and I feel like I really got to know her after that experience. Now, what were you saying, Brad?"

He nodded, and raised his can of Jack Daniels and cola, knowing he had been beaten at his own game. Jenny squeezed high up Iain's leg under the table, to thank him for saving her modesty.

Jenny relived their goodnight kiss all the way home

as she drove through the still drizzling rain, alone. Despite her overwhelming tiredness she had experienced a wonderful night, and felt as if she'd not so much made a lot of friends, as expanded her family circle. It was an unknown concept for her as her mother and father had relocated to Melbourne, for their careers, when Jenny was nineteen and studying hard at University. Other than semi-obligatory visits and phone calls, it was as if Jenny lived her life as an orphan from that day forward. She had not much more than her mother's sayings to remind her she even had parents.

Jenny's family had never been emotionally close. Her father was a surgeon and her mother an ear nose and throat specialist, and they had pounded their children with their beliefs that future happiness and security, only came from studying hard toward a career goal. That involved forgoing friends, and more especially for Jenny, boyfriends.

But now with the soccer players, who to a man welcomed her with open arms into their group, she felt a thrill of belonging, and with Iain, a sense of contentedness in her life.

Once home, before she allowed herself the sheer joy of crashing into bed to sleep, she sat at her desk and wrote the first instalment of her diary. She intended to do this at every opportunity, because, she felt great sorrow for the person she would leave behind when she departed back to the future. Without a diary, she would wake up confused, disorientated, and lost. It was a horrible thought; she would have absolutely no recollection of the previous thirty-three days. Possibly enough to drive her mad. No, she owed it to herself not to let that happen.

By eleven, she was nodding off at the desk, and she hadn't yet got to the point where she made love with Iain. She wanted to do that justice, and made the decision to go to bed. She could take the diary to work, and continue to write it up during free periods at university.

Her phone stayed silent with no telltale message tone announcing incoming words of love from Iain. She debated whether to send him one herself, but decided against it. If she sent one, then he might reply, then two hours would slip past, with them texting like teenagers, and she was just too tired for that.

Chapter 7
Passing Time

May 12th 2247, Berlin, Germany.

Heinrich Abraxist could not believe the reports sitting on his desk; it was impossible! He stared into space, unseeing, almost in a daze. How could some of his test subjects tell such a similar story?

Clearly, it was ludicrous that they had somehow teleported back in time as they stated in their initial interview. It was just laughable. His first reaction was to think the group had all shared some type of drug related hallucination. But, to complicate things further, they lost their memory within a few hours of waking up. That made full investigation and interrogation impossible. It was frustrating that in each case, they forgot what had occurred, but they also could not remember their earlier admissions of traveling back in time to their younger selves.

His superiors were rushing him for a result from his latest round of testing; they could stop his funding at any time. It had been his hypothesis the use of a combination of psychotropic drugs he had discovered, could aid in the treatment of various chemically imbalanced psychological disorders. He had long dreamed of curing violent psychopaths and sociopaths, the incidence of which over the previous two hundred years had grown to near epidemic proportions. He often thought of such violent tendencies to be rather like an unstoppable virus.

The problem he faced in being assured of continued funding was the world was facing dire food shortages because many plants across the world were diseased with the Blight. Resources were being funneled from existing programs into finding a cure for the Yellow Spot before it was too late. Already some of the countries where the incidence had spread to plague proportions, were abandoned with refugees starving at the borders, unable to be admitted to neighboring countries, who had their own shortages.

Even the wealthier nations were in serious trouble. The disease didn't stop at boundaries, and with ever-increasing shortages in feed for animals, even meat was rare and too expensive for normal working families to buy.

Heinrich believed that if he could chemically regress his patients back mentally and emotionally to a time before their symptoms took hold, he could cure them. If he could then find an immunization to stop the violence before it began, he would be a candidate for a Nobel Prize. If the population of the world died of starvation, his cure for mental illness would be meaningless; there would be no one left to save.

These reports of the interviews with the test patients on waking were a mockery, surely?

There was nothing else he could do; he must inject more subjects with the same physical and mental profile. Then focus all his resources on finding the truth of the effects of #ASX101, despite the memory loss that would follow. The team would have to work harder and faster when these people woke up, to get to the bottom of things. He felt better for having made the decision, he just hoped he would have enough time to finish, before his superiors pulled the plug on him.

****

Day Nine, 10th August 2016

Jenny raced home from the university and firstly made her bed, which she hadn't found time for that morning, having spent some more time working on her diary. She tidied her small but comfortable town house, fed Mr. Sanchez, and prepared herself for Iain's impending arrival. She had luxuriated in a hot shower, dried her hair and put on her new black underwear set, again raising her eyes to the ceiling and thanking Janet for helping to dress her, and making her feel more feminine than she ever had before. Over them she wore a simple red cotton T-shirt and blue jeans, with her hair, thanks to Janet's advice, long and flowing.

She was ready and sipped a glass of wine with an FM radio station playing softly in the background by five minutes before six. When the doorbell sounded its cheerful chime, she flung the door open wide and jumped into his arms before he could drop the overnight bag he had in his hand. As they kissed, Iain waddled inside with Jenny's legs wrapped around his hips. He kicked the door closed.

With the bag on the floor Iain's hands were free to roam up and down her back as they kissed. "I missed you so much." She moaned between breaths.

This time she was sober and was aware of his every touch. He slipped his left hand inside the back of her shirt to touch her bare skin, while his right crept down over her bottom. His hand was so big it could cup her cheek while his fingertips rubbed her intimately through her jeans. "I missed you too," he gasped breathlessly in reply.

She could feel his hardness as he ground against her; she wasn't hungry for dinner; she wanted him. She stared into his eyes, and saw his obvious passion lurking there. She undid the buttons of his cream linen shirt. "We don't have to go out, Iain; we could stay here and order pizza. After you've made love to me, that is."

She loved the feel of his bare chest under her hands as she kissed him again, not giving him time to reply. With his hands under her buttocks, and her legs tight around his hips, he walked her backward, toward her bedroom. She was incapable of resisting, not that she wanted to; she wanted him to use her body, any way he desired.

She had left the bedside light on, which spread a warm glow across the room, and once there she lowered her feet to the floor and let him strip her. He took his time; firstly, he peeled her shirt up and over her head and tossed it aside. His eyes were ablaze with desire as he drank in the view of her chest covered only in her new black bra. She thought he would take it off, but he didn't. Instead, while he kissed her mouth, his hands covered her lace-covered breasts, gently at first, squeezing and fondling her, making her nipples beg for attention.

She was delirious with passion and desire. Her breath became labored as he lowered his head to kiss her breasts, suckling her through the material, the lace making her nipples stiffen further as he sucked and bit them each in turn. She yanked his shirt open all the way and jerked it down over his shoulder and arms. He wriggled and helped by disengaging his hands letting the garment drop to the floor before she felt him fumble with the button and zipper on her denims.

"Oh my God, yes Iain." But he didn't peel them down over her hips straight away. Instead his hand slid inside her panties, searching through her pubic hair, down and under her. His finger rubbed her, with a heady mixture of gentleness and roughness. She could feel how wet with desire she was as she moaned and bit his shoulder. He rubbed her harder; gaining speed and friction.

An orgasm rocketed toward her like a comet across the night sky, and she welcomed it, panting deliriously, moaning: "Yes, yes yeeesssssss."

He held her tightly as he coaxed her closer to the precipice, her world disappearing in an ever-closing spiral. She was incapable of rational thought and may have fallen without Iain holding her as her body trembled from head to foot; the climax radiating out from her center in wave after wave until she could take no more.

Jenny weakly grabbed his wrist to stop him, the pleasure too much, her skin over sensitive, and she collapsed against him, panting breathlessly.

Time passed. She phased out; only vaguely aware of him whispering he loved her, as he gently stroked her back. He stepped to the side and picked her up in his arms. She cradled hers around his neck, staring into his eyes with love as he carried her, and kneeling, softly laid her on the bed.

"Oh my God, Iain. I love you more than life itself."

He smiled then stood while looking down as he undid his jeans. She couldn't help herself, lowering her lustful gaze, as he wriggled his jeans and underpants down as one, his lovely hardness springing free in all its glory. She stretched out a hand to stroke him, while he stood on one foot then the other, peeled his shoes, socks and jeans over each foot in turn to leave them on the floor.

Once he was nude he bent at the waist and slipped her shoes off. In one of those momentary flashes of random thoughts, she realized no one had taken her shoes off since early childhood, and she smiled. Then he lifted each foot in turn and removed her socks and she reveled in the look on his face which seemed to be a heady mixture of love, affection, and sexual excitement, because he wanted to see her body, all of her body.

Despite his rampant hardness, and clear need for his own release, she loved him for his gentleness and for taking his time. It appeared he was enjoying every single moment, as if he were locking away in his memory banks each precious second of the unveiling of her body.

She lifted her hips so he could slide her jeans off, and she was surprised too he didn't want to take her panties off at the same time. Again, he was in no hurry. She lay there, looking up at him. He stood up straight and softly murmured, "You're the most stunning woman I've ever known, I want to be able to remember this moment, just as you are, for the rest of my life."

His words took her breath away, and she had to blink back tears of sudden emotion as her heart swelled to almost bursting point. She opened her arms wide. "I love you, I love you, Iain."

He lay alongside her, on his side, sliding his left arm underneath her neck and kissed her softly and slowly but gaining in intensity while his right hand was free to roam on a voyage of discovery all over her skin. She felt as if he wanted to touch every curve, every soft section of her body. He treated her as if he had all the time in the world which was so unlike the two sexual encounters from her past. In comparison, they had been rushed, frantic, and so very disappointing.

When the kiss broke, he lowered his head to her throat and she tilted back to give him access. She would deny him nothing, he was free to do whatever he wanted. It seemed to Jenny, the thing he desired most was to gain his pleasure by increasing hers, and he softly kissed, nibbled, and licked her neck, which caused her to shiver and tremble.

With his fingertips, he slipped a bra strap from her shoulder and slid it down her arm, kissing a trail down to the upper swell of her breast. She gasped loudly as his lips closed over her nipple, already so hard, as he worked on making it even stiffer. His teeth nibbled as he alternated between sucking and biting her, taking her ever higher. Her hips lifted and rocked involuntarily as she squeezed her thighs together, trying to scratch the itch inside her panties.

Her hands roved over his back arms and shoulders, feeling his muscles; her nails making white lines down his skin, but going deeper when he sucked her nipple hard. She lifted her torso off the bed, wanting him to get more of her breast into his mouth.

He suddenly stopped and her nipple dropped free, wet, and turgid, the cool air making it softly throb. He kissed lower, wriggling his body downward, as he trailed the tip of his tongue down her skin raising goose bumps as he traveled south. He stopped at her navel, licking, and she felt his hand on her vagina, outside her panties, rubbing up and down then stopping to make a circle at the top, around her clitoris.

She bit her lip, stifling the moan. *Oh my God, what is he doing to me?* She felt his lips going even lower and her eyes opened wide in shock. *No, he can't want to do that, surely?* Then his tongue was at the top of her panties and he softly, but firmly forced her right thigh away from her left and licked lower. *Oh, my God, he is.* She felt his mouth cover her and suck through the damp spot in the material.

She had been told, and read of such things, but in her sheltered world she'd never experienced being licked before, or even imagined. Her two encounters with spikey haired, university students, when she was much younger, and trying to fit in with the 'in' crowd had left her wondering what all the fuss was about.

It was "just sex" as one of her lovers explained when she had plucked up the courage to ask why he hadn't wanted to see her again. He didn't want to "marry her."

She looked down as Iain positioned his body so he lay between her open thighs as he looked up, and their eyes met. His fingers worked the gusset of her panties aside, and still as they stared into each other's gaze he lowered his head until his mouth engulfed her. The sight of one breast exposed while the other was still covered in black lace, and Iain looking up while he could feast on her, only heighted the sensations she felt. She planted her feet flat on the bed, entwined her fingers in his hair as she gripped his head, and without conscious thought lifted her hips so she could use more of his beautiful tongue.

"*Oh my God!*" she screamed as her second orgasm hit her, rolling like a traveling thunderclap across the sky. She clung to the back of his head, forcing him in deeper and lifted her hips against him. She could not get enough of his wonderful torture, and he too wanted more from her. He wouldn't let up, or give her time to recover, even when she vainly tried to force him away, he would not relent. His hands slid to her hips, and as if she were a bucking bronco he gripped her, trapped with both strong hands, and rode her to a second orgasm, and then a third.

Only then, did he stop, as her head rocked from side to side, delirious with pleasure, until she floated above a plateau of Nirvana she didn't even know existed; where time stood still. She drifted, in a sky filled with white cotton candy clouds, a gentle warm breeze blowing across her naked skin, while in the far distance she could hear the tinkling of tiny cymbals. Everything was serene; her body was at peace with the world, more relaxed than she imagined possible, until slowly, she drifted back to earth.

She opened her eyes to see Iain knelt back on his haunches, smiling. He had been blowing his breath up and down her body to cool the sheen of sweat she wore. "Welcome back, baby. You are so beautifully responsive. I love you."

This man has been sent from Heaven, just for me. "I love you too, Iain. It's never been like this for me before. I'm only this responsive for you, only you. Hold me."

She opened her arms wide and willingly as he positioned his body on top her. He snuggled in, taking his weight on his knees between her wide spread legs, and his elbows. Her arms instinctively wrapped around him to hold him close, while her hands softly trailed tickle lines along his back. They kissed, this time lovingly and gently. His need for his own release must be close to the bursting point, and she wanted to feel him deep inside her when he reached it.

Vaguely she remembered her pledge about using condoms, but she felt so close to him. Surely, one more night couldn't hurt, could it? *I will get the morning after pill this time.*

She loved him so much she ached, and she decided to discuss it with him, calmly and logically tomorrow, or perhaps even later that night, when they ate, but for now she wanted this gift to be for him, to show how much she loved him. *Am I being foolish to want that? Maybe. But, for now, I don't care. I hope I understand when I read my diary after I wake up.*

She snaked her hand between their bodies as they kissed, and found him. She broke her kiss and whispered: "Oh, baby, this time it's for you, Iain."

Her panties were still skewed to the side, so there was nothing between them. Their eyes locked together as he slowly slid inside. "I love you," he whispered.

"I know," she replied and removed her hand from between them and cupped his bottom cheeks and pulled him deeper. He stopped with his full length inside her willing body, and she shook her head in wonder. "Oh my God, Iain. I never knew it could be like this."

"Jesus, Jenny, this isn't going to take me long, I will make it up to you next time, I promise." He withdrew, then immediately thrust back inside, once twice then three times and moaned loudly. She stared into his eyes, and her heart nearly exploded along with him.

"I love you," she whispered, adoring the look on his face. She marveled at the way his eyes dilated, his lips formed a grimace, his brow furrowed, as his hips jerked erratically.

****

May 27th 2247, Berlin, Germany

Heinrich Abraxist took a deep breath in preparation for the meeting he was about to have. On his lap were nine files encased in blue folders with the subject's names emblazed on the front covers. Three were from the first round of tests, but six were the results of a separate series he had conducted in private, with only his two trusted aides who had been sworn to secrecy.

As each test subject woke from taking the ASX101, they were bombarded with identical questions about their experiences, and the results were remarkable. From the previous round Heinrich was aware he would have very limited time to glean as much detail as he could. He had spent hours coming up with the set of questions to be asked in the same way so as not to give hints, or lead the interviewees into giving similar answers. Secrecy was paramount because days before he had been ordered to stop all experiments on ASX101 due to the crisis in food production facing the world.

All research companies in the world had been tasked with finding a solution to the pandemic Blight, regardless which field they were in. The spread was unstoppable, and every pesticide known to man had failed. The most recent shock was the devastation to the Tulip crops in The Netherlands.

It was clear now no plant could avoid attack. Tree

losses in the Amazon Rain Forests were being recorded with acres every day showing yellow spots before eventually crashing to the ground to rot.

As things stood, within twenty years there would be nothing left growing, anywhere, not even weeds.

Werner-Bundt Pharmaceutical; employer of Abraxist, and one of the big four drug manufacturing giants in the world, had been ordered by the Government to cease all research into drugs and switch their considerable scientific brain power to the most serious problem to face the populace, even though they were not botanists. If the answer couldn't be found by traditional means it was time to try the unconventional.

As he waited to be summoned, Heinrich remembered back to when his radical idea struck him.

It was 4:52 in the morning when he sat bolt upright in bed, startling his second wife, of fourteen years. He had woken from a dream; in which he alone was the savior of mankind, and he used ASX101 to do it. He sat and shook his head, 'no, it couldn't possibly work, could it?'

He got up, put on his dressing gown, refusing to answer Gerda as she asked him what was wrong. He acted as if he couldn't hear her, which he couldn't; his mind was racing with possibilities. She had seen this before with him; when he had an idea he needed to think about it, a bomb could go off in the next apartment and she doubted her husband would hear it. She left him to it, and lay back down under the covers and was asleep again within minutes.

Heinrich sat at the dining table, having first clicked on the coffee machine. Soon, even that would become too expensive to buy, as the Blight had affected production of the humble coffee plant too.

He had the kernel of an idea, from his dream. He initially rationalized it was totally ludicrous, but it tugged at the corners of his over active mind. If his theory was correct, maybe it wasn't so ludicrous after all. Thirty-three years was the key.

The coffee machine beeped its readiness, but Heinrich didn't hear it, he was furiously making notes, because he always worked best when he wrote his ideas down.

When the sun rose, he stared at a notepad filled with cryptic notes, dates and numbers, and the year 2016 surrounded by so many rings he had almost worn through the paper. He sat back, dropped the pencil on the table, and stared at his notes.

He must disobey a direct directive from his employer, which, if he was caught, would end his career. But if he was right and he could run one more batch of tests for which they already had the six volunteers lined up who fit the desired profile, then maybe, just maybe he could solve the world's problems.

He met and explained his scheme to two of his most trusted assistants, over a ludicrously expensive lunch at a nearby café. To their credit they immediately saw the possibilities. If they could prove that time travel within a stream of consciousness was possible while under the influence of ASX10, then perhaps a person could be directed what to do, back in the past. That held definite possibilities.

He had not ordered them to assist him, but they readily agreed; realizing if the Destaine Blight could not be halted, mankind had no hope for survival.

Together, they drew up their plans.

The six volunteers were injected in two lots of three, six hours apart, starting on Saturday morning. By Sunday night they had the proof they needed as all six admitted they had traveled back in time thirty-three-years, to inhabit their own bodies, for a period of thirty-three days.

Why that period, and for that long, he did not know. If he had more resources and time he could play around with the dosage and see if he could extend it, but there was no time. Unfortunately, he had attempted to send one of his previous volunteers back for a second trip with specific instructions. Success could prove his point beyond doubt. He did it in total secrecy, and not even his assistants were involved. The man had woken up, not after twenty-four hours as the others did, but within minutes, and he was totally insane.

"Herr Abraxist? You may go in now; the Board of Directors are ready for you," Claudia, the pretty personal assistant to Willie Werner, the Managing Director, announced.

Suddenly, sweat beads sprung up on his forehead, and he doubted he could stand due to nerves. This was to be the single most important meeting of his life. They could fire him instantly, and think him mad, or they could permit him to further investigate his plan. He wanted to send a series of people back in time two hundred and thirty-one years. Back, to two thousand and sixteen, to stop Bradley Destaine from making his discovery.

He nodded to Claudia, and thanked her, then stood and prepared to meet his fate.

Chapter 8
Time for love

Day Ten, 11th August 2016

Jenny lay awake, with her head resting on Iain's chest, listening to his heartbeat while he slept. Her mind raced with conflicting ideas. She was in love, and the feeling was incredible, wonderful, thrilling and at the same time frightening. She had so many problems to face, more than she could possibly have imagined. Maybe even more than any one person should have to bear.

She had wanted to get to know Iain, that was true, but only to be able to gain his trust so jointly they could have some chance of talking Brad out of making the discovery he was destined to make. But, she had fallen deeply, madly, head over heels in love with him, and he had fallen for her too. She couldn't work out if it was for better, or worse.

Soon, she would have to tell him the truth, and risk his anger at her deceit. He might feel she had used his emotions against him, and he probably wouldn't want to see her again, so she was terribly conflicted.

All too soon, she would wake up, and only have her diary to understand what had transpired in the preceding thirty-three days. She had to admit that to Iain as well. Assuming he wanted to stick around her once she bared her soul, which she doubted he would, she wouldn't know him! How unfair? If she made Iain angry and he dumped her for lying, young Jenny would never get the chance to experience the love she now felt.

Then, an even more terrifying thought hit her. If Iain left her and refused to help, could she bring herself to somehow murder Brad if she could not convince him of her honesty? She didn't think so, not now she had met him, yet she must consider the alternative. Losing Iain would devastate her, but she could not lose sight of why she had made the "Leap" in the first place. As much as falling in love was the single best thing that had happened in either of her time streams, it was down to her, and her alone to save the world by making Brad see the error of his ways.

They had spent the night alternating between drinking white wine, eating home delivered pizza, and making love. Each time it had been mind-blowingly good. It wasn't just the orgasms, though they were lovely, it was the closeness, the intimacy, and the sharing of love for each other. If she hadn't climaxed at all, she would have still have adored the genuine depth of feeling Iain so beautifully showed.

But, it was now, approaching four in the morning, and she couldn't sleep for worry about the future, both the near and far one. The thing about having experienced something so wonderful, was she didn't want it to end. And sadly, end it must for her older self, who would wake up as a lonely sixty-eight-year-old spinster, again, soon. A tear trickled down her face as she drifted back into an uneasy sleep.

In the morning, she made him crumpets, with

butter melting into the hundreds of little surface holes, soft boiled eggs and coffee, while Iain showered. He wanted her to shower with him, but she giggled and danced away, waggling a finger. His powers of recovery were wonderful, he wanted her all the time, and while she loved it too, she wanted them to be about more than sex, so she opted to be dutiful and make him breakfast instead.

The sun was coming up; it was going to be a warm day, so she served their breakfast on the back veranda, he wearing his hi-visibility work shirt, jeans and steel capped boots, and she in her nightdress and dressing gown. Hardly sexy and romantic attire for both, but it supplied a much needed sense of normalcy, after a full night of lovemaking.

"Iain, I have a question: Do you ever worry about the future?"

He stared over the rim of his coffee cup and considered his answer. "Babe, of recent times I've just been living from day to day, so no I really haven't worried too much other than helping Brad get through University, to gain his degree, and into a career. Why do you ask?"

"Oh, nothing I suppose. But I worry about it all of the time."

"Anything specifically, or just things in general?"

"Lots of things, pollution, global warming, the growing incidence of super resistant bacterial bugs, the rising crime wave and increasing number of serial killers. And, in the last couple of days, the worst thing of all; you might tire of me."

He looked at her, open mouthed for a moment. "I think you are far more likely to tire of me, long before I could ever get fed up with you."

It was her turn to feel surprised. "Why on Earth would you think that?"

"Hmm, well, let me think, I'm older than you, you are university trained and I'm just a truck driver, I come with a ready-made family, I still live in a house I shared with my late wife, you are beautiful and I'm going gray."

"Oh, is that all? I thought you were going to be serious." She smirked. "Well, let's just look at those things, shall we? Your age or graying hair doesn't faze me in the slightest, if anything I think it's a good thing, and you are one good-looking guy. You will never be *just* anything to me, least of all *just* a truck driver. You own your own contracting business, you've battled as a single father to get your son through University, and I know how much that costs. You are so much smarter, and more interesting than any other man I know, or have ever met, I think your son is amazing and your home is just that: Yours and Brad's home. I'd think less of you if you had sold it just because you lived there with Simone. Meanwhile, I'm mousey, intelligent maybe, but not smart, I'm so not as beautiful as you think, I've had no real-life experience with men, or anything really, I'm dull boring and uninteresting, and God alone knows why you are here. I'm not very experienced in bed, which, I'm sure shows as clear as a bell."

"You really believe that, don't you? You genuinely don't know how amazing you are?"

"Please don't make fun of me, Iain."

He stood and crossed to her side of the table, squatted and hugged her. "Darling, I promise you I am not making fun of you. I would never, ever toy with your emotions. Do you know what? Your lack of, shall we say experience, is just one of the many things I adore about you. I feel like I am the first for you, and it means more to me than you could ever imagine. I love you, Jenny. Those words hardly seem enough, but they are the only ones I have. If I were a poet, or a song writer, maybe I could express myself better, you deserve that. You are amazing Jen, it's no joke, I truly believe it, and mean it."

She hugged him back, so choked with emotion she was unable to speak. He couldn't possibly be telling the truth, could he?

****

March 18th 2115, Diamondback, Northern Territory, Australia

Jerimiah Spry laughed uncontrollably before swallowing at the same time as breathing in and choked almost to the point of vomiting. He finally caught his breath, which at seventy-two years old, took a while. "I barely know you, hombre, and you want me to take some drug you cooked up which you assure me will send me back in time? That's some good-assed story. You're kidding me, right?"

"Jerry, you have a unique chance to do two things. The first is to be one of a very select few who will be able to time jump and go back for a short holiday to your old self thirty-three years ago. Now, won't that be more fun than sitting around waiting for your slot to come up in the nursing home?"

He nodded slowly, before taking another thoughtful sip from his bottle, this time without choking. "Yeah, hombre, if I could believe this miracle drug you say someone else from your future taught you to make, could do what you say it can do. But what's the second thing?"

"You've heard of this yellow spot disease which is popping up all over the world destroying plants and crops? You can help stop it and be one of seven people who will save the world from extinction. Because, a few short years from now, nothing left will grow, and we all die. Everyone dies Jerry. Now wouldn't you like to be one of the Magnificent Seven, and help re-write history, *hombre*?"

****

The day was one of those perfect days sent as a precursor to the start of spring. It had got to twenty-six-degrees Celsius and was sunny, as winter threatened to throw off its cloak and hurry back the warmer weather. But, in the late afternoon, the clouds gathered, and wind picked up to show nature had only been kidding, winter wasn't yet over.

The first drops of rain hit Jenny's car as she drove to soccer training, her windscreen wipers working overtime to let her see the last of the congested evening traffic as she drove to The Queen's Park Club.

Her day had passed uneventfully after Iain left for work starting with a hurried cleanup of the breakfast things, before she took her shower and dressed for work. She had amassed enough laundry to put a load in her front loader washer drier machine and set it going. Then she sat down and did some more work on her diary.

She did not start a text conversation with Iain which would have distracted her from stopping at a pharmacy, and purchasing the morning after pill. It had cost her the outrageous price of thirty-six dollars for a single tablet. *Great inducement to stop unwanted teenage pregnancy; it's going to be condoms from now on, Iain.*

The day dragged by, as all work days seemed to since meeting him, but her mood was good, and she didn't feel as tired as she thought she would. Maybe she was adjusting to getting by on minimal amounts of sleep, or maybe it was just being in love, either way it was wonderful.

At the club, she drove into the car park and the rain was still teeming down. She got drenched just making her way from the car to the clubrooms, cursing herself for not having an umbrella. If it wasn't for her feelings for Iain she would have turned tail and gone home; the weather was so miserable.

Iain greeted her with a delighted look on his face and hugged her, even though she was wet and he wasn't. "I've only had three texts to say they can't make it. In this weather, it's almost a record. I think it's because they all like my sexy helper," he whispered in her ear.

"Yeah, right, that's what it will be all right." She shook her head at his silliness.

"Or, it could be because of Saturday's game, it's a big one. Floreat are top of the league, and they always beat us, but this time after our last game I think we may have a slim chance," he conceded.

"You've got more than a chance, Iain, you're going to win, two goals to nothing."

He lifted his head back from the extended hug he was giving her to look at her face with a quizzical look. "Are you just saying that to give me confidence or is this another one of your visions?"

"You're going to win. A sports editor for the newspaper will describe it as 'the best game of the season, and a pivotal one for both teams in their quest for the title.' You're going to catch them off guard with your four-four-two formation." She had absolutely no idea what that meant, but that was what the sports writer wrote about the game, which she had read while sipping white wine in her future.

Iain stared, his eyes narrowed, but before he could say more, they were interrupted by Brad.

"Hi, Mummy-Jen, could you put my father down now please, and let him join the rest of us, we're freezing here?"

Jenny nodded imperceptibly to Iain, then stepped back from his arms, and turned toward the team. "Hi Brad, hi guys, how are we all doing, ready for the big one on Saturday?"

There were several shouted "hi Jens", and one or two dispirited sounding groans. They were all dressed in training T-shirts, shorts, long socks, and football boots, and she could well see how they would be feeling the cold. "Oh come on now, don't be like that, something tells me you are all going to play a blinder."

Iain took charge, as if to stop her saying anything more about her prediction. "Right boys, one full lap jogging around the ground to warm up, then we meet in the change rooms for a meeting. I want you to jog as a group, so your pace will be only as fast as the slowest runners, who will realize they are slowing the rest of the team down. Remember this is a team sport so work together and encourage each other. The focus on tonight's training will be about teamwork, and talking to each other about what's going on out on the pitch, now let's go."

The rain didn't ease during the warm up run and it was thirteen bedraggled out of breath men, and Jenny, who filed into the change rooms afterward. Some removed their saturated T-shirts to wring out the excess water and Jenny could see steam coming off their young fit bodies. She wasn't sure where to avert her eyes and she felt uncomfortable in a room full of fit young men, barely dressed, though the guys themselves didn't seem to mind her being there at all.

Iain had listed the starting eleven men on the chalkboard, and there were no real surprises there for the team. He cleared his throat and began his talk. "Right, listen up, guys. As I think some of you know, the latest addition to our team 'family,' Jenny, sees glimpses of the future, and she tells me this coming Saturday, we are going to win."

Jenny turned red with embarrassment as to a man the guys all yelled out comments. Some were celebratory yells and whoop whistles, others fired direct questions, but it was hard to pick individual words to reply so, so she stayed silent. She hadn't told Iain, so he would pass it on to the others, it was an example of her giving him information so when she told him her big secret later, it would be more believable. Iain held up his hands for silence.

"You can all talk to Jenny yourselves after training, maybe even ask her to read your palms, or do a Tarot reading for you, but for now let's focus please. As you all know, I've never been a lover of a four-four-two line up, I prefer a stronger midfield and a lone striker, but, Jenny has convinced me to try it for this game because

Floreat won't expect it. They will think we will build attacks from defense through the midfield but I want Brad and Simmo as a joint strike force, to force their defenders back, and make runs in and behind them every time we get the ball. So, when we get possession, lift your heads, look for Brad or Simmo, they will already be on the run, so play long balls in front of them for them to run onto. Get it?"

There were nods of assent and murmurings of agreement. "Defense, you have to hold them out. We know they are a good side; the best in the league, and they will think we are easy beats. But, by winning the ball and playing it long immediately, they will be running forward and backward non-stop. They should tire and get frustrated, and then they might make mistakes. I want to upset their flow and rhythm, make them play our game, and not us play theirs. So, hit them, and hit them hard.

"Jenny has told me they won't score, but, even if they do, the only way to beat the top side in the league is to do what?"

"Score more goals," they said as one.

"I can't hear you, what?"

"*Score more goals!*"

"Right. Okay we've set up a half pitch I want to split into two teams Brad and Simmo Stand up, take turns and pick players as team captains. Now guys I want you to be focusing on the tactic we've talked about: long balls in front of the strikers to run onto. We only have one keeper, and we have an odd number so Jenny has kindly offered to go in goal. Anyone who hurts her answers to me. I will referee so don't let me catch you within ten yards of her, and remember: she is doing her best in the pouring rain to help you guys out, so be gentle, okay?"

Some clapped their hands, and other cheered her for 'volunteering' while Jenny sat open mouthed. She was shocked. She had been press-ganged into playing a game she barely understood, let alone was any good at. But the way it had been done gave her a warm glow of pride and love for Iain, and admiration for the guys who welcomed her into the club.

As if they were in a schoolyard choosing teams, the two main strikers stood and picked their sides, while Iain passed Jenny a pair of gloves and winked. He silently mouthed the words: *I love you.*

At least my hands will stay dry. She gave her best smile back. Brad's side wore red bibs, while Simmo; a lovely young man with thick curly hair and an unfortunate stutter, and his team wore white.

All the better to see each other. Then Brad called her name to join his side, and, more than anything else, that made her heart swell to the point she thought she might cry. There were still four players whose names were yet to be called, yet Brad had picked her! Oh, my God, isn't he wonderful? Like father, like son. Even though she didn't have a clue how to play, she determined she would do her absolute best, because she was Brad's goalkeeper, and she didn't want to let him down.

When they walked outside, under the harsh floodlights, the rain was still pouring down, as if to mock them. They were using one of the junior pitches, with considerably smaller goals than the men's, which made Jenny feel better. Within minutes she was soaked through to her skin, her track pants, T-shirt, and jumper were not designed to keep the rain out, but for once in her life, she didn't care. She was part of a family!

She took up her position in front of the nearest goal, and thought back over her life, and it dawned on her; other than taking part in a debate once, she had never been part of a team. *What a sad life I've lived.*

Her rambling thoughts were interrupted by Iain blowing his whistle, and the scratch match began. Her view of the game, from one end, was a bit weird, and she lacked perspective. The raindrops running into her eyes didn't help and she blinked rapidly to clear her sight. Suddenly, a ball was played toward her from a defender on the opposing team. Big bad Simmo was running full pelt right at her, with the ball as if by magic, at his feet.

Eeek! She froze in a dead panic. She didn't have the faintest idea what she was supposed to do. Suddenly the whistle sounded, and Iain called out, "Offside, Simmo, but it was a great play, and exactly what I want, well done."

Simmo was within ten paces of Jenny and he good-naturedly stopped, waggled his finger at her, and winked. "Th-th-that were never off-fuckin-side, ref," he yelled back. Jenny sensed he was only kidding for her benefit.

The game continued, while the rain cascaded down, and it became obvious to Jenny that Iain was protecting her. In a way, she was disappointed, though at the same time grateful. She could see how Brad peppered the goalie at the far end with shots; he was not holding back. If he were permitted, Simmo would probably do the same. No one kept score but her team were several goals to the better, and it made her feel bad for the losing side. How could they score when Iain wouldn't let them? She wanted to feel a part of it all, and even if she was hopeless, she wanted to be able to try her best.

By watching what the keeper was doing at the far end she thought she could have a go, and when they broke for a half time breather she grabbed Iain's arm and hugged him. She tilted her head up, blinked away the rain drops, which streamed down her face and said: "I love you to bits, but you have to let them try to score, otherwise it's not fair for them. I will be fine, don't worry. I'm freezing my boobs off, and I have nothing to do but stand here in the belting rain, let me get involved, please?"

"Are you bonkers, Jen? These guys are highly competitive; I don't want you to get hurt."

"Iain, I've never felt so alive, so wanted and so loved since I met you. I'll be fine, trust me. I've been wrapped in cotton wool all my life, unwrap me, okay?"

"All right, if you are sure. But don't try to stop the ball, Simmo has a fearsome left foot, so if he shoots, try to avoid it, don't get in the way, promise me, please?"

She grinned impishly. "Trust me."

He needn't have worried, during the second half, it was as if Simmo was playing with his mother in goal. While he did score, several times to Jenny's chagrin, he was always very careful not to kick the ball too hard, or anywhere near her. Once or twice he even rolled the ball toward her in an exaggerated manner so she could make an easy save, then applauded her as if she were playing in the World Cup.

When the final whistle blew, Iain called everyone back into the change rooms, and thoroughly saturated they stood, sat, or leaned against the wall dripping wet, grinning, and lampooning Jenny as a front runner for the league's goalkeeper of the year award. She never felt so wonderful. She glowed inside and out and wondered for the umpteenth time since she made her "Leap": *What have I done with my life before this? What have I been missing out on?*

Iain entered with what looked like a club tracksuit on a hanger and a towel and called for everyone's attention. "Okay guys, I know we are all wet, in need of a shower and desperate for a beer, but we have a presentation to make. As you all know whenever we greet a new player we present them with a training top and tracksuit. Tonight, Jenny made the grade from helper to makeshift player and she is as wet as the rest of us, so I want us all to thank her as I present her with her outfit, so she too can go to the other change room and get dried and dressed."

He handed a shocked and stunned Jenny the hanger and a clean towel. Tears of love and pride welled in her eyes, while all the men stood and clapped. One of the guys, Martin, yelled out over the noise, "Well, coach if Jenny is now part of the team, I think she should shower with the rest of us."

This was greeted with wolf whistles and hooting, and Jenny turned the brightest shade of red, being completely unused to being the center of such sexually charged banter.

Brad rescued her. "Shut your mouth, Marty; that's my future mum you're talking about." This only forced more whistles and cheers from the men, while Iain gave her a conspiratorial grin.

She cleared her throat; it was clear she was

143

expected she say a few words in response. "I want to thank Iain for coming to my rescue with something dry to put on, stupid me didn't give a thought when I left home. More importantly, I want to thank all of you for making me feel not only welcome, but a part of your team. I am loving every minute of it. You will win on Saturday, I have every faith and confidence in you, and if you ever need a goalie again; I'm your girl."

Once again, they erupted with cheers and catcalls, but this time added stomping of their studded boots on the concrete floor which reverberated around the room.

Iain held up his arm for quiet. "Okay guys, one last thing. You all trained well tonight; just don't forget that's how we will play on Saturday. Brad and Simmo, I want one goal minimum each from you, and if you don't get it, you buy the squad a beer afterward. If you do score they shout your drinks. Let's hit the showers, get warm and dressed, I'm told Brenda has made a curry so hot it will melt your teeth and a Stroganoff with rice and fresh bread rolls, I know I'm hungry. Jenny, you will find some privacy and a shower next door in the away team change rooms, and we will see you in the clubhouse afterward. Thank you once again for helping out."

****

As wonderful as a hot shower would have been, after one look at the bathroom area of the away team change room, she shook her head. *Nope, no way, Jose, I'm not showering in there.* It wasn't so much it was dirty, though it was far from clean and sparkling, but there were spider webs in the corners. The light was dim, the chocolate brown color bricks and cracked white tiles didn't help, so the overall impression

144

was…grubby.

She did undress down to her underwear, and gratefully dried herself with the towel Iain had so thoughtfully provided before putting the Queens Park training shirt and tracksuit on. Her hair was beyond hope, but she dried it and brushed it out as best as she could and reluctantly put her wet shoes back on. If she was to keep going with this club, she would need soccer boots, and that thought made her pause.

In three weeks' time, I won't remember this club. I will be able to read all about it in my diary, but realistically, being the kind of person I am, how will I be able to show my face here again, feeling like a stranger?

She wrung out the excess water from her old clothes sadly. It was so easy to slip into the joy of her new life, but she had to keep reminding herself why she took this "Leap." It wasn't to fall hopelessly in love, though what a joy it had been. It was to save the future from Bradley Destaine's good intentions.

She smiled at the noise of the guys next door laughing and kidding with each other as they unselfconsciously showered. No matter what else happened, she had been given a wonderful vacation, and she had to admit she was glad she made her "Leap". Iain was going to be emotionally hurt, and he deserved better from her. It bothered her deeply. But more importantly, father and son were destined to die in a car accident in three years' time. Could she at least stop that, should she stop it?

There was another irony. One of her options was to murder Brad, yet here she was intending to save his life from the car accident.

She muttered: the whole bloody thing is a cluster-fuck. Her father once used the phrase when she was a child and hadn't been aware she could hear.

She sat on the wooden slatted bench which ran along the wall and considered things. *There are too many variables to know what the outcome will be when I tell Iain and Brad why I traveled back in time. One thing is for sure, though, Iain won't want to hang around someone who so blatantly lied to him. He will think I deliberately set out to make him fall in love with me, knowing his feelings would ultimately be hurt.*

There was no point in hoping it may turn out any differently, in her mind that would naturally be the end of it. The least she could do would be to give them both the gift of life, no matter what.

Maybe I could write them a letter and entrust the Dean of the University to see it is delivered in time. Nope, that's no good. It's only the inner me vacating, I will still be here physically, so how do I explain that to him? He would wonder why I don't send it myself and think I'm mad. I will just have to make sure I write about it in the diary, so I know to mail it to them so they receive it before the fateful day.

In it, she could implore them that even though they would hate what she had done to them, they must not take the car trip. Suddenly, she felt a little bit better about things. *What's the point of knowing the future, if I can't save the life of the man I love?*

Then another thought occurred to her. What about fate? If they are destined to die on that day, and they don't get in the car, might they not be killed some other way, because it had been pre-ordained? But, wouldn't that infer the future was set in stone? And if it is, then it means there is no way to stop the Destaine wheat from killing everyone. *It may just be called something else if I stop Brad; like The Smith, or Jones Wheat Strain, when someone else makes the discovery. No, I must proceed on the basis the future can be changed, otherwise there is no point to anything, and I can pack up now.*

With that thought, she gathered up her wet things and put them in her car before heading into the warmth of the clubrooms.

"'Ere she is: The newest addition to the women's team, welcome 'our Jenny' what'll it be Missy?" Geordie called out from behind the bar.

"Believe me, Geordie, the women's team goalie is under no threat from me. I need something warm inside me, so I might have a little scotch and diet coke, if you have it." She loved the gentle ribbing, and once again enjoyed belonging in the wonderful family atmosphere.

"For you, Missy, I'd pop down the bottle shop myself to buy it if we had run out. Luckily we haven't though." He poured a very generous amount of scotch in a very small glass with ice, and placed a can of diet soda alongside, while she took some money from her purse to pay for it.

"Jeeze, Louise. If that's a small scotch thank goodness I didn't ask for a large one. Are you trying to get me drunk, Geordie? I'll take a scotch for Iain too, you know how he likes it."

"Now, don't you get your knickers in a knot. Brenda's curry will burn off the alcohol on your breath in no time flat. She makes a very good Vindaloo does our Brenda."

"Well, can I at least have a bigger glass then

147

please, Geordie? That one is far too small for all the coke I will need to dilute the scotch."

"Aye, you can." He searched under the bar and took out a one-liter beer stein; a glass so big it thudded on the timber bar top when he put it down. Then he turned and poured an even larger measure for Iain than he had for her and put three cubes of ice in the glass. Jenny burst out laughing and stared pointedly, waiting until he relented and found a schooner size tumbler. He tipped her drink from one to the other, with a smirk on his unshaven face. Jenny topped it up with coke from the can.

"You'll ruin a perfectly good scotch with that amount of coke. And another thing, why does a woman with a figure like yours need bloody diet drinks to ruin the taste?"

"Why Geordie, are you flirting with me now?"

He blushed and blustered, which looked remarkably cute. "Did you ever stop to think that maybe I have this figure because I do drink diet coke? Not that this old body is special anyway?"

He leaned on the bar and leaned closer, in a conspiratorial way. "You know lass, if I were just twenty years younger I'd be competing with Iain for your favors, make no mistake."

"Oh, I'm sure Brenda would have something to say about that. Though I must say, Geordie, I'd be very tempted if you were." The irony of his comments was not lost on her; she was thirty-three years younger.

"Well, maybe then, it's a bloody good thing I'm not, aye?"

"I'll drink to that." She picked up her now well-diluted drink, and raised it toward Geordie, and took a sip; but it still took her breath away and burned her throat. He took her twenty-dollar note and dropped the change into her cupped palm.

Suddenly the door flew open and the horde of players piled in all calling out their drink orders at the same time. "Now you know better, my boyo's, one at a time or I'll serve none of you," Geordie said, reverting to his false grumpy manner.

Jenny sidled away from the bar, carrying the glasses to make way for players, and sat at one of the big round tables with the two drinks to await 'her man's' arrival. He wasn't too far behind his team and she waved as he entered. She loved the immediate smile which crossed his face when he saw her and made his way to the table.

He kissed her cheek as he sat next to her, "Wow, babe, do you ever look good in that tracksuit."

She blushed. *Chink there goes another little piece of my heart.* "How come you always know the right thing to say to make me feel good?"

"Obviously, when you did your hair, you weren't looking in the mirror, or you wouldn't have to ask. Jenny, you are beautiful, no matter what you wear. But you have this amazing knack of making whatever you do dress in, look spectacular."

She shook her head and smiled lovingly. "So, Iain, just how long have you been having these hallucinations?"

"Well, it must be ever since I met you." He took a sip of his drink and winced as the liquid burned its way down. "Now that hits the spot. Thanks for the drink. Have I told you today I love you?"

"Hmm, let me think. Yes, I think you've told me

quite a few times, but I never tire of hearing it."

"Good, because I intend to keep telling you. Now, this coming weekend, I have had an idea."

"Sounds dangerous." She placed her hand, very high on his thigh, under the table and squeezed and almost giggled when he flinched.

"You slide your hand any higher and it will be very dangerous. Now, where was I? Oh, yes, this weekend. Ages ago I won a raffle prize at a fund-raising night for the club, and it wasn't a meat tray for once. It was a weekend stay in a King Spa Suite at the Crown Casino Resort. So, I was wondering if you were up for a weekend away. I can pick you up Friday night, after work. We can go to the resort, check in, have dinner at The Rockpool and a late-night spa together with a bottle of wine. Saturday, we have to go to the game, but we can go back there straight afterward, for round two. It comes with a late check out, so after lunch somewhere there we can go back to your place, or mine, Sunday night."

Jenny was speechless, stunned into silence, and stared at Iain with wide eyes, and a dry mouth. *Oh my God. He wants to take me away for a weekend?*

He took her silence as a refusal, and he looked very sad. "Yeah, I'm sorry, umm, I didn't mean anything by it, probably a bit too soon, forget I asked."

"Iain," she whispered hoarsely, "you stop talking like that, right now. No one has ever wanted to take me away, anywhere, ever. I'm quiet because I am speechless, you goose. There isn't a single person in this world I'd rather go away with for a weekend, than you. Yes, I would love to go. Do you know I have never even set foot inside the Crown?"

Players appeared and filtered in twos and threes to their table, with glasses, and jugs overflowing with beer in hand, but it didn't stop Iain's incredulous question: "What, seriously, you've never been to the Casino, not even with some girlfriends?"

She bowed her head. "Iain," she whispered for his ears alone, "I don't have any girlfriends. I'm far too nerdy for the other women on campus, and most of them who are my age are married. I don't have any friends at all really. My life is work, more work, and in my spare time I tutor and mentor students, oh, and look after Mister Sanchez of course."

"Well, looks like I arrived just at the right time then." He smiled, and she smiled back.

"Yes, you did."

"Am I interrupting anything important here, Dad and Mummy-Jen? I hope so," Brad said as he sat next to Jenny. In his hand, he held three glasses, one with scotch on the rocks which he handed to his father, one that looked suspiciously like another scotch and diet coke in a tumbler size beaker which he put in front of her, and an empty beer glass for himself. He filled his glass from one of the jugs. "Cheers." He drank down half of it then licked him lips.

"What is it with the men in this club all trying to get me drunk? Thanks, Brad, but I'm not sure I can drink it all. I have to drive."

"Maybe we want more predictions from you, Mummy-Jen, so we want you tipsy. Any more lotto numbers you can give us, horses to bet on, or locations to find gold nuggets?"

"Ah, now I get it. You only want me for my fortune telling. Hmm, hang on. I do have something I can tell you. Forgive my ignorance, but what are the Wallabies?"

"What are the Wallabies? Mummy-Jen, where exactly do you live, the moon? The Wallabies are the Australian Rugby team; they are in the news now because they will play the New Zealand All Blacks in Perth in a couple of days. There hasn't ever been a game of such magnitude played here before. They will cream us, as they always do."

"No, they won't. Not this time. The final score will be eighteen to nine, Australia's way, and I think they haven't won for several years. Is that right?"

The table had filled up with players, yet they all sat quietly, open mouthed until Brad broke the spell. "That's a good joke, you had me going there. No way in the world will they win. I reckon if they did, it will pay three or four dollars, minimum."

"Four dollars fifty I think. And they will win, you can be sure."

Brenda arrived carrying a huge vat of her curry by the handles. Geordie was behind her and put a massive oval tray full of steamed rice. The wonderful smell hit Jenny and everyone forgot about her prediction. Brenda spooned out curry and rice into the bowls and players passed them around.

Jenny's eyes watered from the heat, but it was so good, she couldn't stop eating, despite her mouth being on fire. "Oh, Brenda, you must give me your recipe for this; it's divine," she said when Brenda returned with a woven basket full of bread rolls."

"Aye, I'll be happy to write it down for you, lass."

There were several other compliments from the players, and everyone wiped their bowls clean with torn off pieces of bread. To follow Brenda and Geordie placed two large roasting trays on the table with chicken wings coated in a rich peanut satay sauce with slices of fresh chili clearly visible sprinkled over the top. When that too was empty, the players sat back in their seats with happy looks on their faces. Having gotten so cold outside on the pitch, Jenny now felt wonderfully content.

Brad had been staring at his phone for a couple of minutes when he lifted his head and in a very serious sounding voice said, "Jenny, I'm looking at the write up and odds on the upcoming rugby game. The Wallabies haven't beaten the All Blacks in sixteen years, and the odds are exactly as you said: Four dollars fifty. How do you know they are going to pull of such a miracle win?"

Jenny looked around the table and everyone was staring at her, awaiting her response. She took a deep breath, and very slowly and deliberately replied. "Because Brad, I'm from the future, and I read the match report online."

There was silence for a full thirty seconds before the laughter started. "Good one Jenny," Col called out "Yeah, brilliant joke," someone else said. But Brad said nothing, neither did Iain, and Jenny picked up her glass and took a long sip of her ice-cold scotch.

****

Later, cuddling naked in Jenny's bed, having made love slowly and tenderly, this time using a condom, Iain broached the subject again. "Really, Jen, how can you predict things so accurately?"

She could have told him then; part of her wanted to. But, something inside told her not to, not yet, it was

153

too soon. "Iain, I'm so tired all I want to do right now is fall asleep in your arms. I've had a wonderful night; every night is wonderful with you, and I love you so much. We will have a talk about it all one day, but for now, just let me drift off in the afterglow, please?"

"Okay, no problem, I'm tired too. But the four-four-two formation? I would not have done it, if you hadn't said I would. So how could you know?"

As Jenny drifted toward sleep, her confused mind pondered on the problem. She had read the match report, which did remark on Iain's use of the new attacking formation against a clearly stronger side, which took Floreat by surprise. Yet, if Jenny did not mention he had done it, he wouldn't have of his own volition. How could that be? How could she alter an event which could only happen because she changed it?

Before she could figure out the answer, the alarm clock switched on the cheery morning announcers at seven am. Iain had left for work, and once again, Jenny had slept through his shower and departure.

Chapter 9
Time away

November 5th 2139, Chengdu, China

In her office at the Panda Research and re-settlement Station on the hillside at Chengdu in South West China, Mini Lee Min wore a very worried frown. The bamboo was dying. In random spots across the province, and even in other places in the country, plants were withering, which meant her beloved Panda Bear colonies were in grave danger.

For many years, the Chinese Government had done all in its power to protect and guide the rare black and white bears from the very edge of extinction. With love, hard work and breathless dedication to the cause, they slowly built their numbers back up to sustainability. It was due to the scientist's efforts they had bred and achieved the buoyant numbers among the several colonies the Research Centre managed. Often over the many years they had been in operation it seemed they would fail.

For over a century the bears themselves resisted all human help to aid in their welfare. They would refuse to mate for years, and consequently suffered very low birth rates, which meant they could not keep pace with the death rate. It had mainly been due to hormone replacement therapy, championed by Mini's own mother, which built some virility back into the males, and helped the females conceive. For over thirty years since they discovered the drug, the Panda populous enjoyed growth. But then, the dreaded yellow spot disease hit the bamboo forests, and no matter what they tried, Pandas, it seemed, would rather die than eat anything else.

At current rates of spread, the Pandas would run out of natural food within ten years, and then, quite simply, they would become extinct.

****

Day Eleven, 12th August 2016

Jenny suffered a minor panic attack when she tried to decide what clothes she would take for the weekend away, as she dressed for work in the morning. While she hadn't visited The Crown personally, she had seen advertising and pictures, which showed it was a luxurious hotel and resort. She had nothing she thought would be appropriate to wear. She owned a few casual dresses, but in the main, for work she wore pants and shirts, and she imagined they would not be suitable for dinner at The Rockpool. Colleagues at university had talked about the renowned restaurant, and that it was a superb place to dine. The kind of restaurant you dressed up to go to.

On a whim, she opened her handbag and searched through it until she found what she was looking for. *Yes, I haven't lost it.* It was Janet's business card, and before she could panic herself out of asking for help, she sent the mobile phone number displayed a text message:

—*Hi Janet. You probably don't remember me, but I was in a few days ago and you helped me out with some amazing underwear, for which I will be eternally grateful. Yes, they worked like a charm. ☺ The man concerned wants to take me to The Crown for the weekend including dinner at The Rockpool and seriously I don't have a thing to wear. Is there anything you can do to help me if I drove down in my lunchbreak? Jenny O'Brien.—*

Jenny didn't expect an answer anytime soon and had just sat down to work on her diary when her phone chirped to announce the reply.

—Jenny, of course I remember you. I'm so glad you made contact, and that my suggestions made a good impression on your man. I'd love to help, honestly I would, my sister has a clothes shop here. What's your budget, and what time can you be here? Put yourself in my hands—

There was a problem she hadn't considered. How much should she spend on a couple of outfits for the weekend? *Whatever it costs.*

—Thank you, thank you Janet; you're a lifesaver, I'm just not used to this. How much do you think I should spend? I probably need one swish nice outfit, and some nice casual things, not too over the top, but not cheap either. Would $500 be enough? I'm happy to put myself in your hands. I can be there about 12:30.—

—With $500 I can make you look like The Princess of Monaco. I remember your size, so I will see you then.—

Jenny, again, was amazed at the things which were happening to her, and the people she was meeting during her "Leap." She hoped after she departed back to the future, her younger version would take note of the diary she would leave behind, and make some serious

157

changes in her life, before it was too late.

There was no doubt in her mind Iain would dump her for lying, but her youthful self wouldn't feel the pain of the breakup, because she would have no memory. She hoped her diary would convince her to make some lifestyle changes. If a relationship with Iain was impossible, maybe, she could meet someone else, if she were receptive to the possibility.

So, clothes were arranged for the weekend, thanks to the wonderful Janet. She put a load of washing on so when she got home her nice underwear would be clean and dry. She made a mental note to pack her condoms. She hoped they would need lots of them. She giggled at that naughty idea and realized she would soon have to buy more.

A random thought flashed across her mind: I'm going to have to make sure Mr. Sanchez has plenty of food.

****

Two things happened of note during the day, and both caught her off guard. The first occurred just after her first lecture when one of her students, a young woman named Veronica Myers approached, when everyone had left the lecture hall.

Veronica was one of the students Jenny usually tutored two evenings a week and was destined for great things. She was studying for a double Master's and could go a very long way in life.

"Ms. O'Brien, may I have a quick word please?"

"It must be quick; Veronica I have to get across Campus. What's up?"

"Well, I know you said you needed to take a month off your tutoring, but I really feel like I need it, and I wondered if you would consider just taking me back on, so I don't fall behind. I promise I won't tell any of your other students."

Jenny felt dumbfounded and looked deeply into the young woman's eyes. Suddenly, she was looking at a twenty-four-year-old version of herself, and that thought was strangely worrying. "Veronica, may I ask you a very, very personal question? Don't feel like you have to answer, only do so if you feel comfortable to, okay?"

'Umm, yes, all right, ask away."

Jenny looked around to make sure they were alone. "When is the last time you had a good night out with friends, or better yet, with a man?"

She immediately blushed, and looked down at her feet, which were encased in very sensible shoes. "Oh, I don't go out much at all really. And I umm, haven't met anyone yet to date, you know?"

"I thought so. Listen to me. Recently something happened to me which has caused me to take stock of my life and where it was heading. I was just like you at your age, all I did was study, and learn, then study some more, that's how I got my three Masters Degrees. Now I realize a couple of things about myself I don't like. Firstly, I wasted the best years of my life, and you don't get to re-do them. Once they are gone, they are gone. I'm not saying you should stop studying; you are a very intelligent and smart young woman. But you are also a very beautiful one, and I am emphasizing the word woman. Please, Veronica, don't do what I did, wake up at sixty-eight years old and realize you wasted all your good years. Oops, I mean thirty-five years old, obviously."

"I'm not sure I understand what you mean."

"I've met a man, a wonderful man, and I know it's probably not going to last, but hey, it's fine, because when we are together, oh my God, Veronica, it is un-bloody-believable. I've got involved in a soccer club, of all things, and for the first time in my life I have not only a man who loves me, but a whole bunch of really, good friends. Suddenly, I've learned what is important in this life, and it's not studying all hours of the day and night."

"You are my tutor, and suddenly you are telling me to stop studying? Throw it all away, all my years of hard work? And for what?"

"No, Veronica, I'm not saying that at all. I'm trying to tell you to find a balance. Have some 'me time' Yes, build a career, but have some fun along the way, live a little. Because, one day you will look back and wonder where it all disappeared. When that day comes, I don't want you to feel like you've wasted your life, like I know I've wasted mine. Now forgive me, I must go. In four weeks' time, I will begin after hours tutoring again, but it will only be for one special student. If you want that to be you, then you have three weeks to earn it. Show me you can find your balance and place in the world. All right?"

Jenny gathered up the last of her things, and left a confused, befuddled-looking student.

The second thing occurred when Jenny was rushing to get to her car at lunchtime so she could get to Claremont. The Dean called out from twenty yards away: "Oh, Jenny, I'm glad I caught you, do you have a moment?"

Fuck, fuck, fuck; no, I don't. But what she said was

"Of course, Dean, how can I help you?"

"Oh, it's nothing serious; it's more of a personal thing." He caught up and walked alongside her toward the staff car park. "It's just, I and others have noticed a bit of a change in you over the last few days. You look and act more, well I don't quite know, more alive I suppose. Not the same old Jenny we've all known for years, and I wanted to ask if everything was all right with you."

"Oh, Dean, thank you for noticing. Yes, I'm perfectly fine. The thing is I've met someone, and he has quite swept me off my feet." She beamed her most radiant smile in his direction. "I should have done it years ago."

"Well good for you, I'm delighted to hear it. There is a staff social function coming up in about four weeks, I hope you will be bringing him along so we can all meet the man who has turned your head."

Four weeks, would be after she woke up with no memory, but she could hardly tell him that. "Well, Dean, it's all very new at this stage, but yes I hope he will come along. We must wait and see though; I don't want to jinx anything. Now if you will forgive me, I must get to Claremont to pick up an outfit for tonight, he is taking me to The Rockpool."

"Claremont for an outfit? The Rockpool? Are you really the same Jenny?" He laughed.

She laughed back as she unlocked her car. "No, Dean, I'm the other Jenny, the one from the future."

****

"Oh my God, Janet. I can't wear that!"

She stared open mouthed at one of the most stunning gowns she had ever seen in her life. But it had

161

no back! Janet held it up off the floor on a gold sparkly colored hanger, turning it front to back, and then back again. It was the loveliest shade of red, but the non-existent rear of the dress stretched all the way down to just above where the top of her panties would be. The dress would suit someone with stunning looks and a body to die for, not mousey Jenny O'Brien. *And another thing, I won't be able to wear a bra, and that's unthinkable. I haven't gone without a bra since I was thirteen.*

"You said you trusted me, Jenny. Now come and try it on. You will look breathtaking; there won't be a man at the Crown who won't want you. You really have no idea how gorgeous you are, do you?"

"But, Janet, I couldn't wear a bra, there's no back to the dress."

"Darling, I saw you the other day changing, you do not need a bra. Your boobs are perfect without one, come on come and try it on, then I bet you'll believe me."

A few minutes later the two women stood in front of the large mirror in the change room, and Jenny had to agree, the gown was beautiful, and looked spectacular on, but *is it me?* She turned from side to side firstly to make sure there were no glimpses of the sides of her breasts; that would have made it impossible to wear. Secondly, she needed to make sure her underwear wasn't on display.

"Oh my God, is it me?"

Janet shook her head and placed both hands on Jenny's shoulders from behind. "Jenny, where have you been? You act like you are an ugly duckling, when you are a beautiful swan. Look at you. Seriously girl I could introduce you to a hundred women who would die to have your looks and body.

Is it true? Jenny looked at her reflection, studied herself. "I don't want to take it off. I'm scared I'm going to wake up and this will all have been a dream. You've made me look, well, unbelievable, Janet. I barely recognize myself, how can I ever repay you?"

She smiled back at Jenny in the reflection of the mirror. "Babe, the look on your face is thanks enough. It's like seeing you wake up. Now I have some other stuff for you. Every woman with a body like yours needs nice dressy jeans, and I found you some incredible white ones with silver trimmings and studs. Also, a couple of tops to go with them, and a dress. It's quite short and could double as a cocktail dress or nice casual. Its yellow, your favorite, and with your coloring, it will look fantastic on. Come on, get that dress off, and let's try the other things on.

As she was about to leave fifteen minutes later, Janet stopped her. "Oh, oh, oh, I nearly forgot, there is one more thing you need, and this is a gift from me." She bent down behind the counter and then stood up holding in her hand a tiny red see-through G String. "You'll need this."

Jenny gasped. There was nothing to them. *It will be only one step away from being totally nude under the dress.* "I may as well be naked, Janet."

"Exactly. Trust me, you are going to feel as beautiful as you are. And your man, Iain? He won't know what hit him when he sees you. Then later, when he gets to unwrap his Christmas present, you are going to blow his mind."

Those words were enough. She gratefully took

them from Janet's hand and tucked them into the shopping bag. "I will never, ever be able to thank you enough. I know I keep saying that, but you've changed my life, Janet."

"Just do me a favor, come and have lunch with me next week, and tell me all the juicy details. Will you do that?"

"I will."

Jenny hurriedly left the shop to get back to the campus, clutching her bags full of the indescribably beautiful clothes. She was five hundred dollars poorer, but she felt so much wealthier for the clothes, and the way they made her feel about herself. Janet told her the bill had come to four hundred and sixty-six dollars, but Jenny insisted on making it up to the higher amount as a tip for the fabulous service, and friendship.

****

Her bag was packed, Mister Sanchez catered for, and she had showered, shampooed, trimmed, and dressed in the red outfit with miniscule underwear. She left her hair down, the 'bun' was a thing of the past, and now she stood in her bedroom, in front of the mirrored door of her wardrobe with mouth agape. She just could not take her eyes from her body as she twirled to the left and right, watching the filmy material swirl around her legs.

Several times she thought of taking the dress off, and putting on the white jeans with silver trimmings which would be so much safer, but Janet's words echoed in her head and she resisted the urge. She had to admit, the woman in the mirror was not the same one from a week ago. This person looked taller, held her head more proudly, and had a confidant air, and, most importantly: looked darn good.

Of course, Janet's choice in clothes was to be thanked, but there was no denying, there was another element to the change in her. Was it just she was in love? Was it there was the wisdom of a sixty-eight-year-old mind in a thirty-five-year-old body? Or, was it that she had always been better looking than she gave herself credit for? Perhaps, she wondered, it was a combination of all three.

She needed to steady her nerves and to have a glass of wine while she waited for Iain's arrival. She was determined not to repeat her mistake of a few nights ago and get hammered on too much wine and too little food in her tummy, so she had stopped off at the local supermarket which featured a very nice small goods counter, and bought some cheese, smoked meats and cherry tomatoes. She had cut everything up, put it on a small platter, and covered it with cling film. It was sitting in the fridge, while she nervously waited for him to arrive. Her idea was that just a little snack and a drink before they left, would be nice. She even bought a six-pack of Iain's favorite beer at the bottle shop, which now resided alongside the snacks.

Her self-doubt still niggled away and she wanted to make sure Iain was happy with the dress. If she sensed he thought it was too, well, too anything really, she could get changed into something more sanguine, and more in keeping with the old Jenny.

As she poured the wine into her glass she saw she had a slight tremble in her hand. *Nerves, I guess, and why wouldn't I be nervous?* So much had happened to her, and this coming weekend was like climbing her own peak of Mount Everest.

In no time at all, she finished the last sip in the glass, *wow, where did that go?* She topped it up while admonishing herself for drinking too quickly. *Slow down, take a deep breath, there's the whole night to go.* Her thoughts were interrupted by the doorbell, and suddenly the flood of fear she had been trying to hold back like a sandbag levy wall collapsed. *Oh, my God, what if he doesn't like the dress, maybe I should call out I'm not yet ready and just go and change?*

But it was as if Janet now resided in her head and her calming voice, told her not to worry, the dress would 'knock his cotton socks off.' So instead she dashed back to her bedroom mirror for one last twirl, then before she could change her mind, bit her lip, and let Iain in.

He looked dumbstruck when she opened the front door. He stood with mouth wide open, his eyes as big as pennies, and finally when he spoke, he stammered, "J-Jesus Christ, Jenny. You look unbelievable."

She had him, mostly, but still she worried just a tiny bit. "Unbelievably good or unbelievably bad?"

And, bless him, he looked even more surprised she could say such a ridiculous thing. "Jenny, I truthfully don't think I've ever seen a more beautiful woman, and that dress? It does things for you, makes you look...I don't know how to say it, like a movie star on a red carpet somewhere."

Her heartbeat sounded deafening as she stepped back and did a slow spin. There was no denying the hunger and desire in the look on his face as she faced him after her twirl. It seemed to be something more than him just wanting to get her clothes off, he looked, spellbound.

"I bought it today, with my new best friend Janet, especially for you, I was so worried you wouldn't like it."

"You were worried? About how you looked in this dress? Seriously? Jenny, you are stunning. Heck you knock me out wearing a wringing wet tracksuit, but this? Now, even more I believe I'm not in your league. I feel like you are a Queen, and I am just a foot servant."

That did it, it was like a small light bulb turned on inside her mind, he did love her. *The silly man thinks I am too good for him?* She gripped his upper arm, and without a word steered him, abruptly, inside her home. She shut the door with her free hand and, still wordlessly, guided him inside, her bedroom. There she stood alongside him before the mirror.

"Iain, for the first time in my very long life I am learning things about myself which terrify me, but in a good way. I've never been even remotely interested in looking good, dressing up, attracting a man, or falling in love, until I met you. You, Iain. You seem to think you are not good enough for me, but what I see when I look at you is the most amazing man in the universe. I see someone who I think couldn't possibly even notice me across a room, let alone want to be with me, yet you do. I think the word dysfunctional fits us both. You have your reasons for being that way, which, let's be honest, are far better than mine. You lost your wife and life partner, but me? I've wasted my life studying, mentoring, and tutoring; lost in this world I call Academia. There is nobody on this planet I'd rather be with than you, you are so not my foot servant, you are the man I love."

They stared at themselves in the mirror, her arm through his, both deep in their thoughts. Iain dug inside his jacket pocket and took out his phone, and still without a word, took a picture of their reflection. When he slipped it back into his pocket he turned and wrapped his arms around her and kissed her softly, and lovingly. The kiss went on, and on, and on; their hands roaming, caressing, and cuddling each other, while the tips of their tongues made their own intimate love.

His hand close over her left breast. *Oh, I want him. I want him now, and repeatedly, and then forever.* She broke the kiss and looked up at face, loving the feel of his hand molding and gently, but firmly playing with her nipple which was so hard under his ministrations. "I want you, but if we start now, we will never make it to the restaurant in time for dinner, and then I will have bought this dress for nothing. I promise you can do whatever you like to me later."

She put her hand over his and squeezed it; a promise of things to come, then taking it from her breast she led him back to the kitchen and out of sight of her bed, and temptation. Back in the kitchen she took out the plate of food and placed it on the breakfast bar, "Would you like a wine or a beer before we go?"

"I want to make love with you, bugger the drinks and food."

He was smiling not sulking. *Chink, there goes another little piece of my heart.* "I see you've already started with a wine, so I will have one with you, please." He answered as he sat on a barstool. "Seriously, Jen, I can't believe how great you look tonight."

"Thank you, kind sir, you look pretty sensational

yourself." And, he did, he wore black pants, a pale blue shirt with a dark tie and cream jacket. The jacket gave him a distinguished look, one she found very attractive. His cologne was heady, and it was as much as she could do to not relent and let him take her to bed. But they had all night for lovemaking and she was looking forward to experiencing the casino, and the opulent Rockpool restaurant.

"Wow, this ham is fantastic and the smoked cheese too."

"Well I'm no expert, but the lady told me it was Parma Ham, apparently the best you can get, and I figured you were worth the best." She held up her now topped up glass for a toast, "Here's to my first ever weekend away, I hope I'm worth it."

"You are." He clipped his glass against hers, gently and they both sipped.

Jenny had never felt so happy, and as fears rose in her subconscious about the truth of her future confessions, she thrust them back down, not wanting to spoil the night. There would be time enough for the bad news, this weekend was hers, a gift from whatever God had sent her from the future. This was her moment in the sun, and she was absolutely committed to enjoying as much as she could, while she could.

****

They drove past angle parked Ferrari's, Lamborghini's and a Bentley, but Iain's car was only months away from showing rust and paint deterioration, yet he had booked valet parking.

"Err, yes sir, do you have a reservation?" The attendant asked.

"Yes, Destaine is the name. The Maserati is in the

workshop so I borrowed the gardener's car tonight." He kept a straight face long enough for the concierge to not know if he was being serious or not.

"Permit me to get that for you, Ma'am." A porter said as Jenny tried to get her bag from the rear of the car, and she stepped back, feeling very out of place.

Jenny had seen ads and pictures of the Crown hotel and casino; you couldn't live in Perth and not be aware of it, but she was unprepared for the sheer beauty of the cavernous entry of the hotel foyer, when they entered through the revolving door. A massive curved glass wall stretched around the external side and stretched up to the heavens, while shade sails crisscrossed each other to filter the heat and sunlight on hot days. As the sun had already set, Jenny noticed the lights highlighting the shade sails changed color, from white to warm blue, and then slowly to red. It was, spectacular.

It was a long walk across the foyer to the check in desk and there were lots of people sitting in comfortable looking seats or heading toward one of the restaurants which were dotted around the inner circumference of the building.

There were shops selling expensive clothes, jewelry, and pearls off to her left, and two glass lifts which raced each other up and down between the mezzanine floors to deliver guests to the rooms above. Slowly the porter led them to the check in desk where an extremely attractive woman of Chinese appearance greeted them. "Welcome to the Crown Metropol, did you have a reservation, sir?"

"Yes, we did, Iain Destaine, for two nights."

The procedure took a few minutes while an imprint of his credit card was taken, and the form signed, before a porter led them to the glass elevators. When it arrived, they were taken to the fourteenth floor, to the sound of softly playing music from the speakers.

The porter opened the suite door with a plastic card inserted into a slot, and they stepped inside. He slid the same card into a location on the wall just inside. The lights turned on and Jenny gasped.

The Jacuzzi spa was in in the center of the suite, with shutters which could be closed, surrounding it, should privacy be required. They were currently open, so from the huge spa bath they would be able to look out through the windows across the Swan River toward the city. The bed was massive, which was off to the right of the huge picture windows, while to the left was a small couch, desk and swivel mounted huge TV. On the walls were beautiful prints, and the whole experience was one of total luxury, which took Jenny's breath away.

On the marble sidewall of the two-person spa bath was an ice bucket with a bottle of French Champagne protruding from the top, and alongside it was two fluted glasses.

She looked around the room, to take in the view, and the magnificent man she was sharing it with. She suffered a panic attack. This wasn't her on a Friday night at seven thirty! Usually she had a bottle of white wine by her side, her cat, either Boof, or Mister Sanchez—depending on the time stream, on her lap, watching a crappy movie on her satellite TV, while she marked assignment papers.

Iain gave the man a tip. He said thank you and tucked the bank note in his pocket, then discreetly left. Jenny stood by the glass wall with the million-dollar view over the city, feeling clammy with sweat.

"Iain, this is so beautiful, but I'm sorry, it's so not me. I'm just a lecturer, I feel terrified."

"Babe, I get it, I'm just a truck driver, and it's so not me either, but guess what?"

"What?"

"I won this weekend in a raffle. It's not going to be our lifestyle, so what does it matter if it's us or not? Let's just enjoy it for what it is, a little holiday, nothing more, nothing less. Oh, and by the way, in that dress you look every little bit like you belong here."

"It's just a dress, Iain, and one I didn't even find myself. I could never have found the nerve. It took someone else to get it for me."

He nodded, thoughtfully. "Honey, if you are having a miserable time, just say the word and we can go immediately back to your place."

"I could never have a miserable time with you, and I'm so sorry if I am raining on your parade, I'm just telling you I would be just as happy, if not even happier, curled up in your arms on the couch watching a movie, than here hob-knobbing with the millionaires."

"Hon, maybe you didn't notice, but as we walked across the foyer, just about every person there was staring at you, and I do mean staring at you. You deserve to be here, I don't. But, I am so happy to be anywhere with you. I thought this would be a little break away, just the two of us, and so what if it's in a place neither of us could afford, nor even want to be here in the future. It's just that: a little break. But, I want you to be happy, and if you're not, we can get back into my car, and we go home, right now."

"I'm being stupid, aren't I?"

"No, you're not. You are just feeling a bit like a fish out of water. And, I hope you'll get over it. We can go and have a nice dinner, then maybe a wander around the casino, just for fun and place a bet or two. Then we come back here, turn the lights out, have a spa and look out over the city while we drink our champagne, and feel like just for once, we are the millionaires."

She stared back at him. The love he had for her shone like a beacon. A tear slowly meandered its way down her cheek. "I love you more than life itself Iain, I don't deserve you, but I am so glad I found you. Yes, let's stay, I'm sorry for being silly, it all just got a bit overwhelming for me, that's all."

He walked toward her, and took her in his arms, and she felt calm again. He didn't try to kiss her, he seemed content to just hold her against him, and they stood, silently with her body feeling every inch where his touched hers. If he attempted to take her dress off, she couldn't, or wouldn't have stopped him, yet he didn't. It appeared as if he wanted to give her comfort and confidence that she did belong in such a place.

"I love you," she whispered in his ear.

"I love you," he replied.

****

After they unpacked their bags, Iain took her hand and they left the room to go exploring before dinner. Once back in the foyer Iain pointed out if they walked to the left they would see the ballroom, convention rooms and theatre, then outside was the Crown Promenade Hotel. Because there was nothing to see to interest them in that direction, they turned the other way, toward an art display, which they paused to look at.

The first few canvasses were Aboriginal pieces which were quite beautiful. They were full of vibrant colored dots portraying images such as giant turtles, snakes, and lizards. Next were some stunning landscapes of the harsh Australian outback, and one took Jenny's eye.

In the foreground was a ramshackle abandoned farmhouse. The timber walls were rotting away and the corrugated iron roof was rusty with one or two sheets which had blown away in the wind. The stone chimney was still standing but such was the detail the artist had captured, Jenny could see the mortar had worn away in the wind, showing it wouldn't be standing for too much longer. The two windows at the front of the once habitable home were smashed which further let the elements inside, and would hasten further deterioration.

In front of the house was a fence made of tree saplings, but that too was falling with decay. Poles lay among large rocks covered in lichen and a stone built well lay in ruins.

It wasn't the house which caught her eye, though in its own way it was beautifully replicated, it was what was around it and spreading into the distance as far as the eye could see. There in the late afternoon sun, lay acres and acres of ripening wheat.

It was a harsh reminder of why she was there, and the coincidence of seeing such a picture, with its desolate, abandoned house surrounded by the healthy crop was not lost on her.

"Don't look at it too long," Iain said quietly. "The price tag is eight thousand dollars."

She turned from the picture and shook her head. "Just for a moment, Iain, I saw something else, role reversal, for want of a better expression. The house was magnificent, but the wheat was dying and rotting. It was quite horrible and gave me a bit of a start."

"I think you need a glass of wine. Come on, let's go to the bar and get one. That will cheer you up."

She tucked her arm through his and allowed herself to be led away. "What a good idea." She replied, not wanting anything to spoil their night.

They kept walking toward the sound of a piano. A woman stood alongside it singing a song made famous by Tina Arena. Jenny couldn't remember what it was called for a moment, but then it dawned on her: Sorrento Moon. Off to the right was a bar, and they made a bee line for it. Iain ordered them both a drink while Jenny looked across to where the white grand piano stood. The pianist was wearing a tuxedo, while the stunningly beautiful woman, dressed in a spectacular black ball gown, sang. They kept exchanging glances with each other, and Jenny suspected the familiarity meant they were probably married.

What a great relationship to be in, one where you could share your interests. It would be like if she stayed involved in soccer with Iain if they married, or he got involved in her environmental interests. *Like that would ever happen; it's going to have to be soccer for us as a couple, for three more weeks, anyway.*

They sat in a low back couch and listened to the music for a while and chatted, but both were distracted by the soulful voice of the singer, who was very, very good. When they took a break, the woman walked straight over to a very startled Jenny.

"Excuse me, I hope you don't mind me interrupting

your night out." She said in a softly spoken voice.

"Umm, no, not at all. We loved your voice, you really are incredibly talented."

"Thank you, that's very kind. May I join you just for a minute?"

Iain stood up, always the gentleman.

"Of course, please do."

Just for a moment, Jenny felt a little angry at the interruption. *Oh, my God, I'm jealous?*

But the woman sat next to Jenny, not Iain, and placed her hand on Jenny's arm. "I hope you don't mind me asking, but where did you get that dress? I have to have one."

Jenny was flabbergasted. She looked from the singer, to Iain, who looked like he was struggling to conceal a laugh, and back again. "Wow. Really? You want to know where I bought it? Sorry, but it's not every day a beautiful, and talented woman like you asks my advice on clothes. In fact, no one has ever asked me a question like that in my life. I honestly don't know which shop it was, but I know it's in the Claremont Quarter."

She explained about Janet, and that it was from her sister's shop, and recommended she contact her for finding out the location, and her styling suggestions, and lingerie.

They chatted on for a few minutes, she introduced herself as Madeline, and the pianist was her husband Don, as Jenny had suspected. Just before she left to start the next set, Madeline stood up and said: "Don't leave before the next song; it's going to be just for you both." Then she smiled and with her long gown twirling, she turned and walked back through the tables and people, to the piano.

"You know me, Jen, I'm not one to say I told you so, but that dress? I'm pretty sure I told you so. You look amazing in it," Iain said, smugly.

Before Jenny could reply, the waitress arrived and asked if they would like another drink. "Oh, I think we have enough time to fit one more in before dinner, two Moon Dancer Sauvignon Blanc's thank you, oh, and please take a drink to the singer from us please, whatever she is drinking."

"That's nice of you, Iain, to buy her a drink; she's a very nice woman."

"Believe me, it was worth every cent to have seen the look on your face when she asked about your gown. I thought your eyes would bug out and you jaw would keep dropping until it got to your knee." He laughed.

Madeline spoke into her microphone. "This next song is dedicated to two new friends sitting over there:" She pointed at them and Jenny turned as red as her dress, when every person turned to look at them. "The beautiful Jenny, and her partner Iain, the song is an old favorite of mine by Chris De Burg; it's called 'Lady in Red.' "

Oh, my God, she is singing to me!

"I think maybe, she fancies you, babe, this is a song between lovers, dancing cheek to cheek and all."

"You can't be serious Iain, I'm not the slightest bit gay, and she is married. Plus, this song is about the way you look tonight. Mind you, if I were that way inclined…."

She laughed at Iain's look of shock that appeared on his face. "Gotcha."

****

Jenny's sense of being a fish out of water returned as they entered the restaurant for their eight-thirty booking. Everywhere she looked gave the appearance of luxury and excellence. The kitchen was open to view to show impeccably dressed Chefs working tirelessly to prepare fare in plain sight of the customers. The dimmed lighting gave the impression of peace and tranquility, and the sheer size of the place was surprising. It was very, very impressive.

They were led to their table by a hostess, who welcomed them warmly. Once seated, she placed a napkin on their laps and pointed out the wine menu, which, she told them, contained over thirteen hundred different wines from around the world.

Jenny bent her head and struggled not to have a fit of nervous giggles, as she recalled a skit from a comedy show from the future. It had been set in a restaurant which also boasted a huge wine list, but when the customer, plainly trying to impress his date, ordered a wine, the waiter came up with more and more ridiculous reasons why it was unavailable. For a while the phrase: "Have you tried the stringy-bark merlot?" was mimicked by most of the young men around campus. The show was due to air in thirty years' time. Remembering that cured the threatened giggling fit, as it reminded her again, her time here was limited.

The feeling of melancholy passed; she was determined not to spoil her night

They both chose the clam and mussel chowder as entrée, and for mains Iain selected an aged Wagyu steak, informing Jenny the place was renowned for them. Jenny stayed with seafood, and the crispy King George Whiting sounded divine.

"Well, Iain, you've taken me out to dinner twice, and you've shown me both ends of the spectrum. With the wine, this meal is going to cost a fortune, so please let me pay for half."

"Thank you for offering, but no. This is all new for me too. I haven't been out for a long, long time, and I am having a ball. Don't worry about the cost, just enjoy the night. I just love the way everything is like you are discovering something brand new for the first time. I could watch your face for hours."

"Is it that obvious?"

He nodded: "Of course, in most things you are very much a woman, yet in others, when something new happens for you, it's quite childlike. It reminds me of Brad, and how he used to be at Christmas, when he saw his new bike, skateboard, or chemistry set." He smiled.

"If you could travel back in time, Iain, would you? To be with Simone and Brad when he was younger, even if it was just for a short while?"

"That's an odd question. There is no way to do it, so I'm not sure how to answer; time travel is impossible."

"Supposing it wasn't, though. Say you could take a drug and wake up in your old body several years ago, but with your consciousness from now. Like a do-over, a second chance to be with Simone again, tell her things you maybe didn't get a chance to before. Experience new things too."

He looked both bemused and whimsical at the same time, and took a long drink from his glass. "This is really nice wine. I suppose my perspective has changed, about a lot of things, since meeting you. Before you came into my life I would have said yes, because other than making sure Brad got through the loss of his mother, my life pretty much stopped. If I could have say, gone back in time every weekend, I would have done it. But now you've shown me life is for the living, not the dead. You are not Simone reincarnated, you are nothing like she was, and that's a wonderful thing. Being with you it's like things are happening for me for the very first time again too. I love you, so for me to go back in time now to be with her, would be being disloyal to you. I've only just got my head around the fact that seeing and making love with you I am not being unfaithful to her, or my memories of her, to be more precise. So, the answer is no; I wouldn't go back; I'm having far too good a time right now, with you."

"Iain, that is the most wonderful thing anyone has ever said to me, and I wasn't fishing for compliments, I promise, but thank you so much. The thing is, I believe, in the future, a form of time travel will be possible, and hopefully it will give us an opportunity to go back into the past and alter things we did that became catastrophes. At least it's my fervent hope we will, because I think we are making a complete hash of looking after this planet for our children and children's children, etcetera."

"Hmm, that's deep. But doesn't it conflict with what you were saying the other night about people changing the natural order of things through good intentions? Is it not the same thing?"

"Well no, not really, not to me anyway. I hope we get the chance to try things, and if they don't work, then go back and stop them from happening in the first place?"

"I'm not getting you, what do you mean."

Here goes, I'm about to bait the hook. "Well, let's take Brad for example. He wants to genetically modify food sources to make them grow more efficiently to feed the starving millions; which is a wonderfully noble ideal. But, what if he gets it wrong somehow; instead of feeding the world, he kills it?"

"How could that happen, hypothetically, of course?"

"Oh, I don't know, it's a bit like when I talked about cane toads the other night. They introduced them to solve a problem, a serious one from a productivity point of view. But all it did was create a far more, wide-reaching, issue which has now achieved epidemic proportions. Wouldn't it be great if we could go back in time and stop them doing that somehow? Go back to the guy who had the brilliant idea to import a toad that, because of our ecology, was fundamentally destructive. Millions of native animals have perished because of the cane toad and some are near extinct. So, suppose Brad could change the structure of his grain, but the nature of the change allows some otherwise hitherto unknown disease to grow, and spread only because he modified it from its original structure."

"But surely there are safeguards in place to stop that very thing happening? If somehow it did occur, they would just change it back, or find a cure."

"Iain, you can start a bushfire by lighting a match, but blowing it out doesn't stop the conflagration, does it? In this theoretical discussion, maybe the change would occur so slowly, and in such a diverse way, it takes years for us to track down the source of the disease. And, unfortunately, by the time we do, it's too late; it would have spread to all sorts of other food sources. You can have all the safeguards in the world, but when industry sees a way to make a lot of money, it's funny how often those rules and safeguards are ignored. We have seen it happen all too often. Thalidomide comes to mind. That was a drug developed to help pregnant women with morning sickness, and wow wasn't there money to be made from a wonder drug like that? Thousands of children were then born with deformities or were stillborn. It was horrific."

"You keep saying 'we' and 'us' like you are from the future..." He looked at her, strangely, and Jenny just stared back, her head tilted slightly to one side as she gave a small shrug. She took a sip of her wine, choosing to neither deny nor confirm his suggestion.

He suddenly laughed. "You had me going there for a minute, Jenny."

Their discussion was interrupted by the arrival of entrees, and they ate in silence, both lost in their own thoughts. Jenny could tell she had sewn a seed in Iain's mind, which was all she wanted to do. While he wasn't morose with her, he seemed just a little bit thoughtful. Her plan, such as it was, was to plant a series of them over the next few days before she dropped her bomb. She was not looking forward to that day which was looming ever closer. But no matter how much she hated what was coming, she had to do it.

****

The meal was superb, so good it had enabled the subject to be changed from the future, time travel, and ecological disasters to much safer and less troubling subjects. The chowder was fantastic and it was a disappointment when their bowls were empty. The flavor was creamy, delicate, and warming. They told each other how good it was several times.

Their conversation revolved around the food, the restaurant, and the people they observed. They joked with each other about what kind of jobs each thought other patrons held, and their bottle of very expensive French Chablis slowly emptied from the ice bucket into their glasses. One very serious looking man in a gray three-piece suit, sat opposite an incredibly tall woman with jet black hair. Iain told her in very hushed tones, he was an ASIO spy, and the woman was with the Russian Consulate. From there people's occupations became more bizarre as they kidded with each other.

The service was impeccable and when the mains had been served, Iain declared his steak was the best he had ever experienced. Jenny, savored every mouthful of her Whiting, saying the fish too was fantastic. They swapped a forkful of each other's meal and nodded both were, amazing.

Iain suggested they skip dessert, as they still their bottle of champagne waiting for them in their room, and Jenny was feeling a very nice buzz from the wine they had already drank, so she readily agreed. The thought of a long hot spa, more wine, and the chance to be naked with Iain was infinitely more appealing than sitting in the restaurant any longer.

****

She stood in the middle of the room, silent, as her eyes followed Iain as he opened the drapes so they could capture the view, then turned the taps on the huge spa bath. It was all so surreal; a luxury hotel, with a million-dollar view, and a man she idolized. This was not her; it was as if she was watching someone else's luxury lifestyle.

Soon his preparations were complete, including two glasses of wine poured sitting waiting on the bath ledge, and he turned and smiled. "I love you," he whispered, his voice a little breathless.

To Jenny, it was just simple, and that complicated. He loves me, and I love him, what else matters right now? Soon enough their relationship would end, she would return to her boring life with Boof, while he would…well, she didn't know what he would return to. But for now, this was real, it was tangible, he wanted her, and, she wanted him.

He quietly stepped, cat-like, across the room and suddenly he was there, in front of her. "I've wanted to do this all night," he whispered, as he took her in his arms, and she felt at home. This was where she belonged, with Iain. Nothing else could feel so right.

"I love you so much, Iain." Her hands found his shoulders, and she looked up into his eyes, while he placed his on her hips and she instantly felt his warmth, like mini bolts of electricity.

"You looked amazing tonight—that dress made you look even more beautiful. But, all I've wanted to do was take it off you."

She silently bit her lip, and raised her arms in surrender, as if trying to touch the ceiling.

His hands, still at her sides, slowly, slid her gown up. Firstly, bunching the material at her waist before working it upward, gently over her full breasts, then her head and she shook her hair free. All that remained were her shoes and ridiculously tiny thong, and she felt wonderfully naughty.

He knelt before her, and softly slid her panties down. She put her hands again on his shoulders to help keep her balance, and she stepped out of each leg hole feeling giddy. He didn't stop there. He lifted each foot in turn, unbuckled her shoes, and took them off, but before he lowered them to the floor he caressed and fondled her feet.

Jenny was beside herself; the eroticism of being stripped naked while Iain was fully clothed made her feel like some sort of strumpet. When he put her foot down his eyes slowly traveled up her body from his kneeling position, lingering at the junction at the top of her legs, then onward to her breasts.

Jenny could feel her own desire. *Iain must be able to smell my need.* Still, he stayed on his haunches, content to drink her in with his eyes. Her nipples, already hard, firmed even more as he openly stared at them, and she wanted him to hold them, suck and bite them even, but he didn't.

Eventually he stood and took her hand in his and led her to the spa bath which neared its full point. He helped her step in it, and she slowly lowered herself into the bubbles, her skin glowing from the heat.

Jenny felt indescribably good, the wine, the bath, the man she was with made her wonder if life could get any better than right at that moment. She lay back, gazing up at Iain as he stood staring back at her. Her breasts were partially exposed, and to tease him further she parted her legs as an invitation.

"I've never seen a more beautiful sight," he said quietly. "May I take a picture; I swear to you no one else will ever see it?"

She bit her lip, and nodded. He took his phone

from his jacket pocket, lined up a shot and Jenny lifted her hips ever so slightly so her pubic mound would be clearly visible.

Jenny had always hated her picture being taken, and here she permitted him to have a nude shot of her. When she wondered later why she had allowed it, she realized what they were sharing could only be temporary, and she did it for him to have something to remember her by.

He undressed, unhurriedly, never taking his eyes from her, and she watched eagerly. He slid his underpants down last of all, the bulge in front looking quite comical as his rampant manhood struggled to burst free. Finally, he was naked too, and she crooked a finger for him to come closer, her eyes never wavering from him. Now was the time. He was clearly very excited, and she thought she would take this chance to do something she had only ever dreamt about in the darkest recesses of her mind.

He stood at the edge of the huge tub, and her hand found him. He made to step in, but she stopped him with her other hand on his hip. She turned in the water so she was kneeling in front of him. She adored him and loved the feel of his erection as she slowly caressed him.

"Iain," she whispered. "I've never done this in my life before, but I want to do it for you more than anything." Her eyes never left his face as she leaned forward and kissed the tip. Instantly she was aware of his smell, the manliness of him, and it was a heady scent. A bead of moisture had appeared at the tip of his penis and it clung to her lips.

"Oh, baby." He moaned as she took him in

between her lips and sucked him.

It felt so naughty, yet so right. *What a perfect fit it is inside my mouth.*

His face, as he looked down at her, was the most incredible mixture of pleasure and sexual excitement she had ever seen, or could have ever imagined. She reveled in her ability to make the man she loved feel so good.

She worked her tongue, instinctively, her only desire to try to heighten his pleasure. The velvet hardness was unlike anything she had experienced before; so hard yet spongy soft. She felt his hands first on her shoulders, then work their way up to hold her head as he made involuntary small thrusts.

She enjoyed herself, the act so natural, and she loved him so much. He moaned louder and louder, and all too soon his thrusts turned more fervent; shorter and faster and it dawned on her he was about to ejaculate, and for a moment she panicked. *Eek, now what do I do?*

"Baby, baby, baby." His thrusts were erratic, his eyes were wide open, and she chose not to spoil his orgasm, and let him finish. If she didn't like the taste, she could always spit it out, but she was determined this be her gift of love to him.

She moaned too, hoping he would know her moan meant for him to continue, and with a loud gasp that turned into almost a squeal, Iain flung his head back, gripped her head tightly and orgasmed. It seemed to be endless, and Jenny remembered poets called it a 'little death.'

The taste isn't horrible, but it's far from ice cream or honey. It's bearable, but only just. She never felt more like a woman, or more feminine. She loved her man, and she had done something for him, and she enjoyed every moment of it, even though the taste left a lot to be desired. She smiled adoringly, feeling more than ever the warm glow of her love, then picked up her glass and took a sip of the Champagne. Then she lay back in the water while Iain climbed in to join her.

He held her in his arms, and she could feel the beating of his heart. What a wonderful feeling it was.

"I love you so much, baby. That was incredible, you blew my mind."

"Oh, I thought it was something else I blew," she joked, feeling very proud of herself.

Slowly the wine disappeared, as they lay in the spa, looking out through the windows toward the city lights and talked of inconsequential things. They topped up the water from time to time, to keep the temperature up, and luxuriated in the streams of bubbles.

Chapter 10
Match Time

Day Twelve, 13th August 2016

They had left the window drapes open and Jenny was woken by the sunlight streaming through. Iain was already awake. He lay on his side, facing her with his head on one hand, and he stared at her, with a happy contented look on his face.

She fluttered her eyes and smiled as she became aware of him. "What's wrong?" she whispered.

"What on earth could be wrong? I've had one of the best nights of my life, with the most incredible woman, who doesn't have any idea how beautiful she is. I've been watching you sleep, trying to convince myself this is all real."

Chink, there goes yet another piece of my heart. She wrapped her arms around him, and he lowered himself to kiss her. *Oh my God, how I love him.*

Slowly, almost languidly, they made love and Jenny bit his shoulder as they both reached an earth-shattering orgasm at the same time. A single tear rolled down her cheek. Suddenly she felt an overwhelming feeling of loss, the relationship was doomed, and it was so unfair.

He noticed her sadness. "What's wrong, beautiful?"

She shook her head and buried her face in the crook of his neck so he wouldn't see how upset she was. She desperately got herself back under control. *I have a purpose, and that is why I am here. All my life I've studied the environment, taught people to help keep our home safe from harm and I have a chance to save the planet and the entire population. I must prevail, the future demands I do. I love this man with all my heart and soul and this will come to an end, but I have a job to do, and that must come first.*

"I'm fine, I'm sorry. Sometimes this all gets a bit much for me. I've never been in love, and I feel like I'm flying by the seat of my pants. It's okay, nothing to worry about, just me being silly.

"I know what you need; breakfast. Let's shower and go and eat. Then I thought we could go into town and look around the city shops. I can't remember the last time I did that on a Saturday morning, but it would be a lot of years ago."

"You and me both, and yes, that sounds like fun."

They breakfasted from the buffet at the Atrium restaurant, and when Jenny walked back to the table with some fruit and yoghurt, she noticed a huge grin on Iain's face. "What's so funny, coach?" She asked as she sat down.

"You won't believe me, but every man in here watched you strut around, you look incredible in those white jeans. You have a fantastic bum and legs."

Chink. "Oh, I don't think so," she scoffed, but deep down wondered if he was telling the truth. She had put on Janet's jeans with the silver trimmings and a simple red blouse, and she had to admit, when she looked at the combination in the mirror after their extremely erotic shower together, she thought she looked okay. She was beginning to wonder if her definition of her looking 'okay' meant it might be something more than that.

"Babe, I'm telling you, every man here wants to be with you, you can see it in their eyes. I feel like I'm the luckiest bloke alive because you chose to be here with me. Next time you go up to get something, look around you; I promise you, men are looking at you."

"I think you had too much wine last night, and you're still drunk." But deep down she felt a groundswell of pride and pleasure in the comment, even though it couldn't possibly be true. *As if any man here wanted me, other than Iain.*

But when she got up and walked to the buffet to get her poached eggs she looked around with quick glances and did notice one or two men turn their heads away guiltily. *Oh, my God, they are looking at me, Janet I'm going to send you some flowers to say thank you.*

****

November 3rd 2188, County Cork, Ireland

Bryony O'Shaunessy had tears streaming down her face, and her husband was not far behind her. They faced ruin.

They lived in County Cork, Ireland, and only the year before they borrowed heavily from the bank to purchase the adjoining property on their Western border when the owner, James Pickle, had died. They were potato farmers, and they stood in a field, surrounded by other fields, containing dead and dying plants.

At first, when they noted the yellow spots on some of the green leaves of the millions of healthy plants they, along with the bank owned, they foolishly thought the potatoes below ground would still be fine as they only had six to eight weeks to harvest.

They dug down below the surface on test plants all over their property, and checked, and things looked normal. Even the stems and leaves above looked fine, except for the array of tiny yellow spots, which in some cases, you needed to be wearing eye-glasses to see.

But, only three weeks later, the leaves withered, though under the surface the 'praties' still looked all right, growing bigger and healthier in the soil. They nervously watched and waited, and hoped all would be well in the end.

A further four days later, as far as the eye could see was brown, dead plants, and when they ran from spot to spot digging, they found the potatoes shriveled to one third their size so they now resembled rotting walnuts. Financially, they had lost everything.

****

Jenny and Iain walked slowly along the city mall, hand in hand, stopping to look in shop windows now and again, to talk about what lay within. The weather was fine and sunny, though not too hot and there were people everywhere. With the noises from music playing and spruikers trying to cajole buyers into their stores, it felt like a carnival atmosphere.

They stopped to watch the buskers, and Jenny had a childlike interest in each performer. She had no need to venture into the city center previously so had no idea it was like this, with such a huge array of extremely talented street artists.

Of special interest was a magician whose sleight of hand skills were extraordinary. She was so entertained she gladly donated a ten-dollar note from her purse when he asked her to. Then he made it disappear, then reappear in the other hand, before it disappeared for the last time. It was only later she saw it sticking out of Iain's shirt pocket.

Seeing such perfectly executed tricks from so close was a wondrous experience, and the magician, who had a broad Irish accent, targeted her for his humor, as he seemed to be able to tell she was an instant fan.

'Snibbo', the magician, took one hapless man from the growing audience and stood alongside him. Then while keeping up his continual patter and touching the man on the arms, back and chest he offered him back his own belongings that had been stolen, one at a time. His wallet, handkerchief, car keys, and even his watch continually were taken by the man only to lose them again and again. Jenny held her hand over her mouth and laughed hysterically as the perplexed victim kept taking his things back from the 'pickpocket' only for them to be removed again.

That was the highlight of the show, and his finale. Solemnly Snibbo announced, "Ladies, gentlemen and children, let this be a lesson to you. I did this only to show everyone there are pickpockets about in this very city. Often, they are attracted to large gatherings, just like this one, so please right now, take out your purses and wallets, and make sure you have them safe and sound."

The audience did, and once they had them in their hands, Snibbo took his cap from his head and walked around the gathering holding it out so people could put money in it. He humorously derided them if he believed they weren't donating enough.

Next, a young man with a straggly beard and hair

which was almost as long as Jenny's, created a piece of art, while all around him were more of his paintings for sale. His specialty was science fiction pictures of desolate planets with weeping waterfalls of lurid colors, stark mountain ranges, erupting volcanos, and weird moons in the night sky. He could give not only a sense of reality to these imagined far-off worlds, but a very strong feeling of things which were there but couldn't be seen. It was as if aliens were hiding from view, or a rocket ship was parked behind the rocks. He used spray cans of fluorescent paint and an assortment of empty tin cans, plates, and cardboard cutouts to create shapes as he worked with extraordinary speed. From start to finish the piece was done within ten minutes, and he then conducted an on the spot auction. His girlfriend tacked it into a frame for the eventual buyer while the auction went on. While his work was beautiful, and very different to anything Jenny and Iain had ever seen, the art would not have suited either of their homes, so they elected not to bid. Jenny was pleased to see it made two hundred and ten dollars.

"Not bad for fifteen minutes' work," Iain whispered.

Jenny wondered if he was being mean, but when she looked up Iain displayed a genuine smile; he seemed as pleased as she was, that the struggling artist had made a sale. *Chink*.

They stopped at a small shop which sold ice cream, supposedly made to an old Swiss recipe. They ate the beautifully colored flavors from crisp waffle cones, as two Asian children, sisters they presumed, performed. One played violin, and the other a clarinet, while a very proud mother stood off to one side nodding encouragement to the two very nervous little girls. Soon they amassed quite an appreciative crowd and the school cap on the pavement in front of them filled with coins and small denomination notes.

As they walked away to find a taxi rank to get back to the hotel, Jenny once more contemplated the shortcomings in her previous life. The simple things, such as a visit to the city to watch the buskers and window shop with someone you loved, was hitherto unchartered territory.

****

They arrived at Floreat Athena's home ground in Iain's Commodore an hour before the scheduled kick off time. Both were in a happy, loving mood. Jenny had a wonderful morning, topped off with a lunch of smoked salmon, French cream cheese and salad baguettes from the café alongside the pool, back at the Crown Resort, and had relished every mouthful.

They separated, Iain to be with his men, and Jenny to fill out the team sheet paperwork. Once alone her mood changed and became somber. Even though the outcome of the match was obvious, she was nervous. When the game finished, knowing that she had predicted the score line Iain would want to understand how she could have known it so accurately, on top of the other predictions she had made. She still had plenty of time, there was no need to rush to tell him everything too soon, but his curiosity could cause problems if she told him deliberate lies now in reply to direct questions.

She was on the horns of a dilemma; she loved him, and not being truthful railed against everything she held dear to her heart. Honesty meant everything, and she hated herself for hiding the real facts from him and doubted she could tell him an out and out lie.

But, she asked herself, what were her alternatives? She could tell him everything now and be done with it. But, deep down, she sensed it was too soon. He would not believe her and possibly think she was mad, or he could be so angry for the deceit he might not listen to reason.

Sooner or later he would learn she had met him under false pretenses and that her only reason for contacting Iain, was to stop his son from destroying their planet. Might that be better later rather than now? Her thoughts raged against each other, sometimes yes, others no.

She hadn't intended for them to fall in love, just have some emotional attachment to help Iain know she was sincere. She had no doubt he would blame her for permitting it to happen if she admitted the truth too early. He would believe she knew there was no possible hope for them to remain together and should not have permitted their love to flourish. What had she been thinking? While she sat on one of the bench seats surrounding the ground, filling out the sheet to give to the referee, her mind raced with self-doubts and recriminations.

Iain is a good man. He didn't deserve to be manipulated so I can gain an ally to convince Brad to change his, and the world's future.

But, don't the lives of the many outweigh the lives of the few? Should one person die to save many more? And who should be the arbiter of such decisions? If Iain's feelings are hurt badly through my lies and deceit, is that fair?

No, it's not. But, neither is it fair that my feelings

will be hurt.

But I won't remember what happened, therefore not feel the pain of separation and loss Iain will.

Jenny looked up to watch her newfound 'family' of players going through their warm ups with Iain out on the pitch. It hit her then, like a thunderbolt. What bothered her most, was her own regret that all of this would end. She wanted to stay, with Iain, marry him and give Brad a brother or sister, but she couldn't, that would be denied her.

Life is so cruel to do this to me; show me I have wasted sixty-eight-years, yet not permit me the means to change it. I'm going to wake up soon, in the future, alone with only Boof, too old to find love, too set in my ways, and no memory of my time with Iain.

She sighed deeply. *One day at a time, that's all I can do. I will not tell Iain a deliberate out and out lie, but I will still try to avoid telling him everything too soon. If I can please have one more week of happiness before I bring it all to an end, don't I deserve that?*

I will tell Iain next weekend, that way I can have enough time to work on Brad. Boy, if Iain will be a tough nut to crack, what about him? Brads lifelong dream is about to be smashed by no proof other than my promise a series of people from the future traveled back in time with only one goal in mind.

****

December 1st 2211

While outbreaks of 'Yellow Spot' disease had gained a firm foothold in all countries in the world by 2211, the spread had been extremely slow to show its hand as the massive problem it would ultimately become. There were many reasons for this, not least of which was human greed and the extent men and women will fight for their own survival. Such traits had caused people to hide the effect on their own crops, and to even deny its very existence to the outside world until it was too late.

When senior government officials were made aware of outbreaks, and the seriousness of them, they quarantined farms and destroyed crops with potent sprays and burning. That had traditionally been successful in halting the spread of diseases in the past. But those drastic measures were the same ones that made most farmers decide to hide that their crops had contracted the Blight. Therefore, it spread.

In many of the outbreaks, destroying the crops worked, when it didn't, neighboring farms were burned too. In severe cases, authorities cordoned off entire areas including townships. They blanket sprayed powerful pesticides before burning all affected plants as well as all nearby healthy ones.

Such tactics stopped the onslaught, often for many years. The areas that had been laid to waste never regenerated, not even with weeds, and slowly the wind eroded the topsoil to leave barren desserts. But the wind also spread the spores.

Eventually, Yellow Spot popped up somewhere else in a completely different type of plant. It was adept at mutating and hiding its presence until it re-appeared. Each outbreak was more destructive than the one before, though often many years passed, which had lulled everyone into thinking it had been defeated.

Governments allocated funds to agricultural agencies to investigate and find ways to stop it, and many times there had been celebrations. They believed the Blight had succumbed to a spray, or airborne dusting program.

Scientists eventually understood that while the bacterium was essentially the same when it re-appeared, it had mutated and was immune to the spray or pesticide that beat it previously.

On the first of December 2211, the United Nations took the step of declaring the Blight as 'A Disease of Global Significance.'

A huge multi-national task force was set up to investigate outbreaks and study affected plants, no matter where they occurred. This force was given extraordinary powers, and army support, to be able to enter any place, anywhere, and investigate rigorously. That would result in the immediate closure of the infected property and others within a ten-mile radius. Within that radius, everything was burned.

Backtracking to find the original source was a vital and major focus of the team. By locating the origin of the bug, they could find a way to defeat it. It was always believed the initial source of the outbreak had been in Zimbabwe, Africa. It took time before they discovered that that was not the case. It was the original genetically modified 'Destaine' wheat that had been the catalyst and provided the perfect growing host for what had become the yellow spot spore.

Over the many years the bacteria, which was a bi-product of the new grain, had mutated, to become a true 'superbug.' At a cellular level, it had grown a thick protective shield around it so the most potent herbicides, even ones which were banned for damaging the environment, could not penetrate to kill it. All that could be done was to destroy the host plants, and hope.

And so, it grew and spread by airborne spores, and adapted to attack more and more diverse plant life, slowly and with deadly efficiency, because that, was how it had been engineered.

****

Fifteen minutes into the game Iain stopped prancing up and down the sideline and sat next to Jenny, under the sheltering canopy. "It's not working, Jenny, I'm going to have to change the formation and go more defensive, they are killing us back there and they look like scoring every time they go forward."

"But, Iain," she whispered back earnestly, as she gripped his arm, "they haven't scored, have they? Our guys are playing the game of their lives. Encourage them, show them you have faith in them, if you change now, you will destroy their self-confidence."

He stared, and she could clearly see the doubt in his eyes. She nodded and silently mouthed the words *I love you,* and he smiled back.

"You're an incredible woman. You win; I won't change tactics unless they score."

"They won't score, Iain, trust me. I've read the match report; our men will hold them out and five minutes before half time Brad will get the first goal. Now go back and yell encouragement at them." He shook his head and looked perplexed. Jenny could tell he wanted to know more from her but now was not the right time to ask.

Wave after wave of attacks by Floreat forwards were repelled, by the Queens Park goalkeeper and his defenders. They belligerently tackled and then, as they had trained, kicked the ball long toward Simmo and Brad. The defenders then ran forward toward the midfield which meant that if the ball bounced back almost immediately, as it often did, the home forwards were frequently caught offside.

Thirty minutes in, the tactics Iain had planned showed signs of working. Their forwards appeared frustrated and sometimes made silly fouls out of anger. Yellow cards were shown, and at one point, Jenny thought the game looked as if it could turn ugly, as tempers almost boiled over into fights.

Iain's defenders rallied superbly. They must have realized the opposition attackers were tiring and slowing down. They were getting on top of the other team, and their passes forward, when they won the ball, became more accurate.

Twelve minutes from half time Simmo ran through a gap in Floreat's defense and shot at goal. It was the first time a Queens Park attack had broken through, and it was only the athletic goalkeeper making a miraculous save; palming the ball around the post diving full length, which saved them from going one down.

The shot was enough to show everyone two things. Queens Park realized they had taken the upper hand and could win. Meanwhile, Floreat were aware that the visiting team they originally thought of as inferior could beat them if they didn't lift their intensity.

Just as Jenny had predicted, right on the forty-minute mark, Brad received a long pass on his chest and nudged it down to his feet. He turned to his left and dummied, then sprinted to the right before charging direction again goal-ward. He spun around one defender, then a second. As if the Red Sea was parting, suddenly he was one on one with the goalkeeper who ran out with break-neck speed.

Calmly Brad looked up as he sized up his options. Gently but firmly, showing consummate skill, he lifted the ball over the approaching keeper's head. The ball bounced, once, twice, then three times, as if in slow motion, into the open goal.

The Queens Park team erupted, as did their traveling supporter base, in sheer delight. Floreat players stood with hands on hips, while some yelled abuse at each other for permitting the goal to happen. Their coach screamed at his hapless men, trying to cajole them into lifting their heads and taking charge over the visitors.

"They were just 'lucky.' We can score ourselves if you stop mucking around." He shouted.

The game restarted with less than five minutes left in the half, and, if not for a great goal-keeping save after a furious Floreat attack, they would have equalized within the first thirty seconds. But, the save motivated the visiting players further, and once again they took charge, as if they believed they were invincible.

At half time, in the change rooms, the two coach's speeches were diametrically opposite to each other in delivery. For the first minute, Iain's team could clearly hear the angrily shouted swear words coming from across the passage while he held his finger to his lips to indicate he wanted silence. As one, they listened to the berating the home side was getting from their coach.

Iain, stood alongside Jenny in the center of the room, then slowly turned three hundred and sixty degrees, and looked at each of his players in turn, who were sitting on the benches. Some were drinking from water bottles, while others wiped sweat from their ruddy faces.

He cleared his throat to speak. "Guys, let me tell you: I have never been more proud of you, and your efforts than I was during the first half. You took everything they could throw at you, stuck to the game plan, and reaped the rewards for it. They think they are better than us, and you showed them they are not. Brad? That was a sensational goal, Piggy? Great pass to set it up, and Simmo, fantastic effort in nearly getting the first one on the board. Their goalie will never make a better save in his life, than the one which kept you out.

"Now, let's not kid ourselves here, these guys are going to come out in the second half fired up after being shouted at, and throw everything but the kitchen sink at you. Can you keep them out, and Simmo, can you get the second goal Jenny tells me you will score?"

They all said 'yes' in varying voice levels, and of course, Iain said he couldn't hear them, so they shouted louder back.

"What?"

"Yes!" was the more eager reply, repeated over, and over again, louder and louder until the walls rocked with their unanimous voices. After ten screamed 'yeses' Iain once again stood with hand on his hips and slowly turned around, nodding silently at each of his players. His silence, reinforced his confidence in them, and Jenny glowed with inner pride at his masterful way with his players.

Jenny was very close to tears. Her feelings were in turmoil; as she was carried along by the emotion of the moment.

****

The whistle blew for the second half and Queens

Park kicked off with a set piece start which involved Brad passing to Simmo who passed back to Mikey, while the two forwards took off at a sprint toward goal. Two Floreat players attacked Geordie's son, Mikey, but miraculously he turned a full circle and for a second he found himself in the clear. A second was enough and he played the perfect looping pass up and over players to land ten yards in front of Brad. The defenders were caught out, and once again Brad was one on one with the goalkeeper. But there was a burly defender who made a diagonal run to intercept just as he got to the ball.

Brad was two paces inside the eighteen-yard box when the slide tackle hit him from his right. The raised foot missed the ball, but connected with Brad's ankle which forced him down, screaming in pain, to writhe on the pitch.

Jenny and Iain instantly leapt to their feet shouting to the referee, who had already blown his whistle for a penalty, as Brad writhed on the grass holding his foot.

Players converged from both sides as tempers flared once again, but the offender knelt at Brad's side apologizing loudly how sorry he was. He looked distraught that he may have broken bones.

It seemed to Jenny, it was this gesture, of genuine remorse, which calmed the tempers, and influenced the ref into handing the player a yellow car, rather than a sending off red. The official frantically waved to Iain he should come onto the pitch and Iain headed off at a run to see if his son was all right, with Jenny only half a yard behind.

"F-f-f-fuckin hell, r-ref. He was one on one with the f-f-fucking goalie. Should be a red not a f-f-fucking yellow," Simmo complained.

"You mind your language or I will give you a card too, for dissent." Was the curt reply.

Jenny and Iain dropped to their knees beside Brad. Iain had got to him first at his near side and the offending player stepped away, wringing his hands, to give them room. Jenny was worried, for Brad's ankle but also because she did not read that this had happened in the match report. Surely a serious injury like this would have been newsworthy? The second goal didn't come from a penalty, but from a defense mistake which gifted Simmo an easy chance.

"Oh, Brad, are you all right?" she asked frantically, her head bowed over him.

In a low voice, Brad replied, "I'm fine, he barely touched me, I just wanted to make sure we got the penalty, so Simmo can take it, and Mummy-Jen's prediction will come true."

Jenny looked up sharply at Iain, who could barely contain the smirk on his face. "Oh, you little..." But she saw the funny side before she could complete the insult.

"Brad, you are the official penalty taker, it's your responsibility, you train for them, Simmo doesn't," Iain reminded him.

"Too sore, Dad." He winked. "Simmo will be fine. Don't you believe in Jenny's fortune telling ability?" Brad stood on supposedly unsteady feet, and hobbled theatrically back to his team, who all clapped him on the back and congratulated him. Brad pointed to his striker teammate, and then to the penalty spot. Simmo looked incredulous and shook his head, no. But Brad just nodded more firmly yes, then limped off outside the area, which left Simmo with no alternative.

The ref turned to Jenny and Iain and pointed back to the sideline. They jogged off the field as Simmo reluctantly picked up the ball and slowly, deliberately walked to the spot.

The ground was hushed. Both sets of supporters couldn't believe what they were seeing. Queens Park were about to go two to zero against the league leaders, and current champions, at their home ground.

Jenny's thoughts were frantic inside the safety of her own mind. This should not be happening, yet it was. She had caused a paradoxical change. Brad admitted to altering his normal behavior only because of her prediction, and her mind swam from the inferences of that. Did it mean the score line would not be the two to nil she had read in the match report if this penalty scored? If she had affected one change, could that cause a cascade of others?

Simmo now looked calm as he positioned the ball and slowly paced backward seven steps. He did not look up at the goal, and Jenny knew it was because he didn't want to give the goalkeeper any inkling of where he was going to aim. His concentration appeared only on the ball as he stood rock still.

The referee blew his whistle; Simmo leaned forward and began his approach. Almost as if in slow motion, he ran at the ball and kicked powerfully with near perfect timing. The goalkeeper dived to his left, and too late realized he got it wrong. The ball rocketed past his feet and ballooned the net. Simmo had aimed to his right.

Iain was on his feet clapping and cheering, while Jenny worried about the implications. Paradox: What was the definition? Something which couldn't be, yet was. *What do I know about paradoxes?*

As play resumed, Jenny's mind returned to her student days, when a lecturer meandered into a discussion which had nothing whatsoever to do with the subject matter at hand. But, because it was interesting, the class had sat silently and somewhat in awe.

Paradoxes are philosophical ways of thinking about a situation which contradicts itself. One example is The Theseus Ship. If a timber ship, over time, had every piece of it replaced, would it still be the same ship? Another example has become a bit of a joke: If a tree falls in the forest, but no one was there to observe it, did it fall then? And of course, there is the famous example of the Grandfather principle, as it related to time travel. If a person traveled back in time and killed his own Grandfather, before he conceived either his own mother or father, how could he have been born to travel back in time in the first place?

Such theoretical problems, while fascinating from an abstract point of view, Jenny always found, weren't concrete enough to hold her interest beyond a cursory glance. Her subjects back then had not included philosophy.

But in this football match, there have now been two paradoxes' which could not have occurred without my prior knowledge and intervention.

For some reason, it both worried and pleased her. The worry was from knowing she had altered the natural course of events by her interference. In this game, she influenced its outcome. Iain never would have changed formation if she hadn't told him he had, and Brad faked a penalty which did not happen in the original game because she told him Simmo would score the second goal.

Floreat had still gone on to win the championship for the third year in succession despite the loss. *But supposing, I told the team they were going to win it? Supposing, buoyed by their recent form, and my false prediction, they then won more games and took out the league? Could such a thing happen?*

Does it matter?

Surely, it was not her place to decide what mattered in life, or not. She was not a God, just a simple lecturer with one purpose for being in this time stream, and it wasn't to help Queens Park win an unlikely football title.

On the other hand, it pleased her to know she had the power to alter the natural course of events and change events in time itself. That was the point of her taking her "Leap". She now had proof she held the means to save mankind by making Brad not genetically modify the wheat. She smiled, she had the power to save both of their lives from the accident. All she needed to do was tell them not to take that trip on the appointed day, simple.

Except, it wasn't quite so simple. She, and by that, she meant the current consciousness she inhabited, would not be around to tell them not to get in the car.

Well, that's a problem for another day.

"Hey Jen, you're missing one hell of a game here, are you okay? You seem really distracted." Iain asked, as he sat down beside her on the bench.

"Sorry, my love. I'm fine. I just remembered something I hadn't done at home I should have." There it was, her first out and out lie to Iain. She hid by leaping to her feet as a Floreat player shot for goal and missed by inches.

Somehow, Queens Park survived the rest of the game without conceding a goal. The attacks from Floreat were relentless, and at times brutally overwhelming, yet resolutely the defense stood firm. Repeatedly, attacks ended without result with the ball flying wide of the post, over the crossbar, or safely in the goalkeeper's hands. A total of eight yellow cards were handed out by the referee for fouls, and when the final whistle blew it was a tired, battered and bruised Queens Park team who were the victors, as Jenny had told them they would be.

But still the result troubled Jenny. The paradoxes were themselves worrying in their own way, but of greater concern was that while the nature of the second goal changed, because it was not scored by way of a penalty in the match report she read, the overall result hadn't. She needed time to process what had happened in her compartmentalized brain.

Despite joining in with the celebrations with the team on the pitch, in the back of her mind she struggled to come to terms with what it all meant, and how it applied to her 'mission'.

Jenny elected not to go to the change rooms after the game with Iain, feigning a slight headache. Instead she walked to the upstairs bar and ordered herself a white wine. Ostensibly she waited for the team, but she needed time to think. She sat at a table which looked out over the pitch, sipped the chilled wine, and let her mind wander.

So, what does it all mean? Is this game a metaphor for me trying to save the world? Does it mean even if I can change Brad's mind, so the wheat isn't discovered by him, someone else will do it anyway? Are things, after all, just pre-ordained? Is there some higher power that while it permits some minor alterations in the time stream, it will not allow big ones?

I need more information, but there is nowhere to get it from. So far as I know time travel has always been just a myth, therefore there are no studies or reference books on the subject I can check out of the library, or Google. Plus, if someone had gone back in time, and made a major change, it would itself become the new reality; therefore there would be no record of it being made in the first place.

Her brain swam with possibilities, and she eventually understood there was simply no way for her to understand the physics behind what she was attempting to do. *I can't allow myself to get bogged down, I have a job to do, and I will do my best to achieve the goal set by those desperate people from the future. Time itself would be the arbiter, not me. No matter what I can cause to happen I will wake up in thirty-three years to success or failure, and within a few short hours not remember what it was all about anyway.*

Ergo, I will never know if I succeeded or failed. Making Brad stop won't affect my life in the slightest, only the lives of people in the distant future.

While that sounded all very cozy, and for most people she was sure it would be enough, for Jenny it wasn't. She was an activist who passionately believed in the environment, and its sustainability. Here she was, with an opportunity to do something about protecting the future, and there was no doubt left in her mind it was why those wise men from two hundred years hence, had selected her out of all the possible people, for this job: she believed in what she was doing.

Her wine glass was empty, and she felt like she needed it topping up.

A full one third of her allotment in this time stream had gone. True she had a wonderful time, and would continue to do so while she could, because she deserved that. But, if today's events taught her anything, it was she had a very serious job to do, and must at all costs do it.

****

Despite how hard the game was played on the pitch and the number of yellow cards handed out, in the bar, after the players had showered and changed, the atmosphere was totally different, and friendlier.

When Iain approached her table, having detoured via the bar so he had a fresh drink for her and a scotch for himself, the opposing coach was with him. "Jenny, this is George Koutsakis, George this is the light of my life, Jenny."

"Jenny, it is a pleasure to meet you, you are without doubt the most beautiful women to ever grace our touch line. I think it's your fault we lost the game— you mesmerized my players." He took her offered hand and to her complete surprise he lifted it to his lips and kissed the back of it.

Oh my God, he kissed my hand! She blushed and stammered her reply: "Obviously, umm, George, you've not had very many women on your touch line."

Iain, thankfully joined in and rescued her, as George still hadn't released her hand, which made Jenny feel uncomfortable. "You know, George. It was Jenny who was responsible for making me change the formation, and what's more; she predicted that if I did, we would win two nil."

His eyes clouded over as he frowned. It did have the desired effect: he released his grip of her.

His reply shocked her all over again. "Jenny we need you in this club, you are wasted with Iain and Queens Park, come and join us; we're a much bigger club. *No*, it's all right, I'm only joking. You should have seen the look on your face." He laughed uproariously at her discomfort.

Jenny didn't like him. He had been an obnoxious pig during the game, and her opinion hadn't changed with meeting him after it. "George, if ever I want to change clubs, which I promise you I won't, I will let you know." She retorted, diplomatically. She noted Iain was smirking out of her peripheral vision as he sat down.

"I can tell I've offended you, and I didn't want that, please forgive me." The insincerity in his voice was obvious to Jenny.

"I promise you I was not offended. I lecture at a university; trust me I've been insulted by experts and they would leave you for dead." She smiled sweetly with as much aplomb as she could muster.

He shook his head and looked almost pathetic. "I can see I'm well and truly out of my depth then. It was a pleasure to meet you Jenny. Iain, next time you won't be so lucky, thank you for the game."

The men shook hands, but Jenny didn't offer hers because she didn't want it kissed again. She nodded her goodbye, and then watched his retreating back.

"Meow," Iain said, seemingly on the verge of hysteria.

"Oh my God, do you think I was rude to him?"

"Oh no, no, no, noooo…Yes. I'm so proud of you. You know I love you, right?"

She smiled and raised her glass. "I love you too, but I have to say what a rude, obnoxious prick of a man he is. Not at all like you."

"Ah, but to be honest, I will never be as good a coach as him either, he is single minded, that's for sure."

She took his hand in hers. "Does that bother you, Iain?"

He tilted his head to one side as he contemplated the question. "Well, of course as a coach I'd like to be more successful, but does it bother me I'm not? Hmm, Well, when I first started out it was only because when he was a six-year-old player, Brad's team was to be disbanded because none of the parents would coach them, so I held my hand up for the job. I've been doing it ever since. The team could do a lot better with a manager who knows his stuff, like George, for example. But, the club is happy with me, and I think most of the players are too. So, truthfully, no it doesn't bother me."

"Iain, because you are the man you are, I've fallen in love with you. I could never with someone like George. I had to count my fingers when he finally released my hand to make sure he hadn't stolen any when he kissed it. Seriously, who kisses a women's hand these days other than sleazy old, fat used car salesmen?"

Iain burst out laughing. "Oh, Jen, you are priceless. But you know what? You're right that's exactly what he reminds me of, a used car salesman."

Slowly, in two's and three's, the team wandered over with jugs of beer, and dragged up chairs to join them. Brad led the charge, as he always did. "Mummy-Jen, you are without a doubt a wizard. You know centuries ago you'd have been burned as a witch for fortune telling?"

"And you, Bradley, should have won an Oscar for acting."

"Touché."

"I know Iain told you all far better than I could, and I am very new to this team, but boys I was really proud of you today, the way you all played. It was a tough game."

There were varying mumbles agreeing it had been a tough game. "You're our lucky m-m-m-mascot Jenny," Simmo said.

"Yeah, we can't lose with you on our side." Mikey joined in.

Jenny sighed inwardly. Unfortunately, that wasn't true; they were due to lose next weeks' game to Subiaco three goals to one, but she wasn't going to tell them. Yet, she wondered if she could somehow use her knowledge to see if she could change the future. Oh, what a head spin. Can I get them to play differently and try to create a new outcome? She needed some time to come up with a plan, and this was a celebration. She would find time for thinking about how she could try, later.

She raised her glass to toast them. "You guys did all the work, not me, but I'm so glad I was here to watch. Congratulations." Jenny took a sip of wine, as the team, as one, drank their beers in a return toast.

They stayed for an hour longer, then made their

preparations to exit, and go back to the resort, which both thought in a way was a shame. Other wives and girlfriends had turned up along with some of the home supporters who stayed on. There was a real party atmosphere building. There was talk of going to a Chinese restaurant in Northbridge, and as Iain squeezed Jenny's thigh under the table, he explained to the others they had a dinner date.

Brad couldn't help himself. "Don't believe him, boys. They are having a dirty weekend away at the Crown. Had to drag themselves out of bed to get to the game and they can't wait to get back there."

His lewd comment drew whoops and laughs, and a blush from Jenny.

"And not one of you can blame me for that, can you?" Iain asked, as he stood up.

****

Iain suggested they eat somewhere less formal, after the grandeur of the meal the night before. They lay in bed wrapped in each other's arms back at the hotel after they had made love. Jenny was on her side with her head resting on Iain's chest while he slowly ran his fingertips up and down her spine putting her body in a state of bliss. She had been treated once again to a wonderful orgasm and now with Iain's touch she hovered in a state of total relaxation; not quite asleep but as if she were drifting on a cloud of feathers.

"Mmm sounds wonderful," she murmured. "But if you don't stop tickling me I will be asleep in minutes."

"I love you, Jenny. You can fall asleep if you like. I can wake you later, when my tummy starts rumbling."

She lifted her head to look at his handsome face. "Where have you been all of my life?"

"I've been waiting, for you to join me."

She kissed him, softly and lovingly. Her hand touched his cheek and felt the light stubble, as the tip of his tongue gently entered her mouth.

I love the way we kiss. I could do this for hours. His hand slide down her back to cup her bottom and squeeze it before following the curve downward to where she had only just stopped quivering from the last time. He's insatiable, I love that he wants me so much. She lifted her hip to give him access and his finger slowly and languidly entered her wetness, again.

She broke the kiss and looked down his body and smiled as the sight of his beautiful penis, still wearing its sheath from making love earlier. She touched it and loved hearing Iain whisper a gasp. She lifted her body to sit up, never losing touch with him, and turned onto her knees, then straddled him.

Their eyes locked once more as she guided him back inside her warm and willing body before closing hers and biting her lower lip. His hands cupped her breasts, and she let out an involuntary moan of her own. He twirled and pinched her nipples and the sensations were fighting the feelings from her womb as he lifted his hips to drive into her, gently but firmly.

She had her hands on his chest to help keep her balance. She looked down once again; she wanted to see when he neared his peak. Jenny wouldn't be able climax again; she didn't need to. This was for him and she wanted to watch his face.

She had so little to give him, and knowing she would break his heart soon, she wanted to be everything for him, while she could. "I love you, Iain." She whispered.

He slid his hands downward from her breasts to her hips to hold her at just the right position, then lifting his lower body his movements became harder and faster. His face grimaced, his eyes opened wide and pupils dilated, and his penis expanded. "Oh, yes, baby." She clenched instinctively to heighten his pleasure.

****

They walked through the casino, hand in hand, which they hadn't found time to do the night before. Iain carried a scotch on ice while Jenny nursed a long-stemmed wine glass with beads of condensation clinging to the bowl. She was immediately struck with the vibrancy of the place.

The colored lights, mechanical noises from the electronic gaming machines, and the hustle and bustle of people made for an atmosphere of excitement. It was noisy too; there was music playing in the background but it failed to exceed the noise of people talking and occasional raised voices when some had a win.

There was a diversity to the crowd, from visitors like themselves, to hardened, seasoned gamblers, representing the huge array of multi-cultures and nationalities. But the thing she noticed mostly was that most people looked happy.

Jenny and Iain walked hand in hand, proudly displaying the love they felt for each other, and Jenny was content to 'people watch' until they found somewhere more relaxed to eat. In one of the huge gaming table areas there was an open looking, very casual 'noodle house' restaurant. They both looked at each other with the same idea: Chinese would be perfect. Plainly the restaurant did not take bookings as there were thirty or more people standing in a line outside, sipping drinks and chatting while they waited for a table.

They joined the queue which only took fifteen minutes to clear, and they were led to a small table by a young Asian man wearing gold-rimmed glasses, who wore a broad smile on his face. Jenny ordered another glass of wine, and a prawn and vegetable stir-fry, while Iain chose a satay noodle dish.

After a couple of minutes of looking around at the other diners, it dawned on Jenny, there was an awkward silence between them. She wasn't surprised when eventually Iain broke the ice. "Jen, after the game, you looked troubled, and you were far from your usual self. Even since, every now and again you seem very distant. Have I done something wrong?"

How like him to blame himself. She leaned forward to take his hand, and only then did she notice he wasn't wearing his wedding ring. *Oh, my God, he has let go of Simone.*

"I'm sorry if I seemed a little troubled, I promise you it's nothing to do with us, and no you most definitely haven't' done anything wrong. It's nothing, I promise you."

"Jen, I'm head over heels in love with you, and it just keeps growing and growing. Please don't shut me out. If something is on your mind, talk to me about it, don't exclude me."

He looked so forlorn. *Chink.*

"Well, it was to do with telling the future. I told you I had read a match report on the game and you changed formation and won two goals to nothing. I also told you who would score, but I never mentioned how they would. You then told me you wouldn't have changed formation if I hadn't mentioned it, and if we believe in time travel as in premonitions of things to come, it throws up a paradox. But that wasn't the only one."

"What's a paradox?"

"A paradox is like something that is, but can't be. For example, from a vision of the future I told you that you had done something, but you wouldn't have done it if I hadn't told you. It's the age-old question: what came first, the chicken or the egg? But then, it wasn't the only paradox in the game."

Iain looked perplexed, and took a sip of his drink, Jenny thought, to try to hide it. "The second goal in the match report I read, did not come by way of a penalty, but a defensive error which gifted Simmo the scoring chance. Because I foretold it was two to nil, and that Simmo would score it, Brad then engineered a penalty and got him to take it. Something he shouldn't have done, and it conflicted with how you coached him. He even admitted the only reason he faked being hurt was that I foretold the result. So, by doing so he created another paradox. But in this case, he changed the future by that act, even though the overall result was the same. The second goal I read of simply didn't happen. So, it got me thinking about the science behind it all. That's all, nothing to do with us, or you, just my brain going into overload to try to make sense of a situation I couldn't understand. Don't mind me, Iain, it's the academic in me." She smiled sweetly to show she meant it.

"But, you are talking as if it is actual time travel rather than just a vision, and we know time travel isn't real."

"What are visions of the future if not a form of time travel? Who can say if years from now traveling back in time is possible, and if it was, how would we know? Any changes made in a time stream becomes a new reality, so from that point of view, we wouldn't know if they were doing it anyway."

"This whole conversation is spinning me out. I know you have these 'visions' and you have been remarkably correct in every one you have shared with me. But I just sort of thought they were like lucky guesses, not actual glimpses of the real future."

Jenny nodded, sipped her drink, and wondered. She was so close to admitting everything, but something told her in the back of her mind to wait; this was still too soon. "Iain, I believe in time travel, at least in the concept of it, and the things I've told you, so far as I am concerned, actually happened from that perspective. Think of it like time being a stream of water that's always there, flowing down a hill. It's like I dropped a boulder in the stream and it took a different course, but still downhill. I cannot stress enough that for me, they were not guesses. The things I've told you are only the tip of the iceberg, and I can, and will tell you a lot more things. They are not just random shots in the dark which luckily turn out to be true; I told you I had read a match report from the future for the last two games, and I have. I've also read next weeks."

"Don't tell me I change the formation again?" He smiled, but looked worried at the same time so it looked more of a grimace.

"You know I love you, right?"

"Yes I do, and I love you."

"So hopefully you know I wouldn't lie to you?"

"Yes." But he looked less sure of himself.

"Okay, you sound unsure, but that's fine, I understand. So, if you don't believe I am seeing the actual future, which I believe not only I am, and it can be manipulated, surely you don't want me to tell you about next week's match, no matter how bad it may or may not be, do you?"

He sat back in his chair and looked torn. "Yes, I do. Call it the curiosity that killed the cat, but I do want to know."

"But supposing it's bad news? The only way to stop something bad happening would be for me to tell you about it, and for you to make alterations which might affect the outcome. But you don't believe in time travel, so there's no point, is there?"

"I'm lost."

Jenny looked up as their meal arrived, steaming and aromatic; the smell of hot garlic caught in her throat and she realized how hungry she was. When they were alone again she picked up her chopsticks and ate a piece of broccoli.

"The thing is, if I told you, and you acted on it, it would be different this time. It would be a complete attempt to alter an event which has already happened, remember the stream I mentioned. I'm just not sure how it would all end, if you and I threw another boulder in, but it's a fascinating problem."

"Jenny? I'm not one of your students, I left school at seventeen. I don't have the faintest idea what you are talking about. Try using words of no more than two syllables."

"I'm sorry. I guess it must sound a bit like double Dutch. Okay, look: when I said, you beat Floreat two nil it was because that was what had already happened if we think of time as a continuum. I read the match report ergo in that stream it had already happened, do you see?" He nodded, though still with a skeptical look on his face, as he sucked up some of the noodles.

She put her chopsticks down, here goes,

"Next week you're going to lose, three to one. The report said your team looked lethargic after their win the week before. You had gone back to your lone striker formation, and Brad rarely saw the ball. Some played with niggling injuries from the battering they took by Floreat, and because of that, they were too slow. It was as if the reporter watched two different teams from one week to the next, he wrote."

Iain sat open mouthed. "You can't be serious?" She nodded; she most definitely was. "But, Subiaco?"

She nodded again. "I wish I could just give you just good news about the future, but that's not always how this works." She popped another prawn into her mouth, to give Iain time to think.

"I'm really struggling here. You are saying these visions you've shared with us, for you, is like you have traveled into the future and read about these events which have already happened?" He asked a full two minutes later.

She nodded, enjoying her stir fry, and feeling pleased with how things were going so far. She had worried how she would broach the subject of time travel, but so far, *knock on wood*, it was going well.

"But you are saying in the case of today's game the future got re-written to some extent, without changing the overall match result?"

This time her nod was less pronounced. If he was

222

going to freak out, now was the time. "Why have you told me all this, Jenny? It seems to me there is more to it all than you are letting on."

Oh, my God, he is so smart. Should I bite the bullet and tell him everything? She gazed back, her brain working overtime, as he looked at her. *Should I, or shouldn't I? No, not yet, don't be stupid. What about the air plane disaster?*

She tilted her head to one side, stretched out for his hand again, but this time he didn't acknowledge it. "Because I love you, Iain. I didn't know, or even imagine a love like this was even possible, certainly for me it never was before. If I could I would spend my whole life with you, and I want to share everything about me with you, and this is a very big part of me."

"So, it's just about the team and the results then?"

She shifted uncomfortably in her chair, deciding to duck the question. "Iain, I don't know if the future can be changed, maybe no matter what we do the guys will lose next Saturday's game, three goals to one. If we don't do anything, trust me that is what will happen. But, we do have that knowledge. We have a chance to do something about it, and I would love to try. Maybe it's my brain wanting to learn more and experiment, but it's not just that, it's because I love you, and I love the guys in the team. The way they have made me feel so welcome, I want to try to help them win."

"But how? If it is the future, rather than just a dream you had, how can we change it?"

"Well, Iain, my love. That's your job, you are the coach; I'm just your sidekick."

He shook his head, he looked unsure, and troubled, and she feared she was losing him.

"Do you doubt me, Iain?"

"No, no it's not that. I know you believe what you're saying, I just can't really accept its actual time traveling rather than just some rare gift of clairvoyance you have?"

"What's the difference? Well, I suppose, there is a difference. If I were a clairvoyant I could go out there and pick which hands to play at in blackjack, or which spins of a roulette wheel to bet on number twelve. I can't do that. But, I can tell you things which have happened in this continuum we are already on.

"If you want to know what is bothering me more than anything else: it's tomorrow morning an aircraft will be reported missing. A China Air A330 on route to Singapore from Beijing will vanish. It will be two days before they find wreckage in the South China Sea." She looked down at her plate and using her chopsticks, towed a piece of carrot around in the delicious sauce.

"Jesus, Jenny. You can't be serious?"

She stayed silent, her appetite gone. When she had studied the current historical events in her own time, this was one of the clashes of conscience she faced, and one which she had questioned her tutor from the future about. "Simon, why can't I use my time to save more people? Yes, I can see why I must stop Bradley Destaine; that makes perfect sense, but this air crash kills two hundred and thirty people, I could try to stop it, and other things too."

"Jenny, I was told the reasons they selected you for this mission was your love of humanity, and your environmental beliefs. It's natural you would want to save lives, which is a wonderful thing about you. But there are other aspects to consider. Is it more important to save two hundred and thirty lives than every living person and thing on the planet? No, don't interrupt, think about this. How would you stop an air disaster? By telling the police, or the airline you are from the future and you know for a fact it will crash? But you are not actually from the future, only your consciousness is. Would they believe you? And if they didn't and the crash happened anyway, they would then suspect you were some sort of terrorist. They would lock you up, that is what authorities do when they don't understand something. They will think: 'she knew about the crash; therefore, she must have had something to do with it.

"You only have your allotted thirty-three-days. You cannot save the world from inside a prison cell. Those people are already dead, that plane crashed, and yes that's sad, but you cannot risk the mission by trying to save them from a death they have already suffered."

Now she sat, in a restaurant, and she was going to have to convince Iain she couldn't tell anyone or try to stop it from happening, but, when the aircraft disappeared the following morning, he would be forced into believing she was telling the truth. Then later, she hoped, it would make it easier to convince Brad.

"You have to stop it from happening, Jenny. If what you are telling me is true, you have to do something about it."

"What can I do, Iain? Who should I tell, who would believe me? They would lock me up in a mental hospital. The flight would go missing anyway, and then they would think I was somehow the cause, a bomber maybe, or I had prior knowledge of terrorist activities. But I'm just me. I know what I know and it's my cross to bear. Hell, I'm having trouble convincing you about a soccer match, how can I tell an airline to cancel a flight to stop it crashing into the sea?"

"We have to try. I believe you now, we must try to do something, and we just must. What flight number is it, I will phone the police."

"And what will you tell them, Iain? My girlfriend, who I have known just over a week, tells me she can see the future and she knows this plane will crash? They will lock us both up. How do you think I feel? My whole life has been in the pursuit of saving the planet, don't you think I want to save their lives, but I can't, why can't you see?"

She loved him, more than ever for wanting to shoulder the responsibility and go to the authorities himself, but she was also angry with him, yet she didn't know why. "I want to help those people, but there is no way they will believe me, they will just think I am mad, until afterward, then they will think I'm a criminal."

"Okay, Jenny. I see what you mean. But we must try something. What about an anonymous phone call?"

"I thought of that, but they would trace it if I used my mobile phone, and there is CCTV everywhere you look so using a public phone is risky too. The only thing that might work is an email, sent from an anonymous address, in a public place, like a library, but these days they have cameras there too."

Iain snapped his fingers. "I've got it, that's a brilliant idea, Jen. In town, today I saw internet café's everywhere, we could find a quiet one, open an email account, and send it from there."

She was elated, and hopeful. "And, if it doesn't work at least we will have tried." She nodded and looked at her watch. "We better hurry, the plane is due

to take off in about five hours' time."
                    ****

Jenny felt as if they were thieves in the night on a raid, as they parked Iain's Commodore in a multi-story car park. They had made their plan in the restaurant and while driving there. Iain insisted he would go to the internet café alone as he believed he would be less conspicuous than Jenny, and even less than if they entered as a couple.

They entered the Staple Bar, which was busy with customers and noisy with a three-piece band playing jazz in the corner. Jenny found a table toward the rear and Iain slipped through the crowd and was gone. Nervously, she sipped her white wine, delivered by a young Scandinavian waitress, and pretended to listen to the music.

From the news reports in the future, the cause of the crash was a suicide from a desperate Chinese pilot whose wife had left him and taken their three children with her. She had learned of an affair he was having with one of his cabin crew. The loss of family and shame drove him to take his own life, and all the passengers on the plane with him.

She and Iain had written out what he would write in the email, on a napkin in the Noodle House.

To the Management of China Air

Re: An imminent problem with flight 746 departing from Beijing

Your pilot, Captain Cheng Gong Chew is suffering from a mental breakdown following the failure of his marriage due to an indiscretion with a cabin crew member. Mr. Chew is intent on taking his own life by crashing Flight 746 into the South China Sea. He has made all preparations. He blames his wife for leaving him and taking his children. You MUST take all steps to remove him from the flight crew of this aircraft.

He has confided his intentions and I cannot permit him to take this action and murder two hundred and thirty innocent passengers.

From

A Concerned Citizen

Twenty minutes later, Jenny frantically looked from left to right searching the crowd. Suddenly there was Iain making his way through the milling people to her table wearing a huge grin on his face. He bent and kissed her as if he arrived for a pre-arranged meeting with her. "Thank God you're here," she murmured in his ear as they hugged. "I've been going around the bend. How did it go?"

He sat next to her and held her hand. "Like clockwork. Taking gold coins with me, was a master stroke because as we discussed, I didn't have to go to the counter for change to buy time. The computers were on one side of the Seven Eleven on Hay Street, and no one paid me any attention when I walked in. I had those spare thin inner goalkeeper gloves in my pocket so I didn't leave any fingerprints. I remembered to wipe the coins before I used them too. I gave some fake information to open a free Gmail account, and it's done, the letter is sent. I got out of there fast, as soon as I hit send in case it raised a red flag."

"Have I told you I love you?"

"Yep, but don't let that stop you from showing me back in our room. Come on let's go, we will leave out of the other exit, arm in arm with heads bowed low, so if they search street CCTV film they won't pick up our faces.

The feeling of euphoria stayed with her as they left the bar. Such elaborate planning and subterfuge may not have been needed, but they agreed it was better safe than sorry. Jenny's tummy felt as if a swarm of butterflies had flocked in, and she hugged Iain's arm tightly as they walked briskly back to the car park.

Once in the car Iain kissed her again, and she responded, hungrily. Her need was growing as was Iain's and it took all her willpower to stop him making love to her right there on the front seat. She had grown a lot since coming back in time and meeting Iain, but having sex in a public car park was still one step too far.

Like teenagers they touched each other while Iain drove back to the Crown, building each other's excitement, and once inside their room they tore at their clothes frantically. As one they fell to the bed, a tangle of arms and legs, and such was their urgency it was only afterward they both realized, Iain had once again not worn a condom.

Chapter 11
A Nervous and Sad Time

Day Thirteen, 14th August 2016

Jenny and Iain ate breakfast from the buffet, though neither of them felt hungry. They hadn't talked a lot, after their frenzied lovemaking the night before; both fell into silence, lost in their individual thoughts, before Jenny slipped into an uneasy sleep.

She didn't know why Iain was so quiet over breakfast, but she was worried. She felt it was a defining moment in their relationship, having shared knowledge about the time travel and he had had time to think about it. The previous night he reacted, without considering the consequences, but today he would have. It was wonderful he had joined in, or to be more precise, taken a leadership role in trying to save all those lives. But now, he had overnight to digest it. She didn't know if he regretted the possible ramifications of an anti-terrorism police investigation, that could result in them being questioned, if their identities became known.

Another worry was the possibility in the cold light of the new day, he now disbelieved the prediction as being too fanciful. Possibly he simply got carried along with the momentum of things last night, and today he doubted her.

She wondered if he harbored regrets about even knowing her. Maybe it might be too hard coming to grips with someone who foretold future events. The 'spy versus spy' cloak and dagger trip to the internet café may well have been the right thing to do in the heat of the moment, even exciting, but that moment had passed.

Does he regret being involved with me at all? She didn't know, and when she had asked Iain earlier what was wrong, he shrugged away her questions. But, it was obvious he was deeply troubled, and she wished he would talk to her.

And the plane crash? If it still happened it could mean there was no way to stop future events from happening, and the purpose of the trip back in time was futile. *Maybe it means I can't stop Brad. And, if by some chance we did save all those people will Iain believe the aircraft was never going to crash anyway? Would he wonder that I either made it up or am a delusional nut case?* What had seemed like a good idea last night, now looked like a huge mistake.

What little she had eaten turned to acid in her tummy from worry. "Iain, have I done something wrong? You're treating me like I've upset you."

He didn't look up from his plate. "No, you haven't done anything wrong. You are who you are, and I've fallen in love with you. I'm just kind of struggling to get my head around it all. It must be horrible for you, seeing these disasters, death and destruction, I'm just not sure I can handle it. I'm just a simple man, who drives a truck for a living."

She stared back, horrified. *Is he dumping me?*

She had always known he would extricate himself

from her, but she thought it would come when she told him the truth about Brad, and the reason why she had contacted him. "I shouldn't have told you, I should have kept it all secret. I'm sorry, Iain, just forget it all, please."

"You've done nothing to be sorry for, this is about me, not you. We couldn't have gone through life together without you sharing your abilities with me, but now you have, I don't know if I can handle it."

Her world spun, and she felt as if she could faint. She swallowed bile, trying to avoid being sick. She wanted to cry, to beg, plead, grovel, do, and promise anything to make him stay, but she remained silent. One realization suddenly broke through like a beam of sunlight on a cloudy day. *I deserve this. This is how Iain would have felt in a week when I broke his heart.*

"I'm sorry, Jenny. I think I need some time to take all this in. I know I love you, and you are an amazing person, who turned my life upside down. It's just all this other stuff I don't know if I can deal with."

She nodded, holding back tears. He still wouldn't look at her, while she was lost in a world of pain the like of which she had never known before. Being in love had been wonderful, but this was hideous, unbearable. She wanted to crawl off and die.

She picked up the room key card from the table, and before the dam wall of her tears burst its banks. She stood up from the table and walked away.

Thankfully the glass elevator was empty as she rode it up to the floor their room was on, crying uncontrollably. She had only one thing on her mind: to grab her things and get out before Iain could confront her and make things worse with his words of love, when all he wanted to do was leave her.

Hurriedly she threw her clothes and things from the bathroom in her bag and almost ran back to the door. Opening it wide she stopped for one final look around to make sure she hadn't forgotten anything. The last thing her eyes focused on was the unmade bed where they had frantically made love the night before. Seeing it only made her tears fall harder.

Her luck held and her lift was empty. She rode it down toward the lobby and instinctively turned to the other one which was going up, and there was Iain. He didn't see her, which just as well. He was looked intently at the numbers announcing the floors the lift passed.

How appropriate. He's going one way, and I'm going the other.

****

She was in the cab when her phone rang. *Iain.* She hit the ignore button on the side and dropped it back in her handbag. A few seconds later the message tone announced she had a voice mail message. Maybe later she would be able to force herself to listen to his voice, maybe, though she doubted it.

Jenny made it home blinking back tears but they spilled out as she paid the cab driver. "You okay, lady?" he asked, and she just nodded her reply.

Once inside her town house, she tossed her overnight bag, and handbag to one side and ran sobbing to the bedroom and threw herself down. Her world had fallen apart. She had no idea love could hurt like this. She cried, and cried, and cried.

****

Time passed.

Somehow in her world of screaming agony, Jenny slept. Her dreams were troubled and involved running through rotting fields of wheat, chasing Iain, who kept looking back over his shoulder, a look of horror on his face. She screamed out his name as she ran, desperate to catch up, but she never could; he was always just out of her grasp.

When she woke, it was early afternoon. Her mouth was dry, and her head ached. She sat up, and took stock of herself. Her heart was heavy, and fresh tears were only a heartbeat away.

I need to get a grip. I'm no lovelorn schoolgirl; I'm a sixty-eight-year-old woman.

But, I miss him so.

She stood up and shuffled miserably to the kitchen and got herself a glass of water. She then unpacked her bag so she could brush her teeth. The crumpled red dress lay forlornly in the bottom of her overnight case, and she fought back tears all over again, as she remembered how happy she had been when she wore it. She held in in her hands, feeling the softness of the material, remembering the hunger in his eyes, and how he had wanted her.

But he doesn't want me anymore.

There was one good aspect to her misery: in several days' time, none of this would matter, because she wouldn't remember it. There was her journal, but she deserved to be judicious with the truth. Though the question crossed her mind: was there any point to writing it?

Her mission to enlist Iain as her ally to help convince Brad had failed. Now she had to make new plans to convince him on her own. That was never going to be easy, but now it could well be impossible. All she could do was tell him the truth. She would give herself a week or so, then try to see him in private to plead on behalf of the future.

As she brushed her teeth she stared at herself in the mirror. Her eyes were bloodshot, and her hair was a mess. *What on earth did he ever seen in me in the first place? Mousey, too intelligent for my own good, and saddled with a mission I wish had gone to someone else.*

After rinsing her mouth, she decided to complete the job and have a shower and wash her hair. *When the going gets tough, the tough take a shower.* Her humor fell flat.

As the water streamed down over her body she wondered if she had any ice cream in the freezer; she felt like she could eat the entire tub. *Yeah, and follow it up with chocolate cake, why don't you?*

By the time she dried herself her skin glowed pink and she admitted she did feel a bit better about things. She dressed in her plain boring underwear, track pants and T-shirt then sat at her dressing table to brush her hair. In the distance, the message tone of her phone sounded and her heart soared. *Maybe it's him. Maybe he wants me back.*

Yeah, right, like that's going to happen.

She sighed and decided not to even look at her phone till tomorrow. *Let him worry at the lack of response, bastard.*

Oh, my God, I'm angry with him for dumping me!

She shook her head. *No, I have no right to be angry. I made the situation intolerable for him. No matter how I wish it hadn't happened, it did, and that's all there is to it.*

She walked back through to the kitchen and switched the coffee maker on, that would help cheer her up, a nice cup of coffee. She flicked on the radio and listened to one of her least favorite songs about a murder on the dance floor.

Murder…The word echoed in her mind. Would it come down to that? She had nibbled around the edges of that piece of cheese before. If she couldn't convince Brad, could she make herself kill him as a final solution? *Even if I could, how would I? Can I condemn millions of people to death, simply because I'm too lily livered to eliminate the threat?*

Then an idea stuck her like a hammer blow. She couldn't kill an innocent person, but she was sure there were some who could. Could she find someone to do it?

Yeah right, just Google Murderer's R Us and hire a hit man.

Hang on, hold the phone. Okay I'm no killer, and I doubt I can find one for hire, but…I can tell Brad, if he won't listen to reason, the people in the future will send other "Leapers" down the line. The next one will be a murderer. In fact, Simon had said something about that, didn't he?

Her head was spinning, trying to remember what he told her. The machine beeped; it was ready, and she made a cappuccino.

The song reached its end and a male voice announced:

"This is Brendon Wilkins here with a special news bulletin. Just a few minutes ago China Air listed flight 746 on route to Singapore from Beijing as overdue. Its last known position was over the South China Sea and grave fears are held for the two hundred and thirty people on board.

"So far it is believed there were no Australians on the flight, however China Air are not able to confirm or deny nationalities of the passengers until all family members have been notified, which could take a further twenty-four hours.

"This is the third such flight to vanish in the last three years, the first has still not been found. The possibility of a terrorist attack has not been ruled out, but a spokesman for China Air say they are pursuing a specific line of inquiry.

"The spokesman has asked for calm while the search and investigations continue for the sake of families of the missing passengers and crew. China Air are working with authorities and will make all information available to the public when it comes to hand.

"We will have more news in our next bulletin at the top of the hour."

****

So, there it is, the whole thing was a waste of time. The future is set and cannot be changed. She cried again, sat in her chair, coffee cup in hand, her shoulders shook as she sobbed.

She cried for the loss of the people in the air disaster, for her broken heart, and loss of Iain, and she cried for the millions of people who were doomed to die of starvation in the future. What a complete and utter waste.

Mister Sanchez jumped up on her lap, and she cuddled him, thankful for the company and the softness of his fur.

Her phone rang again. *Oh, for God's sake, leave me alone.*

She put the cat down, along with her coffee cup, and sauntered slowly over to her hand bag where her phone lay within its cluttered depths. She walked slowly, quite deliberately, so the four rings were up by the time she got it in her hands and the call switched through to her message service. Of course, it was from Iain, as the display showed.

She sighed; she owed him a return message. If he was doubtful about seeing her before, he would most certainly be definite, now the plane had gone missing. Her 'prediction' had come true. He wouldn't want anything to do with her now.

The way I feel right now, that's just fine and dandy.

—Iain. You made your feelings clear this morning, and I don't blame you. This is my cross to bear, not yours. I'm sorry I burdened you with my problems. Thank you for the last few days, they have truthfully been the best of my life. All good things must come to an end, and we have run our race. Please don't message me again; this is final. Good luck to you, Brad, and the team. Please say my goodbyes for me. I will love you until the end of time itself.—

Chapter 12
Time Flies

Days Fourteen to Eighteen, 15th to 19th of August 2016

For Jenny, it had started out as the week from hell. She alternated between being miserable and crying at the drop of a hat, to being angry with everyone and everything in her rotten life. Murphy's Law was alive and well, and anything that could go wrong, did.

While she sipped from a glass of wine on the Friday night following the break up, with Mister Sanchez on her lap, she permitted herself to cast her memory back over her week, itemized, and dated, in her usual academic way.

Sunday Night

She staggered into bed drunk, but then spent the latter part of the night being sick in the toilet and wanting to die. She had not eaten. She finally got some sleep around four in the morning, and then slept through her alarm clock.

Monday

When she woke with a pounding headache she was already an hour late for work. She dragged herself to the wall phone in the kitchen and called in sick. She blamed a tummy bug.

Jenny had not taken a sick day in years, so the

Dean sounded concerned. Jenny was not in the mood for a long drawn out conversation about her health and wellbeing, so she feigned the need for another dash to the toilet to get him off the phone.

By eleven she managed to eat some crackers with lots of water and kept down the four headache tablets she swallowed with it. By twelve she felt vaguely human again. But, that only made her thoughts return to Iain, and how much she was going to miss him.

By one in the afternoon, she couldn't stand the idea of moping around any longer, so she showered, dressed and drove to the local supermarket to buy some groceries. Still she didn't feel like eating, but it was something to do, and would hopefully distract her from thinking of her lost love.

In her car, she started the engine and the radio played a love song. She turned it off, shaking her head muttering 'typical', and drove in silence to the shops. As she was slowly driving through the car park looking for a bay, a Ford backed out of a spot straight into the rear passenger side of her car, scraping the paint and causing a small dent.

A middle-aged Indian looking woman jumped out and accused Jenny of causing the accident. In a state of shock, Jenny wondered if she had done something wrong. When it dawned on her she had not, she flung her door open and leapt out, screaming her own abuse back.

The angst and depression she felt after the end of the affair with Iain combined like an erupting volcano inside her mind, as the rage found an outlet. The woman, seeing a furious Jenny storming toward her, feared for her safety. She hastily backed away, placating Jenny, who could not stop herself from hurling abusive insults.

Seeing the retreat, only made her angrier, and she screamed louder. For the first time in her life, she could have resorted to violence, such was her mood. A tradesman, wearing green overalls, who pulled up behind Jenny's car, intervened.

He ran over to the impending melee. "Calm down, love, its only minor damage, I saw the whole thing and will be a witness for you if you need one."

"Stupid, stupid fucking woman," Jenny screamed. "Where did you get your fucking driver's license from?"

It took some time, but slowly between the kindly calming tones of the man, and the terrified look on the face of the woman, Jenny regained her composure. When she did, it was with a dawning horror, she had taken her bad mood out on the other driver, and was embarrassed by her behavior.

The woman offered her contact details so she could pay the costs, and Jenny took the piece of notepaper, knowing in her heart she wouldn't bother. The damage was only minor, and she felt terribly guilty for losing her temper like a common 'guttersnipe.' That was another of her mother's sayings, of which she had no idea of the meaning.

In a way, the loss of temper helped Jenny. She should have taken her rage out on Iain, or better yet, Simon, but the woman had been a decent substitute. While she was a long way from being her 'normal' self, the release valve in her head had let off excess steam, and she no longer felt near suicidal. She continued her shopping trip, and even stopped for a coffee in the café, but still couldn't force herself to eat anything.

She sat at an outside table across from a newsagent sipping through the chocolaty froth of her cappuccino and saw the headline of the daily newspaper in the hands of a man eating a toasted sandwich, three tables away.

Flight CA746 Still Missing
Grave Fears Held For 230 Passengers

Her heart sank a little lower, not that she imagined it could sink any further. It was the same story she had read thirty-three years in the future, so didn't need to see the rest. The search was on, and in time they would find wreckage, and bodies. She, with Iain's help, had tried her best to save lives, and she couldn't think of any more she could have done. The unbelievably selfish act of one desperate man took two hundred and thirty innocent people, and she felt her anger rising like cream to the surface all over again.

She spent the afternoon cleaning her house from top to bottom to keep herself busy and to stop wallowing in self-pity. In the evening, she warmed a frozen lasagna she had bought and ate it with a salad for her first meal since the break-up. She wanted another wine, but was strong enough to know she had drunk enough the night before, and didn't want to go down that track again.

With Mr. Sanchez on her lap she watched a movie on TV but got angry with the constant ad breaks. *How do cats always when know when their owners are sick or unhappy?* She wondered as she idly stroked his fur.

Once again she slept an uneasy sleep full of troubled dreams of dead and dying plants, but this time she searched for Iain in a huge field full of oversized wheat, rather than chase after him. But, no matter how hard she looked she could never locate him; he was gone. At 4:15 in the morning she got up, unable to sleep anymore for fear of the same dream returning. She made herself a cup of Chamomile tea and sat in her darkened living room watching a black and white Fred Astaire and Ginger Roger's musical.

Tuesday

Somehow, she got through her working morning without screaming at, or punching a student, but it was a very closely run race. Every one of them seemed to want to rile her. She was short tempered and at one stage almost, but not quite; threw a red whiteboard marking pen at one student who had the temerity to send a text message on his phone while she tried to teach. Fortunately, she resisted the urge, and instead, with as much sarcasm as she could muster, asked the boy to share with the class what he found so 'Goddamned' important to text about that he could do it while she lectured about frogs, and their importance to the ecology.

As the bell sounded for the break, she heard her name paged to the Dean's office, and she felt as if her heart sank below the level of the floorboards.

What the fuck does he want?

She contemplated pretending she hadn't heard the announcement, but years of respect forbade her from doing that. She gathered up her things without saying goodbye to her class and stormed off. If she was angry before, she felt incandescent then.

She knocked but didn't wait for a reply. She opened his office door and entered. She would never have been so rude before, but Jenny was besides caring about the niceties of life. Hers felt like hell in a hand basket; that was another one of her mother's sayings.

"Dean, you wanted to speak with me? I do have another lecture so don't have a lot of time."

"Jenny, please come in and sit down, as it happens you don't have a lecture this afternoon, I've asked Mr. Bradshaw, who had a free period, to take it for you."

Of all the things, she could have imagined he would say, that would have been her last pick. "You did what?" Her rage built to eruption point, and she was just in the mood to let him have it with both barrels.

"Jenny, I can tell you are angry with me, and I understand that, but please come and sit down. The fact of the matter is we are all worried about you. You may not think it's true but people here like you, they respect and look up to you. It's obvious to all of us something has gone wrong in your life. I wanted you to know we are here to support you, because you are the opposite of the woman I spoke to the other day."

His words registered in only a part of her brain; the part that just momentarily wondered if he was being nice. But, the more dominant side of her thought of him as an interfering busybody, and she seethed at his temerity.

"How dare you take a lecture away from me without prior consultation? You can keep your holier than thou interfering bullshit out of my affairs, thank you very much. If you want my resignation, you can have it right now. I've never been more insulted in all my life than right now. If I do or do not have a personal issue I am adult enough to work through it. You may be my boss, but that does not give you the right to treat me like this."

"Treat you how, exactly, Jenny? Like I actually care for you and want to offer my help and support?"

Oh, you sneaky bastard. She remembered he did hold a Bachelor of Science degree in psychology. She could well be out of her depth in a debate about her wellbeing, when blind Freddy could see she was not at her best. She took a slow deep breath and forced herself to calm down.

"I apologize, Dean. Thank you for being concerned, but it's quite groundless, I'm fine."

"Jenny, I'm sixty-three years old, and I've been married for thirty-eight of them. One thing I have learned is when a woman says she is 'fine' she most certainly is not. I'm not trying to pry, if you want to discuss it I would love to be a shoulder for you to lean on. And, if you don't that's fine too. Just know we do care about you, and want to help you through a tough time if we can, and, if you permit us. You are one of the finest lecturers this University has ever had, and we do not want to lose you. I've never seen you so angry at everything, some of your colleagues are very worried about you, as am I."

For the first time, it dawned on her she was angry at everything, and far from 'fine.' She didn't need a councilor to tell her she was suffering from an overload of guilt over the plane crash, grief over the loss of her relationship, and a sense of hopelessness because she believed she could not make major changes in the time stream to save the future.

Her tears sprung unbidden, and she dropped her folders on the floor as she raised her hands over her eyes. She was aware of his arms going around her, and she felt glad of it. She hugged him back and sobbed uncontrollably.

She stayed that way for minutes on end, so grateful for the human touch and kindness. "I'm so sorry, Dean. You are right I have not been myself. I apologize to you and the faculty for my behavior."

"That's more like the Jenny we know and love. Welcome back."

Despite her subsiding anger, she had to smile. She took a deep breath and stepped back to see him holding out a box of tissues from his desk. She gratefully accepted the gesture, snatched three out, and bunched them up to wipe her eyes.

"Tell me to butt out if you like, but is it a problem with your new man?" He asked gently.

While she was in no mood to talk about it, she owed him some sort of explanation, and nodded back. "Yes, we broke up on Sunday. Call me stupid and childish, but it's actually the first time I've been in love, and umm, I didn't realize how much it would hurt when it was over."

"I think you are neither childish nor stupid. We can't control who and when we fall in love, Jenny. Whether you're sixteen or sixty, it hurts when it ends. You need to be kind to yourself and give yourself some time to grieve the loss."

She nodded. "I can see why they made you Dean. Thank you for the support. I will be all right, I promise. I've not slept much the last couple of nights, and I think I'm very, very tired, which is not helping my cause."

"Jenny, I want you to take a couple of days off." He held up both hands to stop her interrupting. "Hear me out. You are one of my most valued staff members; the work you do after hours mentoring and tutoring makes you a standard bearer in my opinion in the world of further education. Now, I can cover you for the rest of this week, no problems whatsoever. I have a little place up at the Moore River, it's just a small holiday home, and I want you to pack up a few good books, and your cat, and go up there and relax. Come back Friday or Saturday, then back to work next week, how does that sound?"

He held out a key. She was flabbergasted at his kindness and couldn't speak. "The spare room is the one to the right of the family room and has its own bathroom. You can walk along the beach, drink red wine, read a good book or two, and just re-charge your batteries."

"I don't know what to say."

"I do, just say yes. I've written down the directions here, and there is a list of do's and don'ts. Just replace anything you use and leave the place as you found it.

****

Later that night Jenny sat ensconced in the Dean's riverbank home away from home. She felt a lot better about herself, and her life, due in part to the large wine glass which approached being empty, for the second time.

She looked up at the large ornate clock above the breakfast bar and realized the time. The team would be at training. That thought forced her tears back to the surface all over again, and gulped the last of her drink down.

There was an awful lot wrong with her life, and not being with the wonderful bunch of young men at the club was high on the list of things she missed terribly.

Jenny didn't want to think about Iain, but unbidden

she remembered the way his arms felt around her, the smell of his cologne, the way she could kiss him for hours, how he used to look at her body. She stood up abruptly, to stop that train of thought. She did NOT want to think about the lovemaking.

She looked over at Mr. Sanchez, who seemed quite content on the rug, fast asleep, and decided to go for a walk. It was past eight, she wasn't hungry, and it was a cool but still night. A good night to walk off her thoughts of sex with a man who had taken her to the peak of pleasure, time after time.

Jenny walked along the river bank toward the mouth of the river and the towering sand dunes which held back the ocean, trying not to think about Iain.

Blinking rapidly to avoid crying, she passed a father and son on the bank, fishing for Bream, they said, when she stopped to ask. Once again Jenny remembered a memory from happier days with Iain. She would have loved to have a child with him, a little brother for Bradley. Perhaps if they had, one day they would have been fishing here, father and son, with her watching, sitting on a blanket.

Her melancholy returned worse than ever, and she sniffed back her tears. She left them fishing and headed off once more toward the sand dunes.

Wednesday

After she cleaned up the mess from her breakfast of toast with poached eggs, she felt bored. Jenny had never been a big reader, unless it was student's assignments. Those she had read by the thousand over the years. Consequently, she had not taken any books to read, and when she discovered daytime TV was rather akin to Chinese water torture, she opted to go down to the local general store to see what they had to offer.

She walked to the one and only shop four hundred meters away. Once inside, the fly screen door banged noisily behind her, which made her jump. She saw a book rack and started to make a beeline toward it.

"Hey, Doll." A large woman wearing a fluorescent orange T-shirt that looked two sizes too small asked, "watcha after?"

"Oh, hi. Sorry I didn't see you there. My name is Jenny and I'm staying for a couple of days, and I forgot to grab something to read. So here I am. Do you have something you could recommend to get my mind off my troubles?"

"Troubles, Doll? Now what sort of troubles would a gorgeous thing like you have? Nope, don't tell me, it's to do with a man, isn't it? Yep, I thought so. You know something a woman once said to me? She had come to stay with some girlfriends and she was a self-confessed gay liberation activist."

The last thing Jenny wanted, was to get into a conversation about her disastrous love life with a nosy parker stranger, but for some reason she did want to hear what the gay lib feminist had said. "Sure, what did she say?"

"She stood right where you are now, holding a book by someone named Germaine Greer, and said: 'A woman needs a man, like a fish needs a bicycle!' "

Jenny couldn't help it, she stared back at the woman and quite suddenly burst into laughter. "That's the daftest thing I've ever heard, even if it is true."

"Yeah, that's what I thought. My name's Marion, Doll. Do I have something I can recommend? You bet. Best damn trilogy I've ever read, and you're in luck all three books are on the shelf. Let me get them for you."

"I may not get through one book, let alone three of them, though I must admit you've got me intrigued."

"Doll, I'll have a little friendly bet with you. If you get through book number one, you will not be able to resist the other two. Are we on?"

"We're on, Marion." Jenny felt herself warming to this wonderfully colorful, overweight woman with thick dirty blonde hair.

"Okay, here's the bet, if you truthfully don't like the first one, I will give you your money back, but if you read all three, you owe me a carton of beer."

"Marion, if you can get me to read three books you deserve more than a single carton beer. I'm happy to accept the challenge. What are the books?"

Jenny waited for her to return to her spot behind the counter. Once there she placed the first book face up. Jenny recalled the title from somewhere before, though she couldn't remember where.

"That my girl, is the best damn thriller you will ever read: The Girl with the Dragon Tattoo. If it doesn't make you forget your man problems, nothing will. Then you read this one: The Girl Who Played with Fire, and then the coup de grace: The Girl Who Kicked the Hornet's Nest.

"I remember the first one, but not where from, and definitely not the other two. Where would I have heard about it, I wonder?"

"Well, Doll, it can only be one of three things. First someone may have said to you these are the best thrillers ever written. Second they made a movie with Daniel Craig for the first book. Or three: It could be because of the tragic story concerning the author."

"Oh, now you say that, it could be. Refresh my memory please, Marion."

"The author's name was Stieg Larsson. I say was because after presenting the three books to his publisher, he died before they were released. He never saw how successful his novels became. The estate is worth millions and millions of dollars now. Bloody shame because if he was still alive I reckon people would buy his shopping list just to read it."

"Wow. Well that's a much better story than the one about fish riding bikes." She smiled broadly, and Marion laughed back.

"Tell you what, Doll, when you finish the first book, come and have a beer with me, I live out the back on my own and would love the company. We can talk about how much you enjoyed it, and about how you are chomping at the bit to get into the second one. Doesn't matter what time it is, just tap on the side door if the shop is shut."

"Okay, I will, that's a date."

****

By the time Jenny was a hundred pages in, she was hooked. She was totally absorbed with Lisbeth, though not so much Mikael. Perhaps, she mused, while lying in the veranda hammock reading as fast as possible, it was because she identified with her. Like Lisbeth she believed she lacked the social skills necessary to be popular and successful, yet she was totally loyal and loving to someone she put her faith and trust in.

The more the story unraveled, the more deeply involved with the beautifully drawn characters Jenny became, and the more she was desperate to know how it would end.

When she closed the finished book, she had tears streaming down her face, her wine bottle was empty, and she was hungry. *Oh my good God, what a story*, before following it up with *What a stupid idiot Mikael is. He should hang on to Lisbeth and never let her go.*

I'm so bloody hungry. And when she walked into the kitchen and looked at the clock she could see why. It was after nine-thirty, and she hadn't eaten since her poached eggs on toast that morning. She wavered between fulfilling her promise to go and see Marion or having something to eat. Such was her love of the book; it was a no contest decision. She grabbed her keys and locked a meowing Mr. Sanchez in the house. She half ran, half walked down to the shop.

No sooner had she tapped on the door and it was opened by a smiling Marion. "Right on cue, Doll, I thought you'd be here about now. Come in, tell me all about it. Want a beer?"

"Oh my God, Marion, *what* a story, what characters. I cannot thank you enough for recommending it to me. The only problem I have now is I can't see where the next instalment goes, surely it's all over?"

"Oh, babe, no, it's only just begun. What did you think of 'our' Lisbeth?"

"I love her." To Jenny it was simple. She wanted to hold her, protect her, and give her the love that had been missing from her life, and had been replaced by tragedy, rape and dishonesty. "Umm, I don't really drink beer, I should have brought a bottle of wine down with me, forgive me, I was in such a hurry I didn't give it a thought. I haven't even eaten since breakfast, that's how much I enjoyed the book."

"It's okay, sit you down over there, I think I've got some wine, and I've got some chicken pieces and pasta here too, let me warm them up for us; I've not eaten myself."

Thursday

By nine in the morning, Jenny nursed a minor white wine headache. She had eaten some toast and marmalade and was back in the hammock with the biggest cup she could find in the kitchen, filled to the brim with coffee. She was reading the second installment of the trilogy.

Never could she have imagined becoming so involved in a story. It twisted and turned and evoked such a range of feelings within her soul. Lisbeth Salander was her heroine, and deep down, despite the awful things that had happened in her life Jenny wished she was like her. Everything that happened to Lisbeth, Jenny felt. She cried, smiled, laughed, and hurled abuse at those who would hurt her.

Even when she stopped to make a second, then third cup of coffee, The Girl Who Played with Fire was clutched in her white knuckled hand. *Why are they doing this to her?* Jenny screamed in her head. *How can one person be subjected to so fucking much?*

The sun was going down when the second instalment was finished and her opinion of Mikael had improved out of sight, for his attempts to help Lisbeth.

She heated some party pies and crumbed squid rings from the freezer and wrapped them in foil before heading to Marion's with a bottle of her favorite wine to discuss the book.

She was half way there before she stopped in her tracks with a sudden jolt. She had gone the whole day and NOT thought about either Iain, the end of the world, or the two hundred and thirty dead airline passengers. *What a sad loss to the world this Stieg Larsson is; pharmacies could sell his books as cure-alls.*

With a grin, she headed off once more.

****

Jenny returned to Mr. Sanchez before ten p.m., with a lovely buzz from the alcohol and fantastic company Marion turned out to be. They had talked non-stop about the two books, as they ate and drank, dissecting the main characters as if they were real. To Jenny they were real, particularly one Lisbeth Salander.

At one point during their discussions they both admitted if they were gay, Lisbeth would be the woman they would want to spend their lives with. This was a revelation to Jenny who had never, ever, harbored a homosexual thought about another woman.

In Marion, she found a kindred spirit, another who would fiercely fight to protect Lisbeth, and they talked around and round in circles as they ate and drank. Jenny kept pressing Marion for what would happen in book three; at the end of the second instalment Lisbeth had been shot, buried alive and found by Mikael. She had to know if she lived or died and wanted Marion to put her out of her misery.

"Jenny, Jenny, Jenny. If I told you it would spoil it for you. Enjoy the experience, read it, word for word and find out if she survives. No, don't pout and get mad at me. I know you want to know, and I'm guessing when you get back to the house you will be reading tonight, won't you?"

"You bet your boobies, baby. Oh, my God, my dad

used to say that." They both laughed.

"Hey doll, I know you are going back home soon, to your world of academia, and I'm guessing your man, but do me a favor? Come back and see me sometime, you're welcome to stay here, I haven't had this much fun in months."

"I won't be going back to my man, as you call him. And for reasons I can't go into, you possibly won't see me again. But I want you to know that's not because I wouldn't want to come back, only because I can't."

"Well, that sounds all very mysterious. I will always think of you as my own version of Lisbeth. I think, like her, you are damaged goods with a beautiful heart."

"Oh, Marion, you have no idea. That's just about the biggest compliment anyone has ever paid me in my life."

"Okay, so it's your last night tomorrow, come and have dinner with me, I'm guessing you will have finished The Girl Who Kicked the Hornet's Nest by then, and we will have lots to talk about. You know they say Stieg planned ten books in this series? Sadly, we will never see the other seven by his hand, though I believe someone else has jumped on the band wagon."

"Okay, it's a date. I will bring the booze. How about a nice Red wine?"

"Nah, like my pappy I'm a simple girl. You drink the wine; I'm happy with beer."

"Before I go, I've had just enough wine to say this to you, I hope you don't mind. When I arrived here I was a mess emotionally, you and Stieg Larsson have turned my life around, and I can never thank you enough, Marion."

"Nah, no worries, Doll. I just wish you would come back and see me sometime."

"I promise you if I can, I will."

"Okay, Lisbeth, I believe you."

****

By ten o'clock, she lay snuggled up in bed, a steaming mug of coffee sitting on the bedside cabinet, reading the final instalment.

The first book was great; no question. The second: incredible, but the third was indescribable, as Lisbeth, with Mikael helping from the outside, lay imprisoned in a hospital bed. They fought against not only the police, but the government services themselves. Everyone conspired against the poor woman, yet, she held strong, stuck to her beliefs and fought for what was right.

If Jenny could have met Mikael, she would have kissed him for helping Lisbeth. In fact, *scratch that*, she would have let him do whatever he wanted to her, just for saving her heroine.

Never had Jenny experienced such euphoria over a story. It was five thirty in the morning as she closed the finished book. She wanted to sing and dance and shout out to the world 'her' Lisbeth had been saved.

She fell asleep, cuddling *The Girl Who Kicked the Hornet's Nest* to her chest, a smile on her face, and a wonderful feeling in her heart. Her last thought before sleep overtook her, was if Lisbeth could survive all the shit life had thrown at her, then Jenny could.

Friday

She woke mid-afternoon, feeling wonderful, and glad to be alive, with Mr. Sanchez sitting purring on her chest. She ruffled his ears and stroked his back, the way he liked.

It was raining outside, and the wind howled around the eaves. This was her last day, and she had things to do. Firstly, she cleaned the house, then showered and made up a shopping list of things she had used so she could replace them. Armed with the list she headed off to the nearest 'big shops' where she raced around buying things.

Back at the house she put everything away and re-made the bed. She had washed the sheets before she left, and she took them out of the drier. She intended to get off reasonably early in the morning, not that she had anything to race back for, but she felt her trip away was at an end and it was time to get back and deal with things.

She still had to make some decisions about Brad; should she still try to convince him? Yes, she should. She had nothing to lose, and the future had everything to gain. She intended to talk to him about the folly he would make. She would do it as soon as she could pluck up the courage; which could take a while.

By seven o'clock she finished her wine, and her mental re-cap of her week, and was ready to visit Marion for her last night, and the invited dinner.

Jenny drove her car to the shop because of the three cases of beer and bunch of flowers she had bought for her host. They had a lot to talk about, most especially the awful people who wanted to destroy an innocent Lisbeth whose only crime had been to try to protect her mother from a hideous sadistic monster.

The hours flew by, and it was after midnight when Jenny thought she should go back to the house, and said so to Marion. She hugged her new dear friend as she said goodbye, saddened in her heart to know in a couple of weeks she wouldn't remember her. She would hold a special place of honor in her journal, and she hoped the Jenny staying behind would pluck up the courage to visit with her, though deep down she doubted she would.

Far too drunk to drive, as she walked back Jenny mourned the fact she never had a true girlfriend in her life, yet since making her "Leap" she had met two who she would dearly love to continue to know, Janet and Marion. Life was cruel, but, she reminded herself, nowhere near as cruel as it had been for Lisbeth.

Chapter 13
Time to Return

Day Nineteen, 20th of August 2016

As she drove back home the following morning, Jenny listened to a very troubling news bulletin on the car radio. While not completely unexpected, it was deeply worrying.

The police were now investigating a potential local terrorist connection to the now known crashed China Air disaster. A man of whom the only had the vaguest description, and who police would like to interview, sent a warning email to the airline three hours before take-off from a seven eleven internet café in Perth. 'Police sources' believe this was a terrorist plot to destroy the plane, but theorized one of the terrorists had got cold feet and attempted to stop it from happening.

This news bulletin had not happened in her future, and was another example of a paradox she had caused. Because she had known of the disaster, her attempt became newsworthy where it wasn't before. *Does that mean I can change the future?* She didn't know, but it strengthened her resolve to try to stop Brad.

She was naturally concerned for Iain, who was totally innocent, and she desperately hoped she had not gotten him into trouble. He did not deserve that. As her thoughts returned to him, she realized while she had spent a couple of days distracted from her loss, she still very much loved him as much as ever. She would still need to talk to him about Brad, and her heart sank once more when she thought about that.

She switched the radio off and made the rest of the trip in silence with her day dreams only of Lisbeth and Mikael, which was safer than contemplating her own life. It was so much more enjoyable as she imagined a fictional world where Mikael married Lisbeth.

At eleven fifteen she drove into her carport and saw a car parked alongside. *No, it can't be, surely?* But, it was.

Brad climbed out of his car as she parked, and he didn't look happy. She was not ready for this confrontation, and if he hadn't seen her, she would have turned tail and ran. But, he had. There was no alternative but to talk to him.

She got out of her car and opened the back door and took Mister Sanchez in his travel box out. "Hello, Brad. Are you all right?"

"Hello Jenny, yes I'm fine, but dad isn't. What are you doing to him?"

She stopped in her tracks, key half way to the lock on her front door. "What am I doing to him? Is that what you said?"

"Yes, he is frantic. You ignored all of his phone calls, you ran away to God knows where, he is beside himself with worry over you, and I've never seen him so miserable."

She stared open mouthed. "Now, just hang on, Brad. He dumped me, or didn't he tell you that? My boss sent me away because, quite frankly, I was a bloody mess and couldn't do my job, so don't you dare

260

come around here and tell me about your poor father."

He shook his head with a sad look on his face. "Don't you know he loves you? I've never seen him so happy in years as when he was with you. When you were together it was like he was complete, and now he's shattered into pieces and I can't do anything to help him. He didn't even go to training on Thursday, that's the first session he has ever missed since I was six years old. He is drinking too, and I'm worried. He says he is going to the game today but we are going to lose anyway, that you told him we would, so why should he bother? I don't know what happened between you, but I know he has been trying and trying to get you back. You've ignored all of his calls and text messages."

She opened her door, put Mr. Sanchez's box down, and crooked her finger toward Brad to follow her. She pointed at the breakfast bar, there in plain sight was her phone; she had not taken it away with her.

Silently she crossed to it, and looking at Brad, turned it on. Within seconds, it started beeping to show the missed calls and messages, and a single tear rolled down Jenny's left cheek. He missed her and had phoned to make amends. In her pig headedness, and self-pity, she had ignored him.

"Brad, he dumped me. He sent me a couple of messages which I admit I couldn't make myself read. Then I responded once, telling him he had made his choice and it was over. I even asked him not to call again, that's how badly he hurt me, I just needed to be alone. I missed a day at university, and when I tried to work the next day I was in such a state they refused to let me teach. The Dean loaned me his holiday house to go to, and I took his offer to try to save my sanity. I stupidly left my phone here. I didn't think he wanted me, Brad, and my world kind of died. I tried to find some balance again, and I found it, thanks to an amazing woman, and an author. I love your father with all of my heart and soul, but he hurt me, and I believed he didn't want me anymore."

He nodded slowly. "Amazing, isn't it? He loves you and is miserable without you; you love him and are miserable too. Yet you are both too pig headed to fix the problem. Jenny, he is lost without you, it's pitiful to see. It's worse than when he lost mum. Has this got something to do with you telling him about the future?"

She didn't reply, how could she?

"Yeah, I thought so. Look I don't understand this gift you have, though I suspect sometimes it's more of a burden than a gift. Whatever it is you've seen, please, I'm begging you don't let it destroy my dad."

"What is it you want me to do, Brad?"

He looked at his watch. "Come to the game, let him see you do still care, because right now, he thinks you hate him. He doesn't know you didn't get his messages, he thinks you did and chose to ignore him."

"Brad, I can't go to the game, I'm just not that strong. My God I've never been in love before and I'm quaking inside with you being here, let alone going to see everyone at the club, and your dad. I will send him a message later tonight. I need time to think. I thought I was getting over him, but now this. You've opened up all my wounds all over again."

He nodded. "You have to do what you feel is right. Please, just one thing. Don't ever let on that I spoke with you; Dad's pride wouldn't allow his son to plead his case. He would hate me for interfering, but I love him, he's my dad. When mum died, he put his whole life on hold, just to make sure I was all right and I got through it. I owe him everything. It's been just him and me against the world since mum passed away. He never went out, never put himself into a situation where he could meet anyone, but, then you entered his life. Mummy-Jen, you swept him off his feet." He turned away but at the front door stopped. "We all love you, Jenny, I wish you'd come back, so do the guys on the team, and Dad? Well he's just a shadow of the man he was, now he is without you."

****

One question rocketed like a pinball around and around in her mind. What would Lisbeth do? The answer was not as obvious as she at first thought. Lisbeth Salander was loyal and would lay down her life for someone she cared for. But to anyone who did her wrong, her vengeance was swift and complete. She was incapable of forgiveness or mercy.

That's all fine and dandy, but what if Mikael truly wanted her after all they had gone through together, would she forgive and go to him?

There was no easy answer, and she wished she could phone Stieg and ask him.

****

The match report Jenny read said the game was over at half time, three goals to one. From that point Subiaco turned ultra-defensive to stop Queens Park from trying to get back into it. The reporter said their spirits had been so broken they looked incapable of getting the goals anyway, and the game ground on until the final whistle.

263

At half time Jenny, feeling terrified, but because of her belief Lisbeth would have done the same, walked into the change rooms, wearing her Queens Park tracksuit. The home team sat with elbows on knees, on the benches, dejectedly mumbling and grumbling to each other. Iain stood with is back to them in front of the old wooden chalkboard. He looked as if he were trying to come up with a strategy that might help his dispirited men, but Jenny noticed his shoulders were sagged and he looked every bit as miserable as his charges.

Jenny, had swallowed every ounce of her pride to go to the game. She walked up behind Iain, as the team fell to a hush. She tapped him on the shoulder while the members of the squad sat in stunned silence. Iain turned and without giving him a chance to say a word she wrapped her arms around him.

"I love you," she said, in her quietest voice.

Iain's response was drowned out by the team screaming in delight. They clapped and stomped their boots on the concrete floor.

Jenny felt as if she had come home, and tears welled within her eyes and spilled down her cheeks, but she didn't care who saw them. She was right where she needed to be, in Iain's arms, and she could feel him quivering as he too cried.

A whistle sounded and the referee called out through the open doorway: "Time's up home team, take the field, please."

As one the men stood up, but Brad held up his arms to stop them. "Guys, Jenny is back, let's get out there and show these bastards how much she means to us, let's do it for Jenny."

"Yeah, f-f-f-fuck em. Let's kill the b-b-buggers," Simmo yelled, and everyone screamed their assent and ran out of the change room, leaving Iain holding Jenny.

"You came back. I never thought I'd see you again." He said, blinking rapidly to hide he had been crying.

"I didn't think you wanted to see me."

"But the messages I sent you, I told you I was wrong, and how sorry I was."

"Iain, I was away, I had to. I left my phone behind. I only got those messages today."

He hugged her tightly again. "Please, please don't ever go away again."

She didn't answer. How could she tell him in less than two weeks this version of her would be gone forever?

****

They walked hand in hand to the team bench to watch the second half, though the final score was beyond doubt.

Subiaco's tactics of having every player with a role behind the ball made it very difficult for Queens Park to break through, even though they played with a vigor which hadn't been mentioned in the article.

"*Oh my God!*" Jenny suddenly stood and screamed in delight. Simmo had volleyed a crossed ball out of mid-air, from outside the eighteen-yard box. The multi-colored ball dipped and curled majestically through the air and into the top left hand corner of the net, beyond the diving goalkeeper's outstretched hand.

"T-t-take that, you f-f-f-fuckers," Simmo shouted so loud Jenny cold clearly hear him over the noise of the appreciative crowd, He stood with his arms held high in the air, as the tumultuous roar from the stunned sideline supporters echoed across the pitch.

It was three goals to two. Jenny turned to Iain, 'It can't be!"

Yet it was. The future had been changed.

Oh my God, oh my God, oh my God. She felt deliriously happy as she jumped up and down, fists clenched. Not only was she back with the man she loved, it was possible to alter the future, and that realization made her feel overjoyed. If she could just convince Brad she was truthful, she could still save mankind.

Like the fairy tale her life had become, Jenny and Iain's pumped-up players scored again four minutes later, from another Simmo long range shot. If the players and crowd seemed happy before, they were now delirious. Everyone screamed and cheered, urging the team on. There was still time to steal an unlikely win.

Jenny had never experienced anything like the excitement of a soccer team that had been down and out, to then claw their way back to a draw, and the emotion of the crowd was infectious.

With barely a minute left on the huge clock on the wall of the club rooms, the unthinkable happened. They goaled yet again. Simmo had scored a hat trick which gave Queens Park the unlikeliest of wins. From three one behind to four goals to three in front.

The final whistle sounded. Jenny couldn't help herself; she ran out onto the pitch as the team converged on Simmo and she jumped into his arms, taking her turn along with everyone else, and hugged him. She whooped and hollered and screamed her delight in his goal scoring efforts. The euphoric feeling was contagious as Iain joined her, and the smile on his face was priceless to Jenny.

Brad, stood alone, away to the side. He nodded to Jenny signifying he was willing to give Simmo his moment in the sun. He grinned like a Cheshire Cat at her and she ran to him. "Come here, you," she delightedly yelled and hugged him frantically.

Quietly, so no one else could hear, as she squeezed, she whispered: "Thanks for coming to get me, Brad."

"We couldn't have done it without you, Mummy-Jen." He replied and she wondered, if that was true? Would she ever know?

Simon, once told her, any change she made in a time stream would become the new reality. It was only she, and Iain because she had told him, who would ever be aware the future had been altered.

"Can I cut into this dance?" Iain asked, and an embarrassed Brad let go of her and ran off to go and be with the team.

"He's right you know, if you hadn't come back we would have lost the game as you predicted, three, one."

"Yes, Iain, but do you see what happened, we changed the future? We couldn't stop the plane crash, maybe they thought the email was just a hoax, but we can change the future, isn't that fantastic?"

"I'm just glad to have you back, love. Whatever your talent is I truthfully don't understand, but I love you, Jenny, and I want to spend my life with you. No matter what the future holds. I'm never letting you go again."

Oh boy, I sure hope you still feel that way when I tell you why I'm here.

****

267

"Welcome back Missy." Geordie said as he thrust a very strong looking drink in her hand, and gave her a wink. "I'm guessing you came back for Iain, and not to get me?"

"You were a very close second Geordie, if you hadn't been already married, it could have gone the other way." She held out a twenty-dollar note, but he just stared at it.

"Nay Missy, your money's no good here. I'm not as dumb as I seem, it was you walking into the change room that fired those buggers up, we only won because of you, so drink up, it's on the club."

She raised her glass to him, smiled her best smile, and took a sip before almost choking at the amount of scotch in the drink. "Geordie, did you put any diet coke in there at all?"

"Aye, plenty."

She stared back, holding the glass out. Eventually he smiled and scowled at the same time, and topped her glass up to the brim with coke.

The team wandered in in twos and threes following their showers, and after buying jugs of beer at the bar, joined her at the large round table she had commandeered.

Jenny worried about how they would treat her, after having disappeared without saying goodbye, and missing two training sessions. Yet no one made a fuss or said a word. It was as if she had never left. Iain was the last to arrive and when everyone sat down at the table he cleared his throat.

"Guys, it's been pretty obvious I've not been at my best this week, so much so I didn't even turn up on Thursday for training. I want to apologize to you all by buying a round of drinks. I've left two hundred bucks on the bar, so make sure you all get a drink out of it. It's a big celebration because I've checked results from other grounds, and with today's win we've gone top of the table. Floreat lost to Mandurah, and we're now two points clear."

The team cheered, and Jenny felt stunned. It was further proof that the future could be manipulated. Queens Park should not have won, and even though Floreat lost they should have still stayed top in the original reality. There was no version of the future Jenny had read that this team ever achieved league leader. This meant, it could have a flow on effect; she now had no idea of next week's result. Could they go on and become champions?

****

When they left the clubrooms later that evening, after one of Brenda's fiery curry's, Jenny was unsure what to do. They had no time to be alone to talk before Iain walked her to her car. She stopped at her door and turned. Before she could do or say anything she was in his arms and they were kissing. It flooded back what a wonderful kisser he was.

"Come back to my place, Jenny, please?"

"I didn't pack any clothes or anything."

"That's okay, I will run you back to your place to change and feed the cat in the morning."

Oh, my God, he wants to make love in Simone's bed. "Are you sure, Iain?"

"Never more sure of anything in my life. Its time. Simone is gone, you are my world now."

Chapter 14
Time for the truth

Day Twenty, 21st of August 2016

Jenny awoke laying on her side, naked, facing the window, with Iain snuggled against her body from behind. His arm was around her, the crook of his elbow touching her breast and his hand on her shoulder. His groin was warm against her bottom, and his legs followed the contours of hers. It felt as if he had wanted to touch her in every single place he could, and it was wonderful.

She could feel his gentle breaths on the back of her head and neck as he slept while the air was full of his scent she had missed so much. There was also the smell from their lovemaking, she had missed that too.

She had given herself little time to think, and plan what to do next, and she knew she must. There remained only a couple of weeks to make sure Brad was stopped, and that would take time, as he would naturally rebel against the idea of abandoning his lifelong goal to feed the world.

There was the same amount of time to enjoy Iain and the love they shared. Having only just got back together she was in no rush to have the conversation that would lead to them parting again. She accepted it was selfish on her part, but she still felt she owed herself this special feeling, for as long as she could.

Idly, her finger tips softly stroked the back of Iain's hand at her shoulder. She loved everything about him, he was a wonderful man, and in a way, she was grateful that when she finally woke up after her travels, she would not suffer the pain of separation all over again.

He is my Mikael. I wonder if he has ever read the books?

Probably not. Maybe it should just be 'her thing,' as some of her teenaged students spoke of these days. Everyone was entitled, apparently, to have 'their own thing' meaning, their own special idiosyncrasy. Well, Jenny certainly had that in spades, having come from the future, now that was a heck of 'a thing.' She almost giggled.

She wondered idly if Iain would feel like making love when he woke up. She wanted him again, as she recalled the orgasms she had experienced the night before when they made love in the bed he used to share with his wife. The first was from the tip of his tongue, while the second and third while he thrust deep inside her, her hips propped up by a pillow—another new experience.

Iain wriggled in his sleep to lie on his back, and Jenny took the opportunity to turn to face him. *God, he is handsome, what does he ever see in me?*

She had a mischievous idea, and slowly so as not to wake him, wriggled down the bed, under the sheet. There was enough light creeping through to see his manhood laying on his lower tummy, resting. As if it was an omen, it pointed toward her. Before she could chicken out, she leaned forward and using the tip of her tongue lifted it so it could slip inside her mouth.

I can taste me on him, what a wonderful combined flavor we make.

She softly suckled him, her own excitement building as she was again being so naughty. Slowly she felt him grow and harden as he quietly moaned. She loved what she was doing, giving him pleasure as he was always so intent on giving her. She positioned her hand to cup him in her palm, closed her eyes and lost herself in the eroticism of the act.

She decided she would leave it up to him, as he rose to full erection. If he wanted to finish that way, she would take it, willingly. His hands touched her; he was awake. He explored what parts of her body he could get to. One hand worked its way between them to hold her right breast, while his other stroked her head and neck, his fingers combing her hair.

"Oh, baby," he moaned, spurring her on and used her tongue more, to make it as good as she could for him.

"Jenny, you better stop soon. Baby, baby, oh baby." She could tell by the way his hips were jerking, while he may say he wanted her to stop, he didn't really. And neither did she; she loved him with all her heart. Suddenly he lifted his lower body up off the bed, and she could feel him shudder all the way up and down his torso.

****

Iain made her sit at the kitchen island bench and do nothing to help, as he prepared breakfast. Brad and Lyndsay soon appeared as the smell of a cooked meal wafted through the house. Lyndsay wore a thin filmy dress with a bright orange bikini underneath, and Brad wore board shorts and a Star Wars T-shirt. Jenny had borrowed one of Iain's shirts and wore her tracksuit bottoms.

"I hope you didn't sleep in your tracksuit, Mummy-Jen." He said with a smirk, while Lyndsay glared daggers.

"Oh no, Brad, we took it off." Iain said from the fridge as he took out eggs. Jenny blushed deep red, still unused to the sexually charged banter between father and son at her expense, even though it made her feel like part of their family.

"Good to hear," Brad replied, but clearly he was not to be outdone. "Lyndsay can loan you some clean underwear if you like."

"No, it's fine Brad, we took that off as well." Jenny said, knowing if she didn't respond playfully, Iain would have said something equally embarrassing. "Have any of you guys read The Girl with the Dragon Tattoo?" She asked, as much to steer the conversation away from her sex life, as find out if they had.

"Nope, not me, but Lyndsay and I saw the movie. Great film, loved it, and what an actress the woman who played the girl is."

"I don't get much time to read these days." Iain joined in, raising his voice to be heard over the sound of sizzling bacon. "Why do you ask, love?"

"I read the trilogy while I was away, and fell in love with them, I could never imagine reading three books in virtually a single sitting, but that's how good they are."

"Was that the film with the guy who plays James Bond, Brad?" Iain asked.

"Daniel Craig, yes. Very un-James-Bond-like, but a great story. I didn't know it was a trilogy Mummy-

Jen. I thought it was a one off."

"Books two and three focus mainly on Lisbeth, and her upbringing, why she is the way she is, and what happens to her with her sadistic father, and the State Secret Services."

"One or two eggs, Jen? Maybe we should see if it's on download and watch it tonight, sounds intriguing, and anything you like, I'm sure to enjoy as well." He smiled over his shoulder at her.

Chink. How wonderful is this guy? "I'd love to see the film, Iain, and ummm, you know what? I'm famished so two eggs please."

"How come you're so hungry, Mummy-Jen, what have you been doing all night?"

"That's quite enough of that sort of talk thank you, Brad, otherwise I might tell them about our sex life." Lyndsay grinned, and Jenny gave her a smile of thanks.

"What sex life?"

Brad ducked as Lyndsay threw a hand towel at him.

I wish I could stay a part of this family forever.

"Brad, can you set the table please, it won't be long now."

He stood up and crossed to the cutlery drawer.

"I'll give you a hand, even though you don't deserve it after that last remark." Lyndsay grabbed the place mats and began spreading them out.

"Lyndsay, as you well know it's my job to do the jokes around here, that was: a joke. You remember joking, don't you? It was big a few years ago."

A few minutes later Iain placed a plate in front of Jenny. It was piled high with bacon, sausage, hash brown, mushrooms, grilled tomatoes and two eggs, sunny side up. "You said you were hungry." He smiled at her and winked.

"Oh my God, Iain. I can't eat all this."

"Mummy-Jen, you have lots of endearing qualities, and that is one of them; the way you say oh my God all the time; it's cute. And, if you don't eat all your bacon I'm willing to help out."

Breakfast was spent laughing and joking, and not one word was said about foretelling the future. It was as if it was a no-go subject by agreement, without the agreement having been voiced.

After breakfast, they all pitched in to do the dishes and tidy up.

"What have you guys got planned for today?" Jenny asked Brad

"We're going to the heated pool for a swim, then its study, study, and then some more study. Final exams are looming ever closer. I still have to pass to finalize the job with CSIRO."

Jenny needed clothes, and underwear, plus Mr. Sanchez would be desperate to be fed, so Iain offered to drive her home. They all left the house at the same time.

Once in the car and underway, Iain appeared nervous, and Jenny noticed he kept biting his lower lip. "Iain, what's up, you look troubled?"

He turned his face toward her and grinned. "Sorry, I was just wondering how to ask you something. And if I do pluck up the courage to ask you, I'm worried you might say no."

"Sounds ominous, fire away, I can take it." She exaggeratedly gripped the consul with one hand and door handle with the other.

"Will you move in with me? I love you, I never want to let you go again, I don't care about the future telling side of things, you're the one I want to spend my life with."

She was taken completely by surprise. She didn't know how to answer. She was overwhelmed with conflicting thoughts. Of yes she wanted to, and no she shouldn't.

"Iain, have you thought this through, and how does Brad feel about this?"

"Yes, I have thought this through. And Brad is delighted. I asked him after the game last night when we were at the bar alone. He told me I could never find anyone better, and he also said he really liked you, and that you were good for me."

"But there are so many things we need to think about, discuss, I mean for a start, what about Mister Sanchez?"

"You're really clutching at straws if that's the biggest hurdle you think we have. He comes with you, obviously. We don't have a dog, or any reason why he can't fit in with us. What's the next problem to overcome?"

She sat silently for a while, her hyperactive brain in turmoil. This was akin to a marriage proposal, a trial period before the question was popped. There was no one in the world Jenny would rather marry, but first, she had to tell him the truth. She could not begin living with him under false pretenses.

"We need to talk, there are things I must tell you, and once I have, if you ask me again, I will say yes."

"Jenny, there is nothing you can say to me that will affect how I feel about you, I want to spend my life with you. I never thought I would feel like this after Simone; I'm just so glad to be alive now. When I wake up with you the feeling I have in my heart is indescribable, and when I watch you just before you fall asleep, I know I'm the luckiest man alive. You can tell me what you need to, but it won't change how I feel about you."

Jenny turned her head to look out the passenger side window, so he wouldn't see her cry, but as if he sensed it he carried on: "When we broke up, over me being stupid, it was because I was scared. I was frightened of the future, but now I welcome it. Trying to live without you in my life made me realize you are the single most important thing in it. I was frantic without you, more depressed than when I lost Simone. I know now, you are the one for me, and I don't want to think about life without you in it."

"Take me home, I have a lot to tell you." She said while trying but failing to hold back her sobs. Part of her felt wonderful because of their love and him wanting to live together. Another part was relieved that shortly the lies would be over, she would tell him the truth, and their love would either survive it, or not. But the biggest feeling was that of depression. She had always known this day would come. Now it was here he would leave her, again, of that she had no doubt. She had believed that from the beginning, and now she would find out it was true.

They entered her house, to the sounds of a very angry Mister Sanchez, who stalked around in full fury. Jenny fed him to the sound of constant meows, while Iain patiently sat on the couch. When that chore was done, Jenny slipped off her tracksuit top, then sat cross-legged on the floor, facing her lover, and began.

"This will not be easy for me to explain, and possibly even more difficult to understand. Iain, but please stick with me. Boy, where do I begin?" She paused to gather her thoughts and Iain gazed back.

"I am a 'Leaper.' I am the last in a line of them who all took a leap of faith to take on a very, very important job. A job, which if successful, would save the future of every living thing on this planet. If I fail, we as human beings will eventually become extinct."

"Okay. I don't know what I expected, but this all sounds very science fiction, what exactly is a "Leaper"?"

"I am genuinely from the future. Well, when I say I am, this consciousness you are talking to is from the future, not this actual body. I didn't predict those things I told you, like the game scores, or the plane crash. I studied them in my history from thirty-three years' from now. They were always going to come true, because they already had in my continuum."

"You're not making much sense here, Jenny, this is kind of freaky."

"No, I guess I'm not. I've dreaded this day, and I think I'm making a complete hash of it. So, let me change tack. In the future, a man by the name of Heinrich Abraxist will invent a drug. We are talking two hundred and thirty years from now. He will be trying to find a cure for serious psychological and mental disorders such as schizophrenia. He will believe he has come up with a psychotropic concoction that works, and he will conduct some clinical trials to prove it. But he won't just find a potential cure for psychopaths, he will also discover that in people over a certain age, who weren't mentally ill, something weird and totally unexpected will happen. Their consciousness will travel back in time thirty-three years, for a period of thirty-three days. Now this represents only one day in real time, please don't ask me why or how, I don't know all the technical explanations. But, however it works, those people woke up in their younger bodies, Iain, and got to re-live their past for thirty-three-days with their older consciousness holding the reins."

"But that's incredible, why haven't we been told of this wonder drug?"

"Because it doesn't happen for two hundred and thirty years."

He stared at her, seemingly dumbstruck. Clearly he was trying to understand, keep an open mind and believe her, and by the looks of things, Jenny believed, he was failing. "This is sounding more and more like a plot for a movie." He said, shaking his head, and Jenny felt sad for them both.

"I know it sounds incredibly far-fetched, and I don't blame you for doubting me, but what I am telling you is true. In the future Heinrich Abraxist discovers a way to send a person's consciousness back in time thirty-three years. But that's not the most incredible thing. You see, that discovery could not have come at a better time for the world. It is a time when whole nations are dying of starvation, and we are not just talking third world countries like Africa. There is a terrible Blight, a plant disease which jumps from one genus to another, but very slowly over many years. It ducks and dives, disappears for decades then comes back again even stronger. Scientists and the government cannot stop it, and slowly it destroys any and every plant to the point it cannot re-grow. They try every type of pesticide imaginable, they try re-growing plants in laboratories with built in immunities, but nothing, nothing works for ever. They think they succeed, but the Blight just pops up somewhere else, a different country on a different type of plant. Sooner or later the disease always comes back. The world as we know it, in two hundred and thirty years, is dying, Iain."

"Why are you telling me this, Jenny?"

"Because you asked me to move in with you, you need to know I am one of the people who took this drug so I could come back in time, to try to save the future of mankind."

"So you are from two hundred and thirty years' from now?" He looked incredulous.

"No. Only from thirty-three years' time. To travel back to now from then took seven of us. Imagine us playing a time traveling game of leapfrog. The first person traveled from the year 2247 to 2214 with two jobs to perform. One was to manufacture the drug for the next "Leaper" to take and the second was to convince another person to take ASX101 and do the same thing all over again. That's why we are called "Leapers" because it took an incredible leap of faith to believe a total stranger who said they were from the future, and they were to take this drug they had manufactured. And why? To try to help save the future population from starvation. It was tough to do, I was told. But each person had been selected by people in the future who studied history. The "Leapers" they chose, it was believed, would do it. Not everyone did it for the same reason. That would be too hard and remember each "Leaper" had only their thirty-three days to achieve their goal. For some it was an adventure, for others it was a chance to win a lottery and change their lives, and for others like me, agreed because we are passionate about the environment. We want to make a difference to the world and make sure we leave something behind for our future children, and their children."

He stared back at her, his eyes dark and hooded, Jenny couldn't read him. Was he angry, or just confused? When he spoke, it cut to the very core of the problem. "So, who exactly am I talking to?"

She sighed, this wasn't going at all well, and this was the first major issue he would have to face. Mentally she was sixty-eight years old.

"I'm me, the thirty-five-year-old Jenny you fell in love with, and the one who fell in love with you. I'm everything you see in front of you, I'm the one you hold, the one you kiss, the one you make love with. It's only my mind that has traveled back in time to re-inhabit this body. In my future, I'm sixty-eight years old, I'm single, I've always been single, Mister Sanchez long since died but I have another cat, called Boof. When I told you I've never been with a man like you, it's true, this is the first time I've been in love in sixty-eight years. I got to the age I did and all that's in my life is teaching. I do it by day and at night I tutor students and mentor them as well. I sit alone, at night, drink white wine and cuddle my cat. And, for me, coming back to now has been a revelation. I got to meet you, and fall in love, and you, Iain, you have shown me the life I had was wasted. It's this that's important, its being in love, it's not wanting to live without another person, its having someone to hold and kiss and talk to. To share dreams of a future, together, you have done that for me Iain. I traveled in time to do a job, and made the most wonderful discovery imaginable. I fell in love, with you. And if you will have me, I would like to spend the next thirty-three years with you."

He stood up, then sat down again. Then stood up and walked to the window and looked out over her small but pretty courtyard garden. "So, exactly why did you come back in time? Not to meet me, surely. And why did you know the match scores. I'm really lost and confused here, none of this is making much sense."

"Iain, do you believe me? That's the most important question. My feelings for you are so deep, so real, I've thought many times about abandoning the job I had to do, just to be with you so I didn't risk losing you. But, there is a problem with this drug I haven't told you about."

"Jenny, I just don't know what to believe right at this minute. It all sounds so fanciful and I'm just trying to make sense of it all. But I can tell you believe what you are saying, and you did predict things which tells me you had prior knowledge, like the air crash. What's the problem you've not told me about?"

She took a slow, deep calming breath. "I told you I can only stay for thirty-three-days, then this consciousness goes back to the future. That's how long the drug lasts for with the dosage I took. I'm over half way through, and when my time is up, this body will have no memory of anything that happened during my "Leap".

"What?"

"I won't remember you, or anything we did

together. I won't be in love. I won't have had the most incredible sex with you. My life will for the preceding month be a blank canvass. I'm writing myself a journal, because apparently when I wake it will be like I've had a thirty-three-day blackout, and I will want to know what happened during the time I cannot recall."

"You won't remember me at all?"

She shook her head. "Apparently not. What I'm hoping, is you will be around to help me through. It will be tough for me."

"But, I'll be a stranger to you? You'll wake up wondering who the hell has invaded your bed? You'll want to call the police."

"Yes. I'd never thought of it quite like that, but it's true. It's part of the price I was willing to pay to come back and try to save the future of mankind. I'm hopeful that while I will not have a memory, I will still have some feelings; that the emotion bleeds through for me and I never forget the love I feel for you. That's, of course, if you decide you still want me in your life. If you don't, then I will have no hope of experiencing this again. I love you, Iain."

He stood staring out of the window for long time, before speaking again. "So let me recap what you are trying to tell me so I'm clear in my mind. You came back in time from thirty-three years into the future because you believe you can save the world from starvation. But when you arrived, you accidentally met me, and fell in love with me. But at the end of your journey you won't have any memory of anything, including our relationship."

Now I'm in trouble, here is where it ends. "It wasn't exactly an accident, Iain. I turned up at Queens

Park specifically to meet you."

"It's Brad, isn't it?"

"Yes. The name of the genetically modified wheat Brad modifies, will be called the Destaine. He will engineer it so well, that when it begins to mutate, no one can stop it. It will continue to change and adapt and give incredible results and your son will be hailed the hero savior of the modern world. But it is harboring the Blight inside its cellular structure and will mutate to the point where in time it will kill us all. Initially I wanted to contact you, to help me convince Brad to not release this strain of wheat. I had no idea we would fall in love."

"Don't make me chose between my son and you, Jenny."

"I would never do that, I love you, and I feel incredibly close to Brad. It's not about choosing between you, it's about whether you believe me or not. If you do, then you must help me, the future of our planet depends on it. If you think I'm mad or lying for some reason then you won't help me, and not only will we part company, but you are condemning millions of people to death."

"So now it's my fault?"

"Iain, it's no more your fault than it is mine. I care about people and the planet we live on, and I know you do too. Remember that first dinner we had together, when we talked about the road to Hell being paved with good intentions? Brad has a good heart, and he is a wonderful person with an ideal to feed the world. But, if he continues, his wheat will kill everything and everyone. Do you think he would want that if he knew?"

"So you used me to get to Brad."

"Iain, you know me by now, hopefully. Do you think I am the kind of person who would use anyone? That I would somehow make you fall in love with me for an ulterior motive? I've never even been in love with a man, let alone be clever and smart enough to trap someone emotionally. I'm not that kind of person Iain, and I'm surprised and hurt you would think that I was."

"But you've lied to me."

"No, I haven't. I've never lied to you, strictly speaking. I'm guilty of not telling you everything too soon. Let's be honest, if I had told you I was a time traveler straight away you would have thought I was mad. I never planned for us to fall in love, and it has been the most wonderful experience of my life. And one I wouldn't swap for anything."

"But you believed someone straight away when they told you, yet you assumed I wouldn't?"

"Iain, it was far from straight away. And, for all I know, my 'tutor from the future' may have had other alternative people to approach if I didn't believe him. I don't know. I suspect he didn't, but because of who and what I am, they knew I wouldn't refuse to help. Let's not forget I was sixty-eight years old with a chance to go back to being thirty-five again and have a cause to fight for. Who wouldn't say yes? But this is different. I'm not here to try to get you to agree to be a "Leaper", I'm here to ask you to help me with your son. I don't know the formula for Abraxist's drug, and even if I did, Simon told me this is a one-way ticket. I couldn't come back for a second try even if I wanted to. If I took the drug again I would lose my mind and die a blithering idiot."

"So, I've been making love to a sixty-eight-year-old woman?"

She couldn't help it, she laughed. "Do I look that old? No. I am thirty-five. My mind is older, but it's still me. Safe to say between my age now and when I made my "Leap" in thirty-three years' time, nothing changed for me. I didn't have a man in my life, not because I didn't want one, I was just too busy with my environmental beliefs, and teaching to find the time. It took meeting you to show me how bad a lifestyle choice that was. Men have never been a priority for me; in sixty-eight years, I had two lovers, both when I was a student, and both were disastrous. I was just trying to fit in because I was a geek. I have a triple degree; my idea of a fun night was studying. Plus, let's be honest, I'm not one of the pretty ones, I'm one of the less than average looking ones. But, then I arrived here in 2016, and met you, and you knocked me for six. You said I was beautiful, you were attracted to me, as I was to you. It was like magnetism, an unfathomable force of attraction."

Finally, he turned from the window and looked down at her, still sitting on the floor, but he looked so sad.

"Iain, I love you. I didn't plan to fall in love, and no-matter what you chose to do about us, this has been the best thing that has ever happened in my miserable life. If you want me to not talk to Brad about the future devastation he will cause, then I won't. Such is my love for you; if you ask me to, I will abandon my mission."

"And, if you did, Jenny. If what you are telling me is the truth and not some fantasy, who else will they send? Someone to kill him and make it look like a mugging or robbery gone wrong?"

"I don't know. The idea has crossed my mind. Possibly the death of one man is better than the death of millions. At some point, they may take that approach, Simon did mention Heinrich had warned of the possibility. I'm not privy to the emergency plans of the future, I am not a killer and if I fail, I fail. I was asked to come back as an environmentalist, who believes in the sanctity of life, to reason with him. In trying to do that, I have fallen in love with you.

"I want to believe you; I just don't know if I can. It's just so incredible. But one question seems obvious to me: why didn't they approach Brad himself in his future, then send him back to fix his own mess."

Oh, my God, he asked me that?

"Iain, they couldn't, there was no way to speak to either of you. Brad will release the Destaine wheat in trials in 2019, and it will be hugely successful. But, in July in two thousand and twenty, you and Brad, while on your way home from a soccer game, will be killed in a car accident. That was another of the reasons I wanted this job: to save your lives."

****

It was all too much for Iain to take in in a single session, and when Jenny opened her mouth to add more he put his hand up to stop her. "I'm a simple man, and I need to time to digest all this, it's just so incredible, it's making my brain spin."

"Do you believe me, Iain?"

He looked sad, and she could see the hurt and confusion there. "I think I do. I can't imagine why you would make it all up, and it's so bizarre, I tend to think it must be true. You have predicted things no one could

287

have known, and with yesterday's game, somehow the future was changed. The air crash rocked me, in fact it terrified me. I always imagined life was just a series of now's, but clearly it's some type of ongoing stream. My biggest fear is if you were lying, that would mean you don't love me, and I don't think I could bear that."

"Oh, Iain. I love you with all my heart, with everything I know, and everything I am. I couldn't lie about that. Now, please tell me, should I pack some things, or shall I come back with you to retrieve my car?"

She sat up on her knees, and wrapped her arms around Iain, her face was level with his stomach. She held on, trying desperately to show him she loved him, praying for the right answer.

Chapter 15
Time to Think and Plan

He ran his fingers through Jenny's hair, while holding her. With her head to one side she could hear his heart beat as she waited for his answer.

Eventually he whispered: "How many days do we have left?"

She looked up, as she blinked her tears away. "We?"

He nodded, "We. I hope there is enough time to just chill for a while, be a normal couple. Let me digest things, enjoy each other's company without all the intrigue and talk of the future. In a few days' time, we can talk again, and work out how we will convince Brad to abandon his dream. That's not going to be easy. Then, we need to plan for when you lose your memory. Just one thing, I don't much care for myself, especially if I am not with you, but I do care for my son. How can I save his life?"

"I'm no scientist or mathematician, I'm just like you, I don't understand any of the technicalities of time travel, but, then I don't think anyone else does either. It's not like there have been studies done I could read up on, it's all just theoretical. When we couldn't stop, the aircraft crashing I worried that perhaps significant events in time couldn't be changed. For example; like how the type of goal was changed against Floreat, but not the overall score line. But then yesterday, wonder upon wonder, somehow the team changed a result which was supposedly set in concrete. So, to answer your question, how do we save his, and your life? Stay home, don't go to the game, remain in bed, just don't go anywhere near a car on that date.

"But how do we know we are not swapping one type of death for another?"

"I can't answer with any knowledge. But one thing occurred to me after yesterday's game is this: Once an event has been changed, it may well have changed a whole heap of other things that follow it. For example, you won a game you shouldn't, the time stream changed, and the win put you top of the league ladder. When I read up on this season, that had not happened. The guys are playing now with a confidence and spirit they haven't had before, so who knows where you go from here? Because that one event was changed, it may have a flow on effect; you may win other games and end up league champions. When I read up on this time, you finished third, and never, hit the top spot. Yet here you are, Queens Park are the leaders. My thinking is if we can get you to dodge your deaths, it changes your entire futures. So, I can't see you just dying by some other means on the same day because you take a different route. Further proof, I think are the paradox's that have been set up which we talked about; we can change the future, it is not finite."

"Jenny?

"Yes, my love?"

"Can I make love to you?"

"Mmm, yes you can, but, I need a shower first, why don't you join me?"

****

Mister Sanchez spent the first ten minutes sniffing his way around his new home while Jenny set up his litter tray. Once satisfied the house was acceptable to his discerning tastes, he found a spot on the carpet where the sun streamed through the window, turned around twice, lay down with his head on his paws, and promptly drifted off to sleep.

Iain made drawer and wardrobe space and together they unpacked her suitcase, which helped Jenny feel welcomed. This was a big step in her life; and on top of all the other momentous things which occurred since she volunteered to take her "Leap" she marveled at who she had become.

Iain stood by the bathroom watching her put her toiletries away, smiling. "It's been a long time since this room had the feminine touch of deodorants, body sprays, shampoos and conditioner. Not to mention the hygiene accoutrements and a second toothbrush alongside mine."

She turned from the vanity sink, "Are you happy, Iain, I mean really happy to have me here?" She could not stop a life time of self-doubt from bubbling up.

He smiled and nodded. He didn't answer with words, just crossed the small space between them and took her in his arms.

In the car driving back, they agreed not to talk of the future, time travel, the end of the world, or anything dangerous until the following Sunday, when they would broach the subject with Brad. Jenny thought he made good sense when he said: "We deserve some time to ourselves, I have no idea how Brad will take it, but a few days with you being in the house first can't hurt, can it?" Jenny readily agreed.

She broached the subject of paying her way and bill sharing, but Iain again made a good point: "Jen, don't worry about the small stuff just now, the bills I'd have whether you were here or not, the house itself has been paid off with Simone's insurance payout, so really financially, there is nothing to be concerned about. In a few days from now you will lose your memory and I must try to help you fall in love with me all over again. I hope when we cross that bridge you decide to stay. Assuming you do, then we can formalize things and decide about who pays for what, what to do with your place and all the other things that come with us living together as a couple. How does that sound?"

So, they had agreed; a holiday for them both. A time to be alone and enjoy the love they shared. Jenny lightened the mood as they hugged in the bathroom "Hey, you know there is one problem we haven't really talked about."

Iain lifted his face away to look at hers, and looked troubled, though he didn't take his hands from her body, "What's that?"

"I'm a useless cook. I've lived alone all of my adult life, and when you do you tend to eat quick meals, frozen dinners and sandwiches."

He let out the breath he was holding, "Jesus, Jen, I thought you were being serious." He laughed as she gave a mischievous smile. "Well, I'm not too flash myself, but we will manage. It's something else we can do together. It's a timely point. How about we go to the supermarket now, it's usually the day I do, we can stock up on things you like rather than just the normal stuff I get for Brad, Lyndsay and myself."

She nodded. "Grocery shopping with my man, who'd have thought that would ever come? Yes, let's go, but I'm paying that bill, I insist."

In the car, once they finished shopping and were on the way home, Jenny idly stoked his thigh, thinking her life was now perfect.

Iain glanced toward her. "How about we stop in at the video store to see if they have a copy of the Girl with the Dragon Tattoo movie to watch at home after dinner?"

"I'd really like that, yes please, Iain."

"I haven't been in there for ages, but I still have my membership tag on the key ring."

"Funny how it's all DVD's these days, but we still call them video stores."

He smiled, "True, I'd not thought of that before."

They approached the young man at the counter to ask where they might find the film located as there were aisles after aisles to choose from."

"Do you want the English version or the original Scandinavian?"

"We didn't know there would be a choice, I guess the Scandinavian one has subtitles?" Iain asked, "I always find that a bit distracting; while I'm reading the dialog, I'm missing what's happening on the screen."

Jenny just shrugged, she just wanted to see her heroine on screen, so was happy with the either cut, but the young man hadn't finished. "The U.S. film is just the one movie, they didn't make films out of books two and three, but if you are a true devotee, we have the full trilogy in subtitles. I recommend it, it's very good acting, you do get used to reading the dialog, and it's always been thought they more closely mirror how the author would have wanted it told. But of course, we will never know for sure. The originals have a much darker, more somber feel to them, Daniel Craig is very good in the lead, but for my money the Scandinavian versions are better."

Iain looked at Jenny. "We won't have enough time to watch three films in a single sitting tonight, so how about we get the American version for now, and maybe next weekend make a day of it, and watch the three films back to back?"

"Good idea. I know I'm going to love them all, but if you are not keen on the first one there wouldn't be much point in making you sit through the others."

"Good choice," the young man said. "Was there anything else you wanted? I know exactly where it is, so if you want to grab some popcorn and stuff I will get the DVD for you."

He turned and opened the flap in the counter and walked off. He returned shortly with the plastic box that contained the DVD in his hand. Jenny had grabbed a small packet of caramel, while Iain selected the salted, butter popcorn.

Back at the house after the shopping had been put away, Iain said he wanted to mow the lawns, and Jenny volunteered to get started on making the Shepherd's Pie she had suggested for dinner. When she finished her preparations, she looked out of the kitchen window. Iain had removed his shirt as he worked. His upper body was covered with a thin film of sweat as he walked up and down pushing the mower. Her breath caught in her throat as she felt aroused at the sight of the muscles on his lean body shimmering in the dappled sunlight.

Her life in this time stream was a never ending source of amazement, and feeling sexually excited at the site of a man with his shirt off was no exception. The things other people and couples would find normal, Jenny found highly unusual, and she couldn't remember a time when the physical attraction she felt had ever happened before. Perhaps she experienced it when she had been a student, but if she did, she couldn't recall.

He is so handsome and sexy; God only knows what he sees in me.

She wanted to lower her hand to touch herself, and that was most certainly unusual. When they were alone in bed, later, the memory of this vision would be more than enough to light her kindling. She smiled, then got a glass of filtered cold water from the dispenser on the face of the refrigerator to take out to him.

He had his ear muffs on to stifle the loud noise from the mower, so he would be unable to hear her approach. She waited patiently, holding the iced water, for him to mow his way to the end of a run, then turn back toward her. He smiled when he caught sight of her, and she loved the look of delight on his face.

Lyndsay and Brad surfaced from the bedroom just before dinner was ready, and both remarked on the lovely smell that wafted through the house from the baking casserole dish. Jenny was pleased; she had worried her first attempt of making a family meal might be a disaster, but she needn't have been concerned.

They ate the shepherd's pie with steamed vegetables and a small garlic bread loaf. There were beers for father and son, while the two women drank white wine to accompany the meal. Rapid fire humorous banter traversed the dinner table as they ate, interspersed with 'compliments to the chef' and similar remarks made Jenny's heart soar.

Everyone helped to clean up the kitchen after the meal, still laughing and joking. Brad and Lyndsay said their goodnights as they had seen the movie. They were going to watch TV in his room, leaving Jenny and Iain alone.

"I thought you said you weren't a good cook," Iain remarked as he walked up behind her as she finished at the sink. His hands gripped her sides, just below her bra. "That pie was sensational."

"Thank you, kind sir. I enjoyed making it." She turned into his arms and put her hands on his shoulders while his dropped to her jeans covered hips. "In a way, it's a shame you showered after cutting the grass, I'm in the mood to have washed your back, and front, and sides, and everywhere else."

He cupped her breasts and stroked his thumbs over her nipples. Jenny moaned softly. She hadn't lost the feeling of wanting him since she'd watched him earlier through the window. She loved that even through the material of her shirt and bra, she could feel how he teased her, which raised her desire even higher.

It was as if he could sense her need, as he tweaked and pinched her now very erect nubs, harder. "Why, Jenny, I think you are just a bit horny. Of course, I could have another shower, or we could cut to the chase and go straight to bed."

He undid the top two buttons of her shirt, then slid both hands under her bra straps and down covering her bare skin.

How does he do this to me? Oh, my God I want him to take me right here, up against the sink, jeans and panties yanked down.

"I love you. You can do anything you want to me," she said breathlessly, as she gazed deeply into his eyes.

"But what about the movie?"

"What movie?"

****

Just over an hour later, they sat down to watch The Girl with the Dragon Tattoo with their respective bowls of popcorn. Jenny felt wonderfully relaxed and felt content having climaxed powerfully under Iain's ministrations. For the time being the itch she had felt ever since the afternoon when she had seen Iain shirtless, had been scratched.

As they sat on the couch, she still felt the need to touch him, and she made sure she cuddled in with her head on his chest so his arm could be around her while his hand softly stroked and caressed her back and side.

For the next two hours, they barely spoke, as Mikael Blomkvist and Lisbeth Salander solved the mystery of the missing Harriet Vanger, and the unmasking of a serial killer. For Jenny, it was so much more than enjoying a good film; it was the visualization of the characters she had only imagined, and she was deeply fascinated and satisfied with the result. The film accurately followed the storyline of the book, and she could see if the viewer didn't know there was another two stories in the series, they would have no indication from the film. Lisbeth, had thrown away the present she bought for Mikael after seeing him with his past lover, and rode off into the night on her motor bike. There the story left Lisbeth, heartbroken and alone once more, but incredibly wealthy, and the viewer could make up their own minds as to her future. Only by reading the books would a reader discover what happened next, and more importantly; what had happened in Lisbeth's past which haunted her.

"That was an excellent film, I enjoyed it." Iain declared. "I can see why you like the girl so much; I think she's a bit like you. Troubled, naive, and the sort of person you want to just hold and cuddle, if she would only just let you. Mind you, a man would never want to knowingly hurt her, she would stab him in the back, and front, then slit his throat and probably drink his blood."

"What makes you think I wouldn't too?" She giggled at the look that crossed his face.

Iain had grossly exaggerated, of course, but Jenny felt, he had hit the nail on the head in some ways. "I'd really like to see the other three films. You're right, I somehow do see some of myself in Lisbeth and I guess I feel a kinship with her. I just have this overpowering urge to know more. Unfortunately, because the author died, there is no more than the three books, but the final two instalments in the trilogy focus very much on her, her past, and the struggles she must go through, I think you'd enjoy it, even though it's subtitled. Can we watch them, please?"

"Of course we can. I'd like to watch anything that means so much to you."

Chink. Is there a better man in the entire world? I don't think so. She turned around and kissed him, and his hands wandered over her body. She felt so loved, so wanted and needed, it was incredible. She would have let him undress her totally but they were interrupted by Brad clearing his throat from the doorway.

"Is it safe to come in?" He said, comically holding his hand over her eyes. "You're not having a naughty, are you?"

"No, Brad, we have our sex in bed, unlike someone else I know."

"You're never going to let me live that down, are you, Dad?"

"Nope."

He smiled, good naturedly. "Well I just wanted to say good night to you both. Lyndsay has fallen asleep already, but I know she wanted to thank you too, for the fantastic dinner tonight, Mummy-Jen. You aced it. Much better than Dad's attempts. And, umm, on a more serious note, can I just say something?"

"You being serious? Jesus, this I have to hear." Iain said.

Jenny elbowed him, sensing Brad had something to say that shouldn't be trivialized. "Yes Brad, what is it?" she asked.

"Well, it's just that Dad was lost when you guys broke up. He was amazing when you first dated him, because after mum died he suddenly came alive again, for the first time. Then when you broke up, he died all over again. So, I just wanted to say I'm glad you sorted out your differences. And, umm, I wanted you to also know, Jenny, so far as I'm concerned, this is your home, for as long as you want it to be. Please don't think I resent you being here."

How much like his father is he? She felt so many emotions flood through her at once: love for Iain, and Brad, hurt that this was soon to end, and the unknown of what would happen when she confronted Brad about the future. Somehow she cleared her foggy brain when she noticed the concerned look on Brads face. No doubt due to the tears in her eyes

"Brad, that's one of the most wonderful things anyone has ever said to me. Thank you, I mean that more than you will ever know."

****

Day Twenty-One, 22nd August 2016

Jenny arrived at work feeling in a fantastic mood. She parked her car and remembered something from her student days that one girl had said about another in her earshot: "There goes a true bachelor: he comes to uni from a different direction every day."

This was the first time she had come to work from any direction other than from her home, and she felt good about it. She chuckled at the memory as she turned and almost walked straight into the Dean.

"Well, it's good to see you smiling again, Jenny, the little break looks like it was just the ticket."

"Oh, Dean I cannot thank you enough for your understanding and use of your lovely house. I had a wonderful time. I made a new friend and discovered an author who took my breath away. And, umm I made up with my boyfriend. In fact, I'm delighted to report, I've moved in with him."

He clapped his hands together as a sign of genuine delight. "Jenny, that's wonderful news. It's so good to see you back to your normal self."

As unprofessional as it was, she threw her arms around him and hugged for all she was worth. He had always been so stuffy and officious, but he had displayed a human side, and Jenny, wanted to show her appreciation.

When she stepped away, he had returned to his normal self, and stuttered. "Well err, yes I'm glad you found your true balance again. Glad to help, of course, any time and all that."

"Thank you, Dean. It was just what the doctor ordered. Now I better to get to my first lecture. Oops, I nearly forgot."

She opened her bag, located his house keys and handed them over.

"Jolly good. Keep smiling, that's what we like to see around here."

During her midmorning break, she remembered a promise she had made but hadn't fulfilled. She stopped walking on her way to the common room and fished out her phone from her hand bag. The first thing she saw when she powered it up was a text message from Iain, which made her smile:

—*I can't stop thinking how good life is now you are a part of it.*—

Chink. She fired of a reply of undying love, and then dialed Janet's number which answered after three rings. "Hi Janet, its Jenny. Are you free for lunch?"

"Jennnnyyyyyyyy, it's great to hear from you, how did the dirty weekend go?"

"Meet me for lunch and I will tell you all about it, as promised."

"Deal, we can grab something at Salt and Peppa Café, only a few shops away from mine; what time will you be here?"

****

Jenny ate a pink salmon salad plate, while Janet ordered the pasta of the day. The weekend away was discussed at great length. When she got to the break up, Janet stretched her arm across the table to hold her hand in a gesture of genuine friendship, and concern. Jenny did not explain why the sudden split, only that they had a stupid argument which got out of hand.

"I'm so sorry it didn't work out for you, I really did have my fingers crossed and I've been thinking about you in that red dress ever since."

Jenny sat back in her chair, and smiled warmly back at her new friend. She was a good friend. Why was that? *How could I have got to sixty-eight years old, and not had one good, solid, girlfriend?*

Jenny talked about her few days away at the insistence of the Dean, the discovery of the adventures of Lisbeth, the making of a new friend at the general store, and finally, the resurrection of the relationship with Iain, thanks to Brad's intervention. The genuine affection concern and shared pleasure was etched into Janet's face.

"So, umm, I've moved in with him."

"Get out of town, you have not!"

Jenny nodded. It was so good to be able to talk to someone, and for that person to not only listen, but care. She made a commitment to herself to write a very strongly worded diary note: she must continue to cultivate the friendships with Janet, and Marion.

Lunch finished all too soon, with an agreement they would catch up again, soon. Perhaps go out to dinner as a foursome, so Janet could meet Iain, and Jenny could meet Adam, her husband.

Driving back, her thoughts wandered to comparing her before and after life, and the deep-seated regret she felt. Sure, she taught kids, some of whom had gone on to do important work in the world of working in and saving the environment, and she was justifiably proud of her vocation. But what had happened to her personal life? Where did it go? It seemed when she blinked months had disappeared, and when she fell asleep years slipped by. Time itself had flown past on golden wings in her early formative years and then on a rocket powered sled in her later ones.

God, or more realistically, the wise men in the future who planned this trip back in time, not only selected her to save the world, but, had granted her a way of atonement for ignoring the important things in life. She had discovered the incredible side of true friendship, which only two women can share, not once, but twice. And she had found the love of a good man.

Jenny always thought of herself as not so much an ugly duckling, but as a very average one. Yes, when she looked back she could remember boys wanting to date her, but: they hadn't been very persistent, or had they? Maybe her frosty demeanor had frightened them off?

She enjoyed her afternoon at University, even finding time to laugh and joke with one or two of her favorite students. On her way to Iain's house; it was far too early to call it theirs; she stopped at the supermarket to get some things for dinner. Jenny was determined to carry on where she had left off on the cooking front. If they liked her shepherd's pie, they were going to love her grandmothers Tuna Mornay. *That's if I can remember the recipe, of course.*

When she arrived, she entered, using the key Iain had given her, which put another smile on her face. It had been another special moment in her life when he gave it to her. She put the things for dinner in the kitchen and walked through to the bedroom to change. She could hear Iain in the shower, and she smiled mischievously. Quickly she undressed completely and crept into the bathroom. He had his back to the glass door as he washed his hair. Perfect.

Jenny softly opened the shower door and snaked her hand around to hold and gently fondle him. *I love being so naughty.*

He flinched, momentarily, but otherwise didn't move as shampoo streamed down his face. "I hope that's Jenny." He whispered hoarsely.

She wrapped her other arm around him to hold his chest as she stepped into the cubicle. It was so small her breasts were squashed up against his back. "Who else would it be, Scarlet Johansen?"

"Well, if it is, you can bugger off quick smart, my lover is due home soon and she's the only one I want touching me there."

Chink. "You're as hard as a candle, I think the idea of Scarlet touching you is a turn on. Keep your eyes closed, turn around. And you can imagine it's her sucking you."

"Uh huh. I'd rather keep them open and watch Jenny."

And that was such a perfect response, she rewarded him by allowing it.

****

Jenny served the Mornay with asparagus, sweet corn and broccoli, and it was a lip-smacking success, bringing praise from everyone.

"I could get used to these kind words about my meagre cooking skills."

"Well, that's only fair; we could get used to you cooking." Brad replied.

"Please, Jenny, you must give me the recipe, it was delicious." Lyndsay joined in enthusiastically.

After everyone again helped with the dishes and

tidying up, Brad suggested they all play a game called Yahtzee. Iain readily agreed while Lyndsay and Jenny looked questioningly at each other. Iain topped up Jenny's wine glass as he explained the rules. Brad found the game.

He exaggeratedly blew imaginary dust from the box when he walked back in the room. "It's been a while since we played this, Dad."

"Not since your mum was alive." Jenny turned to Iain, worried he might be upset, but he smiled, and winked to show he wasn't.

"Partners and combined scores, oldies versus the young guns?"

"Good call, Jenny and I will whoop your asses, you know that, don't you Brad?"

"In your dreams, maybe."

Lyndsay shook her head at Jenny. "Just in case you hadn't noticed, Jen, they are just a bit competitive."

Just over an hour later, Jenny was caught up in the joking around, as the games stood at one to each team, and were deep into the decider, which everyone wanted to win. Jenny was doing poorly, but so was Brad so they balanced each other's scores. Lyndsay had one Yahtzee on the scorecard at the halfway point, but then Iain got one too. They raced each other neck and neck but with her second last throw of the dice, Lyndsay scored her second major score. Unless Iain could match it with one of his last two throws, the game looked to be over.

He held the cup containing the dice and paused for effect, looking at the other players and finished with Jenny. He winked before rattling the cup and turning out the dice on the green cloth lined container. 6-3-6-1-

1. "Sixes or ones, Jenny?"

He had already achieved his bonus, and getting five ones was the same score as sixes. However, if he failed to convert it, it made more sense to keep the sixes and use his 'chance,' which was the combined total of all the dice.

Before she could answer Brad interrupted: "You can't ask, Mummy-Jen can see the future and it would be cheating."

"Oh yeah, like it's really helped with my game, I'm doing terribly." She smiled back, sweetly.

"Yeah but that's probably all just part of your cunning master plan to lull Lyndsay and I into a false sense of security."

Oh, my God, how close to the truth. "Okay, you're right Brad, I won't tell your father to go for the one's."

"Oh, boo, cheater." But he didn't look angry, he smiled."

"Hmm, something is telling me to go for the one's, but the smart play would be sixes, decisions, decisions." Iain said, seemingly engrossed in looking at the assorted numbers. He picked up the two highest numbers and motioned them to one side as if he wanted to keep them, but at the last moment dropped them into the cup, and the three followed. Then he picked up the two ones and put them to the side. "I hope you're right, babe."

He shook the cup and rolled again: 6-1-4. He now had three of a kind with one throw left. Slowly he took his last turn, and all eyes were on the dice as they rolled. When they stopped. What faced them was 6-6, and Jenny groaned. Her feeling about the ones had been completely wrong.

Iain sounded delighted as he exclaimed: "Oh that's lucky, I didn't need a full house, but the two sixes makes the chance acceptable." He penciled in the correct score.

"You lucky bugger." Brad said as he now picked up the Dice for his turn. "Don't worry Lyn's, you can do it, he needs a Yahtzee on his last go or we are home free."

The turns continued with Jenny, Lyndsay and Brad failing to make anything useful and crossing out their last scores. It all hinged on Iain's final throw. He picked up the tumbler, shook it, then put it down again. "I might just go and get a drink before I throw, anyone want one?"

"Don't you dare," Brad yelled, "you're killing us with suspense here."

"Yeah, but I really need to go to the toilet first."

"Nope, not buying that either. Hold it with one hand, and take your shot with the other."

Iain grinned at Jenny, who smiled back. "Go on babe, put them out of their misery. Win or lose it's been fun, I've really enjoyed it." She finished her glass of wine and sat back to wait.

His first throw was a long straight, with numbers 1 through 5 showing. "You don't see that very often, do you?" He said, with a shake of his head. Jenny thought he was slow playing because he was relishing being the center of attention. She didn't think it mattered too much if they won or lost, but he seemed to be enjoying the fun of it all, as she was. "Come on, baby," she cooed, "You can do this."

"Yes, but which number to keep; that's the question isn't it? I mean the ones didn't work last throw, the sixes did, but I don't have one of those to keep? Should I stay with the low numbers, or maybe a five? What do you think Jen?"

Jenny giggled as Brad interrupted: "Oh for God's sake will you just throw the damn things."

"Patience, lad, that's always been your downfall, lack of patience." He tutted and shook his head while Jenny stifled her laughter and wished she had some wine left. "I think I will keep the five, Jen, or no, wait a sec, the four."

Showing he was in no rush, he slowly removed the four, and picked up the other dice and dropped them in the shaker then rattled long and slow. "Come on babies, speak to me." He spoke softly into the container before tipping them out.

"Oh, good choice Iain," Jenny enthused as she saw 4-4-4-5 appear."

"It's four of a kind, shame we don't need one of those, but four fours mean we just need one more of them to win the game. Exciting, Brad, isn't it?"

Jenny thought Brad was enjoying the charade, but still felt the need to stay in character. "Jesus, Dad, can you go any slower? You're just delaying the inevitable loss. Don't panic Lyn's, he won't do it, its six to one against, the odds are on our side."

"I wasn't panicking, Brad, if anyone is it's you. It's just a game you know, calm down, and take deep breaths." Jenny thought she was enjoying it too, far more than she was letting on.

"Just a game, is that what you said? Just a game? This is the final throw in the 2016 World Yahtzee Championships, we're well and truly in the lead and it's a six to one shot they will take the title away from us, on the last throw of the match. And you say it's just a game? Are you mad, woman?"

"Anyone want a glass of red wine?" Iain asked

"*No, I want you to throw the damn dice!*"

Oh my God, how do I love this family? Iain slowly picked up the last remaining dice and put it in the container. Then one at a time took the 4's from the throwing area.

"So, it's all come down to this?" Iain asked slowly shaking the tumbler from side to side, "Just one more throw. It's been fun guys; we must do it again sometime." He turned out the dice which rolled and slowed and eventually halted, showing a single dot pointing toward the ceiling.

Brad leapt to his feet and strutted around the table, fist pumping, as he chanted: "Oh yeah, oh yeah, who's your daddy now?"

Iain winked at Jenny, who gave him her best smile back. She felt happy they had lost. Brad and Lyndsay had won, and Iain didn't seem to mind too much at all either.

Chapter 16
Running Out of Time

August 4th 2247, Berlin, Germany

Heinrich Abraxist sat with his feet on his desk, looking out of his window at the cloud filled Berlin skyline and thought about his immediate future, and what he was going to do about a very serious problem. The United Nations Committee had sanctioned his plan; and decreed it was viable. They had given resources for the program and final planning had begun the day before.

Some committee members commented the idea was not only viable, it was the only plan that could stop the spread of Yellow Spot. All biological attempts to kill it had failed. Huge tracts of land were now wasteland dustbowls, and it was an ecological nightmare of catastrophic proportions. Even if they now somehow found a way of killing the disease, it was feared it was too late for things to recover. Once crops and forests disappeared, the wind came next, ripping the topsoil from the ground and sending it toward the rivers and ultimately the ocean.

As it was his discovery which provided the glimmer of hope, he had been given the senior role to lead the team of experts nominated. These were mostly made up of historians, charged with finding the seven people who would become their saviors. Of itself this was no mean feat and sparked long passionate discussions as they searched through history, because everyone had a different idea about the type of person who could be relied on to take on such a job. Eventually they reached agreement, and had a list of people they thought would be able to be convinced to take the drug, and take their part in saving mankind.

The first "Leaper" had been an easy choice, as was the last. Leading the charge would be Heinrich himself. He was of the right age, and he reasoned if he failed at the first hurdle, there was little point in going further.

Next he worked tirelessly to find a simple way to manufacture the drug outside the laboratory. It had been a major stumbling block, and he succeeded after long hours of trial and error. He was passionate about his plan, believed in it, and no one was going to deny him his starring role. As he had studied in America, and began working for Diedeck Pharmaceuticals in New York, it would put him in the right country for the second "Leaper" in the team.

The final member had been an easy choice for Heinrich once they found her. Jenny O'Brien was an outspoken environmentalist of her day. She was single, and lived in the same city as the target. They thought if all stayed on schedule they could land her back in 2016, full three years before the launch of the Destaine Wheat.

In her later years, she had become more and more vocal against pollution and several other ecological causes, and had died at a protest rally against fracking, aged seventy-five from a heart attack. Heinrich knew everything there was to know about her, and he believed she was the one. She was a spinster with no surviving family, she was a woman of principles, and the psychologists thought she would be driven to succeed. He believed she would jump at the chance to be able to save the planet for which she had fought for all her life.

Unfortunately, not so all the committee. They did not believe in her as readily as he did. They wanted the final "Leaper" to be someone who could, if necessary, murder the target, and had argued against using any other type of personality. They believed they would only get one chance, and the stakes were so high they could not afford a failure if Bradley Destaine could not be convinced of the result of his discovery.

They selected a man who they believed would be capable of carrying out the 'final solution'. Thomas Harrison, aged fifty-eight had been released from a Melbourne prison in 2016, having been jailed for twenty-eight years for a series of underworld killings for hire. His preceding "Leaper", by using a lottery win, would have sufficient funds to contract him to travel to Perth and commit the murder.

Heinrich had agreed with the principle, even though the idea of murder was abhorrent to him. The final part of the plan could work. The problem, as he saw it, was convincing the other six to go back in time to be a party to a paid assassination at the end of the line.

It was madness to suggest they would all be motivated enough to become willing participants in a contract murder. Heinrich refused to be a party to such a plan, and he carried on with his own ideas for his team. Now, he sat, ready to launch his consciousness back in time and begin the journey.

But earlier in the day, he had been informed of a secret plan by a disgruntled committee member which devastated him. With typical German ruthless efficiency, they had sanctioned a second-strike force of "Leapers" which were going to follow the first team. The secret planning committee, who was forbidden to tell Abraxist about their existence, believed they had found the right set of people who would be willing to conspire to commit the murder.

These were not the benevolent kind Heinrich and his team and tracked down, they were more mercenary. They would be funded by gambling wins and effectively bribed to go back in time to cumulatively purchase Thomas Harrison's services. Heinrich wondered if such people could even be trusted to carry out their mission and not take the money and run back to the future, however, he did not want to take a chance.

It was his drug, and he was outraged it could be used for a sanctioned killing. He could never live with himself if he permitted it to take place. He wanted to carry on regardless, thumbing his nose at his bosses, but he wondered should he tell his "Leaper" of the others potentially following behind?

His confidant had only found out the first person in the chain of murderers, but none of the others. If he told his "Leapers" of the threat, how might they react? Could it not make them scared and possibly not take their place in history, dooming his elaborate rescue plan to fail? Could he take the chance? The answer was no, he could not. He decided he would plant the seed of the possibility of a murderer to the "Leapers" but no more.

Heinrich believed destiny decreed he should save

mankind. #ASX101 was his discovery and it was he who dreamt up the plan to use it. He had spent his life finding drugs to help people, and even if it meant the end of the world, his last act would not be one which condoned murder. The problem he faced, was wondering what he could do to stop it?

The real issue, was if he did nothing, and Jenny succeeded in her mission, sometime later along would come Thomas Harrison and kill Bradley Destaine anyway. Even though he was no longer going to release the modified wheat. It was possible he was still going to die, which would be grossly unfair.

Four hours later, as the rising moon poked its head between two dreary rain filled clouds, Heinrich realized two things. First, and most urgent, his leg had gone to sleep and he couldn't straighten it. Secondly, he had come up with a plan he thought might work.

His first idea he'd discounted after some serious consideration. It had been based around an old debate about time paradoxes. His idea had been to go back, set up his first "Leaper" and when he was sure of success, kill himself. The problem was if he did, how did he know what the outcome would be? If he just ceased to exist, and never got to invent the #ASX101, how could he then use it to go back in time?

His field was drug research, not time travel and he just didn't know what would occur because of such drastic action. Perhaps the strike force would already have left in that continuum, maybe not. Maybe if he killed himself then nothing would stop the Destaine grain, because there would be no #ASX101, and no "Leapers". There were far too many variables to ensure success and the more he considered the idea, the more he felt confused at the myriad of possible eventualities.

He stood up to walk off the pins and needles but almost fell when his leg would not take his weight. He stumbled around until he got his circulation back.

He had some research to do, then he would go home, go to bed and inject himself with the #ASX101 and put his second plan into motion. There was no time to lose because the other team were due to launch their campaign in three days.

****

Day Twenty-Six, 27th August 2016

For Jenny, the week had been like living inside a wonderful dream. It was as close to sheer bliss as she could ever imagine her life to be. Things had been wonderful, and she barely gave a thought to the upcoming weekend's game except for when they were at training. The club would face a rampant Kalamunda Tigers team, which currently sat third on the table, and who had won their last four games. There were only two matches left in the season, which contributed to it being a critical game.

Training on Tuesday and Thursday had been fun, with the tem working tirelessly. Jenny thought the men sensed they could be on the verge of an unlikely championship trophy and they trained with a purpose. She volunteered to go in goal during scratch matches, and this time did make two saves, though she believed Simmo hadn't shot with anywhere near the power he could have. Iain trained the guys ruthlessly. He motivated them by telling them this was the highest in the league the team had ever attained with him in charge. He wanted them to win again and hold on to top spot, and prove they were worthy, but Kalamunda would not be an easy team to beat.

She avoided thinking about the conversation with Brad, which they were going to take place on Sunday evening. When thoughts entered unbidden into her mind, she did her best to ignore them, and distracted herself with other things.

She felt so much in love, and every day had been picture perfect with Iain. She took great delight in the small things which most people would take for granted, like doing the dishes together, watching him as he shaved in the morning, and discussing current events as a family over the dinner table. There was always time for laughing and joking as a family, and at night they made love.

"I've been thinking a lot about what you said about how we've changed an event which had been set in time by beating Subiaco last week." Iain said, during breakfast on the day of the game.

"I love it when you think a lot, it usually leads to you making love to me, not that we have time right now." Jenny grinned, then sensuously licked the tip of her spoon which held some of the soft-boiled egg she was eating.

Iain stared back, at the rather erotic display she was putting on. "I've never known anyone quite like you, Jenny."

"What we you saying about the game tomorrow, Iain?" Then used her tongue again to taste the egg.

He shook his head as if he needed to, to clear his mind. "Well, you said when you studied our history we had lost this game, which made it two losses in a row. But, because of you firing the lads up, they snatched a miraculous win last week. I need to do something to help keep the momentum going, so I thought I would change the formation again, and it only dawned on me this morning how I could do it."

Jenny stopped teasing him, as this was music to her. Anything which could show her they had the ability to alter the future was deeply fascinating. "Go on, I'm all ears."

"Well, it's pretty radical, but maybe what we need; is to stop being so predictable. Since you joined us the whole dynamic of the team has changed, you got me to change to a more attacking line up. I think before we used to play games thinking we could never get higher than third spot, and now we are the leaders. So, what I'm thinking, is let's go all guns blazing and try an even more attacking style."

Her eyes sparkled with pride, she just nodded because she didn't want to trust her voice wouldn't tremble.

"In this league, and most teams throughout the world, play with a line of defenders, called a 'flat back four', which as you might imagine means four guys in a straight line. You've taught me to have faith in my defense, so what I'm considering is, to reduce it from four to three. One of the guys, probably Mickey, I'd push up into the midfield, and then Scotty, our current center-mid, I would make a third forward. If we can stop them scoring with just the three guys at the back, then we should be able to beat them. And if we did, then there is only one more game in the season, and that should be a relatively easy one.

"I'm so proud of you."

He looked genuinely surprised. "Why? It's you who have been the catalyst for all this change in form, without you, nothing would have altered."

"Well, even given that, your coaching of the team has been incredible, and you've shown you can alter tactics for different circumstances. Everyone resists change, it's human nature, but you've welcomed it, and I love you for it."

She squeezed his hand, and noticed he looked a little embarrassed. "I'm not used to anyone being proud of me. Jenny. In a few days' time, when you won't remember me anymore, will you be the same kind loving person you are now? I'm scared I will lose you, forever."

The question stung her, and saddened her all the way down to her soul. She had felt the same fear, but each time it raised its ugly head, she forced it back down again as a thought too painful to consider. "Iain, all I really know is what I've been told. When the test subjects woke up back in the future they were questioned closely before they lost their memory, which apparently takes between six and twelve hours. For that time, they were befuddled, not remembering fully either stream. Apparently, it's like the two sets of memories are fighting each other. My recollections of the thirty-three days versus the ones my older body continued with in the thirty-three years since. They all had some recall on waking, but, when they lost those memories they could only recall what had happened in their lives before, and after, but not during. They described it as a month-long blackout. My only hope is none of those people fell in love during their stay in the past, as I have. I just so hope my love will seep through the loss of memory, and help me, I want it more than anything else in the world. I've been keeping my diary up to date, as you know, and you must make me read it. I think you will need to be patient with me, but, I fell in love with you once, I know in my heart I can do it all over again. Iain, I am essentially the same person, I've never changed much at all, really, until you. What you see is what you get, I hope and pray it will be fine, but, it might take time."

He nodded, and gave a lopsided smile. "I hope so, I will be lost without you."

****

The night before, they had returned to Hoy Anne's Vietnamese restaurant in Leederville, with Brad and Lyndsay, and had a wonderful night. Tuyen made a fuss over Brad from the moment they arrived to the time they left. She always served him first, and poured his drink before everyone else's. It was amusing, and heartwarming, for Jenny to watch.

Tuyen remembered Jenny too, much to her surprise, at one point asking if she still wanted to see a menu. She drank the traditional toast on three separate occasions with them. The meal was again, superb, and while Jenny knew what to expect, it was Lyndsay's first time, so Jenny took great delight in seeing the surprise on her face. She was sure it was the same look she wore with Iain during her first visit.

The main course of garlic, chili and ginger beef with the freshest of crisp stir fried vegetables had the perfect combination of sweet, sour and spicy heat, while the noodle soup which preceded it contained perfectly cooked scallops and prawns, adding depth of flavor.

They caught an Uber cab home laughing and joking at Brad's expense, telling him Tuyen had the hots for him and to watch out for her husband, in case he chased after him with a meat cleaver. It interested her to see Brad at first joking along, but under relentless teasing get slightly annoyed, though not enough to spoil the night.

For one so intent on joking at other people's expense he can't take it as well as he dishes it out.

At home Jenny mastered the coffee machine, and made hot drinks and served them with a blueberry cream cheesecake she had bought on her way home from work earlier.

****

It occurred to Jenny, more than ever that she had become a solid member of the team, as she stood alongside Iain in the change rooms before the game at Kalamunda's ground. The guys all got changed in front of her. She avoided looking, but she was surrounded by young healthy males in various stages of undress, though thankfully they kept their underwear on.

Luckily, no one talked to her because she was worried about how her voice would sound if she had been forced to answer. Eventually they were all dressed in the team colors and sat on the benches to listen to what Iain would say to them. He walked to the chalkboard, turned and looked at his men.

"S-S-So, J-Jenny, are we going to win today?" Simmo asked

She paused for a moment and looked around at the expectant faces. "Yes, you will. Iain has come up with an incredible game plan, and if you stick to it, they won't know what hit them; you can do this guys, I promise you all."

This statement was followed by hoots, whistles,

and stomping of boots on the concrete floor, until Iain held up his hand for quiet.

"Guys, listen up. We have two games left in the season, and if we win both we will be champions, for the first time in more years than I can remember. You have got us to this point, and you can finish this off. Today's game is the toughest one left, so how are we going to win?"

Everyone expected the question, and gave the usual chant: "Score more goals!"

"That's right, and here is how we are going to do it." He turned to the board and began writing up names in the formation he wanted them to play. The murmurings started when he chalked up only three defenders, and became a mini cacophony when he finished with three forwards.

He turned back to the team. "Defenders I am relying on you to hold them out, and don't take any chances by trying to play it out of the back line. If you have a clear pass, then of course take it, there are four mid-fielders. Otherwise, we have three guys waiting up front for you to play long balls ahead of them. Win, lose or draw, we are going to finish this season by trying to win games, as opposed to not losing them. I want you all to have fun, enjoy the moment, and let's kick some Kalamunda ass."

As one they cheered and stood to go outside and warm up but they were halted by Brad's raised voice. "How many goals Mummy-Jen?"

"Three." She called back, without hesitation, even though she had no idea what the score would be. She wanted to help them keep the positive frame of mind.

While the guys jogged off to stretch, and go

through some warm up exercises, Jenny completed the team sheet and walked over to find the opposing coach, and then the referee. Once her formalities were out of the way she took her seat on the sideline which was bathed in warm sunshine and looked at 'her' team. She loved being involved, and earlier in her latest diary entry urged herself to keep going with the team after she woke up, describing the deep sense of belonging, and of being wanted and welcomed.

Her reveries were disturbed by a touch on her shoulder and she turned to see Geordie and Brenda behind her. He was holding out a bottle of orange juice with beads of condensation on the outside, which she gratefully accepted. "Thank you Geordie, that's very kind of you, it's rather warm sitting here today. I suspect it will be very hot for the players having to run around in it. Hi Brenda, come to watch the boys?"

"Aye he dragged me along, by the scuff of my neck."

"Don't you believe her, Missy, she was desperate to watch the boys win today and get one step closer to winning the league. Oh, just so you know, I put just a touch of vodka in your juice, but best keep mum about that, no alcohol is allowed be drunk outside the bar area."

She simultaneously smiled and groaned inwardly at his kindness. The groan was because she could imagine just how much his 'touch' of alcohol would be. "Thank you, Geordie, I will go and buy another two bottles of juice to water it down then."

He smiled. "You know, Missy, there's a lot of talk around the club how it's you who are responsible for the resurgence in the team. That you've motivated them somehow when Iain couldn't. Those of us who watch week after week have all noticed they seem to be playing with more of a purpose, like they know something the rest of us don't."

"Maybe it's just having a female touch, what do you think Brenda?" She replied, feeling uncomfortable with being singled out, and not wanting to get into a conversation about foretelling the future.

"Well, maybe it is, and maybe it isn't. And maybe it's Iain who is the motivated one." She winked knowingly.

"Aye, well that I could understand, our Jenny is a catch." This comment forced a blush from Jenny and a glare from Brenda, but they were interrupted by the referee blowing his whistle for the captains to toss the coin.

Jenny looked around her while she absent-mindedly took a sip of the orange juice. While it was cold and refreshing, the Vodka burned her throat all the way down.

The Kalamunda club was a very pretty place, nestled in the hills above Perth and the ground itself was surrounded by huge native trees such as Red Gum, Wattle and Eucalyptus. The sun shone, and with so few games left in the season this one had attracted a large crowd of supporters. Iain told Jenny earlier, the league champions would come from one of three clubs, and two of them were playing each other here. Floreat Athena would be hoping for a Queens Park versus Kalamunda draw; giving each one point, while a win for them would see them join the league leaders on points. If that were the outcome the superior goal difference Floreat possessed would mean they would retake the top spot. A win by Kalamunda would see them leapfrog Queens Park to be one point ahead. This match was a pivotal one for all.

Iain sat down beside Jenny and the three substitutes as Geordie and Beryl wandered off to the spectator area as the game got underway. The tone of the game was set in the first thirty seconds when a Kalamunda player fouled Scotty as he passed the ball forward. By the five-minute mark, Jenny believed the instructions from the opposing coach to his players had been if they couldn't win the ball fairly, they should win it by committing fouls. Clearly, they did not want Queens Park to find their rhythm and play the game their way; they were to be stopped by any means.

Slowly though, Queens Park exerted their dominance. To Jenny it looked as if they wanted to win, while the opposition's intention was to stop them. The combination of three attacking forwards wore down the home team's defense, and Jenny felt there was a sense of inevitability, who the eventual winner would be.

Yet, when the half time whistle sounded the score was still locked at nil, nil, and the Queens Park players looked tired and heat affected. Iain and Jenny met them on the pitch and instead of taking them into the change rooms they led them to the shade of a huge, majestic red gum tree, where he had already stashed a chest full of ice, water bottles, energy drinks, and cold face cloths, which were soaking in the melting ice.

He distributed the drinks and cold cloths to each player and waited until they had cooled down before he spoke in a calm, and confident voice. "You men are playing like the champions you deserve to be. I'm proud of you, and that won't change, win lose or draw.

You three guys in defense are awesome, so far Kalamunda have not taken a shot on goal and I don't think they can if you keep it up. Mid field, fantastic job, and I'm pleased you haven't been drawn into fouling them like they are trying to do to you. Stay strong and you will prevail. I know it's hot, and you are tiring, but hang on just for another forty-five minutes. If you are tired, so are they. For them to overtake us they need to win and the way they are playing they don't have a hope in hell, so long as we stick to our game plan. Forwards; what's going on out there, you've had five shots on goal, and missed each time, if we can turn that around it's in the bag."

There were a few mumbles of assent, but Brad sat with head held in hands with elbows on knees. He looked exhausted.

The breeze blew gently rustling the leaves in the tree above, as Iain silently walked to the ice chest, filled a plastic beaker then approached Brad from behind and poured the cold water down his neck.

"*Jesus.*" He yelled and stood up.

"Are you okay, Brad? If you are not up to giving a hundred percent, I can take you off. I know it's tough out there, and you've been a star all season. There would be no shame in playing half a game here."

"Nah, I'll be all right. It's just a combination of the heat, and them being so physical. That defender Robbins is all over me, he won't give me any time with the ball, and if he doesn't tackle he leans, shoves, kicks or trips me." He sounded annoyed before sitting back down, though Jenny didn't know if the annoyance was from Robbins tactics, or his father dousing him in iced water to wake him up.

"I get that, they are treating everyone the same way, it's the only way they know how to play. But if you drop your shoulders and slow down, they may score on a counter attack, so let's not get suckered into playing their game, we want them to play ours. The key is to move the ball around quicker. Don't take them on, pass and move, then pass and move again. I want one-two's, long balls and first touch passing. This is what we train for, this will be your toughest challenge, so, lift your heads, you are so much better than them. Yes, it's hot, so let's play smart. Find space, pass quickly and make them run. Can we, do it?"

Jenny smiled as the team agreed they could do it, but of course it wasn't said with enough gusto for Iain, so he asked, again, and again, until the men were shouting agreement back.

"That's better. Now who wants a league champions medal, and who wants to quit now without winning one?"

Again, there were a series of chants, and Jenny felt in awe at just how good a motivator Iain was because to a man, they all looked animated and determined.

"Okay. So how bad is it, really? You are top of the league, you played the first half brilliantly and a goal is just around the corner. Stay patient, keep your shape, pass the ball quickly and make them do all the running. You can do this, I have faith in you, and so does Jenny. Are you sure you are right now Brad?"

Brad nodded, a steely determined look to his face, and stood up, "You're right, Dad. Come on guys, let's teach these guys a footballing lesson." He then proceeded to pour more water over his hair, then shake his head like a dog at the beach to flick the droplets off.

The others all followed suit, tossed the bottles toward the chest, then jogged back out onto the field to prepare for the second half.

Jenny busied herself by tidying up, not trusting her voice not to quiver with pride and love for Iain if she spoke.

It was the constant attempts to foul the Queens Park players which caused the inevitable goal twelve minutes into the second half. A free kick was awarded near the half way line and on the right-hand wing. Simmo had been forced down by a dreadful sliding tackle which elicited a yellow card for the offender. Jenny thought he didn't look the slightest bit bothered by it.

Simmo kept his temper intact as he rose to his feet and gathered up the ball which had rolled away, then took his time placing it where the referee indicated, so his team could take up their positions. From the training exercises Jenny had seen, when he held his left arm up in the air it meant he was intending to angle the ball toward the far post. He then delivered it with perfect precision. Brad ran in from the edge of the eighteen-yard box and leapt high into the air. He rose to the ball's height, using his knee to strike a defender in the lower back which sent him sprawling, just as Brad's forehead connected with the ball. Cleverly Brad directed the ball downward and back across the goalkeeper to bounce before finding its way into the back of the net.

Both Iain and Jenny jumped to their feet, screaming like jackals with delight, as the team descended on Brad leaping on his back congratulating him while their opponents surrounded the referee complaining of a foul.

The body language of the official waving them away was obvious to even the most die-hard of supporters. It was they who had set the tone of the game by fouling, and, so far as the nonplussed referee seemed concerned, he was not going to disallow the goal.

Iain turned to Jenny and hugged her, "That will teach the bastards to play fair."

There was no way Kalamunda could come back from a goal down, so a win next week would seal the championship for Queens Park and it would not have happened but for her, and Iain's intervention. More than ever, she had hope she could change Brad's mind and reset the future.

After the restart, the spirit of Kalamunda had been broken, and too late they changed tactics to play soccer to score again rather than foul. But it played into Queens Park's hands and they consistently showed better skills. The second goal was scored by way of a one—two pass between Simmo and Brad who curled the ball around the goalkeeper's grasp to record his double.

A third followed. This time it was scored by Simmo who dribbled past three defenders to record an outstanding goal with a booming shot from the edge of the eighteen-yard line. But rather than celebrate with the team he ran over to Iain and Jenny, with the guys trailing behind him. "Th-th-that one was for you, J-J-Jenny; you s-s-said we would score three.

Oh my God, how wonderful are these young men? She jumped up and hugged him in delight. "It's okay," she whispered into his ear. "You can score another one if you like."

Yet they didn't, and while driving home after the game, Iain and Jenny discussed the strange sight of his attacking formation turn completely defensive to stop Kalamunda scoring a goal once they had the three. It was almost as if, the players had agreed, the team was only interested in living up to Jenny's prediction, and no more.

****

Lyndsay arrived at the club driving Brad's car to meet with him. They were going out with friends while Iain and Jenny had a date at the Video shop, where they were to pick up the three 'Dragon Tattoo' movies.

They hadn't intended to watch them back to back, and ordered home delivered pizza after the first film as neither wanted a break to cook a meal. Iain was drawn into the incredible story of Lisbeth Salander and Mikael, and did not want to go to bed without watching till the end. Jenny knew, how wonderful the finale would be from reading the books, but Iain had no idea.

He mimicked Jenny's 'Oh my God' at least three times during the marathon sitting, and told her the subtitles had not been distracting at all. Once he got half an hour into the first film he was accustomed to reading the dialog.

When they got into bed, they couldn't sleep, and felt the need to discuss in depth, the tragic story of Lisbeth and how she had not only survived but fought back, and how well the actress played her part.

Chapter 17
Crunch Time

Day Twenty-Seven, 28th August 2016

They awoke late, nestled in each other's arms. Jenny glanced at the bedside clock; it was after eleven, and when she turned back to Iain she saw his eyes were open.

"How long have you been awake?" She asked in a quiet voice.

"Oh, I'm not sure, fifteen minutes or so."

"Why didn't you wake me?"

"I think I told you once before; I love watching you while you sleep. It makes me remember just how much I love you, and how utterly beautiful you are."

"Oh, Iain. Whatever did I do to deserve you?"

He smiled, "Well, I'm pretty sure you were brave enough to take a leap of faith, and come back in time to save the world. I think that justifies deserving me."

She lifted herself up, and kissed him deeply.

****

They spent the day in family normality, they cleaned, and washed clothes, yet for Jenny, it was happiness personified. They did the grocery shopping and when they got home Iain mowed the lawns and they both did some gardening while laughing and kidding with each other. But as the day wore on, the laughter turned hollow. The hours, and then minutes ticked down to the inevitable conversation with Brad, which she had been dreading.

Jenny cooked a roast leg of lamb, with all the traditional vegetables for dinner, having remembered on one occasion Brad had mentioned it was his favorite. Jenny didn't want to be like his mother, but if it was his favorite, she hoped it would put him in a good mood for the planned conversation after dinner.

"Mummy-Jen, that was superb." Brad exclaimed after he cleaned the last morsel from his plate. I am so full. That was your best meal to date. Dad said you wanted to talk to me, without Lyndsay, about something serious. After a meal like that, if it's to ask my permission for you to marry Dad, the answer is yes, you most certainly can."

"Why thank you, Brad. In a week's time, if your father asks me, and I can remember everything, I will say yes."

He stared back blankly. "Why won't you remember?"

"I will come to that a bit later, but suffice to say seven days from now I will have no memory of this last month, and your dad must help me through a tough time. I know it sounds very mysterious, but you will understand later. Let me ask you a question," she paused, feeling more nervous than any time she could remember.

"The vegetables you had tonight, can you ever imagine a world without them? A world where food is no longer available, because plants have succumbed to a dreadful, all consuming disease?"

"No, I can't, Jenny. But if I could I suppose it

would only motivate me more to continue my work and try to discover ways to make food grow more plentiful, and quicker, so people no longer starve to death in poorer countries."

Jenny stood up and crossed to the kitchen drawer from which she took out an envelope. When she returned to sit at the table, she handed it to him silently.

"What's this? Jenny, you are starting to freak me out a bit here, what's going on?"

"Brad, since you've known me, I hope you've come to accept I am an honest person, and I wouldn't lie to you. I've told you some things about the future, but there have been other things I've told your dad which you don't know of. All those things, they have all come true, haven't they?"

"Yes, they have."

"In that envelope I have written for you a series of events which will all come true over the next three months. I've done it for you so you can see that while for now you might not want to believe what I'm going to tell you, in time I hope you will, because this list of things will be proof of my honesty with you. Unfortunately, something else will come true, if you don't do anything to avoid it, in three years' time. You, and your father's death."

He stood up, angry. "*What*?"

Iain interrupted, "Brad, please sit down, there is a lot more to tell you, but Jenny needed to get your attention, so you'd listen to the rest. I believe every single word she is going to tell you, and I hope and pray you will too."

"This is nuts. Why don't you just spit it out. How do you think you know dad and I are going to die?"

"Because I read your obituaries, and death notices. You were driving home after a soccer game. I've written down for you the location, time and date. A heavily laden truck driver swerved to avoid a car which overtook him and swung back in front too sharply. He lost control, crossed the median strip, and as his truck fell on its side, your dad's car was crushed with you both in it."

"Hang on, this is bullshit. You are using past tense, saying it did happen, but you just said it's going to happen in three years if we don't avoid it."

"Brad, I am from the future. I traveled back to now, so for me it was in my past. I don't just foretell things, I've lived them. I come from thirty-three years from now, and before I leapt I studied you, and your father's lives which had occurred in my history."

He laughed, loudly and looked from Iain, to Jenny as he did, but slowly his laugher died until he stopped altogether. "So, you've got a time machine? Wow Jenny, that's fantastic. Where is it parked, can I see it?"

"I wish I did, then you might believe me a whole lot quicker. No I don't have a machine. It was my consciousness which traveled back in time, my body was always here. Where I come from, I am sixty-eight years old. I took a drug which sent me back for a total of thirty-three days' residency in my younger body. I have six days left, and when I awake, my memory of this trip will be gone. All this will be a blank canvas, and your dad is going to help paint a picture on it, and help me fall in love with him all over again."

"What, you disappear in a puff of smoke? Like here one second and gone the next? This conversation is madness."

"Brad, let's have less of the sarcasm, please. Show some respect, please." Iain interjected.

"Oh yeah, right, show some respect for a woman who has lost her marbles, and convinced you to lose yours too."

"She has not lost her marbles, it's all true. Remember the missing plane which crashed in the South China Sea a few days ago. Jenny told me about it five or six hours before it took off. We did everything we thought we could to try to save all those people. The man the police want to talk to, who sent the email warning them from the Perth Seven Eleven shop? That was me."

"But it's impossible. That can't be true."

"Why would we lie?"

"I don't know, maybe you've both taken up drugs. But time travel is impossible. Even Einstein said it was."

"Well actually he didn't say that at all." Jenny said, shaking her head earnestly. "He said it would be impossible to travel faster than the speed of light, which he believed would be required to bend time. But he always thought time travel was theoretically possible. But again, that's not what I did; I did not physically travel in time and space. I took a drug called ASX101in 2049 and fell asleep. My consciousness then woke up here in 2016, in my own younger body. While I am awake here, I am still asleep there, almost in a coma. A man by the name of Heinrich Abraxist discovers the drug in his quest to cure serious psychological disorders in the year 2247. As you can imagine, the technology in two hundred and thirty years' time is a bit different from now."

"I don't know what's going on here, but I don't believe any of it. I'm sorry."

"Brad, you are going to find a way to genetically modify wheat so it grows faster, withstands all weather, pests and soil conditions, and provides significantly bigger yields. That wasn't even imagined thirty years ago, why should this be a different situation?"

"Because…. Oh, I don't know, it just is. It's called technology."

"Forgive me, but for someone who has dedicated their life to science, and to find new ways to feed the world that doesn't sound like a terribly scientific attitude. Today's mysteries are solved by tomorrows scientists; you know that to be true. Just because time travel is only available in fictional stories now, it doesn't mean the secret of it won't be found in the future. And, it has been unlocked, I am living proof of it. In two hundred and thirty years' time, they discover how to send a person's consciousness back in time by thirty-three years. Like you, Brad, I devoted my life to study. Where you entered the science arena I've been trying to teach people to respect our planet, look after it, make sure it is still there for our children. I sometimes think I've been fighting a losing battle, but then every now and again, my faith is restored in human nature."

"I'm sorry, but this is just all too fantastical to be true. Even though, granted you gave me a few lotto numbers, you didn't give me all of them, only some. And yes, you did predict some football scores, and a rugby outcome. I don't know about this plane crash, I will just take your word for it, but it could have been just some kind of premonition."

"So, you are willing to believe in premonitions, but

not time travel. Brad, I could have given you all the lotto numbers; I had them. I deliberately chose not to make you an instant millionaire before we had this talk. If that is the path you choose, in the envelope, one of the things I have told you is the winning numbers for an upcoming jackpot. You can be the only winner and pick up twenty million dollars, if you want to. I welcome that, if I can just get you to believe I am telling the truth. I turned up here to meet you. And for a very important reason. But, along the way, I fell in love with your father."

He stared back, then looked at the envelope, before raising his gaze to her again. Jenny thought she was starting to win him over, there seemed just a glimmer of hope.

"Let me tell you about what's happening to our planet two hundred and thirty years from now. You will be a micro biologist very soon; this should interest you very much." Jenny sat forward in her chair and linked her fingers underneath her chin. "Brad, our world is dying. And mankind is facing extinction. The reason it's dying is there is a terrible Blight which over the years has learned to jump from plant to plant, genus to genus, and causes what's called Yellow Spot. At first they thought Yellow Spot was a fungal, or bacteriological disease, but it was far, far worse than that. It had been genetically modified, somehow, along with its host plant, and it became a super bacterium. Its cell wall is impervious to all pesticides. When they find a new one to fight it and they think they have succeeded, it just pops up somewhere else, many years later, on a different sort of plant. They burn entire tracts of land to stop it and when it destroys the host plant, nothing will grow in the soil, because it is infested with Yellow Spot spores. African countries are desolate, wind-blown desserts, and everyone who once lived there died of starvation. The rest of the world is battling the same plant disorder on a catastrophic level, it is spreading like an out of control bushfire, leaving immense tracts of land like a patchwork quilt of destruction.

"When Abraxist dreamed up his radical plan to use the ASX101, to go back in time to fix the problem before it started they estimated there was less than twenty years left to the total extinction of every living thing on the planet, because there would be nothing left to eat."

"Why, how, what are you talking about? If this is all true, why are you here?"

"Brad, I am here, to plead with you. To convince you not to genetically modify your wheat, because it is you who inadvertently causes the Yellow Spot disease. While initially you will be hailed as a hero of modern science, and the savior of the starving millions, two hundred and thirty years from now, you will be thought of as the man who killed civilization and destroyed the Earth."

"Oh this is rubbish, absolute crap. What have you got against me? Why are you saying all this? I have no intention of modifying a disease."

"On one of our first dates, I spoke to your father about an old saying: 'The road to hell is paved with good intentions.' Nobody is questioning your heart isn't true, Brad. For many years, especially after your death, you were held in the highest regard for your discovery. You were nominated for a Nobel Peace Prize. Even many, many years later when the plant disease was back tracked to your wheat, no one ever believed you did it intentionally. But your discovery of genetically modifying wheat was so good, it grew so unbelievably hardy in withstanding whatever nature or man could throw at it, somehow, someway, you created Yellow Spot to be the same. There is no way to stop it once it starts, and that is why I am here, now. My job is to beg and plead with you to stop now, before it is too late."

"But hang on, you said you were from thirty-three years from now, but then you said you were from two hundred and thirty years. Which lie is it?"

"Oh, Brad. Can't you see for me this is the most difficult thing I've ever done in my life? My sixty-eight-year-old life that is; I'm not lying to you. I have fallen head over heels in love with your father, and with you too. I like to think of you as the son I never had, and this last week has been the happiest of my life; finally having a family. In my future, I'm a lonely old spinster with only a cat for company. I considered not telling you and letting everyone else die in the future because I love this family life and would love to find a way to keep it."

"Yeah? Well you have a funny way of showing it."

Jenny shook her head. "What possible reason could I have for lying to you?" Brad stared back, and she could tell he was a long way from being convinced.

"For me to come back and see you took seven dedicated people. Each of us believed enough to make the trip back in time of thirty-three years. We call ourselves "Leapers" because we took a leap of faith in the previous person that they were telling us the truth. Each one had to be taught how to manufacture the drug, then convince their target to take it and do the same. I am the last in the line. Brad, you must listen, please believe me, and change your direction. Only you can save every plant, animal and human being. By not modifying the wheat you will create a new reality, one where everyone lives."

"You mean if I buy this crap you are pedaling?"

She nodded, sadly. "Brad, I am not a scientist, I'm an environmental lecturer in university, but I am hoping upon hope I can convince you to make the decision to abandon what you are going to do. I don't know anything about quantum physics, or the theory of time travel, so I don't know at what point the new reality kicks in by you deciding not to go ahead. But, I want to save you, and your father's life. There is one more reason you must do this, other than the humanitarian reason, that is. I think you can avoid the car accident, which my history showed you both dying in. I know there are ways to change events set in time. I've proved it with the soccer team results, even though we failed in stopping the aircraft from crashing. But, there is one more possible way you might die if you do not create that new reality I need you to believe in. You see, Heinrich Abraxist was, or more precisely will be; I still get confused with the right tenses here, a pacifist. But he needed resources and permission to set up his "Leapers". He got it from the future equivalent of the United Nations. He was always afraid they might set up a second team to come back if I failed in my mission. Those people would have a very different agenda, their final "Leaper" would be an assassin."

He stood up, angrily, his face red. He pointed a finger at Jenny. "I don't know what your game is, or why you have turned against me. For a little while there you almost had me fooled. Maybe someone is paying you to stop my research, to release their own version, I don't know. But an assassin from the future to kill me? That is the most ridiculous thing I have ever heard. You are either delusional or you have some nefarious reason for stopping me from achieving my goal, but either way you've failed."

He turned and walked out of the room, Jenny called out to his retreating back. "Brad, please believe me, I only want the best for you, think about what I've said, think about how it is for the people in the future. How it makes sense to kill one person to save billions of lives."

"Brad, don't turn your back on this, come back and talk to us, please." Iain called out, but two minutes later the front door slammed, and then Brads car started up and screeched as he drove out of the driveway.

"He'll come back." Iain said.

But, Jenny didn't believe he would. The envelope was lying on the table, unopened.

****

August 11th 2214, San Francisco, USA

Abraxist was delighted. It had gone so much better than he could have imagined; the committee had chosen well, he had to admit. Not only was his next "Leaper" easy to convince, he was eager to get going and take his place in history. Perhaps as each one leapt down the line it would be harder to convince the next participant, because the Blight would become less and less well known. In 2214, it was publicized, though not the dire seriousness it would become.

Henry Van Anst lay in his bed asleep, traveling

back in time to his younger years from the injection Heinrich administered. Henry was confident he could manufacture the ASX101 with the instructions he had observed and learned by rote. Along with some historical facts he would need to convince the next in line. He felt a burning desire to feel useful, after a lifetime of financial success and wealth, and Heinrich had fed his latent desire.

He did query why they were making a double batch, but Heinrich waved away the question merely saying he had another use for it, then distracted Henry by asking to repeat, for the hundredth time, the formula.

The second dose, sat in Heinrich's jacket pocket, while he rocketed across the stratosphere in Skytracker 417, the aircraft which would take him from New York back to Berlin in forty minutes. He hoped he wouldn't arrive too late to complete the second part of his mission, which was to halt the other team of "Leapers" in their tracks.

Chapter 18
Time's Almost Up

Day Twenty-Nine, 30th August 2016

Brad did not come home, and had ignored all phone calls and messages from Iain and Jenny.

She decided to move out; back to her own house, because she blamed herself for the rift between father and son, and found it impossible to live with the guilt. She told Iain of her decision before training on Tuesday night.

Iain tried his best to placate her. "Jen, he is big enough and old enough to make his own decisions. He has always been headstrong and single minded. No amount of talking will change his mind if he doesn't want to change it himself. Sure, you could make the gesture of moving out and leaving me, but what would that solve? Brad will come to his senses in time or he won't. Either way he is my son, and I love him. He will always be welcome back. But I love you too. You've completed your mission, you've done your best to change his mind, and I think, hope, and pray in time he will realize you've done nothing but tell the truth. Why should we break up forever just because you had to do what you did?"

"Oh my God, Iain. I love you so much, but this guilt of coming between you and Brad is killing me."

He hugged her, and she felt his inner strength. "I love you," he whispered. "Please don't leave. In four days, you will go to sleep and forget me. I need you here so I can help remind you about us when you wake up. Brad will be at training tonight, I'm sure of that, maybe we can talk to him afterward."

Brad did turn up, but was morose and virtually ignored Jenny and his father, though he dutifully took part in the exercises. He didn't stay to shower and Jenny saw him leave without going to the bar for drinks and Brenda's meal. She felt even worse for seeing him that way and ran after him toward the car park to try to talk to him away from everyone else.

"Brad, please stop, talk to me," she called out to his back as he strode purposefully toward his car. His back stiffened, and he turned a cold stare toward her.

"Did *he* send you to talk to me?"

She didn't answer but just launched herself and threw her arms around him to hug him tightly. But he didn't respond. "Brad, I will leave the house, tonight, and never return if you will only make up with your dad. This is killing him, I can tell. I traveled from the future to ask you to save the world, I failed, and I can see that. But please, please don't let me come between you both. I'm so sorry I caused the rift between you, I wish I had never come, nothing is worth this."

His hands gripped her shoulders and firmly forced her away. "It's too late."

"Brad, it's never too late. One thing I have learned during my trip is this. This right here is what's important: love and family. All the things I never had in my other life, I have experienced with you and your father. If you don't make up with your dad now, you never will, and for what? Because he believes in my honesty and you don't? I don't care about the future anymore, but I do care about you two. Please, Brad, please come back and talk to him. You once spoke to me because you could see he was destroyed without me in his life, well I can see he is like that without you there. Please don't do this, please."

A tear trickled slowly from his left eye. "I, I, I need time to think, you have no idea what you've done to me. Everything I lived and worked for you tell me is wrong, instead of saving people I murder them. I don't know whether you are telling the truth or it's all a horrible plot you've created, or what. I'm so fucking confused, and angry with you for doing this to me."

She took the envelope from her tracksuit pocket and tucked it inside his. "Please, read the list of things I've prepared for you, and you will see I could only know these things if I lived in the future. Let me ask you one more thing, do you love Lyndsay?"

"What? What's Lyndsay got to do with this? Of course, I love her."

"Would you do anything to keep her?"

"Of course I would. Spit it out, what are you inferring?"

She stepped back and took a deep breath; this was her last hope. "Brad, soon, a few months before you make your big breakthrough, you've been working more and more hours. Often you even sleep at the lab, because you know you are so close, and the end is just around the corner. Unfortunately, it's a very long corner. You and Lyndsay fight more and more, she is left alone night after night, and eventually she seeks solace in the company of a man she is working alongside, an Irish man named Eamon. They fall in love and she leaves you to be with him. Because you have nothing left, you throw yourself even harder into your work, and when you do finally succeed, it is too late to make up with her. You never recover emotionally, Brad, all you have left then is your work, your dad, and your football, right up until the car accident that takes your life. Please, please believe me. I want you to be happy, not miserable."

"Are there no depths you won't sink to?"

"To save you, and your father? No. I would do anything."

"Why would you do this? Why would you make all this up? Why?"

"I'm not. This is your future, just as I've told you, but it's not chiseled in stone, it can be altered. You alone have a chance to change it, to be the savior of mankind you always wanted to be. You can keep Lyndsay and have your own children with her, and be the father to your son your dad has been to you. He loves you more than life itself. I am giving you the gifts of life and love. All you have to do to keep those gifts is believe in me. If you want me to go, so you can go back to the way it was between you and your dad, I will leave tonight and never return. All I want is for you to make up with him; he doesn't deserve this."

"I need time to think, this is all too much, tell dad I love him, and I will be here on Thursday, maybe things will be clearer by then." He turned, quickly, Jenny could see he was crying, and she let him go.

****

Day Thirty-One, 1st September 2016

Wednesday and Thursday dragged by slower than

Jenny could have imagined. Even when she and Iain made love, there was an air of melancholy between them. Jenny no longer orgasmed with the intensity she had before, but she needed the closeness and intimacy to reinforce their love. They clung to each other frantically as often as they could, as their final days, hours, and minutes as a couple ticked by.

Her diary entries became shorter, she no longer gained pleasure in trying to teach herself how good her life was with Iain, because Brad had still not responded to Iain's calls or text messages.

At the final training session for the season, on Thursday, Brad was not there when they took to the field to warm up, or at the team talk. Iain's heart was not in it, Jenny could tell. He muddled through a speech about how important a win was for the club, and for them in their last game on Saturday. He kept the same formation which had been so successful the week before, and it seemed to Jenny even among the players there was a sense of hopelessness. She thought they too knew there was something wrong, but no one would ask what.

Jenny watched them practice from the sidelines, her head bowed and hands thrust deep in her pockets. She felt such a depth of sadness, all she wanted to do was cry. She had never envisioned trying to fulfill her mission could cause such pain to her, Iain, and Brad.

"Hi, Mummy-Jen." She heard from behind her.

She turned, and the tears that threatened, finally broke free. There was Brad in his training clothes, grinning in that lopsided way. Lyndsay stood alongside him. Jenny couldn't help herself, she hugged him tightly. "Thank God you turned up." She whispered.

"Lynd's wants to talk to you." He mumbled, and then he was gone, jogging out onto the field toward his father and the rest of the team.

Oh, my God, I can't take much more of this.

She dabbed at her eyes with a tissue. "Hi, Lyndsay."

"Tell me the truth and look me in the eye when you do. Are you really from the future?"

She nodded, not daring to speak.

"Does he really destroy the planet?"

Again, Jenny nodded silently.

"And do I really leave him for someone with the unlikely name of Eamon? Couldn't I find someone with a better name than that?"

"What can I say? I didn't write that part of the future, you did."

"My mum always said I was the perceptive one in the family. From the first moment I met you, there was something different about you, something not quite right. I don't mean that in a bad way, but there was always something in the back of my mind which just didn't feel right when I was with you. It was a bit like when you see something out of the corner of your eye, but when you turn there is nothing there. That's how I always felt about you. Now I know why. I believe you, Jenny, and I've just about got Brad to believe in you too. He hasn't opened the envelope yet. He keeps looking at it, wanting to read it, but chickening out. He will though. I won't say he will stop his research, but what I think he will do is change his direction or look deeper into it, to stop the Blight. And umm, thanks for telling him about Eamon, whoever he is, I think that was the final thing that clicked into place. He needs time, maybe a lot of time, but I think you've won.

****

Day Thirty-Three, 3rd September 2016

The Queens Park ground was packed for the last game of the season. It was also to be Jenny's last day in her state of consciousness. The car park was full and even the street was choked with parked cars.

Brad came home after training on Thursday, though everyone felt a nervousness around each other. There had been no further discussion about the future. Jenny's job was done, and there was nothing else she could say or do; he would either change it, or he wouldn't. She could live with that.

Her biggest fear was if another "Leaper" turned up with murder in mind, and she urged Iain to be vigilant, just in case. He promised he would, but it was beyond their control. Some things in the future were best left unknown.

The spring weather was bright and sunny, with a stiff breeze so it wasn't as hot as the previous week's game. In the locker room Jenny stood alongside Iain as the players changed from the practice strip to match day shorts and shirts. The names of the starting eleven were chalked up on the board. They had rehearsed the game plan, and there was little more to be said. A win meant they would finish the season as champions, a loss meant they wouldn't, assuming Floreat won their game, which was being played at the same time at their home ground.

"Well, here we are." Iain began, once the guys had dressed and sat down on the benches. "Last game of the year, and what a year it's been. Who would have thought we would be in this position at the start of the season? If I had to pick a point in time when things turned around for us, I think we would all agree it was when a certain beautiful blonde woman walked into our lives. The team picked up a fantastic helper, whose perceptiveness, enthusiasm, and predictions of the future galvanized us, and turned us from a team content to play well, to one that wanted to win. I learned so much as your coach from Jenny, and I know you all have too. She taught me to be adventurous and change formations. Without her, we would not be here in this position. I've been so lucky to have found the woman I want to share the rest of my life with. So, before we take the field I want you all to stand and thank Jenny for all her help, advice, predictions, constant urging, and positivity."

Oh, my God. She rapidly blinked back tears as to a man each player stood, whistled and clapped for her.

Somehow she found her voice. "Thank you, thank you, thank you, you wonderful men. I have loved every minute of being with you. Now go and win, you deserve it."

"H-h-how many goals, Jenny?" Simmo asked.

"Four."

The roof nearly lifted off with the foot stomping, screams, and yells of delight.

Iain held up his hands for silence. "Two more things guys. One: go out and enjoy yourselves, you deserve this moment in time. Just play the game you know you can, and you will win, I am positive of that. Two: I would like you all to witness something."

From his pocket, he took out something, and to Jenny's shock and delight, Iain dropped to one knee. He opened the small jeweler's box to reveal a diamond ring, and held it out toward Jenny. "Will you do me the honor of marrying me, Jenny, and make me the happiest man alive?"

She could not stop the tears from falling. How could she answer? Tomorrow she wouldn't remember this. She looked from Iain to the ring, to Iain, then turned her head to the left to look at Brad.

"Go on, Mummy-Jen, say yes."

"Yes, oh my God, *yes*."

****

Queens Park were unstoppable. They played skillfully and decisively and like a freight train screaming through the night nothing could stand in their way. They scored three goals in the first half then a fourth in the second. Once they achieved Jenny's prediction, the team stopped trying to score a fifth. Content with the win she told them they would have, and the goals she told them they would score, it was enough for them once again.

After the final whistle, when she finished hugging Iain, he left to run out onto the pitch and celebrate with the team. Jenny chose to hang back, lost in the sheer joy of the moment. Suddenly, there was Geordie holding a drink out toward her, and he looked on the verge of tears.

"Oh, Geordie, you daft bugger, give me a hug."

"Aye, Missy, I thought you'd never ask."

She wrapped her arms around his neck and the sun glinted off the diamond engagement ring she wore. Everything felt right in her world. She had come back in time, and found love, and a place of belonging, the future would take care of itself; she could do no more.

****

350

The crowd of players and supporters celebrated well into the night. It had been twenty-two years since the club had been champions, and there would be many a sore head in the morning. One of the members was a photographer and took a photo of the team holding the cup at the end of the presentation. He left and arrived back later having printed it into a framed poster. He hung it, alongside the bar.

Each player in the squad signed their name over their picture, leaving Brad, as team captain, until last. He took the black permanent maker from Simmo and signed his name. When he had everyone's attention, he wrote in bold capitals across the top the date, and the words: '*Jenny's Team.*' The bar reverberated with the sounds of clapping and cheers.

****

At nine thirty, Jenny felt tired, unusually so, and she beckoned Iain to one side. "I don't feel so good; I think it's time for me to go."

His gaze snapped to her face with obvious concern. "Is it...?"

She nodded. "I'm not sure, but I think so, I'm so tired."

Iain called a cab; he had drunk far too much to consider driving. They said their goodbyes to everyone at the club she had come to love.

****

Jenny and Iain lay in bed, just before midnight, wrapped in each other's arms. They had made love for the last time. She was consumed by a feeling of sadness to which there were no depths. She cried out during orgasm, clinging to Iain as if by doing so she could stay with him, though she knew in her heart she could not.

351

Had she succeeded in saving the future of everyone from Brad's wheat? She did not know and as sleep beckoned its crooked finger toward her, she looked at Iain.

"I don't want to go." She sobbed, but within moments, was asleep.

Epilogue

August 5th 2247, Berlin, Germany

Heinrich Abraxist sat at his desk, distraught, shaking his head, feeling anger, and dismay. He did not have long left; his memories were becoming cloudy. He could just remember what he had done, and why, but the memory would soon be gone. He had to act before it was too late and got to his feet, unsteadily.

He took the vials of ASX101 from storage, emptied them down the sink unit in the lab, and ran the tap continuously. He then smashed the glass tubes into tiny pieces, making sure they were rinsed thoroughly so no trace of his formula could be re-constituted from the remnants.

He called up the computer records on site and at the back-up servers and deleted them, so there was no longer any documentation of how he had invented the drug, or its formula.

ASX101 was too dangerous to be allowed. Man could not be trusted with such a powerful drug. He invented it, and he alone would destroy it. He had to ensure it could never be used again.

He intended to destroy the ASX for two powerful reasons. The committee, by sending a team of assassins back in time, could not be trusted with owning it. No one should be allowed to use his formula to create havoc throughout time by committing murder. Today their intent was to save the planet by any means. Tomorrow it might be for another reason. Who had the right to change history by killing people?

Another fear was what if the formula was stolen? What was to stop anyone going back in time and changing the future without any restrictions? No one had that right, not even himself, after the resultant disaster he had achieved during his "Leap", albeit inadvertently.

He stopped to think, one last time, making sure there was no trace anywhere of the formula for ASX 101. There was only the injector device he now held in his hand which held a quadruple dose which would be fatal.

He walked to the basement where the furnace stood. It was used to destroy lab samples, as well as heat the building. He opened the door to look inside. As he stared at the welcoming flames flickering, he remembered what he had done thirty-three years before.

He knew the date set down for sending back the first member in the second team of "Leapers" which was why he had to complete his mission and get back to Berlin for when Dietrik Wilders made his jump.

He arrived in time, and proceeded to watch his target contact his next "Leaper". Three days later he observed them accumulating the items needed to manufacture the drug in Martin Voehler's kitchen.

He stood alongside, pretending interest in something else and listened to them in the market when they bought the turmeric root, a vital ingredient for the manufacture of ASX. The two men discussed meeting the following day, when Dietrik would show Martin how the drug was manufactured. The conversation sealed Wilders' fate, in Heinrich's mind; he could not permit that meeting to happen.

Heinrich followed him back to the apartment tower he lived in, and stepped into the elevator with him. Fortunately, they were alone, so no one saw Heinrich inject Dietrik with a massive dose of ASX101, his second, which would surely stop him from completing his mission.

Abraxist had spent his life trying to help people, and the taking of a life sickened him. But he believed the killing was a means to an end and justified. Dietrik had shown himself to be a murderer, even if it was by proxy, so deserved his fate. He had stayed his hand in hopes the man may have chosen not to contact his next "Leaper" and make the drug; he had to give him the benefit of the doubt.

Once the meeting took place with Vohler, and they purchased the paraphernalia required, there was no alternative. He must give Jenny the chance to complete her mission, and as he believed she would succeed, he had to save Bradley Destaine's life.

Heinrich left Dietrik unconscious in the elevator, and walked briskly down the corridor to the staircase, which led him down and to the outside. Then he traveled back to the sky port to catch another aircraft back to America so he would be there in plenty of time for when he woke up.

Returning to his own time stream, he raced to his lab before he lost his memory to see if he had been successful. With dawning horror, he read that Dietrik had gone on a demented rampage before taking his own life.

He had armed himself with an array of weapons he kept in his bedroom. He then disabled the elevators and lurched from apartment to apartment and murdered the occupants. When he ran out of ammunition he set fires, and the conflagration roared upward from his floor, trapping and killing everyone else in its path.

There was no explanation why Dietrik Wilders took so many lives, but Heinrich knew why; it was the injection he had given him.

While he could have lived with causing one justifiable death, he could not survive with his conscience, having been the cause of seventy-three innocent people being murdered, if not by his hand, by his deed.

****

Calmly, Heinrich injected himself with his own drug and tossed the injector into the furnace. Within moments he giggled, uncontrollably. He felt the approaching darkness of unconsciousness and his eyelids drooped. The flames beckoned him ever closer. His last conscious act was to bend down, and thrust his upper body so far inside the furnace he was incinerated in seconds.

****

August 3rd 2049, Perth, Western Australia.

Jenny woke up, alone, confused and disorientated.

She stared at the ceiling, wondering at the fabulous, intricate, and beautiful dream she had enjoyed. Her head felt fuzzy, almost nauseous and when she attempted to sit up, the room spun around her.

Oh, my God, what a dream! Her memory of it was haphazard, and splintered, but she remembered being in love. *Me? In love? Now, what a lovely thought that would be, but so not me.*

Then it dawned on her, with a horrified realization, the room was not the same one she had gone to sleep in.

This is not my bedroom in Monument Towers! She sat up abruptly which only made the room tilt and spin the other way. She felt like she could be sick at any moment.

She raised her hands, to rub her temples and wipe at her head, trying to figure out what had happened. She had gone to sleep in her apartment, to...what?

To go back in time.

Suddenly, she remembered. The dream of Iain, her Iain, and the love she experienced wasn't a dream, it had been real, hadn't it? *Oh, my God!*

With that thought, she suddenly remembered she would forget this soon, so it was important to recall things while she could.

She looked slowly around the room, which was far more beautiful than the plain one she had gone to sleep in. The bed was huge, and the quilt cover was made of fine linen, as were the pillow cases. She ran her fingers over the material, lost and confused. She was wearing a nightdress, and not like any one she could remember wearing before, it was...beautiful.

Where am I?

Simon had told her, when she woke up, she would be in a state of fugue, as memories crashed against each other from the two different time streams. Slowly, over the next few hours she would forget what had occurred during her trip and she would begin to remember what occurred after it.

Oh my God, Iain. Whatever happened to you?

She felt so alone, so terribly alone that he was not

by her side. Not trusting her legs to be able to carry her she called out his name as loudly as she could. "Iain, Iain, where are you?"

There was a knock on the door, and Iain walked in and closed it behind him.

That's not Iain. Or is it?

She was so confused and disorientated she wanted to cry. He looked so like how she remembered him, but different; younger somehow. How could it be?

He calmly sat on the edge of the bed and took her hand in his. "Are you okay? How do you feel?"

She stared back, dumbly, his voice sounded like Iain's but again, different somehow.

"Who are you?" she pleaded, her alarm rising.

"It's okay, we knew this day would come, didn't we? We've been waiting and preparing for it. Keep calm. I was delegated to be your first point of contact, to help you remember. You are going to be all right, your memory will come back soon. I'm your son, Larsson. You and Dad named me after your favorite author. My full name is Larsson William Destaine. You always thought I was conceived on your first night with Dad, when you both got so carried away. You've told me many times about it, and you've read me excerpts from your diary of how you fell in love. I always loved hearing your story. It's in the bedside drawer by the way, your diary, in case you need to recap."

"My son?"

"Yes. I was your first, but you just didn't stop with me. Dad had a hell of a time with you, when you woke up in 2016. You screamed and accused him of abducting you. It took some time, but slowly you accepted what had happened, and you rekindled your

358

love together. I always thought it was waking up with the engagement ring on your finger that helped, and your diary, of course. But, either way, to have fallen in love twice with the same man is just about the most incredible tale I could ever imagine. He's always been a romantic, Dad has. You also had another son, Toby, and a daughter Victoria. They are outside on the balcony with Brad and Lyndsay, and their children. They all want to see you, to help you through things, but we decided it might be a bit overwhelming for you if everyone was here at once."

"Oh my God, really? Everything worked out okay?" Her tears fell in earnest; she was incapable of stopping them. She could remember some things, but had to take his word for others.

Larsson hugged her, and stroked her back, as she cried. "It's okay, Mum, I love you. You are such a heroine in this family; you don't know the half of it. You told us it will all come back to you in a few hours, but not the thirty-three days when you were back in the past. But we can all tell you about that, don't worry. And, there's your diary, too.

Suddenly she sat bolt upright. "Brad, did he, is he, did they?"

"Did he carry on and release the diseased wheat you mean? No, he didn't. No one turned up to kill him either, and they didn't die in the car accident. He married Lyndsay though, thanks to you. They have two children, Jenny and Russell. Jenny, well she is just gorgeous, loves ballet, and naturally, is named after you. Russell is quite the budding football star; he plays for the State and they think he might play for Australia one day. Brad coaches him at Queens Park. Brad did win that lottery you gave him the numbers for. He used the money to buy you and Dad this house and form his own company. He does good work, Mum, you are so proud of what he is doing, He is feeding the starving millions, but these days he does it by fundraising and charity work.

There was another knock on the door, and it slowly opened. Iain shuffled in and Jenny's heart skipped a beat. Still the same Iain, tall and good looking, though he walked with a stoop. He had a full head of gray hair, wrinkles that accompanied his advancing years, and a walking stick to aid him. He had aged well, and she still loved him with every fiber of her being. He stood looking at his wife, smiling. She stared back, biting her lip; she wanted him to hold her.

Larsson stood, "I think this is my cue to leave you two alone for a while. Welcome back, from your travels, mum.

Author's Note

I've taken many liberties to tell this story; historical, technical, and geographical. The heart and soul of this book is the love between Jenny and Iain, and my belief that love, family, and friendship is why we are on this Earth. Anything else that comes our way is a bonus.

Is genetic modification of food sources a good thing?

Time will tell.

~S.B.K.

A word from the author…

I was born in the UK, what seems like an epoch ago, and moved to Australia at age sixteen. I was a long-haired rock guitarist and poet/songwriter, before real life got in the way, and I gave it all up for love.

I've always felt I had tales to tell and won short story competitions and published poetry in my wilder, younger days. More recently I've written and published five novels. While they have all been police procedural thrillers, mainly focusing on serial killers, they all have a love theme running through them.

I believe love and family are everything. Anything else you gain in life is a bonus.

I live in Perth, in Western Australia and am fiercely patriotic, and parochial. My wife is amazing in that she not only puts up with living with a writer, but encourages it. I've been blessed with five children, and I adore them all.

http://stephen-b-king.com

Thank you for purchasing
this publication of The Wild Rose Press, Inc.

If you enjoyed the story, we would appreciate your
letting others know by leaving a review.

For other wonderful stories,
please visit our on-line bookstore at
www.thewildrosepress.com.

For questions or more information
contact us at
info@thewildrosepress.com.

The Wild Rose Press, Inc.
www.thewildrosepress.com

Stay current with The Wild Rose Press, Inc.

Like us on Facebook

https://www.facebook.com/TheWildRosePress

And Follow us on Twitter
https://twitter.com/WildRosePress